The
Sleeping Salesman
Enquiry

ANN PURSER

BERKLEY PRIME CRIME, NEW YORK

THE BERKLEY PUBLISHING GROUP
Published by the Penguin Group
Penguin Group (USA) Inc.
375 Hudson Street, New York, New York 10014, USA

USA | Canada | UK | Ireland | Australia | New Zealand | India | South Africa | China

Penguin Books Ltd., Registered Offices: 80 Strand, London WC2R 0RL, England
For more information about the Penguin Group, visit penguin.com.

THE SLEEPING SALESMAN ENQUIRY

A Berkley Prime Crime Book / published by arrangement with the author

Berkley Prime Crime Books are published by The Berkley Publishing Group.
BERKLEY® PRIME CRIME and the PRIME CRIME logo are trademarks of
Penguin Group (USA) Inc.

For information, address: The Berkley Publishing Group,
a division of Penguin Group (USA) Inc.,
375 Hudson Street, New York, New York 10014.

ISBN: 978-0-425-26180-4

PUBLISHING HISTORY
Berkley Prime Crime mass-market edition / May 2013

PRINTED IN THE UNITED STATES OF AMERICA

10 9 8 7 6 5 4 3 2

Cover illustration by Griesbach / Martucci.
Cover design by George Long.
Interior text design by Laura K. Corless.

ALWAYS LEARNING   **PEARSON**

continued . . .

250

Acknowledgments

With many thanks to Anne Sowards, my endlessly patient and skillful editor.

One

"THANK GOODNESS THAT'S over," said Ivy Beasley to her fiancé, Roy Goodman.

She was, of course, referring to Christmas, a season of the year that she had not enjoyed since she was aged five, when she had come downstairs on Christmas morning to find no tree, no presents, and her father shut out to sleep in the shed as punishment for arriving home pleasantly drunk on Christmas Eve.

Ivy's mother was long dead. Ivy herself was in her late seventies, early eighties—take your pick—but still occasionally heard her mother's voice in her head. It was always caustic and critical, and although Ivy knew that sometimes her own voice was exactly like her mother's, she tried her best to be her own self. Unfortunately, that self was sharp and self-righteous, so that when she arrived at Springfields Luxury Retirement Home in Suffolk, at the suggestion of her much younger cousin, Deirdre Bloxham, it was a huge surprise when she met Roy Goodman and they fell in love.

This was not the first time Ivy had experienced romance, but a never-to-be-forgotten suitor had left her standing at the altar. That had been in the village of Round Ringford, where she had spent all her life before moving to the retirement home in Barrington in Suffolk, and she was quite comfortable with a reputation as a tough spinster determined to arrange life as she wanted it, for as long as she was able.

And then Roy! He was a bachelor, already a resident in the home, and most of the time he had grown stiff and dull with boredom. Television, visits from a truly terrible singing group of patronising do-gooders, and the occasional trip out in a minibus labelled with a charity's name writ large on the sides, were the chief entertainments in his life. When Ivy came along, he fell in love for the first time in his life. Properly in love, that is. He had been and still was an attractive man, and had had all the usual flirtations and affairs, but had never even considered taking a girl to the altar.

Now it was all different. He had carried on a campaign to get Ivy to name the day ever since they became engaged, and she had actually suggested Christmas as a time when the home would be festive, anyway, so they might as well make use of decorations and all that nonsense, and celebrate their nuptials at the same time.

But Christmas had come and gone, and still Ivy prevaricated. At last she could resist Roy's blandishments no longer, and said May the fifth would do very well.

Mrs. Spurling, the person in charge of Springfields and a woman with very little patience, had sighed. She had given up all hope of getting this marriage out of the way swiftly and bringing routine and order back into the lives of her residents. However, her assistant, Miss Pinkney, a more gentle soul and a true romantic, persuaded her to begin planning, and offered to take as much of the responsibility off her boss's shoulders as should be required.

Now Ivy and Roy sat in the lounge after lunch and were silent for a few minutes. Then Roy said, "I know you are reluctant to talk about our wedding day, my love, but could I suggest Enquire Within leaves the subject of our next assignment until after May?"

"Certainly not!" said Ivy, with some asperity. "For one thing, what are Deirdre and Gus to do with themselves if we are not usefully enquiring?"

Gus was Augustus Halfhide, a somewhat mysterious character who had moved to the village for no apparent reason, and maintained a protective wall of unwillingness to answer any nosey villager's questions about his past. Along with Ivy and Roy, Deirdre Bloxham and Augustus Halfhide completed the enquiry agency team nattily entitled Enquire Within, and the team had solved several serious crimes in and around Barrington over the past few years.

Needless to say, the local police were reluctant to admit that two old folks in a retirement home, together with a merry widow and an oddly reclusive incomer, could be of any detecting use at all. They had been proved wrong, but still handled Enquire Within with suspicious reserve.

"As always, beloved," said Roy, "I'm sure you are right. Shall we call an extra meeting for Tuesday, and meanwhile reserve some time having fun planning our wedding?"

Ivy, who had unbelievably softened in her approach to this particular man, stroked his hand and said that if anyone asked her, she would say she was the luckiest woman alive.

Two

THE WIND HAD a wintry chill as Ivy and Roy—he expertly steering his trundle along the pavement—made their way up the gentle slope that led to Deirdre Bloxham's strangely triangular-shaped house, fancifully named Tawny Wings. She always described it as a letter "Y" without a leg to stand on. The house had been built by a successful builder in the nineteen twenties and Deirdre's husband, Bert, a motor trade tyro, now sadly deceased, had bought it at a stage in their lives when they felt able to move a few rungs up the social ladder.

"Just as well we settled for hats, scarves and gloves this morning," said Ivy.

"I'm not used to wrapping up, beloved," said Roy. "A farmer has no truck with scarves and gloves when he's out on the fields on a bitter winter's morning. Takes a bit of getting used to being mollycoddled."

"Huh!" Ivy replied. "No one has ever accused me of mollycoddling anyone! But I intend to get you as far as May the fifth in one piece, so just put your coat collar up and do as you're told." To soften this outburst, she bent over and kissed the top of his head, then resumed her smart pace beside him up the hill.

"Hey! Wait for me, you two!" A tall, thin man with sparse hair flying in the wind came puffing up to them. "Morning, Ivy, Roy. You're walking as if you mean business! Pink of health, both of you?"

It was Gus, the fourth member of Enquire Within, and Barrington's mystery man, though not so mysterious as he had been for a year or two after he arrived. Now everyone knew that he was divorced from a dreadful woman who had nearly shattered his life before he fled, and had then turned up again to make trouble, and a case for Enquire Within, not so long ago. Village people were also pretty sure that Augustus Halfhide had been some sort of secret agent working for MI5 or 6, or maybe even 7, if it existed. All very hush-hush, and all, they presumed, in the past.

"And how are you, young man?" asked Roy kindly. Ever the peacemaker, he was good at anticipating Ivy's sharp replies, but not soon enough this time.

"If you ask me," she said, "Gus could do with a daily dose of Deirdre's golfing. Has she got you out on the course yet? Very good for the breathing, golf, so I'm told."

Before Gus could defend himself, they arrived at Tawny Wings, and Deirdre opened the door. "Saw you coming," she said. "Cold morning, folks! All ready for coffee and a brainstorming session?"

"A *what*?" said Ivy.

"Never mind, dearest," said Roy. "All will become clear when we are safely settled in the warm with a cup of Deirdre's excellent coffee."

"NOW, ARE WE sitting comfortably? Everybody got coffee? Then we'll begin."

Ivy straightened herself in her chair, and said, "Deirdre! Will you kindly stop behaving as if we were visiting infants from the village school. Now, Roy, first, shall we tell them our news?"

"Of course, Ivy. Over to you."

"Roy and I," she began, "are going to be married in a quiet ceremony with no fuss on May the fifth."

There was a stunned silence. "But, Ivy," said Deirdre, "last

time you announced your marriage, it was going to be the
Christmas just gone. And it didn't happen. Are you sure
about May?"

Roy said hastily that he for one was absolutely sure, and for
this momentous day in his life he would see that Ivy was the
one standing by him at the chancel steps in the village church.

"Well-done, Roy! We'll get her there if we have to carry
her!" Gus saw Ivy's expression and laughed. "Come on, Ivy
Beasley," he said. "It'll be a great day, and I hereby offer to
give the bride away."

"So who is to be your best man, Roy? Gus can't be in two
places at once."

"Well, I have given it some thought, and as you all know, I
have a nephew who turns up here occasionally and spends half
an hour making sure that I am still alive and my bank balance
is secure. I thought it would be appropriate to ask him. He is
my only remaining close relative, and who knows—may one
day be my heir."

"Are you sure he's a good choice?" said Deirdre.

"Once a businesswoman, always a businesswoman," said
Ivy scathingly. "I suppose you mean that unless Roy has stipu-
lated otherwise, I should be the one to inherit his millions?"

Deirdre bridled. "I'm only being practical," she protested.
"You have to think of these things."

"Exactly, my dear," said Roy, and smiled. "And thank
you, Ivy beloved. I shall give the whole matter some more
thought. Now, shall we change the subject?"

Talk then progressed on general lines, but Ivy was thinking
private thoughts. She had truly not realised that if Roy should,
after their marriage, die before her, without making a will, she
would inherit his considerable wealth. There had been several
farms in his family, now all tenanted, and he seemed to have
no worries about finance. Not that she was interested for herself, as she had benefitted from a pair of miserly parents, who
had left her a tidy sum. But to protect him from unknown
eventualities, she decided to take the next opportunity of asking
him tactfully about his will.

But could she do that? After all, he might get suspicious if
she started talking about making wills. She could be planning
to marry him, poison his porridge, and skip off to the Bahamas

with a scheming toy boy! No, she would just have to take things as they came.

"So what do you think, Ivy?" Deirdre tapped her on the shoulder.

"About what?"

"I knew you weren't listening! About our next case, of course. The man at the bus stop. The one Roy met at the end of our last case. He was having trouble with his wife and suspected foul play from the family. Roy suggested we might be able to help and gave him our details. Wasn't that it, Roy?"

"Afraid I don't remember the conversation exactly. But I think that's more or less right. I think she wanted a divorce, and he wasn't having any."

"As a matter of fact I remember clearly," said Ivy. "It might be interesting to find out more. But how are we to find a strange man Roy met at the bus stop? Did you take his details, Roy?"

"Sorry, no. But I can describe him pretty accurately. I could try being at our bus stop at the right time of day for a few days. He might show up again. Not a very scientific investigation, I realise, but sometimes a simple solution is best."

Ivy frowned. "I can't allow you to hang about the bus stop for hours in this cold wind. It is a ridiculous idea, if you ask me. You others must back me up on this."

"Certainly," said Gus. "Thanks for offering, old man, but this is a job for me. You can tell me what he looked like, and I am quite happy to hang about on the Green or in the shop around the time the bus is due. We've only got two buses to think about, after all! Do you remember what day of the week it was?"

"Not absolutely sure, I'm afraid. Where he was going, or what he was doing, I can't remember that, either. If he told me, that is. But I *do* remember that he wore heavy black-framed spectacles, because I remember thinking how unprepossessing he was, and no wonder his wife wasn't keen. Is that a help?"

Gus laughed. "Of course. But are we sure we want to take on an unprepossessing character with sinister glasses and an errant wife? It's a bit close to our last case, isn't it?"

"No two cases are the same," Ivy said firmly. "Worth a try, anyway. And so long as Roy keeps his promise not to lurk by the bus stop in the middle of winter, I propose we take the first step as outlined. All in favour?"

Roy could not remember giving such a promise, but obediently raised his hand. Gus winked at Deirdre, a wink she interpreted as an instruction to humour the oldies, and they both raised their hands.

"Good, that's settled, then," said Ivy. "So you will be by the bus stop tomorrow, Gus. I suggest half an hour either side of the due time. Then if that fails, we can discuss on Thursday whether it is worth continuing. I have a small thought that might be worth pursuing, but we'll see what happens. Now, is there any other business?"

There were no takers, and Gus said he had to leave soon. He planned to look at some old, affordable cars.

"I have to go into Thornwell," said Deirdre, checking her watch. "Can I give you a lift?"

Brazen hussy, thought Ivy. In my day, girls waited to be asked. Not so for the widow Bloxham. She had got not only Gus in her sights, but also Theo Roussel. Theo was the bachelor squire of the village, and an old flame rekindled when Deirdre had found herself living alone in Tawny Wings, a few hundred yards away from the Hall, ancestral home of the Roussels.

"Thanks a lot," said Gus. "That would be splendid. By the way, team, I can't remember if I already told you about my plan to buy a new car? New to me, that is. Can't afford a brand-new one, but I shall be looking round for a bargain."

"Look no further," said Deirdre, smiling sweetly at him. "My Bert and me were in the motor trade for years, and I still am. I know as much about cars as your average garage mechanic. We shall go together to my showroom, and I shall guard you from being palmed off with an old wreck."

Ivy snorted. "If you ask me, Gus," she said, "you'd be better off sticking to the bus."

Three

THE MORNING BUS through Barrington was not always on time, being occasionally early and often late. Gus decided to take his small grey whippet for a walk around the Green and then call into the shop for supplies and a chat with the shopkeeper, James. That would give him plenty of time to spot the man who had spoken so openly with a complete stranger in a trundle.

As he walked along Hangman's Lane, where his cottage was the last in a row originally built for estate workers, he thought about the man at the bus stop. It was quite likely, in Gus's view, that the whole thing amounted to a husband-and-wife quarrel over breakfast. But at least it was something to occupy Enquire Within until something more juicy and important came up.

"Morning, Gus," said James behind the counter. "Nice to see you. How's Whippy?"

"Fine, thanks. Hooked up outside, like a good citizen. How's business?"

"Quiet this morning, but Saturday was good. A posse of cyclists went through and stopped here for snacks. Took more cash in ten minutes than I usually take in a day!"

Gus slowly stacked up a bagful of groceries, keeping a sharp eye on the Green. "No bus yet?" he said, and James shook his head.

"Late today. There's quite a queue out there."

"Including the man at the bus stop!" said Gus quickly. "Must go, James. See you in the pub tonight?"

There he was, a lumpy-looking man, with a few strands of hair slicked back and heavy, black-framed glasses with tinted lenses, all contributing to a sinister appearance.

Gus was convinced this was his man, and approached with a friendly smile. "Good morning, sir," he began. "Lovely morning!"

"Get that so-and-so dog away from me!" said the man. "I don't know you, whoever you are, and I don't want to. Here comes the bus, so just get out of my way."

Gus recoiled, and stepped back onto the forecourt of the shop. He took a deep breath. Wow! So that was a complete disaster. He watched the queue disappear into the bus, and saw his man sit down at a window seat. The scowl on his face was particularly directed at Gus, and as the bus moved away Gus felt as if someone had taken a potshot at him from behind a tree.

"Gus!" It was James calling from inside the shop. "Here a minute! I should have warned you," he added, as Gus returned. "That charming character is well-known for his dyspeptic manner. Not just you, so don't be upset. He's like that to everyone."

"Does he live in the village? I don't remember seeing him before."

"Do you know that tumbledown cottage up Cemetery Lane? Next to the old smithy. Paint all peeling off the woodwork. Well, that's Alf Lowe's place."

"Lowe by name and low by nature!" said Gus, reviving quickly. "A nasty piece of work, then? I don't think he can be the man I was looking for."

"Didn't know you were looking. Can I help?" James knew just about everybody who lived in the village, and was used to directing lost lorry-drivers to village addresses.

Gus described Roy's brief acquaintance with a man who had trouble with his wife, and James said that as far as he knew, Alfred Lowe was a bachelor. "He may have had a wife years ago," he said, "before I came to the shop. But now I'm sure he lives alone up there. That's what I've heard, anyway."

Gus made his way back home, thinking hard about what had happened. Alf Lowe had answered Roy's description exactly, and yet could not have been further from a friendly chap having trouble with the wife. Ah well, perhaps Alf had a brother. More work needed on this, he decided, and headed for the pub and a lunchtime snack.

"GUS WAS THERE on time," said Ivy to Roy, as they sat working their way through large portions of rabbit pie. "He was seen talking to someone outside the shop."

"Not necessarily our man," said Roy, "but let's hope he has something interesting to tell us this afternoon, then."

"If that was your man this morning, he'll be here early to tell us, but if not, it will be more like teatime, when the afternoon bus has gone. Chances are, anyway, that he won't find your man at first attempt."

Roy, who, along with the rest of Enquire Within, did not feel too much urgency on this new case, changed the subject and said that he had decided to call his nephew to ask if he would be best man, and had caught him just as he was leaving the house.

"Sounded quite shocked when I told him about our marriage," laughed Roy.

"Why shocked?" Privately, Ivy thought she knew very well why his nephew was shocked, but, as she had previously decided, said nothing about Roy's will.

"He said he had thought I was a confirmed bachelor, and at my age wasn't it a bit risky? I asked him to explain, and he huffed and puffed and said what about my weak heart. I said I had no such thing, and if he didn't want to be best man, I could easily find someone else. But then he changed his tune and said he would be delighted, and looked forward to hearing details. Then he signed off, presumably in a hurry."

"Mm," said Ivy, and frowned. "I haven't met him, have I?"

"I can't remember the last time he came to see me. Must be at least six months ago. He did say he'd be over here very soon."

Roy and Ivy, as was their habit, got up to go to their respective bedrooms for an afternoon nap. This was an established routine now, decided on by Ivy, who said that if they were in each other's pockets every hour of the day, no engagement could stand up to it, let alone that of two old codgers imprisoned in Springfields.

AFTER A PLEASANT session in the pub, Gus felt more cheerful and walked home briskly, with Whippy trotting beside him. He had almost made it to his cottage, when his neighbour's door opened and a figure appeared.

"Gus! Missed you this morning! Are you up for home-cooked plaice and chips this evening?"

It was Miriam Blake, who had grown up in the village and since Gus's arrival had conducted a brave campaign based on the saying that the route to a man's heart was through his stomach. In spite of many rebuffs, she still hoped to lead him by the hand to a life of bliss in holy matrimony. And if not that, since Gus was divorced and had vowed never to marry again, then she would be perfectly happy to live with him in unholy sin.

"Thanks, Miriam. Very kind, but I have a prior engagement."

"Not at Tawny Wings, I hope," she said, pouting. "You know she's the squire's fancy woman? Shouldn't have thought you'd want secondhand goods."

Gus forebore to point out that he himself was not exactly a shining example of purity and innocence, and said apologetically that he was free tomorrow evening, if the fish would keep.

Mollified, Miriam agreed, and said that she had just made a pot of good strong tea, and wouldn't he like a cup?

Never gives up, Gus said to himself sadly, and nodded. "That would be very nice. Thank you, Miriam. I'll just put Whippy indoors, and then I'll be round."

"Don't be long," she called merrily, as he disappeared through his front door. "Jam tarts fresh from the oven!"

Four

STEVEN WRIGHT—STEVE to his friends, of whom there were not many—pulled up his car with a spray of gravel in front of his pleasant, pebble-dashed house in the posh suburb of Thornwell. He had had a frustrating day at the office, where he worked as chief departmental manager in a large furniture emporium on the town's new trading estate.

Trade was slow, partly because of the dire economic situation in the country, and partly because, as he knew, it takes a long time for shoppers to change their habits and try new suppliers. His wife saw his grim expression, and quickly handed him a large gin and tonic to match her own. This ritual had developed over the years, and Wendy Wright had come to need support when her quick-tempered husband returned from work, anxious to make her as unhappy as he was.

He was not unattractive, with clear blue eyes and thick gingery hair, which he kept bristly short, not making any attempt to conceal the grey streaks beginning to appear.

"Distinguished-looking, darling," Wendy had said one morning, as he brushed fiercely, showing no mercy to his tingling scalp.

"Naturally," he had replied, and for once waved a cheery good-bye as he set off in his car.

This evening they were due to have dinner with friends, and Steven made it quite clear that he would rather stay at home. "They're your friends, not mine," he said grumpily. "Tell them I'm sick. A bug going round the office. Something like that."

"What happened today to put you in a more than usually black mood?" Wendy was a gin or two ahead of him, and spoke with Dutch courage.

Steven sighed and collapsed into one of his top-of-the-range armchairs. "Uncle Roy happened," he said. "You'll never guess what his call was about."

"Tell me."

"Asked me to be his best man at his wedding in May."

There was a long silence. "You're joking," Wendy said.

He shook his head. "Nope. Absolute truth. He's marrying some old harpy in Springfields residential home, and sounded extremely chirpy."

"Oh my God. And is he likely to live that long?"

"Oh yes. He sounded years younger. I shall have to go over there, and see what's to be done."

"Couldn't you push her into the garden pond and hold her under? Joke!"

Steven did not laugh. "Might come to that," he said. "I have some serious thinking to do."

More silence, and then Wendy said, "You need taking out of yourself. Go and get changed, and we'll hope to be at least amused by our neighbours. It's one of those parties where each couple takes a dish of something. I've done your favourite curried fish, so you can stick to that."

IVY SAT IN her room with Roy in his usual armchair. "Did you invite Steven to come over and hear our banns being published?" she asked.

She noticed his eyelids drooping as now she went through a provisional list of people they would ask to their wedding. She counted up, and made it over fifty. "I think this list is long enough," she said.

"Yes, indeed, Ivy dear." His answer was not much more than a mumble, and Ivy smiled.

"I've decided to call it all off," she said.

"I'm sure you're right, Ivy. As always."

"Roy Goodman! What did I just say?"

Roy snapped awake. "Um, not sure, dearest. Would you mind saying it again?"

"Never mind," Ivy said. "I've just had a count up, and the list stands at fifty-four. Enough, don't you think?"

"Quite. But what did you say before that? Something about the banns?"

"Did you invite your nephew to come and hear them read on Sunday? Steven, I mean. I suppose we should, though I don't much care for the sound of him. Perhaps his wife is more acceptable. Pity we can't have a best woman."

Roy chuckled. "Who do you suggest? Mrs. Spurling?"

"But seriously, Roy, are you sure you wouldn't rather have someone else? I am sure James at the shop would be happy to oblige."

Roy shook his head. "No, Ivy. I think family counts for quite a lot, and Steven is, after all, my last remaining relative. Close relative, that is."

"What about distant ones?"

"Lost touch long ago. Nobody takes any interest in an old retired bachelor farmer, with nothing to talk about but the old days."

"But there are some Goodmans somewhere?"

"Yes, I believe there were some Goodmans farming over Settlefield way. Not one of my farms. Another branch of the family, about ten miles away. But there was never any contact. A feud of some sort, I remember my mother saying."

"Perhaps we should get in touch with them and settle the feud. Often in these cases the new generation has no idea what it was all about. My family were like that. Dad's lot couldn't stand my mother, and wouldn't come anywhere near us. Mind you, I couldn't really blame them!"

"Let's talk about it in the morning," Roy said, struggling to his feet. "Time for my beloved to catch up on her beauty sleep."

Ivy giggled, a rusty, unused kind of sound. "Oh, you!" she

said, and took him by the arm to make sure he got safely to his own bed.

DRIVING BACK FROM a particularly dull evening, Steven and Wendy sat in silence, until Steven said suddenly that he needed a pee. "Don't think I can make it home," he said, and stopped the car. Running for the hedge, he disappeared from sight. Wendy sighed. She had not enjoyed any part of their friends' efforts to entertain them. The conversation was boring, and a couple of guests were an hour late owing to the non-appearance of their baby-sitter.

"You all right, Steve?" she shouted out of the car window.

He didn't answer, but stumbled into sight and returned to the car.

"I chucked up," he said finally. "Must've eaten something. I could taste something rotten. Did I have the stuff you cooked?"

"Oh yes. It was all set out on that big table. I had some of mine, and one or two others did, I think. I'm okay, for one, so I expect you'll be fine in the morning."

"Let's just get home and go to bed." He turned to look at her. "Perhaps next time you'll take my advice and refuse the invitation."

"The end of a perfect evening," said Wendy sadly. As they drove up to their house, she said pathetically, "At least I quite enjoyed talking to the others. We don't get out much."

Without answering, Steven made straight for the stairs, looking to neither left nor right, and after a quick visit to the bathroom, he yelled that he would sleep in the spare room. If he died in the night, she was to make sure that stingy old sod, Uncle Roy Goodman, remembered his promise to take care of his heir's family. "And tell him to find another best man, and good luck to him!" he shouted, banging the door behind him.

Five

"SO ARE WE back to Thursdays being Enquire Within's regular weekly meeting day?"

Deirdre had seen Gus's new car—well, almost new—drive into Tawny Wings and park by the front door. He had insisted on collecting Ivy and Roy from Springfields, saying it looked like snow was on the way. His prime reason for buying the Peugeot Partner, or, as he referred to it, a van with windows, was to be able to take them safely up to Deirdre's house.

"Very useful for a collapsible wheelchair, should you need one, Roy, plus any major shopping we might want."

"If you ask me," said Ivy, alighting with the aid of a hand from Gus, "it's just like mounting and dismounting a horse! But very comfortable once you're in it," she added, seeing his face fall.

When they had all made their way upstairs to the Enquire Within office, Gus headed for the chair behind the big desk. But as usual Ivy got in first, and proceeded to act as unofficial chairman.

"Now, Gus, what have you to report? I gather you made it

as far as the bus stop outside the shop? So would you like to tell us what happened next?"

"I certainly got as far as the queue waiting for the bus, and was gratified to see an elderly man answering Roy's description, but perhaps rather scruffier. Anyway, I wished him a cheery good morning to introduce myself, and got a very dusty answer!"

"Oh, poor Gus!" said Deirdre. "So he wasn't our unhappily married potential client, after all?"

"Let the man carry on, Deirdre," said Ivy. "You can have your say later."

"First of all," continued Gus, "he took great exception to Whippy, who was nowhere near him. Then he said he knew nothing about Roy or me, and didn't want to find out. In other words, get lost. I retreated with my tail between my legs, and watched him push his way into the bus."

"Oh dear, so sorry," said Roy. "Must have been the wrong man. Unless I was totally deceived when I met him. But you said my description was good?"

"Oh yes, it was him, all right. He had a very shifty look, and the minute I started to speak I could see his face close up. I think his denying everything was an automatic reaction. Goodness knows why. I don't think I look particularly threatening; do I? And if Whippy had been a bull terrier, I might have understood. But a small grey whippet is never going to harm anyone."

"Some people are just afraid of dogs in general," said Roy mildly. "But anyway, Gus, I do apologise for leading you into an unpleasant experience. I suppose we should think about whether it is worth trying again on Saturday?"

"Of course it is," said Ivy shortly. "Gus is thick-skinned enough, surely, to approach him again? He will probably have forgotten all about your first meeting by then, Augustus. Maybe just got out of bed the wrong side. Happens to us all now and then."

"Thanks, Ivy. But there is more. As I was standing disconsolately watching the bus disappear into the distance—"

"Get to the point," Deirdre said. "We can do without the literary stuff."

"As I was saying," said Gus. "There is more. James called

me into the shop, and said the old man was called Alfred Lowe and was known locally to be a bad-tempered old sod, if you'll pardon my French. He lives in Cemetery Lane, next to the old blacksmith's forge."

"So you and James went swiftly to the pub to regain your strength with a couple of pints and a game of shove ha'penny?" Deirdre said.

Gus smiled fondly at her. "More or less," he said. "Oh, and yes, there was something else rather important. James said Alf was a bachelor and lived on his own. He'd never heard talk of wives, neither present nor past. So this makes the whole thing a puzzle. I could swear Alf did remember something about meeting Roy, and was his man. I could see it in his face. And yet the story of a cheating wife could not apply, could it, if James was right?"

"Unless," said Ivy with emphasis, "he had been lying when Roy first met him. Sounds entirely possible that he was having a bit of sport to pass the time waiting for the bus. What do you think, Gus?"

"I think I should have another go on Saturday. He can only threaten to send for the police. But I shall be politeness itself. Humble, even. I could offer to buy him a pint. James said he was an occasional drinker at the pub."

"Good. Now, what's next?" Deirdre made a great show of looking at her watch.

"Hairdresser's appointment, might I ask?"

"Well, yes, Ivy. But not for a while yet. Please carry on."

"So, we continue with pursuing the man at the bus stop. Anything else? Something to keep us going if this turns out to be a nonstarter? We haven't come up here on a cold winter's morning for you to send us home after ten minutes so's you can go off to get beautified."

"Now, now, girls," said Gus. "I was wondering, Ivy, how the wedding plans are going? Is there anything we can do to help?"

"If you're implying I'm suffering from prenuptial nerves, the answer's no. Maybe no thank you," she said, relenting. "I must admit there does seem an awful lot to think about, just for a couple of old codgers deciding to get spliced."

Roy reached out and took her hand. "My love," he said.

"Nobody could call you an old codger. And we are all here to tackle problems together. Including prenuptial nerves! Now, as it happens, there is one small thing I would like to ask you all to help with, if it is not too much trouble."

They all relaxed, and Gus reflected that Roy was a national treasure. "Fire away, then, Roy," he said.

"As you know," Roy began, "my best man will be my nephew, Steven. He is, as far as I know, my only close relative."

"And your heir," said Deirdre.

"And, as you say, my heir. As I know little or nothing about him, I feel I should find out more, and at the same time do some research on the Goodman family over at Settlefield. All I know is that generations ago there was a link, but all connections were severed over a family squabble. It could be that there are still some of them over there, and it would be fitting, I think, if I could reestablish good feeling between the two branches of the family. I suppose I would like some family support, and it might be nice for my beloved here, should I go first. What do you think?"

This was a long speech from Roy, and Gus knew immediately that his colleague had been giving some serious thought to all this. For all their disagreements, there was affection between the members of Enquire Within, and certainly when Gus's wife had caused so much trouble, the others had stood by him.

"Of course! We shall enjoy doing a bit of family research. And now I've got the van with windows, we can follow up any leads we might uncover."

Ivy surreptitiously dabbed her eyes with a lace-edged handkerchief, and said that if anyone asked her, she didn't care if there were no other Goodmans in the entire world, so long as she could have Roy.

"Phew!" said Deirdre. "That's got that one dealt with, then. I love delving back into family history, so count me in, Roy. There are lots of sites on the computer that might help."

Roy smiled, and thanked everyone. "I shall expect to pay fees into the agency account," he said, and his suggestion was immediately drowned out by noisy refusals.

"So, Gus is going to the bus stop tomorrow morning, and as there's still time for a last coffee and a Miriam fruit scone, shall we end the meeting there?" Deirdre stood up, and walked towards the door.

"Looks like we already have," said Ivy, a trifle acidly. "Now that Miriam is baking for the shop, there will be no need for any of us to turn on our cookers, will there, Deirdre?"

Six

GUS LOOKED AT his watch. He had overslept, and fumbling for his watch disturbed an offended Whippy, who was still snoozing at the end of his bed.

"Blast!" It was Saturday already, and if the bus was on time, it would be across the Green and outside the shop in exactly one hour's time. He leapt out of bed, stubbing his toe on a leg of the bed. Hopping painfully to the bathroom, he had a quick sluice down, wishing he had not stayed so long at Miriam's last evening. She had, as usual, insisted he stay for coffee and chocs, and he had fallen asleep on her sofa. When he had surfaced at midnight, she was curled up with her head on his shoulder, leaving him in a dilemma. Should he wake her and return home, or should he leave her sleeping peacefully until morning?

He had chosen the first option, and she had been resentful, saying all he wanted from her was her cooking. He tried to find a tactful way of saying she was right, and was more or less shown the door.

Now he dressed quickly. One of these days, he said to himself, you will find yourself in Miriam Blake's warm bed, having been tempted once too often by her homemade primrose wine, and unable to stop her having her wicked way with you. Well, he consoled himself as he pulled a warm jersey over his head, worse things could happen.

He gave Whippy her breakfast, and looked at the clock. Ten minutes to go. "Better be off, little dog," he said, and fixed her lead. "Let's hope Roy's ugly man appears this morning. And if he turns out to be Alfred Lowe, I shall not be put off. Oh God, there's Miriam at the back door!" he added. "Come on, quickly, let's creep out the front way. Good dog. No, no barking! Quickly!"

Once out of the cottage and striding across the Green with Whippy trotting along beside him, Gus's spirits rose. It seemed as if the wedding of the year was really going to happen this time, and he looked forward to a May weekend of jollity. He was fond of both Ivy and Roy, and could think of no reason at all why they should not be very happy in the time left to them. He would call on them after his stint at the bus stop, and see how they were getting along with preparations. His own marriage had been disastrous, but he was not against the institution entirely. Sometimes he even considered asking Deirdre how she felt about it. But her recent reaction when she had quite mistakenly thought he was about to propose had been enough for him to forget it for the moment.

They reached the shop, and the usual crowd of shoppers stood waiting for the bus. It must be galling for James, Gus thought now. His own shop was well stocked with all that anyone could need, whilst not ten yards from his open door stood potential customers in a line ready to spend their all at Tesco in Thornwell.

But hang on a minute! There was Alf again! Why would a miserly old bachelor want to go two days in one week? But then again, why not? The thing to do would be to ask him. Gus took a deep breath, attached Whippy's lead to the shop's dog hook, and returned to the queue with a big smile.

"Good morning, Mr. Lowe," he said. "My name is Halfhide, Gus Halfhide, and I believe we may have friends in common? I am so sorry if I alarmed you, but I really only wanted to say hello."

"Hello," said Alf.

Progress, thought Gus. Definitely a better start than before. "I am sure I remember my old father mentioning your name.

He had a farm in the Cotswolds and was always going on about his brilliant stockman, one Donald Lowe? Does that ring bells?"

Alf stared at him. "Supposing it does?" he said suspiciously. "Now, look here, the bus is just coming, so if you're going into town, come and sit by me and we'll see if there's anything in your story. More likely a trumped-up reason to get me to talk. But we'll see. On you go; you go first."

As the bus started on its way, Gus's arm was touched by a kindly looking matron across the aisle. "Was that your dog?" she said. "Did you mean to leave her hooked up outside the shop?"

Panic! Gus tried to stand up to stop the bus, but Alf pulled him down in his seat. "Dog'll be all right," he said. "Do you want to talk to me or not? I'm not bothered, so you'd better make up your mind. You could get off at the next stop and walk back."

Gus thought for half a minute, and then pulled out his mobile. "I'll get James to take her in until I return," he said.

"Don't know what we'd do without our village shop," said Alf, with the trace of a smile. "So, I'm supposed to have met your friend at a bus stop a while back?"

"Yes, that's right. He said you were having wife trouble—do forgive me if I'm getting this wrong—and he offered the services of our enquiry agency, should you need it. We have just finished a case, and wondered if we could be of any use to you?"

It would have taken a monster not to be softened by Gus's anxiety to please.

"Well, what did you say your name was? Mine's Lowe. Alfred Lowe. Alf to my friends in the pub."

"Barrington pub? Haven't seen you in there. Mind you, I only go in for the odd pint and a game of darts."

"You any good? At darts, I mean."

"Not bad. I fill in if one of the regulars can't make a match in the league. How about yourself?"

"County champ in my youth. Misspent youth, I should say. I'll give you a game someday."

They were silent then until approaching the outskirts of Thornwell, and then Alf asked if Gus had much shopping to do.

"None," said Gus. "If you remember, you abducted me onto this bus."

Alf laughed uproariously. "Very good!" he said. "Now, would you like to be abducted to a café in the marketplace? Then I'll tell you the whole story of my ill-fated marriage."

"So it *was* you who met Roy that day?"

"Roy who?"

"Roy Goodman. He lives at Springfields residential home in Barrington. You must know him, surely?"

"Roy Goodman! Was that him that day? I thought the old bugger looked familiar! Well, I never. Roy Goodman, still in the land of the living! His family used to farm near us. A wealthy lot, they were. Several farms here and there. Goodmans everywhere a generation back, you know. What about Roy? Did he get wed, have children?"

Gus shook his head. He thought he would keep quiet about the forthcoming marriage between Roy and Ivy. "No, he's been a confirmed bachelor, I gather."

"Blimey. When the old man dies, then, there'll be quite a carve-up, won't there?" Gus did not answer, and Alf stirred in his seat. "Now, here we are," he said. "Follow me, and I can guarantee a good cup of tea and the best rock cakes in the county."

Gus frowned. This family information did not quite accord with Roy's oft-repeated denial of any close relations, except for one nephew, son of a now-deceased sister. It could just be true, if all the Goodmans and their offspring were now dead. Except one, and he was to be Roy's best man. Odd, but possible.

When they were settled in a scruffy café in a side street off the marketplace, Gus thought it was time to open the subject of Alf's marriage. But the old man was too swift for him.

"I've just remembered something else about old Roy," he said, with a smirk. "I'm sure it was him who was once engaged to his cousin Ethel. Lovely girl, she was. Quite a bit younger than him. I never knew what happened, but my auntie told my mother that Ethel Goodman was jilted. Roy broke it off, they said. At the altar steps, if I remember rightly. He'd found some rich bloke's daughter who was a better bet, so the rumours said. There was talk of him being sued for breach of contract, but I don't know if that was even legal in them days. Are you sure he's never been married? He must be getting on for eighty odd?"

Gus was astonished. He was sure this had never been mentioned at Springfields, unless Ivy had been told by Roy and they had agreed to keep it quiet. Good heavens! If anyone had suggested that Roy was a dishonest old philanderer, Gus would have staked his life on them being wrong!

"You've gone quiet, Gus. Something I said? Don't you worry about old Roy. Whatever happened in the past is not going to make much difference to an old man in his eighties, is it?" Alf chuckled. "Let's go mad an' have another rock cake. What do you say, Gus? Then I'll tell you the story of my life."

Seven

"WHEN I WAS quite a young lad," said Alf, fishing out of his pocket a grubby red handkerchief and blowing his nose noisily, "I fell deeply in love, as they say, with a gel who was at school with me. We were friends right from infants' class. We used to do country dancing in them days, and Susan was always my partner. Her favourite was Gathering Peascods, where couples stood in a long line and then the bottom pair danced up to the top and so on. You in a hurry, Gus? I see you looking at your watch. There's no bus for a couple of hours, and you said you'd got no shopping to do. Just you sit there and listen to me. You might learn something."

"No, no, I'm going nowhere. You carry on, Alf. Fascinating stuff."

"Then, later on," Alf continued relentlessly, "during the war, we used to get what we called aeroplane glass—it was really some kind of perspex—and fashion it into rings and bracelets and stuff."

"How on earth did you do that?" Gus asked, fascinated by an aspect of World War Two totally new to him.

"Not sure. Cut it, I think. My dad gave me one for Susan,

and it had a blue stone glued into it. I told her it was a sapphire, and I made it myself, and she laughed at me. She was always laughing at me. Anyway we got married eventually."

"Good," said Gus, with some relief. So Alf *had* been married. "And it ended badly, did it?"

"You could say that. She died in childbirth. The baby died, too. It was a boy, a lovely bouncing boy. I suppose it wouldn't happen now."

Gus looked at him and frowned. Alf had a dreamy look on his face, and a half smile, which hardly seemed appropriate.

"Alfred," said Gus. "Are you telling me the truth, or making it up as you go along?"

Alf tried to look affronted, but gave up and burst into a raucous laugh. "Got you going there, didn't I! I always could tell a good story. Known for it."

"So how much of all that was the truth, you old fibber?"

"Not a lot," he replied comfortably. "Susan didn't die, and she didn't have any children. Didn't want them. But she left me. Wanted a divorce, but I'm Roman Catholic, and marriage is for life. So there we are. Husband and wife, but not lived together for thirty years. She gets in touch when she finds it convenient to have a husband, and that's about it."

"Ah, now, is that really the truth? Because if so, that sounds like what you told Roy at the bus stop that day. So, do you want help or not? Seems you've rubbed along reasonably well up to now?"

"But things have changed. She's got her whole family together, and now they're talking again about persuading me to give her a divorce."

"Sounds like a straightforward case for a lawyer. I don't think Enquire Within is well enough qualified to help you, Alf."

"How about another pot of tea? I haven't finished telling you yet. The fact is, as far as I'm concerned, we was married in the sight of God, an' there's no way of undoing that. As long as ye both shall live, an' all that."

"No more tea for me, thanks. But I'll sit with you, if you want more. Actually, I wouldn't say no to another rock cake. As to the divorce, aren't you being a bit of a dog in the manger? You don't want her, but you won't let anyone else have her?"

When they were served, Alf resumed. "The thing is, young

Gus, I think she might have been shacked up with a bloke all these years, and now he wants to marry her. Make it legal, an' that. Maybe put a gun to her head? Well, the more trouble I can make for her, the better I shall like it. She put me through it when we was living together, I can assure you of that. I didn't go to church, an' that, but we were both Catholics, and that goes deep. She knew I wouldn't divorce her then, and I won't now. When I go, I mean to go with my image of a nasty old man safely intact! What do you say to that? Can you keep her off my back? That's all I want. Tell her there's no chance, and she'll just have to carry on like she's been doing. All I want is a bit o' peace, a game of darts, and a couple of pints in the pub. Not a load of legal stuff and notices in the local paper. No, you tell her, boy."

"I'm sure we can help," Gus said, though he was far from sure. "I must take the whole case to my colleagues for discussion, and then I'll be in touch. Roy will be particularly interested to hear about your predicament, you being neighbours in the past."

"You'd better think twice about that stuff I told you about him and Ethel, my old flame."

"Why? Wasn't it true?"

"Ah," said Alf, struggling to his feet. "That'd be telling, wouldn't it?"

BY THE TIME Gus got off the return bus in Barrington, he was still confused. He got halfway home and then remembered Whippy.

"How could you forget her, Gus?" said Deirdre. She had stocked up on chocolate cake and homemade shortbread, and was leaving the shop looking guilty.

"Thought you were on a diet?" he said. "Anyway, I love you as you are, so no need to hide the goodies from me."

"Never mind about dieting," she said huffily. "Did you find Roy's man at the bus stop?"

"Oh yes, I found him, all right! I've spent a happy afternoon trying to sort out truth from fiction. All shall be told at our next meeting, unless Ivy wants to get us together sooner. Here, let me carry those for you."

"No, thanks. You've got a dog to collect, remember?"

"Right! See you soon, Deirdre love. Must go now. Miriam's promised me a slap-up lunch, with a new bone for Whippy."

Deirdre was almost sure that Gus had no evil designs on Miriam, but she regarded him as her property and did not like to hear about her rival's latest move. Bones for his dog now! The woman was pathetic.

"Fine," she said. "Enjoy yourself. I'll think of you on the sagging sofa whilst I am languishing in the arms of the squire in his stately home."

Gus laughed. "I do love you, you know," he said. "In spite of everything."

IVY HAD SEEN Deirdre walking by Springfields, and now saw her returning with shopping bags bulging.

"Do you think she's given up driving the Bentley to Oakbridge to shop at the supermarket? Of course, there's the weekly hairdo as well. But those full bags look to me like weekly supplies. Has she started to think of the environment at last?"

"Probably not, dearest," said Roy sweetly. "I think she stocks up on Miriam's baking once a week, and shares it with us on Thursdays."

"Which reminds me, shall we get together tomorrow for tea? Sunday tea is always nice here in Springfields. Old Spurling is off duty, and Katya loves to bake. We could ask her to serve it by the fire in the lounge. Nice and cosy. Shall we give Deirdre and Gus a ring to fix it? Then we can hear how he got on this morning. He was seen getting on the bus, and Whippy was taken in by James at the shop."

"How on earth do you know all that?" Roy never ceased to marvel at his beloved's talent for information-gathering.

"Katya told me. She went to the shop for supplies, and they were all talking about it."

Katya was one of two Polish girls working at Springfields, and had a special fondness for Ivy Beasley. She had a knack of saying the right thing and treating Ivy with due respect. She thoroughly approved of the Roy and Ivy romance, and did all she could to foster it.

"Guests for tea?" she said now, coming into the residents' lounge. "I have new cookies for you to try."

"You are a treasure," said Ivy. "And yes, Deirdre and Gus will be here around four o'clock."

"Unless we let you know otherwise," said Roy considerately. After all, they had not yet been asked, though he knew Ivy regarded her invitation as an order to attend.

Eight

"YOU'D THINK IVY would say 'please' once in a while, wouldn't you?" Deirdre had met Gus walking down to Springfields and the cold wind had brought colour to her cheeks.

"More like a three-line whip! *Be here at four o'clock, and don't be late!* But it wasn't quite like that. She did ask me if I was free. Good old Ivy. Where would we be without her sharp tongue and passion for giving orders? I was told by somebody that when she first came here she was very unhappy and lonely. She'd lived in Round Ringford all her life up to then. But my goodness, she was soon having them all running around at Springfields, reorganising things for her!

"Well, here we are, then. All present and correct. Let's go in and see what the old thing has to tell us this afternoon. Have you ever wondered what dear Roy sees in her?"

Gus shook his head and took her arm. "Love is blind, so they say. In we go."

They were greeted by Miss Pinkney, who smiled broadly and said that she had with some difficulty turfed out a couple of regular fireside residents and reserved the chairs with

newspapers so that they could join Miss Beasley and Mr. Goodman for tea.

"You look frozen, my dear," she said to Deirdre. "Did you
walk all the way from Tawny Wings?"

"It's all of two hundred yards," said a brisk voice. Ivy
emerged from the lounge and told them to look sharp. "You're
ten minutes late, and me and Roy have waited tea until you
arrived. Tell Katya to bring it in now, please, Miss Pinkney."

"See? She said 'please,' " whispered Gus into Deirdre's ear.
"Good omen?"

AFTER GOOD STRONG cups of tea had been served, with
plates of golden cookies, Gus settled back in his chair and
asked if the others would like to hear how he'd got on with
Roy's man at the bus stop. Most of the other residents had
retired to watch television, and the ones who remained were
stone deaf. Inevitably, the tea party took on more of a meeting
air. Miss Pinkney came in to put more logs on the fire and to
ask them if they would like more tea.

"No, thank you," said Ivy. "I trust we shall be more or less
undisturbed now? There are only three chairs in my bedroom,
and the interview room is no doubt damp and cold as usual?"

Miss Pinkney retreated, shutting the lounge door quietly
behind her.

"Right, Gus. Off you go."

"Well, you know I was having another try with the sinister-
looking man in black-framed spectacles? This time I had more
luck."

"We know you got on the bus with him and disappeared en
route to Thornwell, leaving poor Whippy hooked up outside
the shop," said Ivy. "You can skip that bit, and carry on."

"Thank you, Ivy. I'll make the rest as brief as possible. It
turns out that he is, after all, the man Roy met. His name is
Alfred Lowe, he lives in Barrington in a small cottage, and has
been married but separated for thirty years. His wife is younger
than him and is still living. She has relations who are supporting her in her attempt to get a divorce. He wants us to get them
all, including his wife, off his back."

"Brilliant report, Gus!" said Deirdre admiringly.

Ivy nodded agreement. "Couldn't have done better myself," she said. "But why won't he divorce her? Surely that would be the most sensible course?"

"Straight to the heart of the matter, Ivy dearest," said Roy. "Surely, Gus, that would be the simplest answer?"

"As far as I could understand the wicked old bloke, he wants to make her suffer. But he also genuinely objects because of his religion. He is a Roman Catholic, born and bred."

"Ah, then that is a problem!" said Deirdre. "Do we really want anything to do with this grim old character?"

"Funnily enough," said Gus, helping himself to a last cookie, "I rather took to him. A wicked sense of humour, and sharp as a pin. If we could find a way of helping him, I'd recommend we take him on. It shouldn't take much to settle it one way or another. There's annulment, for one thing. Recognised by the state, but not the RC Church. But it would enable her to have a legal second marriage. Takes forever to get through, and Alf, understandably at his age, doesn't want the hassle."

He was quiet now, trying to decide whether to reveal what Alf had said about Roy and Ethel. Perhaps it would be best to keep quiet on that for the moment. Nothing to be gained by spilling it all out when it might well have been another figment of Alf's fertile imagination. And yet . . .

"I forgot to say, Roy, that he did remember you, and some of your family who'd farmed over towards Settlefield. Did you recognise him at all?"

"What was his name, did you say?"

"Lowe, Alfred Lowe. Bit of a hermit now, so I gather from James in the shop. Doesn't come out much in the village, but goes twice a week on the bus."

"Good heavens! I've got it! The Lowes were a terrible family! Their farm was a shambles. Broken-down fences, sheep wandering everywhere, fields lying fallow for years. I'm not at all sure I want to be mixed up with them again."

"But Roy dear," said Ivy, "this is just one old man, wife deserted him for years, and now wants to wreck his retirement with divorce proceedings, which could be, at the least, lengthy. We've nothing else on at the moment, and it might be a useful assignment for us."

"If you say so, Ivy. It gets my vote, then, so long as it does not prove to be too time-consuming for you to enjoy planning our wedding. And I must say I trust Gus absolutely in his recommendation. Alfred Lowe does sound quite a character. So yes, Gus, I support you."

"So that leaves me," said Deirdre. "I must say he doesn't sound like a man in need of the machinations of the law, church or state. Surely if one of us, maybe me, could go and have a word with the wife? And then I could report to Alf. Try a bit of female charm?"

"Don't be naïve, Deirdre," said Ivy sharply. "Alf Lowe sounds very capable of eating you for breakfast! He's not going to budge from his decision. No, this is going to need thinking out carefully. Gus, you've had time to do some thinking since you got back. Anything occur to you?"

"Not much time, Ivy! I think we should all give it some serious constructive thought and come to a decision at our meeting on Thursday. How does that sound?"

"Excellent," said Roy. "So, now let's talk about something really exciting, like the forthcoming marriage of Ivy Beasley to Roy Goodman, bachelor of this parish!"

AS DEIRDRE AND Gus walked away from Springfields, a few flakes of snow were beginning to fall.

"Fancy a drink?" Deirdre asked.

"Not 'arf," said Gus. "There was more that I didn't tell the others, more from that old reprobate, Alf. I'm bursting with it, so if you swear to absolutely cross your heart and hope to die if you reveal the secret, I'll tell you what else he said."

"How can I resist? Come on, boy, let's get back before the storm. Look at that sky—it's full of snow. You might even get snowed in and have to stay the night, with any luck."

"SO DID YOU enjoy your tea party?" Katya came to collect the cups and saucers and empty plates. She never ceased to marvel at the effect that Miss Beasley had on her associates. They had arrived shivering and miserable from the cold wind, and when she watched them leaving, both Mr. Halfhide and

Mrs. Bloxham had a spring in their step, and marched off laughing, arm in arm.

"Yes, thank you, dear," said Ivy. "The cookies were a triumph. You could market them and make a fortune. I think Mr. Goodman and I will retire for our afternoon snooze now. It is a little late, but we have a great deal to think about. Isn't that right, Roy?"

"Yes, indeed. Foremost in my mind at the moment is when shall we take our usual taxi in to Oakbridge to choose the wedding ring? And after that, I shall decide on which tailor in town will have the honour of making my wedding suit. How about you, Ivy?"

"I shall close my eyes and try to decide who is the best person of us four to contact Alf's wife and persuade her to change her mind."

"Who is Alf, if I may ask? We have no one here called Alf. Is he a friend of yours in the village?" Katya picked up the loaded tray and smiled at them.

"He's certainly in the village, but we have yet to decide whether he is friend or foe," said Ivy, and added, "Come along, Roy. Up we go."

Nine

THE SNOW OUTSIDE Alf's cottage was already four inches deep when he struggled to open his front door and found his wife on his doorstep.

"Go away!" he said, attempting to shut the door. But a ridge of snow, driven against it by the wind, now fell onto his doormat.

"Don't be ridiculous, Alf! Let me in and I'll clear this lot away with a spade."

"I don't need your help, Susan. Just go, and then we'll both be happy. You know whenever we meet it ends in a flaming row. Just go, while the going's good."

"No chance. I haven't come all this way and got wet feet into the bargain to be turned away by my own husband."

"Huh! Some husband. You can't be a husband without a wife, and I haven't had one of those for thirty years."

"Oh, not that old thing! Now," she added, pushing past him into his living room, "where's your shovel? That'll do. Then we can shut the door and you can offer me a cup of coffee. We need to have a talk urgently, and we might as well attempt it without you losing your temper."

"Me! Lose my temper? Not at my age. Brings on a heart attack, you know. You must be thinking of someone else. One of your other husbands, or lovers, or whatever you call them. I'm as calm as can be. So leave my snowy door to me and go home."

But Susan Lowe was made of sterner stuff, and had no intention of leaving Alf without getting him to promise to go with her to solicitors in Thornwell.

She kicked aside the ridge of snow, saying her feet couldn't get any wetter, and shoved the door until it closed.

"Now," she said in a managing voice, "where's your kettle?"

"Where d'you think it is? In the kitchen, of course. And if you want coffee, you can make it yourself."

IVY WALKED ALONG steadily beside Roy in his trundle until they reached the church gate. As if all necessary summons to attend had been issued, the bells stopped pealing and diminished to a single tolling, warning that the service was about to start.

"Good morning, Miss Beasley. And Mr. Goodman! Allow me to help you alight," said the churchwarden, who prided himself on giving his warmest welcome to all churchgoers.

"Good morning. And thank you, but Mr. Goodman is perfectly capable of managing," said Ivy, marching straight past him and up the aisle to the front row of pews. There she stood and waited until Roy caught her up, and then she helped him to sit down. She was still on her knees praying for the whole world, if not the universe, when the vicar entered and the congregation stood with hymnbooks at the ready.

"Welcome, everyone, to our service this morning," said the vicar, the Reverend Dorothy King. She had had enough of Miss Beasley's lengthy prayers, calculated, she was convinced, to make her wait, unwilling to interrupt her devotions. But last week she had waited five minutes, and had decided enough was enough.

"Our opening hymn is 'Who Would True Valour See.' Number four hundred and five."

And as a silent postscript she added that she could do with

a bit of valour herself to deal with the likes of Miss Ivy
Beasley.

The service proceeded smoothly, until the banns were
announced. Roy reached across and took Ivy's cold hand in his
warm one.

"I publish the banns of marriage," said the vicar with a happy
smile, "between Ivy Beasley, spinster of this parish, and Roy
Vivian Goodman, bachelor of this parish. This is the first time
of asking If any of you know cause or just impediment why
these two persons should not be joined together in holy matri
mony, ye are to declare it."

The usual silence greeted this announcement, and the vicar
made a great show of pretended relief. The congregation dutifully tittered.

"First step achieved," whispered Roy. "Now all I have to do
is make sure you don't escape." He leaned across and kissed
her on the cheek.

"KISSED ME IN front of everybody!" said Ivy to Katya at
lunchtime. "I could have died with embarrassment."

"But weren't you a little bit proud?" Katya smiled sweetly
as Roy limped across the dining room to where Ivy sat.

"Proud and pleased," said Ivy firmly, as Katya held the chair
for Roy to sit down. "But I was brought up not to show emotion,
you know We were, in them days. Old habits are hard to break.
Now, what have we for Sunday lunch?"

"Roast pork, applesauce, roast potatoes, and parsnips," the
girl said. "And for pudding, Anya has made for you a Polish
pudding. With English custard, of course!"

After they had cleared their plates, hungry after the excite-
ment of the morning, Roy turned to Ivy and asked whether she
wouldn't like a little outing to celebrate the first reading of the
banns.

"But where shall we go? The pavements are still very slippery. You know you nearly skidded this morning in your
trundle, and I was not too steady on my pins."

"I have checked, my dear. It's stopped snowing, and the lane
up to the cemetery has been completely cleared. We could go
as far as you like and turn around whenever you say so. Sunday

afternoon in Springfields is exceedingly boring, with all the old dears snoring after their heavy lunches, and television churning out endless sporting fixtures. What do you say?"

Ivy agreed reluctantly. She always had knitting or needlework to occupy blank hours, but she did feel that they should mark their day in some way. "Very well," she said. "But we must tell Pinkers in case one of us crashes down and there is nobody to rightle us."

"Like sheep on their backs in a meadow," said Roy.

"Exactly," said Ivy.

They wrapped themselves up in scarves and gloves and woolly hats, and set off, Roy in his trundle and Ivy with a stout stick to keep her steady. They were halfway up to the cemetery when they approached a cottage facing directly onto the pavement. Suddenly the door flew open, sending out a shower of dirty snow, and a woman emerged. She saw them just in time, and grabbed the handle of the door behind her.

"Oops! Look where you're going, you two! You should be safely by the fire at your age, you know. These pavements are dangerous."

"Susan! Just mind your manners! These two kind people live here, and they don't expect strange women to jump out in front of them. Sorry, folks! Are you hurt?"

"Well, I'm off, Alf. I'll be back; you can be sure of that." Susan Lowe stormed off down the lane, slipping and sliding from side to side and only just remaining upright.

"Good riddance, I say," said Alf, smiling at Roy. "Women! Pity we can't do without them."

"I'm afraid I don't agree," said Roy gently. "My name is Roy Goodman, and we have met before. At the bus stop. This is my fiancée, Miss Ivy Beasley. And you, if I'm not much mistaken, are Alfred Lowe."

"Bless me! If it isn't old Roy! I only just heard tell you were living in Barrington. After all these years, eh? We must get together and have some reminiscing. But not now, old chap. Time you were getting back. Your fiancée looks blue with cold. Good day to both of you." He turned back into his cottage and shut the door.

"So that is the nasty old man? The notorious Alfred Lowe?" said Ivy. "If you ask me, he is a polite and pleasant person.

Apart from his views on women, of course. Ready to go back now? We can look for your ancestors in the cemetery some other day. What a useful idea of yours to come up here! If I didn't know you were not a scheming old codger, I'd think you planned it purposely, in the hope we'd meet your new friend Alfred Lowe."

"Never crossed my mind, beloved," answered Roy. "Hold on to the trundle if that would make you feel more secure. Look, there's blue sky over the woods! I can guarantee this slushy stuff will be gone by morning."

They arrived safely back at Springfields, only to find that a perfectly audible row was going on in the office between Miss Pinkney and Mrs. Spurling, who had returned unexpectedly to find two of her residents out in the raw air of a winter's afternoon, unaccompanied and still not returned.

"We're back, Pinkers!" shouted Ivy as they passed the office door. This flew open and Mrs. Spurling came out. "And where do you think you two have been?" she demanded.

"Up to the cemetery," said Roy, and Ivy knew at once what Mrs. Spurling's reply would be.

She obliged. "You'll be up there permanently, if you don't take notice of Springfields' rules," she almost shouted. "Now go and warm up. I'll send Katya with a nice hot cup of tea."

"Whisky and hot water, please," said Ivy. "That's for Roy. I'll have a glass of hot ginger ale and lemon. Now, if you will excuse us, we will go and change our socks."

Ten

AS ROY HAD predicted, the next morning dawned with a clear blue sky, bright sunshine, and not a sign of the dark snow clouds that had gathered over the village.

"There was a frost last night, Ivy," he said, as she sat down at the breakfast table. "I wonder if the roads are suitable for us to take a taxi to Thornwell? We need to go to a jeweller to decide on a wedding ring. And then we can have our usual coffee. I advise boots and warmest clothing. The sunlight is deceptive at this time of the year. Not much warmth in it. But do you know, beloved, I caught a smell of spring in the air when I opened my bedroom window this morning! Farmers have sensitive noses, and I haven't lost the skill."

"I should think pig farmers would be glad to have none of that particular skill! At Ringford, just behind my house, there was a man who kept pigs intensively, under cover. Never let out in the field. And turkeys at Christmastime. The stink! It was enough to turn you up, I can tell you."

"You have no romance in your soul, Ivy dear. After breakfast I shall ring for a taxi, and hope that the sight of a wedding ring will erase all thoughts of pig muck."

Ivy roared with laughter. "That's more like it," she said. "Good honest pig—"

"Good morning, Miss Beasley and Mr. Goodman. How are we this fine morning? No ill effects from your adventure yesterday, I trust?" Mrs. Spurling managed a small smile, but her tone was sour.

Ivy drew herself up in her seat and said if Mrs. Spurling considered a short walk up to the village cemetery an adventure, she must have led a very sheltered life. Roy attempted to smooth things down by saying that the bacon had been particularly tasty this morning, but Mrs. Spurling stalked off, high dudgeon in every step.

THEIR USUAL TAXI, driven by a Presley fan named Elvis, was adapted to carry Roy in his trundle, and arrived promptly at ten o'clock. "Didn't expect you two to be off shopping this morning. We were deep in snow yesterday!"

"Nearly all gone now, though," Roy said. "Don't forget I was a working farmer, Elvis. The world doesn't stop turning for a few flakes of snow."

"Some special reason for going into town this morning?" Elvis had been driving Ivy and Roy around the county for a long time now, and considered them as special friends. He loved the idea of this late romance, and had encouraged it from the time Ivy, spiky and lonely, had arrived in Springfields.

"No, nothing special," said Ivy, winking at Roy.

"Very special," said Roy, refusing to be silenced. "We shall be buying Ivy's wedding ring. She has very pretty hands, and deserves the best."

Ivy looked down at her own hands, and thought that Roy must be blind. They were small, certainly, but knobbly and veined. Still, if he loved them, that was all that mattered.

"Wow! Have you named the day yet, you two lovebirds?"

"Don't be ridiculous, Elvis," said Ivy. "But perhaps it would be a good thing to ask you to reserve May the fifth? We haven't got invitations out yet, but you're on the list. And we might need you for the honeymoon. Yet to be arranged."

"Funny you should mention that date," Elvis said, after thanking them profusely. "The office had a call this morning from a Mr. Wright, wanting to book a taxi for May five, for a wedding in Barrington church. Could that be yours?"

Ivy and Roy exchanged glances. "That's right," said Ivy. "He's Roy's nephew, and going to be best man. Steven and Wendy Wright, that's them."

"Your nephew? Well, bless me," said Elvis. "He used to be one of my regular customers, a year or so ago. Done for speeding, doing a hundred miles an hour on the motorway, and had his licence taken away for several months. I taxied him all over the country. Funny bloke, if you don't mind my saying so. Never said a word, all the time I was driving him. He used to get in, tell me to turn off me radio, open up his newspaper, and disappear behind it until we reached his office. One of them big furniture stores out of town. Still, I expect you know that, Mr. Goodman?"

"I really don't know much about him," said Roy. "He's my late sister's son, and my only living relation. Well, close relation, that is. He comes to see me twice a year."

"His wife was always very polite and nice," said Elvis. "Always thanked me when I brought him home. Pity you haven't got someone a bit jollier, Mr. Goodman. And since you haven't asked, I'm offering to be understudy to your nephew, should anything happen to him."

"Done," said Roy. "Though I reckon Steven has had plenty of experience in looking after himself. I remember my sister telling me that as a young lad he was always sailing a bit too close to the wind. Anyway, we shall see. Now here we are. My favourite old jeweller. Been here in Thornwell for centuries, literally."

"When shall I pick you up again? Are you having your usual coffee?"

Ivy and Roy were unloaded carefully, and waved as Elvis drove off.

"Come along, now, dearest," said Roy. "Let's enjoy ourselves." He parked his trundle and took Ivy's arm. He could manage short distances with the help of a stick, and made the most of this, determined not to be wheelchair bound for good.

The jeweller was a tubby, round-faced man with half-moon spectacles on the end of his nose. His sparse grey hair was carefully combed forward over the top of his head, and he greeted them with a chuckle and a sparkle in his blue eyes.

"Good morning, Roy," he said. "I got your message, and I must say I am extremely excited by your news. And this is—?"

"Miss Ivy Beasley. My dear, this is Oliver Beconsfield. His family have been here since—when, Oliver?"

"Seventeen ninety-eight. I hasten to add that I myself have not been here that long!"

Ivy shook hands over the counter, and thought she had never seen anyone in her long life so like she imagined Charles Dickens's Mister Cheeryble.

Wedding rings of all sizes, shapes, and precious metals were brought out for Ivy to study. She spent a long time looking at them, shutting herself out of the conversation between Roy and Mr. Beconsfield. Finally, rejecting all but one, she turned to Roy.

"This will do very nicely," she said. She handed a plain gold band to Roy and he smiled. "I knew as much," he said, taking her hand and kissing it. "A good plain ring in the best gold. My Ivy, Oliver, my old pal, is the most sensible, practical woman I ever met. Such a pity I didn't find her sooner! She'd have made an excellent farmer's wife."

"You were not short of candidates, if I remember correctly," Oliver Beconsfield replied with a knowing smile. "Even came to me for an engagement ring, didn't you? You must have escaped that one! But now this lovely lady has captured your heart."

Roy coloured and looked extremely uncomfortable. "Our memories play us tricks, don't you find, Oliver?"

"Well, mine don't," said Ivy, "and I seem to remember we plan to have a coffee in our usual café. Let's be off, then, Roy," she added, and took his arm.

Then she turned back to address the jeweller. "I expect you say this rubbish to all the couples who come in for rings, don't you? Well, it's all very well, and much appreciated, but now I've chosen, not only a ring but a husband. So I'll say good day to you, Mr. Beconsfield, and thank you for your help."

GUS HAD ALSO ventured into town this morning, reluctantly, as it happened, since when he looked out of his window and saw the wintry landscape, he put on an extra jersey and piled up logs on his fire, planning a cosy day indoors with

Whippy. But then he recollected his intention to research Roman Catholic marriage laws, and as his computer had crashed and the man who promised to fix it had not turned up, he decided to go into town and do some ferreting in the library. At least he would have something to report to Ivy and Roy at their next meeting.

The library was warm, and the librarian friendly and attractive, and Gus sat down with the necessary books chosen for him. After more than an hour at the library computer and checking facts in hefty books, he sat back in his chair and thought.

The relevant facts to emerge were, one, that the Catholic Church regards its marriages as made in the sight of God, never to be torn asunder. And two, that any attempt to divorce and remarry would be lengthy and difficult. "So if I was a Roman Catholic," Gus said aloud, "my first marriage in church would be a union, never to be dissolved by anyone except God. And that's what old Alf is saying to his wife, Susan."

"Excuse me," said a familiar voice, "are you needing some help?"

The attractive librarian leaned over Gus's shoulder. "Have you found some useful information? I know it is a complicated subject. Are you researching for yourself?"

"No, not for me. I'm not Catholic, and my first marriage has been irrevocably dissolved. No, this is all about a friend who needs the information. The trouble is, I may be wasting my time, as I am not even sure he is really a Roman Catholic! Still, Enquire Within has to enquire. The nature of the beast! Anyway, thanks for your help. Next time I come to the library, I'll ask for you. Your name is?"

"Annie," she said, laughing. "And enquiring is my business, too."

Eleven

WHEN IVY AND Roy arrived back at Springfields, just in time for lunch, Mrs. Spurling intercepted them on their way to the dining room.

"No good looking at your watch, Mrs. Spurling," said Ivy. "We are exactly on time. At least, we shall be if we are not interrupted."

"Dear Miss Beasley," said Mrs. Spurling with exaggerated politeness, "always so precise! No, I have no wish to curb your activities. I was about to give you a message, Mr. Goodman. Your nephew—a Mr. Wright?—is calling in to see you at about three o'clock tomorrow afternoon to discuss wedding details. I believe he is to be your best man. I must say he sounds very charming and helpful."

"Thank you, my dear," said Roy. "Where shall we see him, Ivy? In the little interview room? That would be private. Ears do flap in the lounge if there's anything interesting going on with visitors. Natural enough, I'm sure. But perhaps this time . . . ?"

"Of course," said Mrs. Spurling. Nice Mr. Goodman, she thought. What on earth does he see in this sharp old spinster? Before she came, he was so easy and undemanding, but now—!

"So you'll make sure it is clean and warm for us, won't you?" added Ivy "Now, we must go in to lunch, or we shall be incurring black looks. Come along, Roy."

Ivy sailed into the dining room and sat down. When Roy had caught up with her, she leaned towards him and said in a stage whisper, "Do say if you'd rather see Steven by yourself, dearest. I'm afraid I automatically assumed it would be both of us, but you will say if you think I'm presuming, won't you?"

Roy laughed aloud. "Ivy, you and I are about to be one! I shall be extremely glad if you are with me. I don't feel I know Steven at all. For instance, I knew nothing about his driving ban. He has blown in here over the years, perhaps twice a year, and talked platitudes about the weather and farming—about which he knows nothing—and then disappeared again for another six months. The role of best man is important, I believe, so we must make sure he does it the way *we* want it. Can't have him revealing the sins of my youth in his speech!"

"IT'S SHEPHERD'S PIE today, Miss Beasley, with a lovely crispy potato topping."

"Thank you, Katya dear," said Ivy. "You describe it beautifully, but the fact is that it is usually minced up leftover meat from yesterday's roast. My mother used always to make it on Mondays, and the meat was always grey and gristly."

"But Anya has the magic touch," Katya said. "The meat has a delicious basil sauce, and potatoes are mashed with butter. If you don't like it, I'll eat my hat!"

"Where on earth did you get that expression? Though I must say my mother's shepherd's pie tasted like an old felt trilby." Ivy had cheered up now, and tackled her lunch with a will. Roy watched her make short work of the pudding which followed, and thought how much he loved and admired her. She had changed his life.

"Do you fancy a stroll down Hangman's Lane this afternoon?" he said now, as they left the dining room. "We might catch Gus at home, ready for a short walk with Whippy? He might have something interesting to tell us."

"We certainly have something interesting to tell him," Ivy said. "That woman we saw yesterday coming out of Alf's

cottage was definitely Mrs. Lowe, don't you think? They were
having a real ding-dong. She sounded like a regular fishwife!
I feel sorry for that man, you know. I reckon he's had a lot to put
up with. Good idea of yours. We'll get our coats and go straight
away. Then we can have our snooze when we get back."

They managed to slip out quietly, telling only Miss Pinkney
that they were going and would not be long.

"The sun's really warm now," Ivy said, visibly relaxing once
out of the gates of what she and Roy privately called their
prison.

"Right, and you are looking lovely as ever, my dearest." Roy
sat up straight as a ramrod in his trundle, and they set off across
the Green in the direction of Hangman's Lane.

Gus Halfhide lived in the end cottage of the Hangman's Row
terrace, and beyond were Barrington Woods, a favourite place
for villagers to walk in summer. They were part of the estate
belonging to Theo Roussel, the squire up at the Hall. He was
very tough on trespassers, but as in many English villages, com-
moners' rights were upheld from generation to generation.

Nobody now grazed their cattle on the Green, nor did most
sportsmen shoot game in the woods without permission. There
were still poachers from time to time, but David Budd, the game-
keeper, kept trespassing under reasonable control. He lived at
the opposite end of the terrace with his wife and two small boys.

As Ivy and Roy approached, Rose Budd lifted her head from
brushing slush away from her gate, and welcomed them with
a cheery smile.

"How are you both? It is lovely now, and the forecast is
good."

"We are venturing out from incarceration," said Roy with
a smile. "We dread being snowbound, don't we, Ivy?"

"Afraid the boys' snowman is melting away rapidly," Rose
said. "He was quite something for a while. Are you visiting Mr.
Halfhide? I believe he's at home. We know everyone's move-
ments here in the Lane, I'm ashamed to say!"

Gus was indeed at home, hiding from his over-friendly
neighbour, Miriam Blake. He peeped out of his window when
he heard the doorbell, and was relieved to see Ivy and Roy.

"Nice to see you two! Come on in. You must need a rest
after a long walk."

"No thanks," said Ivy. "We mean to go on into the woods for a bit. Just the path that'll take the trundle. We thought you might like to join us. You and Whippy maybe?"

Gus sighed. He had been planning an afternoon in front of a football match on the telly.

Ivy sensed his reluctance, and said firmly that the fresh air would do him good, and his dog, too. "That Whippy doesn't get nearly enough exercise for the breed," she added. "She should be able to go like the wind, instead of strolling on a lead across the Green to the shop every day."

"I give her lots of chasing after a ball on the playing fields," Gus said defensively. "The vet gave her a clean bill of health at her last checkup. But yes," he added, seeing Roy's silent signal from behind Ivy, "you're quite right. I'll be two ticks, getting my coat. Don't want you catching cold hanging about."

"SO YOU ACTUALLY went out for a walk yesterday, like good King Wenceslas, when the snow lay all around, deep and crisp and even? I must say that was a little foolhardy, wasn't it?"

"Oh, don't you start, Gus," said Ivy. "I don't see what King Thingummy has to do with it. We were quite safe, and until Roy's wheels began to slither about in the slush, we were perfectly all right. Then we turned back, but not before something really curious happened."

"In Barrington? Nothing curious happens down here in Hangman's Lane."

"Must have done once, judging from its name," said Roy. "They say the gibbet was up beyond the woods, at the crossroads. Deliberate, apparently, so that as many villains as possible got the warning."

Whippy was straining at the leash, scenting rabbits in the woods, and they turned off along a flat path leading to a picnic spot. It was colder under the trees, and Ivy said they should turn around and retreat to Gus's cottage for a cup of tea.

"Are you going to spin it out, Ivy, in time-honoured fashion, before you tell me what the curious thing was?"

"Yes," said Ivy. "My feet are getting wet, and Roy's nose is blue. Come on, let's quicken up and get back."

Gus's cottage was warm. He had a small wood-burning

stove in the sitting room hearth, and Ivy and Roy settled down in front of it. Ivy had taken off her shoes, and was toasting her feet in front of the stove's open doors.

"Nice little place, this," Roy said.

"It's hideous," said Gus. "If my poor father saw the depths to which I had sunk, he would turn in his grave." His words were harsh, but he grinned. The cottage was a refuge from his former life, when his private and professional existence had become irretrievably muddled. Now in relative peace, he enjoyed the companionship of people who wished him well, and Enquire Within kept his brain active.

"Yes, well, enough of that. Isn't that the kettle boiling? Hot tea is required, and not too strong for me, please," said Ivy.

"So, the curious happening?" Gus said.

"Right," said Roy. "We escaped for a short while when the snow stopped and everywhere was dripping in the thaw. I had heard that Cemetery Lane was cleared and suggested we went up there, possibly to see the graves of my ancestors, God rest their souls."

"Don't be so silly, Roy," said Ivy. "You don't think about your ancestors from one year's end to the next. Shall I carry on? Yes? Well, you remember our latest client, Alfred Lowe?"

"Of course I do, Ivy. I am the one who tackled him. He lives up there, doesn't he."

"We were just coming up to his house, when his door opened and a woman came out. Tottered out, would be the best way of describing it. Heels four inches high, in this weather!"

"So, Alf had a visitor. That's not particularly curious, Ivy."

"Ah, but this visitor was screaming at him, and her parting words were that she would be back. Then I heard him say something like, 'Stay away, Susan,' and I reckon from the way they were at it, hammer and tongs, that she was his absent wife."

Gus nodded. "Right. That's his wife's name, all right. So not so absent. Did he say anything to you?"

"Oh yes. I introduced myself and Ivy," answered Roy, "and then he remembered me. Said we should get together sometime to talk about the old days. He was really very pleasant."

"Mm, seems he's a bit of a Jekyll and Hyde character. You should have heard him when we first met! Anyway, now you've taken a very important step, and we can arrange to have an official consultation with him. What do you say, Ivy? Happy to take him on now?"

"I thought we had already," said Ivy with a sniff. "Now, we must be getting back, Roy. Our jailer will be sending out a search party."

Twelve

HILL TOP, HOME of the Wrights, high up above the town of Thornwell, had had another flurry of snow, and Steven, already in a bad mood and feeling rotten from his disastrous meal last evening, was swearing bitter oaths at having to clear away a pathway for his car in order to visit his old uncle in Barrington.

"Why didn't you get me up earlier to deal with this?" he said crossly to his long-suffering wife.

"You've made a good job of it now," she said consolingly. But to herself she thought that one of these days she would booby-trap the garage door so that it would come down on top of him and silence his complaining voice forever.

"I shall probably be late back," he said. "This morning in the office, and then over to Barrington to see the blushing bridegroom. Boring old Roy. The whole thing is a complete embarrassment, and I shall do what I can to get him out of it. Probably in the clutches of a scheming old woman."

"Sometimes these late romances are very lovely. Old people can be very lonely, and if they have someone belonging to them to keep them company, it is a great blessing."

"Sentimental nonsense, Wendy. And don't stand outside here in the cold. You'll be going down with flu or something, and you know I have to steer clear of infections."

He drove off without saying good-bye or offering a backward wave.

She returned to the house and decided to have another coffee and start the book she had ordered from Amazon, and which she intended to keep from Steve's prying eyes. She settled down in front of the electric fire in the sitting room and opened the package. "*Murder, She Said*," Wendy read aloud. She chuckled and turned to the first page.

STEVEN'S SO-CALLED BORING old uncle, Roy Goodman, was in fine fettle this morning. He had woken to see snow clouds passing overhead, but up to now it had been fine in Barrington. A good day to plan the next move for Enquire Within, he decided. He picked up the room phone and dialled Ivy's number. "Good morning, light of my life!" he said.

Ivy was scarcely awake, and muttered that as far as she could see her room was in complete darkness, and could she ring him back.

"It's Roy, sleepyhead," he said. "Just wanted to wish you a nice day, as the Americans say. I have some ideas we might talk about. But first wash an' brush up and breakfast. It is quite late, actually. I do hope Katya will have kept something hot for us."

"Do you always wake up so bright-eyed and bushy-tailed, Roy, my dear?" said Ivy.

"Always," he replied. "I do hope that is not going to put you off marrying me? I am afraid it comes from a lifetime of getting up early to do the milking."

"*Nothing* is going to put me off, Roy. I wouldn't have you spending all that money on a ring only to duck out on you. By the way, one of the things I shall be enquiring about this morning is what that jeweller meant by 'plenty of candidates' to be a farmer's wife, and the purchase of an engagement ring? You being the farmer in question?"

"Ah, thereby hangs a tale. All shall be revealed to you over the eggs and bacon. See you in a few minutes, my lovely."

Ivy put down the phone and smiled. She had had so many doubts about the wisdom of getting married at her age, but now she was sure. Roy was like a rock, always so calm and sensible, and she knew she could trust him absolutely. And whatever he had got up to in his youth was nothing to do with her. He was a good-looking old dear now, and must have been wickedly handsome in his youth. Bound to have had romances galore. Well, she had netted him now, and meant to keep him.

GUS HAD NOT seen Miriam for the whole of yesterday, and now he wondered whether lately he had put her off too sternly when she offered lunch, tea, or supper. She was a good soul, if pushy, and he thought perhaps he would take her an olive branch in the form of a box of chocolates. It was a little elderly, but never mind. He could always scribble over the sell-by date. They were expensive Belgian ones given to him by his ex-wife on her last visit sometime ago. He looked at his watch. Just time for a quick walk with Whippy and then, with luck, a decent lunch.

Miriam was arranging a bunch of chrysanthemums she had brought home from the village shop, when she saw Gus pass by her window, and she opened the back door.

"Peace offering," he said, thrusting the chocolates towards her.

"Sell-by date?" she said. "They look suspiciously like that box sitting on your kitchen window in the sun for months, if not years."

His face fell, and he walked over to her wheelie bin and threw them in with exaggerated force. By this time she had come out into the yard and took him by the arm. "Nice try, Gus," she said. "But you were horrid to me yesterday. Still, forgive and forget. I'm cooking fish cakes for lunch. Enough for two?"

Gus accepted at once. He had had an idea that since Miriam had lived in the village all her life, she might well know something interesting about Alf Lowe and his family. And anyway, her fish cakes were always light and tasty, with plenty of delicious salmon in them. His mouth watered at the thought.

He returned to his cottage and Whippy stood shivering at the door. A virtual balloon hung above her head saying "walkies!" and he laughed. "All right, we'll go. Perhaps we'll follow on Ivy's Sunday walkies with Roy up to the cemetery. I do like a good cemetery, as you know."

Whippy barked joyfully. If she had understood nothing else, the word "walkies" was enough.

The village was busy with customers making their way over the Green, its lush grass restored by the melted snow, towards the shop. James, the owner, thought ruefully that it was an ill wind etcetera. He sold twice as much food at the first fall of snow, when people panicked at the idea of not being able to get out of the village.

"Morning, Gus," he said now. "How does Whippy like the snow?"

"Not much. Her coat is thin and she's even more shivery than usual. We're just going up to the cemetery and back."

James turned to the shelves behind him, and brought out a neat pack. "Here's your answer," he said. "Cosy Doggie Waterproof for Winter. Folds up small enough to go into your pocket."

"James, you're a wonder. Is it Whippy's size? Great, I'll take it out and put it on her straight away. She's on your dog hook out there."

"You make it sound as if she's rotating on a spit over hot coals. Allow me, Gus," he added. "I'd like to make sure it fits." There were no other customers at the moment, and he followed Gus out of the shop.

LUNCH WITH MIRIAM was, as usual, protracted and excellent. After a suitable interval, Gus had brought up the subject of the Lowe family, and Alf in particular.

"Turned into a horrible old man in old age!" she said. "Why on earth are you asking about him?"

"Just curious," he replied. "I met him at the bus stop, and we got into conversation. I sat next to him, and he was really interesting. You can't always tell from people's looks, can you, Miriam?"

"Not just his looks!" she said fiercely, "and I know you went off with him to Thornwell last Saturday. Left Whippy behind, didn't you. I was working in the shop and James told me."

"Yes, you're absolutely right. Memory going, you know. Old age creeping on."

"Nonsense! If you'd let me look after you properly, you'd be a new man in no time."

Time to change the subject, Gus thought, and hastily asked whether the Lowes had lived in the village for a long time.

"Always. At least, as far back as I can remember," she said. "Some of his family farmed over at Settlefield, I'm sure. But Alf's father ended up being this village's blacksmith and farrier. The old forge is still there behind the cottage. Full of junk, I expect."

"Is his wife still alive? He looked rather uncared-for, I thought." Miriam did not need to know that he already had the answer to that one. Best to start from scratch.

"Susan? Oh yes, she's very much alive. Much younger than him. Left old Alf in the lurch, and went off to live with a bloke from Thornwell. She's probably dumped him by now! One of those who milk a man dry, and then swan off to find another sucker. Poor Alf didn't turn nasty until she left. Took the heart out of him, she did. He went around swearing revenge for ages."

"You sound very bitter, Miriam. Did you not like his wife?"

"Loathed her," she said. "He was quite keen on me at one time, and though he's quite a bit older, I really liked him. Made me laugh, old Alf. Then Susan came along and in no time he was taking her up to the altar in Thornwell. Mind you, they say he would never divorce her. Roman Catholic an' all that. Out for all she could get, that was Susan Green. Her family are solicitors. It was said at the time that she was marrying beneath her, but I reckon she was already secondhand goods. No better than she should be, that Susan. Left him bitter and twisted, as they say. Now, Gus," she added, "there's an apple turnover hotting up in the oven, and I've got double cream to go with it. Fancy it?"

AFTER LUNCH AND a couple of glasses of Miriam's primrose wine, Gus felt so contented and sleepy that he decided he would have a doze in front of his fire before making some notes on Alf. But then he realised he would probably have forgotten half of it after he woke up, and so thought he would take Whippy into the edge of the wood for some fresh air.

He felt refreshed and alert by the time the east wind had cleared his head, and he was just approaching the wood when a large black car drew up beside him. The window was lowered and a smart-looking man beckoned him over imperiously.

"Hi. Tell me where Springfields is. I've been before, but not for some time, and I've taken the wrong road, I think?"

Gus felt prickles on the back of his neck. It was a long time since men in anonymous black cars had issued orders to him through darkened windows, lowered enough to bark out a question.

"You have indeed taken the wrong road," he said lightly. "You'll have to find somewhere to turn around, and then take a right and a left and it's on the right-hand side opposite the old telephone exchange." And if that doesn't confuse you, nothing will, Gus said to himself.

"How far is it to a place where I can turn round? This god-forsaken lane is getting narrower, and there's still snow under the trees."

"Hangman's Lane, this is, and you'll probably have to go up as far as the gibbet crossroads to turn. I'd hate to think of you backing into a ditch."

The window was wound up without another word from the stranger, who was, of course, Steven Wright in search of his uncle Roy.

Thirteen

IVY HAD CHANGED her dress and shoes after lunch, and combed her hair back into her usual severe bun. She had powdered her nose—her one concession to makeup—and went down to find Roy equally spruced up, sitting in an upright chair and smiling at her approach.

"Very smart, my beloved," he said. "Nephew Steven will be impressed. More impressed than you will be by him! A shifty-looking gent, though perhaps I shouldn't say such things about my own flesh and blood. But my sister married into the Wrights, who were reputed to be gypsy stock. Hence the shifty look."

"Now, now, Roy, I have known some very nice Romany gypsies in my time. Not at all shifty. There are bad apples, of course, but then, they pop up everywhere."

"Mm, well, I used to allow a regular band of gypsies to stop on the farm on their way to Appleby Fair. Great occasion for them. Then they'd stop on the way back, and always brought me useful things for the farm. But there was one year when a couple of brothers stopped, and after they'd gone, so had several of my best tools!"

Their conversation was interrupted by a loud voice asking for Mr. Goodman. Miss Pinkney was on duty, and she very politely asked his name.

"Wright. Steven Wright. He's expecting me. And don't worry; I won't run off with the silver."

"Oh dear," said Roy.

"Not a good start," said Ivy, and turned to look at the tall, heavy man approaching.

"Uncle Roy!" he said heartily. "You're looking splendid. And this is—?"

"Miss Beasley. Ivy Beasley, my fiancée."

"How do, Ivy," Steven said. "Perhaps you wouldn't mind leaving Uncle Roy and myself to have an important chat about your nuptials? Sounds rude, doesn't it! I'm to be best man, and that's exactly what I intend to be. Best man, see?" He laughed loudly, but Ivy did not even smile.

"I wish Ivy to stay with us and have her say, Steven," said Roy. "She already is the better half of the two of us. Now, shall we begin at the beginning? Have you done the job before?"

Steven shook his head. "But the whole thing's bound to be a doddle. I looked up weddings on my computer, and it gives the order of service and all that jazz. I have to look after the ring, give it to the vic at the right time, keep your pecker up in case you're feeling nervous, and toast the bridesmaids in a jolly speech at the reception. Right?"

"There will be no bridesmaids," said Ivy firmly.

"Then I'll toast you instead," Steven said, patting her on the shoulder. She stiffened, and said she believed someone else did that job. But from what he said, she was sure he would be word perfect by the wedding day.

"Next," announced Steven, in a loud voice that carried all round the lounge, to the delight of the other residents, who were watching television with the sound turned down, "next we must talk about a little gift for the bridesmaids. Oh no, no bridesmaids. But perhaps a small gift from the bride to the groom? Are you having rings exchanged, Roy?"

Roy looked at Ivy. He had not considered such a thing, and it did not appeal to him. Luckily, Ivy answered for him quite fiercely.

"Good heavens, none of that nonsense. Roy and I have

already chosen the ring for the bride—me—and if I consider giving him a gift, it will be private, not for all the world to see."

Not in the least abashed, Steven said he had a pal in the jewellery trade who would be delighted to find her something suitable. She had only to say the word, and mention his name.

"Ten percent off, straight away," he said.

"That won't be necessary," Ivy said. "And now, if you'll excuse me, Roy, I have to go upstairs."

Steven heaved a sigh of relief, but Roy looked anxious. "Are you sure, my love? You are very welcome to stay."

Ivy smiled at him. "I'll see you later, and you can bring me up-to-date. Good-bye, Mr. Wright. We shall no doubt meet again." The prospect of this clearly did not please her, and she marched out of the room.

Steven settled back in his chair and nodded his head at Roy. "Odd choice, Uncle," he said, attempting to soften his remark with a smile. "A very sharp lady. In the best possible way, of course."

"I am a lucky man, Steven. She has given me a new lease of life."

"Ah, now, that brings me to a ticklish subject, which I'm sure you won't mind my mentioning."

Oh yes, I know what you mean, young Wright, thought Roy. But you can squirm for as long as possible.

"It's really to do with your being a bachelor, well, up to now. And not having a son and heir."

"And especially an heir?" said Roy, perfectly relaxed.

"I suppose so, yes. But I am sure you have thought of all that. Made a will, and so on?"

"Wills are confidential, until after the will maker's death."

"Oh yes, of course! But you do see that a little advice on the subject would be a good idea for everybody."

"I have a very smart adviser in my Ivy," Roy said, with a soppy smile. "She has tidied up all my affairs, along with my socks and ties."

"It is nice to see you so happy, Uncle," said Steven, beginning to lose patience, "but I mean professional advice. These things can cause a lot of trouble if they are not done properly. You must take the matter seriously."

"If you don't mind my saying so, that is entirely my

business. All I ask of you is to turn up on May the fifth and be my best man. You will be asked to meet our new rector, a very pleasant lady and a true Christian, in my opinion."

"A woman? Oh God, they're getting everywhere. Do you know, Uncle Roy, there are now five women on the board of my company! No wonder the country is in such a mess."

Roy was too annoyed to answer, and began to struggle to his feet. "I must go and order tea for us," he said. "And make sure my Ivy is all right. She will share everything, Steven, joys, woes, triumphs, everything."

"Including your considerable fortune, Uncle," muttered Steven, as he watched Roy hobble out of the lounge door.

IVY SAT IN her room, staring crossly out of the window. What a dreadful man! If only she had met him before Roy asked him to be best man. Anyone would be better than him! Family, indeed! Friendship is more important than family, in Ivy's opinion. Of all the slithy, untrustworthy—!

There was a soft knock on the door, and she opened it to find Roy standing outside, looking humble.

"Has he gone?" she said.

"No, my dear. We are about to have a cup of tea, and I should be so grateful if you would join us. My nephew is beginning to alarm me, and I need your strong and capable arm to lean on."

"Oh well, if you put it like that, Roy dear, of course I will come down with you and tackle Mr. Wright."

"Thank you so much. He is beginning to utter what sound like threats! Oh so softly disguised, but threats nevertheless."

"Oh, is he indeed! Then he shall answer to me. Come along, my dear. Take my arm. We'll soon put him in his place, and if he takes the hump, then there's plenty more best men in the sea. Such as Augustus, for a start. Such a pity you didn't choose him first."

"My fault, Ivy, I know. But I have this thing about family solidarity. Perhaps it's because I haven't had any family of my own, and don't realise the possible pitfalls!"

They stood at the top of the wide stairs, arm in arm. "Don't forget, dearest," said Ivy, "that you are not alone in that. After all, Deirdre is my only relative, and, believe it or not, I have even considered asking her if she would like to be matron of honour."

They descended slowly, and got a good view of Steven Wright sitting in an embarrassed lump, being stared at by curious residents. "Ah, there you are. Tea has been brought in, and the little foreign girl said Miss Beasley would be mother. I told her it was a bit late for that! But she didn't see the joke, and glared at me. Far too many of these foreigners coming into the country, don't you think?"

"Each is a special case," said Ivy sourly. "Now, are you a miffy?"

"A *what*?"

"Milk in first, of course. Some are; some aren't."

"How quaint," said Steven. "As a matter of fact, I have tea without, thanks. So what does that make me, Ivy?"

"A twit, Mr. Wright. A twit. Tea without it."

Fourteen

"DO YOU KNOW what I think?" Deirdre asked Gus. They were sitting in her king-sized bed having a companionable cup of tea. She had forgiven him many transgressions, one way or another, and mostly to do with Miriam Blake, and had asked him round for a potluck supper the previous night. Then, by mutual agreement, they had retired to a night of passion, hindered only by advancing middle age on both sides.

"What do you think, Dee-Dee?" said Gus fondly.

"I think Ivy and Roy would do well to steer clear of that nephew of Roy's. I heard something not good about Wrights when I was having my hair done yesterday. It was just coincidence, but a couple of women were waiting behind where I was sitting. They were gossiping, of course, and I heard the name Wright mentioned."

"In what context?"

"One of the women had bought some furniture at Maleham's store on the new retail shopping park in Thornwell. A table and chairs, I think she said. And when they were delivered, one of the chairs had a big chip out of the back. She didn't notice until they'd gone, and then she found it. She made a fuss on the phone at once, of course, and demanded they replace it."

"Naturally," said Gus, "but what has this got to do with Wright and Ivy and Roy?"

"Patience, Gus! The man the customer talked to on the phone said he was the department manager, and his name was Wright. He was very rude and uncooperative, she said. Told her the damage must have been done by her after the delivery-men had left. She sounded furious."

"So would I be," said Gus. "So what happened next?"

"Dunno. It was the woman's turn to go under the drier then, and she was led away with a towel round her head."

"Extraordinary things they do to you at your hairdressers! But it is an interesting piece of information. Could be relevant It's not a common name hereabouts, is it?"

"The only Wright I'd heard of before Roy's nephew, was the name on a travelling circus that used to come around here every spring. They had a roundabout with Wright's Golden Horses up in lights all round the top. Very pretty, it was."

"Mm. Perhap a trip to the furniture store in Thornwell might be a useful move for Enquire Within? You and I could go today, if we get up before it's bedtime again."

Deirdre slipped out of the sheets and went downstairs to the kitchen. "What do you fancy for lunch?" she called.

"Kippers!" shouted Gus.

"And the same to you," yelled Deirdre from below.

IN MALEHAM'S TASTEFULLY arranged furniture store in Thornwell, Steven was still smarting from his encounter with Ivy Beasley. Who did she think she was? Just a scheming old woman after his uncle's money? Well, he was a match for her. He had stayed awake most of the night planning what to do next, and was tired and irritable with customers. At lunchtime, he had a surprise visit from his managing director.

"Wright? A word, if you please. We'll go to my office."

Steven was reminded of his headmaster's "See me outside my study, boy." He was only too familiar with that phrase, and its consequences, and this interview with old Maleham was likely to be on much the same lines.

"Not to beat about the bush, Wright, I have had a complaint from a customer about the way she was handled during a transaction on a set of chairs and a table. You fit the description she gave. Do you know what I'm talking about?"

Steven shook his head. "It wasn't me, sir." He half expected Maleham to reach for the cane.

But he merely frowned. "Strange. My spies tell me you were heard being less than polite on the phone to a customer with a complaint. Still no recall of this?"

"No, sir. Must've been one of the others. That new chap is a bit of a smart aleck, I've noticed."

"Never mind what you've noticed. Perhaps you should go home, Wright, and sit quietly somewhere and think back. Then come in tomorrow and see me first thing."

"Before maths lesson, sir?" he said under his breath.

"What was that!"

"Nothing, sir. I'll contact you tomorrow. But there's no need for me to go home—"

"There may be no need, but those are my instructions. Close the door as you leave, please."

WENDY WATCHED THE car come up the drive and her heart sank. It must be bad news. Steven never came home during the day. She rushed to the door, and as he came in with a thunderous expression, she asked him quickly whether he was ill.

"Of course I'm not ill. Just a slight migraine, that's all. And I've been feeling a bit sick, still. A couple of aspirin and an hour or two's sleep will do the trick. We weren't busy at the store, and my deputy was happy to fill in. It's a sign of a bad manager if things go to pieces in his absence."

"I'll bring you a cup of herb tea. That'll help," she said, and went off to the kitchen thinking it was not the moment to tell him about the huge bill for the new swimming pool she had ordered. He had confirmed the estimate, but there were various extras that she had since agreed to.

Suppose he was lying, as usual? Maybe he'd been sacked and sent home in disgrace! Then they'd be in real trouble. Oh God, please don't let it be that. She told herself not to be ridiculous. He was a valued employee, and had earned several bonuses since taking the job.

And he did suffer from the occasional migraine, and was sick with it. At least that was true. She could see it in his eyes. She sighed. Nothing to do but make a fuss of him. She groaned. It was a long time since she had done that with any real enthusiasm.

"SHALL WE ASK Ivy and Roy if they'd like to come, too?" Deirdre was dressed now, glowing rosily at the breakfast table.

Gus looked up from his kippers and nodded. "Why not? An innocent trip to the furniture store. Nothing more natural for a couple about to set up home together."

"Don't laugh, Gus. They are very sweet about it all. I must say I'm thrilled to bits for Ivy. She has had a long life of either living with her mother, who was a real old harridan, or on her own in Round Ringford, with only two batty old ladies as her friends."

"What happened to her father?"

"Nagged to death at an early age, I believe. And now there's dear Roy, who couldn't be nicer, and is devoted to her. I hope they live forever."

"Mm."

"What do you mean—'mm'?"

"Nothing, really. I just have this wretched feeling that all will not go according to plan. Something to do with that Wright man. We must find out more about him, and quickly, in case he has an alternative plan in mind."

"What kind of plan?"

"An evil one. I don't like the sound of him at all. Do you want to ring Ivy, or shall I?"

"I'm having second thoughts," Deirdre said. "If Ivy and Roy come with us, and Wright is in the showroom, he'll recognise those two and that will rouse his suspicions. I think it would be best if you and me go on our own. Maybe tomorrow? It's starting to rain, and I've got a meeting with Social Services at five thirty."

"Fair enough. And I suppose I must go back home and face the wrath of good neighbour Miriam. She misses nothing, bless her."

"Could be useful," said Deirdre lightly.

Fifteen

"DO YOU REALISE, Roy," said Ivy, looking out of the window at a grey, misty morning, "that we had a whole day yesterday without talking to either Gus or Deirdre? Do you think they are plotting something?"

"Very likely, my dear. That's why you asked them to join your enquiry agency, isn't it? Plotting has led us to very satisfactory conclusions in the past."

"You are being deliberately obtuse, Roy. I mean plotting something without our knowing. Or being involved."

"I'm sure they will tell us what they're up to in due course, my beloved. Nothing to worry your pretty little head about."

Ivy softened. "Roy, you do say the most ridiculous things. But you are right. If I don't hear from Deirdre by this evening, I shall ring her and ask for information."

"Very wise, Ivy. Very wise."

ON MEETING MIRIAM Blake outside his cottage, Gus had had a sticky conversation with her, in which she had accused him of playing fast and loose with Deirdre Bloxham, a rich and vulnerable widow with no one to advise her. "I know you're not serious about her," she had said to a suitably humble Gus. "Fortune hunting, my mother used to call it."

This had incensed Gus, and he rallied in his own defence. "Unfair, Miriam!" he had said. "And if you don't mind my saying so, I remember a time when your late lamented mother conducted a campaign to marry you off to Squire Roussel. Pots and kettles, Miriam!"

Finally he had escaped with Whippy, and fled indoors to prepare for Deirdre picking him up in the Bentley. They planned to be at Maleham's Furniture Store in Thornwell at around ten thirty, and after sauntering around and asking a few questions, they intended to have a coffee in town and compare notes.

The retail shopping park was newly developed, the usual mixture of end-of-line designer clothes, toy emporia, and discount stores. Maleham's was large and on two floors, and Deirdre, who was wearing a real fur coat and didn't care, walked in, followed by a slightly embarrassed Gus. There were very few customers, and Deirdre said she supposed most people came in at the weekend when both husband and wife would be free.

"Shall we pretend I'm your husband, Dee-Dee?"

"If you like. Mind you, you are nothing like my Bert. He was comfortably tubby, with lots of frizzy grey hair and a lovely smile. You, on the other hand, are tall and skinny, with sparse hair, and most of the time you look as miserable as sin."

"Oh, not true! I am the soul of fun and laughter. Come along, wifey, let's look at beds."

The bedroom section was upstairs, and they wandered from one side to the other, sitting on mattresses and bouncing up and down to test the springing. They split up, thinking this would be the best way of attracting attention, and sure enough, Deirdre was approached by a smart young man in a good grey suit and subdued tie.

"Good morning, madam. Are we looking for a comfortable bed?"

"A preliminary reconnoitre, yes. We have moved into a larger house, and so mean to treat ourselves. We are quite happy to wander about on our own for a bit. But if we need help, we'll ask. Thanks. Oh yes, and do you have dining room furniture on this floor?"

"That's right, madam. All part of our interior design department. Just over there. But our usual manager in that department is off sick at the moment, so we are doubling up. I will make sure someone is available for you. Ah, good morning, sir. I understand from your wife that you are upsizing? If I may say so, you have come to the right place!"

The salesman drifted away discreetly, but kept a watchful eye on them as they continued on their rounds.

"It's all terrible stuff, isn't it?" whispered Deirdre.

"Ghastly. All brass knobs and limed wood. Give me a charity shop anytime. You can get real bargains there, Deirdre. Not that *you* need anything. Bert obviously had good taste in more than Bentley cars."

"Do you think we should ask for Mr. Wright? Or will we know him when we see him? I remember Roy saying there was no family resemblance."

The problem was solved when they arrived in the dining room department. A thickset young customer was marching towards the cubbyhole office, and as they approached they heard him ask in a loud voice to speak to "an idiot called Wright."

Deirdre froze and grabbed Gus's hand. "Listen!" she whispered.

"I'm sorry; our Mr. Wright is off sick today. Can I help you?" said a voice from inside the office.

"He'll be even sicker when I catch up with him!"

"Perhaps you would like to speak to someone else? If you have a complaint, I'm sure it can be put right, sir." The voice belonged to a small, neat assistant, who emerged to face the complainant.

"You'll do, if that Wright is not here. I'm not satisfied with a call from your department regarding a damaged dining room chair, delivered to my house. When my wife called to complain, your Mr. Wright was extremely rude and accused her of lying and doing the damage herself after the delivery van had gone. She was very upset, and has still not recovered. And all I have had is this." He pulled a card from his pocket and handed it to the sales assistant. She read aloud, well within the hearing of

Gus and Deirdre, a formal apology and an assurance of Maleham's best attention at all times.

"Not good enough!" said the young man. "I want a replacement chair delivered free to my house within the next week, or I shall be seeing my lawyer."

"No need for that," said Mr. Maleham, coming up the stairs and approaching them. "I'm afraid I could hear you all over the store! As for the chair, we already have the matter in hand and, as a goodwill gesture, will include a footstool to match your set."

"Footstool be buggered!" said the young man derisively. "Just get my replacement chair delivered, and that's the last you'll see of me. And you can tell Wright I shall be looking out for him."

Mr. Maleham drew himself to his full height. "Take care, young man. I have a duty to protect my staff, and if you make threats in my hearing, I shall be forced to inform the police. Good morning."

"WOW! THAT WAS more than we expected!" Gus followed Deirdre into the nursery department and they were idly looking into cots and pushchairs. "Sounds like Steven Wright forgot the salesman's golden rule, that the customer is always right."

"I don't give much for his chances of staying in that job. Oh look, Gus, at this adorable little teddy bear. I think I shall buy it, just to prove we are real customers."

"But neither of us has any child to give it to. Unless you're keeping secret from me a family of two sets of twins?"

Deirdre put the bear back in the cot. "Not true," she said. "I wanted children, but by the time Bert said we could try for a baby, it was too late. I don't think he really wanted one. Unhappy childhood himself. The usual story."

"Mm, in my case it was Kath who didn't want to share the limelight with another being of any age. Pure selfishness. Still, I'd have been a lousy dad."

"Let's go and get a coffee. No good hanging on here. I think we've done well. Oh look out, here comes Mister Smoothie."

Deirdre pulled her fur coat around her, and said politely that they had had a good look around and would be thinking about what they had seen. Gus added his thanks, and they left.

* * *

"NOTHING DOING THERE," said the smart assistant to his woman colleague. "The ones with fur coats and Bentleys never buy anything, do they?"

"Would you? I don't blame them. It's all a load of rubbish, anyway. By the way, shall we send a 'get well soon' card to Steve?"

"Not likely! He's often off sick. I hope it takes months. I reckon that bloke with the damaged chair could make mince-meat of our Steven, if he finds him. With any luck."

Sixteen

"I HOPE YOU found yourselves something useful to do, Deirdre," Ivy said. "I'm not sure what Gus does with his spare time, but I know you are a great time waster."

"Ivy! That's not true." All four enquirers were assembled in Deirdre's house, with Roy insisting on tackling the stairs to the agency office.

"Don't worry; we made good use of the morning," replied Gus "How did your session with the vicar go?"

"Very satisfactorily," Ivy said. "We were able to settle several matters. The banns will be read on Sunday for the second time of asking. I do hope you two will find time to come? Solidarity means a lot to me and Roy."

So even Ivy is feeling nervous, thought Deirdre. She had a sudden pang of affection for her fierce old cousin. It must have been a hard decision for her to make. So self-reliant and used to managing her life exactly as she wanted it. It was a miracle that she agreed to come to Barrington and Springfields! Probably that bout of flu she had in Ringford weakened her resistance. Still, it had all turned out well, and now she was to have her chance at being a married lady.

"Of course we'll be there, Ivy. Won't we, Gus?"

"Certainly try to make it. Dogs allowed?"

"Don't be ridiculous, Augustus." Ivy smiled at Roy, and said if anyone asked her, she would say that her leg was being pulled.

"Now, you two," said Deirdre, picking up a pen and attempting to look businesslike behind her desk. "Do you want to hear about our expedition yesterday?"

"Told you they were up to something," whispered Ivy to Roy.

"You start, Gus," said Deirdre. "I'll fill in as we go along. I am afraid it's nothing to do with our Alf assignment."

"Well, it was unplanned, actually," he began, crossing his fingers behind his back. "Deirdre needed a new kitchen table, and I suggested we go to have a look in Thornwell at the new retail park. There's a big furniture store there, and as she wanted a perfectly plain table, I suggested Maleham's." He looked at Deirdre and hoped she would remember that Roy would not necessarily approve of information-gathering about his nephew.

"Then I remembered that your nephew worked in a furniture store, Roy," she continued, nodding slightly at Gus. "We realised that whereas you both, Ivy and Roy, had met him, maybe two or three times, Deirdre and I would not know even what he looked like. We thought we might introduce ourselves, but there was no opportunity, and we just wandered about. Deirdre wore her fur coat, to show we had money to spend!"

"Not relevant, Gus." Deirdre frowned at him.

"And then we overheard the most extraordinary conversation. Although shouting match might be a more accurate description. A thickset young man marched in and demanded to see Wright. He was steaming with fury, and it turned out your nephew had been very rude and accusatory to the young man's wife, who rang in to complain. She had subsequently needed sedatives from the doctor, he claimed. Seems they had taken delivery of a table and set of chairs, and after the van had gone, she found damage on one of the chairs."

"And the young man was out for revenge?" asked Ivy.

"Well, actually he was out for a replacement chair. After some argy bargy, the top man arrived and smoothed him down, and he left with a threat that if he found Wright, he would see to him. He was a rough-looking chap. The sort you wouldn't want to cross in an argument."

"Did Steven appear?" Roy's voice was full of concern.

"No, they said he was off sick. Didn't know when he would be back."

"If ever, I reckon," added Deirdre.

Gus nodded. "I agree. The boss said all the right things, but times are hard and losing a customer is a disaster for stores selling furniture that people might want, but can't afford. If this is Wright's first-time offence, maybe he'll be given a warning, but if he's known for it, he'll get the boot. And rightly so, in my opinion."

"Oh dear," said Roy. "What would my poor sister have said? In a way, I feel responsible for him, now she's gone."

"Rubbish, Roy!" said Ivy. "He is in no way your responsibility. I advise you to find another best man at once. Forget all about Steven Wright."

"I'll think about it, dearest. I will certainly give it some thought."

DEIRDRE HAD SPOTTED that Roy was looking very downhearted, and so suggested a break for coffee before they discussed Alf and his problem. She cut a specially large slice of Miriam Blake's butter shortbread, now selling at exorbitant prices in the village shop, and asked whether wedding plans were going smoothly.

"One more thing," said Ivy, "and we might as well decide it now. There will be no bridesmaids or pages or any of that nonsense, but I'm told I shall need some female support, so how do you feel, Deirdre, about being matron of honour, or whatever they call it?"

"Oh, Ivy," she replied, and her eyes filled with tears, "I thought you'd never ask! Of course I will, you silly old thing."

"Here. Not so much of the 'old,' if you please," said Ivy. "Now, can we get back to Alf and his rotten relations? He has asked us for help, and we have accepted, so we'd better get on with it."

"I've done some thinking," said Gus. "And the not very inspired result is that I conclude the big trouble is his wife,

Susan. You've seen her in action, Roy. What did you think might be a way of persuading her to leave Alf alone to be miserly and bad-tempered all by himself?"

"My first reaction," said Roy, cheering up visibly, "is that she is a real harpy, and since all she wants from him is a divorce, he'd do well to get rid of her permanently and leave her for some other man to tackle."

"Sensible advice," said Ivy. "The trouble with that, though, is that I can't see Alf changing his mind. He's one of those obstinate old devils, who won't budge. The more we try to persuade him, the deeper he digs in his toes. Dog in the manger, our Alf. And not only that, we must take his religious objection seriously."

"Well said, Ivy," agreed Gus. "So I thought again, and came up with something that might work." He looked around the others triumphantly, and was met with stony disbelief.

"If we can find out where Susan lives," he carried on, "I am prepared to visit her and play devil's advocate, pretending that I will support her attempts to get Alf to a lawyer. Then I will tell her the deed has been done and she need not pursue him further. Then we can decide what to do next. I could also reveal that I am aware poor old Alf has not long to go."

"Gus!" said Deirdre. "That is the most impractical, unprofessional and dishonest plan I have ever heard! What do you think, Ivy and Roy?"

Roy hesitated, and then said he rather agreed with Deirdre, though thought Gus should have top marks for ingenuity.

"And Ivy?"

"Ridiculous." Ivy's expression was one of lofty determination. "Let's start again."

IN A SILENT bedroom with the curtains drawn tightly across, Steven Wright slept a troubled sleep. With the aid of a double dose of aspirin and a glass of neat whisky, telling himself that he preferred a coma to the continuing pain and sickness of migraine, Steven Wright had finally fallen asleep.

Seventeen

GUS SAT IN his shabby little sitting room, reading the news. He had got up late, and taken Whippy across the Green to buy milk and the morning paper. When he got back, he had met Miriam, who was waiting for him in her front garden.

"Morning, old sleepyhead," she had said, with a fond smile.

So I'm forgiven, Gus thought, and grinned at her. "Morning, Miss Blake, and a cold and frosty one, too."

"That's why I was looking out for you," she had said. "The garden tap is completely iced up, and I know you use it for Whippy's outside water bowl, so I'm offering to fill it up from my kitchen."

"Thanks, but don't bother. I can easily fill it from mine. Only a couple of yards farther to go! Do these cottages get frozen up inside? My winters here so far have not been too harsh, so no burst pipes."

"You've been lucky. Several winters we've been frozen up. Have a look and make sure exposed pipes are lagged. Especially up in the roof. The Honourable Theo might have got it done before you moved in, though I doubt it. Poor as church mice, those Roussels. Are you free for lunch? I've made a huge Lancashire hot pot. It'll last for days."

"Then you won't want me eating it up!"

"Oh, there's plenty to go round. Half past twelve, then?"

Gus had been about to insist on refusal when he remembered his plan. Miriam had talked before about Susan Lowe and Alf, and now she might well know where the erring wife lived. Miriam knew a great deal about everybody who had ever lived in Barrington.

"Thanks very much," he had said. "I'll bring a bottle."

Miriam shook her head. "Plenty of primrose left," she had replied, and Gus groaned to himself. Miriam's primrose wine was lethal, unless you were actually hoping for eight hours' uninterrupted sleep.

IVY AND ROY had been up hours before, and Ivy was first in the breakfast room, staring fixedly at the kitchen hatch as if willing her morning porridge to appear. When Roy joined her, she announced in a loud voice that the service in Springfields was definitely going downhill.

"Didn't sleep well, Ivy dear?" said Roy.

Ivy sighed. "No, I didn't. I'm afraid I was awake half the night worrying about your nephew, Steven. If nothing worse, he sounds like a very unpleasant character. Are you sure you want him to be best man? Gus knows one or two unsavoury characters who could put the frighteners on him."

"Ivy Beasley!" Roy looked horrified. "Steven is family, and I'm sure we can improve him by our wedding day. And really, he doesn't have too much to do."

"Oh, very well. I shall put him out of my mind, and leave him to you. I must get used to that, mustn't I?"

"Yes," answered Roy firmly.

"What shall we do today?" Ivy decided to change the subject. "Any ideas?"

"We could book our taxi and go shopping," said Roy. "Or we could look at some of my family photographs, just to show you what an upright, God-fearing young man I was. Do you have any of your mother and father?"

Ivy shook her head. "I don't remember photos being taken

in our family. My mother wouldn't have approved. But I'd love to see yours. Maybe some fancy women I can recognise. One or two of the old ducks in here look at you in a knowing way. We can get Katya to bring our coffee upstairs to my room." And maybe, she added to herself, I can see whether there's any truth in what old Alf said about the young Roy Goodman.

ROY HAD BROUGHT along albums stuffed full of photographs, sepia and black-and-white, and later on colour snaps of families, prize cattle and sheep, and the occasional oldest inhabitant sitting in the sun outside a stone cottage.

"Your entire life is here," said Ivy, smiling at him. "Perhaps we'll do it in instalments."

"Right, here we go. This one is my great-grandmother, Eliza Jane Wilson, with four of her six children. All girls! In those days you needed at least a couple of good strong sons to help on the farm."

"I think my father wanted a boy," said Ivy. "But there was just me."

"I'm sure he was proud as punch of you, Ivy dear. And here's her daughter Annie on her wedding day. And that's when the Goodman name came in. My grandfather Valentine Goodman was not much of a man. Too fond of the ladies. But he and Annie had three boys and a girl, and the farm went well."

"And one of the three boys was your father? Was your mother a farmer's daughter?"

"No. Her father was a solicitor. I think it was a small family, and she was an only child. But she loved the farm, I remember. Became a pillar of the newly formed Women's Institute, and was a champion bread maker."

"And who is this?" said Ivy, pointing to a bonny baby, staring wide-eyed at the camera.

Roy chuckled. "That's me, aged six months," he said. "Good-looking even then, don't you think?"

"Adorable," said Ivy. "And no doubt spoilt rotten. But what's happened here? Two pages stuck together. Shall I pull them apart?" she asked.

"No, no, don't bother. Plenty more."

But it was too late. Ivy had carefully separated the two pages and was peering at a studio portrait of two young people arm in arm and smiling broadly at each other.

"Roy, is that you?"

He sighed. "Yes, Ivy, that's me."

"And?"

"I forget her name. She was just a friend."

"Rubbish! Of course you remember her name. 'Just friends' don't have special studio portraits taken of themselves arm in arm. Who was she?"

"Her name was Ethel. Ethel Goodman."

"As in the Settlefield Goodmans?"

"As in them, yes. She was a cousin many times removed."

Ivy closed the album, and went over to the window, looking out for several minutes in silence. Then she turned.

"That's enough for today, Roy. Time for coffee, I think. I'll ring for Katya," she said.

Eighteen

IVY HAD SPENT a miserable night and the whole of Saturday avoiding long conversations with Roy, who was obviously upset and puzzled at her attitude. Then last night she had again spent long hours awake and, when at last falling asleep, had been haunted by the pretty, laughing face of Ethel Goodman.

Was Ethel really special to him, and where was she now? At least she might discover whether Alf Lowe had spoken the truth when he said Roy had ditched her when she got herself up the spout. It couldn't do any harm to find out a bit more.

"Morning, Miss Beasley," whispered a voice. It was Katya, bearing her cup of tea and biscuits. "How are we this morning? Yesterday was not a good day for you, no? But the sun is shining and winter is in flight."

"Poetically put, my dear," Ivy said, and shook off an urgent desire to lie down and go back to sleep. "Thank you. I shall be up and dressed very shortly. We have an important church service to go to."

* * *

GUS WOKE, CONVINCED there was some reason why he had to get up, though it was a Sunday. Then he remembered. The banns were being read in church for Ivy and Roy, for the second time of asking, and he and Deirdre had promised to go.

He got out of bed, tripped over a squealing Whippy and made his way to the bathroom.

His telephone rang, and he cursed, rushing downstairs two steps at a time.

"Hello, who is it?"

"Me, silly. You know I said I would ring to make sure you were up and ready for church. You've got an hour to make yourself presentable."

"Oh, Deirdre, do we have to go? No, don't answer that. We *do* have to go, and I shall be ready in suit and tie, so's not to let down the betrothed pair. See you later, and thanks for remembering."

THE CLEAR SKY and bright sunlight had brought out more churchgoers than usual, and by the time Gus and Deirdre arrived, they had to sit in a pew at the back.

"There's Ivy, and Roy beside her," whispered Deirdre. "Dear things. I feel quite soppy about them, don't you?"

Gus shook his head. "Marriage should be avoided at all costs, in my opinion," he said. "Not necessary these days. People can live together and split up without fuss if it goes wrong. No problems. And don't remind me of the vows you make in marriage. Nobody thinks twice about breaking the lot these days."

"Shhh," said Deirdre. "You'll be drummed out! Ah, here comes the Reverend Dorothy. Stand up, you unbeliever."

"I could quite fancy her," whispered Gus.

Deirdre didn't answer, but obediently opened her hymnbook in the right place, and then sang in a pleasant soprano voice. The sermon was mercifully short, and the vicar preached well, even including a few jokes.

"What's her surname?" whispered Gus.

Deirdre thought it best not to answer.

The service was drawing to a close, and there were a few notices to be read out, followed by the banns.

". . . If any of you know cause or just impediment why these two people should not be joined in holy matrimony, ye are to declare it," ended the Reverend Dorothy, and looked smilingly at Ivy and Roy. There was the usual short pause, while the congregation pretended to look around for a challenger.

Then it happened. "I declare it!" came a man's loud voice from the back of the church. "I know a very good reason why that man should not marry that woman. He should be sued for breach of promise to another."

There was a horrified silence, and then the vicar drew herself up in a dignified fashion, and walked with measured tread to the place where the man stood, red-faced and belligerent.

With great presence of mind, the organist began a soothing rendering of a Bach prelude, and the church was full of subdued whispering.

Ivy sat as if turned to stone. Roy reached for her hand, and it was icy. "A silly mistake, beloved," he said quietly. "It will all be sorted out very quickly. You'll see."

Nineteen

NOBODY IN CHURCH could remember such an extraordinary event. Even the oldest inhabitant, an old lady who was blind and deaf, when she had had it explained to her, said she had never known the like of it.

In due course the vicar arrived back into the church, but there was no sign of the red-faced, belligerent man.

"I am sorry about the delay, everyone, and especially Miss Beasley and Mr. Goodman, but I now have to make some enquiries," she said. "It is the law, and must be done, though I am sure everything will be cleared up by next Sunday, and we may proceed with the banns. Now please turn to hymn number sixty-four, 'Fight the Good Fight, with All Thy Might.'"

"And so we will," whispered Roy.

"I'm so proud of Ivy," said Deirdre, moving up close to Gus. "The second time it's happened to her, but she's, well . . ." She sniffed back tears.

"Bloody but unbowed?" asked Gus.

"That's it, exactly," answered Deirdre.

* * *

IVY AND ROY hung back at the end of the service, and the vicar asked them if they would like to come round to the vicarage with her to have a coffee and talk about what had happened. They agreed immediately, and set off on the short walk to the large Victorian vicarage, imposing with its forbidding-looking turrets and tall chimneys.

"Wouldn't you prefer a nice bungalow, dear?" said Ivy, as they walked up the drive.

"To tell you the truth, Miss Beasley, I really would! It is a very off-putting old place, as it was meant to be, to keep the humble peasants at bay. But I like the idea of friends in the village popping in for a chat, and nobody's going to pop in here, are they?"

They agreed, and settled down in the large drawing room, with its wonderful bursts of sparks and warmth.

"Now, the position is this," said Rev. Dorothy, once they were settled with a hot drink. "The law of the church is that if, as this morning, someone declares they know a good reason why the two applicants should not be married, then the claim has to be investigated. Usually this turns out to be a case of spite or envy, and it can all be settled amicably. But occasionally there is a good cause, such as one of the pair being married already."

"Good heavens, that certainly doesn't apply to us, does it, Roy?" Ivy looked astounded at even the suggestion.

"No, of course not, dearest," he said, and turned to Rev. Dorothy. "I am sure we shall both give you all the information you need, and be as helpful as possible. Is there anything we can do straight away?"

"Yes," said the stalwart vicar. "There is one major problem. The man who interrupted duly followed me into the vestry, but when my back was turned, he fled. There is a door out into the churchyard, and he was out of there at such a speed that I could not catch him. You two can go home and forget all about it. Just ignore people if they ask awkward questions, and if necessary, refer them to me. That usually shuts them up. I have to try to find out who he was, and if you want to, perhaps you can do likewise. I shall be in touch daily, to keep you informed, but before you go, can you think of anyone who wishes to spoil things for you? Anyone with a grudge?"

Ivy shook her head. "I've never been a popular person," she said. "But I don't think anyone has wished me harm. How about you, Roy?"

To her surprise, he didn't answer straight away. "Not sure," he said eventually. "I'll give it some thought and let you know."

IN THE AGE-OLD way of villages, by the time Ivy and Roy had returned to Springfields, the news was out and all round the staff and residents. Miss Pinkney, who was always on duty on Sundays, was waiting at the door for them, and as Roy parked his trundle and they came in hand in hand, she gave both a warm kiss.

"Come on in," she said. "Cook was in church, and so everyone knows what happened. I have warned them all that if anyone asks awkward questions, they would be sent early to bed with no supper!"

Roy smiled, and Ivy nodded and said how thoughtful Miss Pinkney had been. "But don't worry, Pinkers; we regard the whole thing as a challenge for Enquire Within. Another case for us to investigate, alongside Alf and *his* marriage problem. Gus and Deirdre were there and witnessed everything, and we have arranged a meeting for three o'clock this afternoon at Tawny Wings to take our first step in the enquiry."

"That's marvellous," said Miss Pinkney. "If you need a temporary short-term assistant, you know where to find me! Now, we have roast Norfolk turkey for lunch, and Anya has made another one of her Polish desserts."

"I hope it's more edible than the last one," said Ivy cheerfully. "We had terrible indigestion, didn't we, Roy?"

Roy was gazing at her in amazement. How did she do it? She'd been through the most awful thing that could have been expected this morning, and here she was, her customary acerbic self, talking about puddings.

"I'll go up and change my feet," Ivy said, "and see you back in the dining room, Roy."

Upstairs in her room, Ivy sat down on the edge of her bed and silently wept for two minutes. Then she looked at her watch, went into her bathroom and sluiced her face in cold water, gave herself a good shake, and set off for lunch.

"IT WAS A good idea of yours to wait for them until after they had seen Rev. Dorothy," Deirdre said to Gus, as they walked slowly back across the Green. "Ivy looked very pale, and I noticed Roy's hands were a bit trembly."

"I wish I could have got my hands on that bloke!" said Gus. "I'd have given him a lesson he wouldn't forget! Of all the terrible, shattering tricks to play on a nice old couple like Ivy and Roy."

"Still, after you'd said we should meet straight away and make it a priority case for Enquire Within, they bucked up enormously. Rev. Dorothy will keep us informed, I'm sure. But if it's more complicated than just an act of sheer cruelty by some maniac with a grudge, then it may take longer. We can go all out in our own investigations, and I know our Ivy will be at her best."

"Good-o!" said Gus. "I'll leave you now and go back to my lonely, freezing-cold cottage, with only a dog to talk to, and see you later this afternoon."

Deirdre laughed loudly. "Nice try," she said, and took his hand. "You over-egged it slightly. But still, I get the point. Come on, we'll share a plump pheasant I left in a slow oven. You can go back and see Whippy for an hour or so after lunch, before we have our meeting."

When they got back to Tawny Wings, Gus asked if he could use Deirdre's telephone. "I think I'll give Rev. Dorothy a ring, and tell her what we've decided to do. We'll need her help, and she might give me some idea of who that idiot was, and if he had any sensible explanation."

"Good idea. Carry on, while I do the potatoes. She's a nice woman, although she may be bound by rules of confidentiality."

Gus went into the little telephone room and shut the door. He dialled the vicarage number and Rev. Dorothy's voice was sharp. "Whoever it is, I am going out and not answering any questions about this morning's church service. And don't bother me again."

"Excuse me, Rev. Dorothy? This is Augustus Halfhide here. Friend of Miss Beasley and Mr. Goodman. We three, plus Mrs.

Bloxham from Tawny Wings, are the Enquire Within team, and, of course, all of us are most upset by what happened this morning."

There was a pause, and then the vicar apologised and said that she had been contacted by both local newspaper reporters on the phone already, and they had been disgustingly insistent and wouldn't give up pestering. "I thought you were another of them," she said. "So sorry. How can I help you?"

Gus explained their plans to carry out an investigation, and wondered if she was allowed to tell him anything about the man who had challenged the banns.

"I will help you as much as I can," she said, "but for a start, I got nothing out of that person except a repeated statement that he knew of a watertight reason why Roy Goodman could not marry Ivy Beasley. He wouldn't give me his name, but said he would be seeing his lawyers, and they would be in touch. I said that his lack of cooperation seemed to indicate nothing but mischief making, and he said if I did not do what he asked—no, ordered—I and the engaged couple would regret it. Then he pushed past me in the vestry and left. I rushed after him, but he had vanished."

"Mm. Much as I thought," said Gus. "I suppose you know that Mr. Goodman is a retired, wealthy landowner? There is a lot to discover yet, and we mean to find out all the facts. Rumour is sometimes helpful, but we try to deal in facts. It would be wonderful if we could work together on this?"

"Only too pleased," said Rev. Dorothy. "Do drop in anytime, Mr. Halfhide, won't you."

"Thank you so much. And please do call me Gus. Good-bye, then, and again, thanks for your help."

He emerged from the telephone room, and Deirdre called from the kitchen that lunch was ready and could he come and open the wine.

"You look like the cat that's got the cream," she said suspiciously.

"Useful conversation," he said. "Augustus Halfhide has not lost his touch with lady vicars."

"Oh, for heaven's sake! Here, take this corkscrew and try not to get bits of cork in the wine."

Twenty

WHEN IVY AND Roy arrived at Tawny Wings, promptly at three o'clock, Deirdre opened the door with a big smile. "Gus will be here soon. He's just gone back to feed Whippy and take her for a lightning walk, and he's bringing his car up so that he can give you a lift back. You can leave your trundle here, Roy, and I shall drive it down to you tomorrow."

"And a fine sight you'll look!" said Ivy. "But thanks, anyway. We shall be glad of a lift this afternoon. It gets dark so early, and the pavements could do with a lot of repair work. I think I'll write to the council and complain."

"But first, our meeting," said Deirdre. "I thought we'd be in the drawing room this afternoon. Our office upstairs is not very warm, and we can relax in front of the fire. My Bert, before he died, offered to fix an electric coal fire, but I said no, you can't beat the real thing. Come on in, both."

Gus arrived five minutes later in his car, and joined them.

"Car going all right?" said Roy.

"Fine, thanks to Deirdre," Gus said. "I reckon I got special treatment, being a friend of the garage boss!"

"Very likely," said Ivy. "Can we make a start on our various investigations now?"

They followed their usual practice of going round the four, each one saying how much he or she knew of the person or persons involved.

"You first, Ivy," said Deirdre.

"I'd rather Roy began," she said. "He's the one who has lived hereabouts all his life, and is likely to know more about past goings-on."

"Certainly, my dear," said Roy. "Well, first, I deny categorically that I have been legally married before, and therefore never divorced, nor never should have been divorced. Secondly, I have no idea who that man was. Never to my knowledge have I set eyes on him before. Thirdly, I have tried hard to think back to a time when I offended someone, knowingly or unwittingly, in a way that would cause them to act so cruelly. I have come up with nothing."

"Now me," said Gus, sensing that Ivy really wanted to be last. "I can honestly say that the possibility of the banns being challenged never once occurred to me. Deirdre will back me up in saying that my own disastrous marriage has turned me against the whole institution for good. But for Ivy and Roy, who so obviously love each other, I am wholeheartedly behind this investigation, and shall not rest until it is solved." He paused, then cleared his throat and said that he had had a useful conversation with Rev. Dorothy, and told them what she had said to him.

"Me next," said Deirdre. "I back up everything Gus said, except the bit about marriage as an institution. I was happily married to my Bert for years, and I wish he'd lived longer. As for this morning's interrupter, he looked a very nasty piece of work, but . . ."

"But what?" said Ivy.

"But I think I've seen him before somewhere. His face was vaguely familiar, and though my memory's not what it was, I think it may come back to me."

"When you least expect it," said Ivy. "Now me. It was a complete surprise, and I was shocked for a few minutes. But Beasleys are a tough lot, and if I'd been a few years younger, that fool would not have escaped. But he did, with threats of the law in action, so that's what we have to deal with. I hope you'll forgive me saying this, Roy, but I think there may be one urgent investigation needed, and that is a roundup of previous girlfriends, no matter how long ago, who were understandably keen on you, maybe more than you realised." She had not forgotten the photo of Roy and Ethel, arm in arm and looking into each other's eyes.

"Well said, Ivy. So now we can begin planning what to do." Gus fished a pen out of his pocket and took up a notebook from the highly polished coffee table. "To work, team," he said.

At this moment, the telephone rang, and Deirdre said she would take it in the kitchen, as it was probably her butcher wanting her weekly order.

The others talked desultorily, until she returned. Her face was pale, and she looked dazed.

"Dee-Dee!" said Gus, rushing over and helping her to sit down. "Who was it? Is it bad news?"

"Come on, gel," said Ivy kindly. "Pull yourself together. There's three of us here to help you, whatever's up."

Deirdre breathed deeply, and cleared her throat. "It was the police. Seems they had tried to get hold of Ivy and Roy at Springfields, and Mrs. Spurling had referred them to my number. They asked if I was willing to pass on the message, and I said of course I would."

"Well, what is it? Out with it, love," said Roy gently.

"It's your nephew, Roy. You see, he's been found dead. They tried to resuscitate him, but it seems that he had been dead for some hours."

"Oh my God," said Gus. He looked across at Roy, who was quite still, and scarcely breathing. Ivy, sitting next to him, took his hand and, to the others' amazement, slapped his cheek lightly, and said, "If you ask me, he had it coming to him."

Roy shook his head, as if to clear his thoughts. "Did Deirdre say Steven is dead?" he asked in a quavery voice.

"Yes, she did. And I said he had it coming to him. Now, this is a bit of a shock, and Deirdre is making fresh coffee, so why don't we all relax and chat for a bit, before we get back to business."

A ghost of a smile crossed Roy's face, now regaining its normal colour. "Don't you think we might have the morning off, dearest? I shall have a great deal to think about, so perhaps Alf's problem with his wife can be put on hold, as they say?"

Gus sat dumbly, watching Ivy's extraordinary handling of her beloved Roy.

"It may well be, Roy dear," she answered, "that Enquire Within will be required to work on Steven Wright's demise. No time like the present. Ah, here's Deirdre. Hot and strong," she said, tasting her coffee. "Just the ticket. Now, where did we get to?"

"DETAILS, DEIRDRE? DID the police give you any details?" After their coffee break, Gus and the others seemed ready to continue. Deirdre refilled cups and then sat down to answer him.

"One or two, Gus. But the main thing is that they will be coming over to Springfields late this afternoon to see Roy. I said I was sure Ivy would want to be with him, and they said that was fine."

"What else?" said Ivy.

"Well, it appears that first thing this morning, when the care-taker arrived, he opened up the store as usual, dealing with all the security systems and so on. Then the first member of staff to arrive was the junior salesman in the beds department. He took off his coat and checked messages and so on. Then he took his usual walk around the department to make sure all was ready for the day's trading. He got as far as a large, expensive double bed and was shocked to see someone lying in it, faceup under the duvet, apparently fast asleep. Then he recognised Steven Wright, and his first thought was that his unpopular boss had somehow got back into the store last night, perhaps drunk and incapable, and stretched out on the bed and gone to sleep."

"Was the salesman sure he was asleep at that point?" said Roy.

"Oh yes. He was really furious and shook his boss vigor-ously. But he couldn't wake him, and it finally dawned on him that it wasn't sleep, but death. Mr. Maleham had arrived by then, and he reported immediately to the police."

"And then?" Ivy was sitting bolt upright, holding on tightly to Roy's hand.

"Mr. Maleham closed the store for the day. All the staff are being interviewed, of course."

"What about Wendy, Steven's wife?" asked Ivy. The germ of an idea was already forming in Ivy's mind. Uppermost in her thoughts was a vivid picture of Steven Wright, and it was not a happy one. She had found him unpleasant and unlovable.

"Don't know about her," Deirdre continued. "I've told you everything the police told me. They thought I should break the bare bones of it to Roy, and then it would be easier for him this afternoon, when the police will be interviewing him."

"Right, well, that's all we can do for the moment. Perhaps we could carry on with Alf's troubles until four, and then Roy and me will be getting back to Springfields, ready for the police when they arrive."

"Right," said Gus, taking his cue from Ivy. Normality was to be maintained until it was time for Roy to be questioned. "I suggest we concentrate our investigation on the identity of the man who interrupted the banns. Someone in the congregation might have recognised him. We'll make a list of everyone we can remember of the few who were in church this morning, and divide them up between us, to see if anyone can help."

"And I'll study all the info about reading banns and having them challenged and that." Deirdre had rallied, and followed Gus's example.

Gus loaded Ivy and Roy into his car, and they waved good-bye to Deirdre, who was standing at her door with a concerned expression.

"What a day!" said Ivy, when they arrived at Springfields. "Good job we're fit and well, and all our marbles are intact. What say you, Roy?"

Roy looked at her with a blurring of tears in his eyes. "What I say, Ivy, is that I love you so much that nothing else matters," he said.

Twenty-one

WENDY WRIGHT HAD, of course, been told the bad news earlier, and now she sat with her neighbour, Marie-Agnes, in her kitchen, drinking one cup of tea after another, weeping bitterly, or speaking in rushes of nostalgia in response to consolation and support from her best friend.

"I thought he was with another woman," she said, after a short silence. "He often spent the night away, and said that he was here or there on business trips. He did some buying for the department, as well as organising his salesmen and doing some selling himself."

"But what was he doing there on a Sunday?" asked Marie-Agnes gently.

"Oh well, the store started Sunday opening a couple of months ago. Apparently masses of stores do it these days, and business is always good. I suppose with big things like furniture, partners like to come and choose together. It meant that Steven had to give up his regular golf four on a Sunday morning, but he didn't seem to mind."

"What makes you think he had another woman, Wendy dear? He could have been telling the truth."

Big tears plopped into Wendy's cup. "I checked up on him once. He told me he was going to Liverpool to an appointment with a big supplier. I knew the name, and phoned to talk to him. I said it was urgent. They knew nothing about his appointment, and were very nice, checking round every possible person who might have been expecting him. Then when he came home, I asked him how it had gone, and he said it had been fine, and he'd given them an order. So I knew."

"Did you face him with it?"

Wendy shook her head. "I said nothing. Didn't see the point. I just hoped it was a one-off."

"I'll make some more tea. Are you hungry? Could you eat a sandwich?"

Wendy shook her head. "Didn't get much sleep last night, wondering where he was this time. Then I got up early and had some cereal and a coffee, and after some serious thinking, decided I was going to leave him. He was a difficult man, as you know, and I had had enough."

"So instead of you leaving him, he's left you," Marie-Agnes said. "Did the police know how . . ."

"How he died? Not for definite. But they were looking at suffocation, they said. Those beds are made up with pillows and such, and apparently it would have been easily done."

"Provided he was already in the bed and asleep. He was quite a strong man, wasn't he?" Marie-Agnes suggested.

IVY AND ROY sat in the interview room at Springfields, holding hands, while a kindly Inspector Frobisher asked them as tactfully as he could about what they knew about Roy's nephew, Steven Wright.

Roy took most of the questions, and answered them honestly and straightforwardly, with Ivy occasionally unable to resist chipping in. But the inspector was a patient man. He knew Ivy Beasley of old, and had considerable respect for her. He had had past dealings with the Enquire Within agency and, though reluctant to believe that they could be of any use to him, had to admit that their enquiries had been extremely useful in previous difficult cases they had taken on.

"What kind of a man was your nephew, Mr. Goodman?" the inspector asked. "Take your time, sir. I am in no hurry."

Roy sighed. "To tell the truth, Inspector, I hardly knew him. He was my sister's son, and she is sadly—or maybe not so sadly, in view of this terrible news—no longer with us. I was very fond of her, and as children we always played together. She married against our parents' wishes, as her husband was known to be a violent man. But they seemed to rub along together reasonably well. He died young, and my nephew was brought up mostly by my sister on her own, so there was no masculine role model, as they say, for young Steven."

"We have talked to his wife, and she says he used to visit you here?"

"Once or twice a year," said Roy.

"And then he would look at his watch after about half an hour," said Ivy.

"And I understand he was your only living close relative?" The inspector shifted in his chair.

"He was my heir, and until I met my dearest Ivy here, he would have inherited everything on my death. When he got married, I was very pleased and assured him that his family would, of course, be special to me."

"And would have shared in what must be a sizeable sum?"

Roy nodded. "Of course. But I am to marry Miss Beasley shortly, and that will mean changes."

"Ah," said the inspector. "Then your relationship with Wright became very important. Could you tell me something about that?"

"I asked him to be my best man, and he agreed. He seemed pleased; didn't he, Ivy?"

Ivy sniffed. "I suppose so," she said.

"And he was due to be in church this morning to listen to your banns?"

"We asked Steven and Wendy, but I don't think they could make it."

"Right," said the inspector, again shifting in his chair. He hesitated before asking his next question, because he realised how ridiculous it was. But it had to be asked.

"You may think this a silly question, sir, but I have to ask you what you were doing from six o'clock last evening to around eight o'clock this morning?"

Ivy puffed her chest out like an angry pigeon. "I'll tell you what he did," she butted in, her face scarlet with rage. "He went over to Thornwell in his trundle, parked it outside Maleham's store and waited until all the staff had gone. Then he crept in through the keyhole, found his nephew, Steven Wright, tidying up the bed department, challenged him to a fight and punched him to death. Then he lifted him into the best bed, arranged the duvet over his lifeless body, and tiptoed out, back through the keyhole, and returned to Springfields on his trundle. How's that?"

Inspector Frobisher frowned and reminded Ivy that this could well be a murder investigation, and therefore extremely serious. "I think that will be all for the moment, Miss Beasley, Mr. Goodman," he added. "Thank you for your cooperation. I shall, of course, be in touch very soon. Good evening."

Miss Pinkney was waiting for him in the reception hall. "Are you off now, Inspector?" she said. "I do hope this will all be cleared up very soon. I really fear for Mr. Goodman and Miss Beasley. Old people should not have such terrible shocks, should they?"

Inspector Frobisher looked her straight in the eye, and said, "Have no worries about Miss Beasley, madam! She has the heart of a lion, and will make sure no harm comes to Mr. Goodman. Good evening."

Twenty-two

NEXT DAY, IVY and Roy sat at the breakfast table in silence, each busy with their own thoughts. Roy was thinking back to when Steven was a boy, being brought up by an over-loving mother. He could have done more to help with his upbringing, he knew, and would not forgive himself for selfishly leaving his sister to tackle it alone.

Ivy, on the other hand, was thinking about her wedding, and how she intended to make her own list of likely people in the congregation who might know the interrupter. The squire, Theo Roussel, who hardly ever came to church, had sat in the front pew opposite them. She knew him from a previous Enquire Within case, and felt happy about asking him for a suitable time when they could talk. Then behind them, a couple of pews back, had been an ancient couple, a famer and his wife, now retired.

As she went through the list, she realised that all that day's churchgoers were in late old age, except for Theo Roussel, and were not likely to be much help. She decided to start with Theo, and, after explaining to Roy what she intended to do, went upstairs to make the call.

* * *

THEO HAD BEEN very helpful, and said she must come along at once and bring Mr. Goodman, too. As they made their way up to the front of the Hall, they remembered how Theo had been the victim of a wicked housekeeper, and Enquire Within had helped to rescue him from her. Now they were concerned with themselves, and when he greeted them at the door and helped Roy along to the sunny drawing room, Ivy felt sure he would be able to help.

"Afraid I didn't catch a good look at him," said Theo, "other than the back view when he went off to the vestry with the vicar. Ran off, did you say, and disappeared? Now, let me see. He was bald and thickset. Overweight, I would say. Jeans and an anorak, and some kind of boots. And, oh yes, he dropped a handkerchief in the aisle."

"Very good, sir," said Roy. "Excellent memory. Now, did you recognise him at all? Someone local, maybe?"

Theo thought hard. There had been something about the man. Who was it he reminded him of? "Just something about the way he walked," he said. "Sort of loped along. Strangely enough he reminded me of an old bloke who used to work on the estate when I was a child. He was the farrier."

Theo Roussel looked out of the window, his eyes seeing another time, another way of life. "We had a lot of horses in those days," he continued. "Father was keen on hunting, and a guest was out with him when the horse tripped and fell. Rider badly damaged. All blamed on the farrier for not noticing a loose horseshoe. Strange that I should have remembered that! Can't remember his name, though. I can see him now, loping across the fields."

Ivy smiled. "That's most interesting, Mr. Roussel," she said. "I am sure we can follow up the family, and it may be of some help. If you do think of your farrier's name, do let us know."

THE OTHER NAMES on Ivy's list, Mr. and Mrs. Bourne, came as no surprise to Roy. His farm had bordered theirs and they had been good friends. As Ivy and he left the Hall, Roy said they should try the Bournes straight away, while their memories were fresh. If they were anything like his own, they had a habit of vanishing overnight.

"Shall we ask Elvis to collect us and take us over there, if he's free?"

"Good idea," said Roy. "We'll ring them when we get back. They may well be at home now. I seem to remember they did up one of the farm cottages when they retired, and I should have their number."

They were in luck, as Elvis was happy to take them, and the Bournes said they would be delighted to see them.

"Off enquiring again?" said Elvis, as they drove along through the slushy lanes to the Bournes' farm. "So here we are. Not far to go. Shall I wait for you, if you're not too long?"

"Fine," said Roy. "This'll take me back, I don't mind telling you! But we'll try not to be long. Soon be lunchtime, and we don't have to tell you how Mrs. Spurling hates latecomers!"

"THAT WAS A bit of a facer, Roy!" said his old friend Ted Bourne. "Never known it to happen before. There's always that little gap, when people look round the church, and that's what me and Mother did yesterday. So we got a quick look at him. Can't say we recognised him, though both of us felt he was a bit familiar."

Roy told the Bournes about the squire remembering the likeness to his father's farrier, and Mrs. Bourne said, "I remember that man. Used to go round all the farms shoeing the working horses. Sullen sort of chap. No wonder, when you think, Roy, what it was like in our young days, when farm workers put in more hours and got less pay than any of the young blokes today!"

After a short and pleasant trip down memory lane, Ivy stood up and said they must be leaving, as Elvis would need to get going. She walked towards the door, and a faded photograph on the wall caught her eye. It was of the hunt meet up at the Hall, and elegant ladies and gentlemen, high up on their horses, engaged in conversation, while the hunt servants busied themselves at ground level below.

"Look at that man there, Roy," she said. "Who does he remind you of?"

Roy stretched up to look at the photograph. "Him on the

left there? Good heavens, Ivy, it could be him! Still, he's no doubt been dead and gone these many years. Come along, now, dearest. Elvis will be getting restive. Wonderful to see you both," he added. "Keep well."

After they had gone, Mrs. Bourne stood looking at the old photograph. "I haven't looked at that for years, Ted," she said. "That man they were looking at, come and see. Isn't that the farrier they were talking about? And it's quite true—he does look like that wicked so-and-so who interrupted the service yesterday. Do you think he could be one of the same family?"

IVY AND ROY had been in Deirdre's thoughts when the phone rang in the kitchen. She had been stacking plates in the dishwasher and humming quietly to herself.

"Hello? Oh, Gus, it's you. Have you heard any more news? I'm really worried about Ivy and Roy. The news about Steven Wright coming on top of that challenge to their banns could be too much for them, poor old things. Are you busy? Do you want to come up for a snack lunch, and then we can talk about it without disturbing them?"

"Good idea. See you in a few minutes. I'll take Whippy round to Miriam, in case we need to go off somewhere and investigate."

"And if she invites you to lunch, please say you have a prior engagement."

"I'll see what Miriam has to offer, and then decide," Gus said, half laughing. Deirdre put the phone down on him.

"WELL? WHAT DID she have on her menu?" she said acidly, when he arrived at Tawny Wings.

"Guess," said Gus, putting his arm around her shoulders. "Lamb with apricots. She's trying them out for James at the shop."

"So what did you decide?"

"I'm here, aren't I?" he said, giving her an affectionate peck on the cheek. "Let's get down to business."

"I've been thinking since I rang you," she replied. "There's a good chance that the belligerent man we saw when we were in Maleham's beds department is a candidate for murderer, don't you think? After all, he threatened to deal with Wright next time he saw him."

"Mm, yes. But he was nothing like the chap who challenged the banns. And wouldn't the bed department be immediately on guard if they saw him again?"

"I don't know. Just because it's obvious, it isn't necessarily wrong. I think we should report all we saw that day to the inspector, anyway. The police can easily find him from the furniture purchase documents."

Gus was silent while he struggled with a nourishing but not particularly appetising vegetarian salad. He frowned and shook his head. "My instinct tells me it wasn't him," he said. "And it occurs to me that we may not have been the only ones to over-hear that quarrel between Wright and the customer. Do you remember seeing other people around?"

"Oh gosh, I'll have to do some thinking," Deirdre said. "Meanwhile, I've had another idea. Steven was his only rela-tive, so far as we know, and his heir, so who's going to bene-fit now?"

Gus stared at her. "Deirdre, you're a marvel," he said.

"I know that," she said. "But answer my question."

"I do remember Roy saying at some stage that there was another branch of the family over at Settlefield, but generations ago there had been a feud and the two lots hadn't had anything to do with each other for years and years. So, Mrs. Cleverclogs, the first thing we do is take a trip to Settlefield and ask around."

"Their name may not be Goodman, but we can look up records. Shall we go now?"

"Why not?" said Gus, "I'll drive you in my car, and establish the correct relationship between us."

"What? You mean the man should drive and the woman be a mere passenger?"

"Correct," said Gus. "You may take my arm."

GUS WAS A good driver, and Deirdre relaxed. "It is rather nice being driven," she said. "Bert always used to drive when we went out together."

"You must miss him still, love," said Gus, neatly avoiding

a splendid cock pheasant stalking across the road in front of them.

"Of course," she replied. "But I often hear him in my head. He was a practical chap, and still keeps me from making unwise decisions."

"Such as remarrying?"

"Certainly that," she said. "But I decided that myself long ago, and I must say with all the kerfuffle with Ivy and Roy, I am not so sure they are doing the right thing."

"Oh, I've never doubted that it is right for them," Gus replied. "But not for us, eh?"

"We take a right turn here," said Deirdre, not answering his question. "Then I reckon the post office in that shop over there is the best place to start."

They parked outside the shop, which was full of customers discussing the morning's news.

"I reckon he went to sleep and 'ad a 'eart attack," said a young man in oily overalls. "Prob'ly bin celebratin' and thought he'd get away with it."

"Oi don' think so, boy," said a motherly lady holding a wriggling toddler. "That don' say that in my paper here. They reckon it were a revenge killing."

"Excuse me," said Deirdre sweetly, "but does it give the name of the murdered man?"

"Wright, dear. Not a relation of yours, I hope?"

"Oh no, no! I heard a bit of the news on local radio at lunchtime, but missed his name. Not a local one, is it?"

"Next, please!" said the shopkeeper, a mousey little woman not much taller than the counter. "There's others waiting to be served."

"Come on, Deirdre," Gus said. "Was it chocolate you wanted?"

They waited until the shop had emptied, and then the shopkeeper smiled at them. "You're not from round here, are you?" she said.

"No, but not far away. We live in Barrington. You had plenty of customers today!"

"Ah, but that's unusual. They were all wanting to talk about the case in Thornwell. Man found dead in bed department of Maleham's store. Funny thing, that. It's a mystery to me how the killer, if there was one, got in and out of the store without being seen. And there must have been a struggle, surely. Unless he was drugged," the small woman added with relish.

"Or drunk," said Gus lightly. "The name's unfamiliar to me, but I'm a newcomer to the area."

"And to me," said the shopkeeper. "There's a lot of new names in the village. Incomers, most of them. There's just one original farming family left now. Well, two, actually. Josslands and Goodmans have been farming round here for generations. Young couple with a new baby. She was a Goodman, and he's a Jossland. Baby girl, I think. The farm's down a long drive off the Oak-bridge road. Were you looking for anyone in particular?"

"No, no," said Deirdre. "But it's always interesting to hear about local people."

As she spoke, the familiar sound of a police car siren got increasingly louder, until it passed through the village at speed and disappeared.

"On their way to Thornwell, I expect," said the shopkeeper wisely. "Now, chocolate, was it, you wanted? We've got a new supply of Green and Black's plain chocolate. Will that do?"

"VERY PROFITABLE," SAID Gus, as they settled back into the car. "I don't think we should look up the Jossland family at the moment. But we can report back to Ivy and Roy. In fact, I think we should do so. It may be important to Roy to confirm he still has relatives in Settlefield."

"I agree," Deirdre said. "After all, it may be really nice for him to know a young couple with a baby are close by, and related to him. Not as lonely as he thought he was. It could lessen his grief over that no-good Steven."

"I don't think he's grieving all that much. But I do see what you mean. Let's go back, and then call in unannounced at Springfields."

Twenty-three

"I MUST SAY," said Gus, "that this chocolate cake makes up for that disgusting salad! Another piece would be so welcome." They were back at Tawny Wings, having a late tea and deciding to call Springfields before dropping in to see Ivy and Roy.

"Are you up to revealing to Roy that he's got blood relations after all?" Gus asked.

"It could make a great difference to his life with Ivy, and cause more trouble than if we kept quiet about it."

"Don't be ridiculous, Gus! Of course we must tell him. For one thing, it might have some connection with the murder of Steve Wright."

"You're not intending to implicate an innocent young couple with a new baby, are you?"

"Of course not, but we do need to know much more about them. There may be more of them, and who knows what plans they might have? Time for some input from Roy and Ivy. Shall we go?"

WHEN THEY ARRIVED at Springfields, Mrs. Spurling was on duty, and barred their way into the lounge.

"Good evening, Mrs. Spurling," said Gus. "Miss Beasley and Mr. Goodman are expecting us."

"It's rather late, Mr. Halfhide," Mrs. Spurling said with a frown.

"What rubbish!" said a voice from the top of the stairs. "Why don't you come up, Deirdre and Gus, and I'll rouse Roy. He's probably not asleep, anyway. He sneaks a look at the crossword to get at it first. We always do the *Guardian* crossword after tea, you know. Keeps the brain active."

Mrs. Spurling sighed. "We really like residents to entertain visitors in the lounge," she said, without much hope of co-operation.

"Enquire Within is not entertainment," said Ivy firmly. "This will be a business meeting. Has Katya been baking? Cookies all round would be welcome."

Mrs. Spurling went back to perusing the Sunday newspaper's jobs section in the hope of finding a suitable appointment vacant in her field of administration.

"THIS IS A nice surprise," said Roy, blinking sleepily as he joined them in Ivy's room. "I do hope there's no more bad news?"

"No, I hope it will be good news," Gus said. "To begin at the beginning, I had lunch with Deirdre, and in talking about your nephew's unfortunate demise, we remembered you saying there was a branch of the Goodman family over at Settlefield. We really need to know about them, since someone is clearly very anxious to stop anyone other than themselves inheriting your fortune. Steven has gone, sadly, and now is the time when a long-lost nephew or niece on another side of the family is likely to pop up and stake a claim."

"I wish I had no money at all," Roy said vehemently. "I have a good mind to will it all to a home for ill-treated donkeys."

"That's fine by me," said Ivy. "They say money is the root of all evil, and there's never been a truer word spoken. Anyway, Gus, all you've told us so far is supposition."

"So we went to Settlefield," continued Deirdre. "The village post office shop was full of folk talking about newspaper reports of the man found dead in a bed in Maleham's furniture store. We listened to their conversations, but nothing interesting was said until the shop cleared and the shopkeeper told us about a young couple farming locally, and—guess what?—the wife's name was Goodman before she married!"

"Well, that's not unexpected," said Ivy flatly. "Could be a distant relation of Roy. I don't know what you're so excited about. Who did she marry?"

"A chap called Jossland. Another farming family, apparently," Deirdre said.

Roy nodded. "It does often happen in the farming world. Sometimes doubles the size of the farm." He looked at Ivy and winked at her. "I suppose the Beasleys haven't got some arable land hidden away somewhere in the county?" he suggested.

"Don't complicate the issue," Ivy replied sternly, and turned to Gus. "So how are we going to find out about the young couple? I should think twice before contacting them direct," she said.

"Ask Alf," Roy said. "Alf Lowe. He knew my family over Settlefield way, or so he claims. He might have some contacts who could enlighten us. What do you think, Gus? Are you willing to tackle the old reprobate again?"

A knock at the door brought in Katya bearing a tray of glasses and a bottle of sweet sherry, and, as requested, cookies. "Good evening, Mrs. Bloxham and Mr. Halfhide. Are you comfortable sitting on the bed, Mrs. Bloxham? I shall bring in another chair. One minute, please."

She disappeared, and Ivy began to pour the tea. "That girl is the best thing about Springfields," she said. "If she ever leaves, then so shall I."

"I trust you'll find room for me?" said Roy. "I shall follow you to the ends of the earth, you know."

"Of course you will come, too," she answered. "I have been thinking for some time that Tawny Wings would make a very pleasant retirement home, and Deirdre could manage it perfectly well."

"Ivy! What are you saying? Hands off my ancestral home! What would Bert have said? No, don't even think of it!"

Katya appeared once more, carrying a chair, which Gus took from her and placed near the window for Deirdre.

"So, Gus is going to tackle Alf. What about the rest of us?"

Deirdre looked quite pale at the thought of Tawny Wings Home for the Elderly, and was anxious to get back to the business in hand.

"There will be a funeral to attend for me," said Roy. "There is no date for it yet, but I must go."

"And I shall come, too, and see what I can pick up in the way of useful information," said Ivy.

"Which leaves me," said Deirdre. "All this talk about over-hearing and gleaning something useful from Alf seems unnecessary to me. I shall try the direct approach. I don't see why I shouldn't, Ivy. You can all get on with things, and I shall arrange to call on Mr. and Mrs. Jossland and their new baby at Hartwood Farm. There is absolutely no reason why I shouldn't introduce myself as a voluntary worker for Social Services—which is true—just calling to make sure they don't need any help. I might even take a small teddy bear with me as passport."

Twenty-four

UNAWARE THAT THEY were the subject of speculation, the Josslands at Hartwood Farm were sitting in their large kitchen, drinking coffee and marvelling at the small miracle in the cot by the window.

"She looks quite like me, doesn't she?" said Bella. "My blue eyes, and those sweet little wisps of blonde fluff are my colour, too."

"It'll all change," said knowledgeable farmer William. "All babies have blue eyes. Then they change colour to what they're always going to be. She could take after your aunt, Ethel, and have brown eyes and ginger hair." He grinned at his young wife. "Maybe we should call her Ethel? Good old-fashioned name."

"It's horrible! She's going to be Faith, after my mother."

"Faith Ethel, then?" said William. "The ancient old duck might leave her some money; you never know. Some say she's loaded, and she never married."

"That nursing home is eating up all her savings," Bella said. "Still, Faith Ethel is a reasonable compromise. Oh look! She's smiling!"

"Wind," said William cruelly. "They all do that. Now, I

must get out to the cows, so I'll see you in a bit. Bye, Faith Ethel," he added, blowing a kiss to the baby. "Looks hungry to me. Better get milking, Bella."

He made his way to the door, opened it and then stopped. "Are we expecting anybody?" he said, as he saw a woman crossing the yard.

"MY NAME IS Bloxham, Deirdre Bloxham. I am a voluntary worker for the social services department in Thornwell, and we try to keep in touch with our new mums, just in case they need extra support." All of this was perfectly true, though Deirdre would have to make sure she organised the paperwork in the office.

"Do you have any proof of identity?" said William. He was large and tough, and he filled the doorway, blocking Deirdre's view inside the kitchen.

"Yes, of course," she said, bringing out a card to confirm. "Is it inconvenient? I could always come back."

Bella appeared, carrying the baby, and said she was welcome to come in. "William has to see to the cows now, so I'll be glad of your company. It's a bit strange, isn't it, when there's suddenly a new little person in the household!"

Deirdre, whose knowledge of new babies was scant, but who had a warm and capable personality, had seen many young mothers through those difficult first few weeks. Now she asked to hold Faith Ethel, while Bella put on the kettle.

"Do you live locally? I don't think I've seen you around, have I?"

"I don't come this way often. I've lived in Barrington for many years, and before that I was brought up in Thornwell. Not really a country girl, you see! But my husband, Bert, owned Bloxham garages. All around the county. You've probably noticed them."

The girl was obviously impressed. "Does he still own them?" she said.

"He's passed on, sadly," said Deirdre. "Much too soon. He loved his business, and was very popular with customers. So now I run them, with the help of an expert staff. Perhaps your husband will have heard of us?"

"I'm sure he will. Now, shall I attempt to put my small

daughter down in her cot? I think she's already decided she'd rather be cuddled!"

"They're very knowing, even early on. Friend of mine claims her tiny son was intellectualising—whatever that means—at one week old!"

Bella laughed loudly, relaxing properly for the first time since the birth of Faith Ethel. "It is really nice to meet you, Mrs. Bloxham," she said. "Apart from Auntie Ethel, who's a hale and hearty eighty-year-old and daft as a brush, none of my relations or William's are left."

"No mother, then, to help you?" said Deirdre. "Or even mother-in-law? Though they can be a mixed blessing, I know."

Bella shook her head. "They were pale, the two families. The generations intermarried a number of times way back. All gone now. My mother had multiple sclerosis, and died a couple of years ago, and Dad had an accident with a tractor. William's parents are both gone, too. He was a very late child—mother in her forties when he was born—and he's a good bit older than me. So there we are, and though I've lots of friends, we are a bit isolated down here. You're not in a hurry, I hope? I do tend to rattle on, once I get started."

Deirdre shook her head. "No hurry," she whispered. "Look, she's fast asleep, little precious. May I just sit here holding her for a bit?"

Bella was only too pleased to have this nice woman keeping her company. She seemed to be a natural with babies. She wondered whether Mrs. Bloxham had children of her own, and asked her tactfully. And then the conversation continued comfortably until Deirdre looked at the old shelf clock and said she would unfortunately have to be getting back.

"I'll give you my address etcetera," she said, "and you must call me at any time if you're stuck on anything. I can usually help. Nothing medical, of course. You must get your doctor or midwife for that. But I'd really like to see how Faith progresses! Have you thought of another name for her?"

Bella made a face. "Unfortunately, I have agreed to the old aunt's name. Ethel Goodman, that is. William's idea, of course. So she's Faith Ethel. Perhaps you'd like to come to her christening in due course?"

"Love to," said Deirdre, really meaning it.

* * *

IVY AND ROY had retired to Ivy's room after lunch, feeling the need to stay together to face the dire happenings that had fallen on them in the last few days.

"You'd think, wouldn't you, Roy, that two old parties such as us could get spliced without any fuss or inconvenience to anybody?" Ivy sat in her usual chair, which enabled her to look out of the window at goings-on in the village street.

Roy reached across and took her hand. "Dear little hand," he said consolingly. "Don't you worry, beloved; we shall have that gold band on this finger in a very short while."

"No word from the others this morning. Deirdre must have found nobody at home at that farm at Settlefield. A barmy idea, if you ask me. You can't just go knocking on doors and expect people to tell you their business straight away."

"She can be very persuasive," said Roy, with a grin. "She can twist our Gus round her little finger. Anyway, she'll probably pop in later."

"And Gus is off tackling Alf Lowe. He's welcome to that job, though I must say there's something likeable about the old man, horrible as he is."

"He can't be both, can he, my dear?"

"Oh yes," said Ivy confidently. "I've known several men like him. My own father, for a start. I don't like to mention the subject, Roy, but I think the most interesting thing brought up by Alf Lowe in his story—untrue, I'm sure—is about your involvement with an old friend of his. I can't remember the name, but there was some woman you were supposed to have been engaged to, and then ducked out of it. There's never smoke without fire, in my experience, and he might be trying to off-load some other bloke's guilt onto you."

Roy's expression was mutinous. "I'm afraid I disagree with you there, Ivy," he said. "I have already explained that the whole thing was a fabrication. I think we are being deliberately led astray on that one. But why? That is the real nub of it."

"Money," said Ivy flatly. "A pot of gold waiting to be collected in the event of your passing on. Little do they know that now I am almost your wife, you are going to be the longest-living person in the world!"

"But who are these 'they'? Steve has gone, so it was nothing to do with him."

"Except that he was one person between them and the pot of gold, and is now removed. Poor old Steve. And if the attempt at preventing our wedding succeeds, then another contender has been eliminated, for the moment. Me, that is. That possibly leaves these Josslands, with a wife who was a Goodman, over at Settlefield."

"You've forgotten the man who interrupted our banns. Where does he fit into all this?"

Ivy was silent for a few minutes. "Something to do with Alf Lowe and his low-life relations? Could be someone hired to do the job?"

Roy frowned. "Ivy, my dearest, do you realise what this means?"

"Yes, of course. It means that whoever is prepared to murder once, might try again. And this time, the one most in the way of he or she inheriting your millions is me. But only once we are married. Do you suppose I should hire a bodyguard?"

"Don't joke, Ivy! I shall be glad when Gus comes back and we can ask his advice. Meanwhile rescue is at hand for all those poor donkeys."

Ivy ignored him. "And then, of course, my love, there is you. It all hinges on getting rid of you, should the murderer be in a hurry. I'm afraid that is the real nub. But never fear; I do not intend to let any harm come to you, and I am sure that Enquire Within, with some help from Inspector Frobisher, will be able to trace the villain very soon."

"I'm glad you're so confident!" said Roy. "I must say I feel more and more uneasy as we uncover new information. Ah, there's Deirdre coming up the path. Let's hope she has some good news for us."

Deirdre was followed by a dishevelled Gus, who looked as if he had been dragged out of bed.

"Sorry to come at lunchtime, Ivy," Deirdre said. "I just rescued Gus from an attempt to clear the brambles at the bottom of his garden, and brought him up here."

"Is it urgent, then?" said Ivy. "La Spurling doesn't like our mealtimes to be disturbed."

"Mrs. Spurling is off duty, and Pinkers won't mind a bit.

She might offer us lunch?" Gus knew that Miss Pinkney had a soft spot for him, and he went off to find her. He returned beaming, saying they were all to have lunch together in the table in the alcove, so that our conversation could be private. "Isn't she a darling?"

"Not many people have called her that," said Ivy. "Poor thing. Well-done, Gus. Come on into the dining room, everyone."

Needless to say, all the other residents were consumed with curiosity. One or two said in very loud voices that it was all right for some. Others had to abide by the rules and stick to visiting times, they said. Gus helped a grateful old lady into her seat, and Deirdre earned undying devotion by tucking an elderly man's table napkin into his collar, and so eventually they were settled. Deirdre began to tell them in detail about her morning's achievement.

"Did you talk to both husband and wife?" Ivy asked.

"Oh yes, and the baby. The sweetest little soul named Faith. I cuddled her until she went to sleep. All warm and smelling of Johnson's baby powder." She paused, dreamy-eyed.

"It's no good you getting broody, Deirdre Bloxham," Ivy said sharply. "You've lost your chance at motherhood. Could we get on?"

"Yes, well, I asked about the family, and Bella—that was the girl's name—said that the Josslands and Goodmans had been marrying each other for generations. But now, for a number of reasons, natural selection, I suppose, there are just the two of them left, plus an aged spinster aunt named Ethel."

"Ethel what?" interrupted Roy, his voice unusually sharp.

"Ethel Goodman," said Deirdre, playing her trump card. "How about that, then?"

"Well, you certainly had more luck than we did. Our investigations yesterday morning included Theo and Mr. and Mrs. Bourne, old friends of Roy. And all we discovered was that there was an old farrier at the Hall years ago, who got the sack because of a loose horseshoe, and who looked uncannily like the man who challenged our banns. Might be worth remembering, if nothing else."

Twenty-five

THEIR CONVERSATION WAS broken up by Katya coming in with puddings. She beamed at the table for four, and said how nice it was that residents felt they could ask guests for lunch. "So much more like an hotel than an, um, old folks' home," she said.

"I'll deal with this," said a voice behind her. It was Mrs. Spurling, back on duty earlier than expected. "I shall not make a scene in front of other residents," she said, "but perhaps you can explain to me how two non-residents appear to be having lunch at Springfields' expense?"

Before any of the others could draw breath, Roy had struggled to his feet. "Please leave us, Mrs. Spurling," he said. "I shall be in to see you in your office in due course, but in the meantime, Mr. Halfhide and Mrs. Bloxham are our guests, so you will charge the expense to my account. I have more to say, but it will be best said in private when we have finished lunch."

There was an astonished silence, and then Mrs. Spurling stalked off. Roy sat down, beamed at the others, and said he felt much better. "Do carry on, Deirdre," he said. "You were just telling us about an aged person called Goodman, who may be a long-lost relative of mine. Isn't it exciting? I do hope she turns out to be a nice person and a new friend for you, my dear," he added, turning to Ivy.

"There's only one Goodman for me," she said, her voice a little wobbly. "And that's you, Roy. That Spurling woman is impossible, and you really put her in her place. And now, Deirdre, what about all the rest of the Goodmans of Settlefield?"

"Well, the baby's father, William Jossland, is quite a bit older than Bella, and his parents have died of more or less natural causes. He was an only child, and he married Bella Goodman, herself an only, and they have produced dear little Faith. Bella's parents are also dead. Mother died from multiple sclerosis, and Father had a fatal accident on his tractor."

"Not surprising," chipped in Ivy. "Those enormous great things are a menace on the road and the field. Get one of those in a ditch and you've had it. And they shake the village houses to their foundations when they go by. So both Bella and William are orphans, so to speak?"

"That's right. And Bella seems to come down in a direct line from the farming Goodmans. Oh, and by the way, I did not mention anything about you and Ivy, or Steven Wright, or any of the people we are investigating. I just established contact, and a delightful contact it was."

"I am really pleased," Roy said. "I must arrange to meet them in due course. I am sure Bella will be a pleasant addition to our family."

"And also an addition to the list of people made vulnerable by possibly inheriting your fortune," said Ivy. "But perhaps you'd like to tell the others about the donkeys?"

"What donkeys?" said Deirdre. "What on earth are you talking about, Ivy?"

"Private joke," said Roy. "Ivy is teasing me."

They finished lunch, and got up to leave the dining room. "Excuse me one moment," said Roy. "I have a date with La Spurling in her office." He hobbled off chuckling.

"So now I must away to think," said Gus. "And visit Alf Lowe and see what he has to say about Miss Ethel Goodman. Not much hope of getting the truth out of him, but I shall try."

When he had gone, Deirdre took Ivy's arm and said she would like to ask her a personal question.

"Depends what it is," said Ivy.

"It's this. Do you know whether Roy has made a will? And if so, and it seems very likely that he has, do you know who are the beneficiaries? I've noticed he skirts around the subject whenever it comes up."

"I have never asked him, and he has never said. As far as I am concerned, I don't want any of it. The donkey joke was because he is so unhappy about all the trouble his money seems to be causing, that he declared he was going to leave the whole lot to look after neglected donkeys."

"Not such a bad idea," said Deirdre. "Still, we have to respect his wish to keep his will private. Hope you don't mind my asking, Ivy, but I'm beginning to get a bit scared."

"Don't worry," said Ivy. "We should hear something soon about the Maleham's furniture store report. Let's hope the police are a bit nearer finding the murderer, if murder it was."

"Did you ever meet Steven's wife?" Deirdre said. "I just wonder if she might know a bit more."

"She might even have done him in, nasty piece of work that he was," said Ivy. "Come on, girl, let's go and ring up Frobisher and see if he'll tell us anything. And after that, we'll call the Reverend Dorothy and see how she's getting on sorting our banns out."

WHEN GUS APPROACHED Alf Lowe's cottage, he was surprised to see Miriam coming down the path towards him.

"Hi, Gus," she said. "Where are you off to?"

"And where have you been?" said Gus, laughing. "I'm going to call on Alf Lowe. He promised to tell me some tales about the Roussels. They've been squires up at the Hall for generations, and since the Honourable. Theo is my landlord, I thought it would be entertaining."

"I could tell you some entertaining stories about the squire," Miriam answered. "More entertaining than Alf Lowe's. I doubt he knows much more than that his old father was given the push as estate farrier, after one of the hunting crowd was thrown off in a field because his horse lost a shoe that had only just been put on. The rider was badly injured and never walked again."

"Good gracious!" said Gus. "There's always a disaster lurking round the corner in this village. So where have you been? No, don't tell me. You've been putting flowers on a grave in the cemetery."

"Right first time," Miriam said, taking his arm. "Mum and Dad are up there. Come on, I'll walk you back up to Alf's cottage. I hope you've not much sense of smell; otherwise you're in for an unpleasant interview."

Alf must have been looking out of his window, thought Gus. He had barely knocked on the door, where paint was peeling off in unsightly strips, when it opened to reveal Alf. "*She's* not coming in here," he said, and began to shut the door.

Miriam put her boot in the narrow opening. "Don't worry; you wouldn't catch me in your hovel, Alf Lowe!" she said. "It's just Gus Halfhide here who wants a word with you. Watch where you tread, Gus," was her parting shot, and she walked quickly away.

"Come in, Halfhide," said Alf. "Can't stand that woman. Biggest gossip in Barrington."

"Her heart's in the right place, though, Alf. She's a good neighbour."

"Yes, well, I've known her longer than you have. Anyway, what can I do for you? And how are you getting on with putting the frighteners on my wife?"

"We are pursuing our enquiries," Gus lied. They had, in fact, done nothing about Alf's case, since the murder of Steven and the challenged banns had occupied the team full-time. He looked around Alf's sitting room and was surprised to see that it was fresh and clean. There were cheerful rugs on the old brick floor, and a bright fire leapt in the polished grate. Old oak furniture had been polished to an enviable patina, and one or two excellent hunting prints adorned the walls.

"You've got it all very nice and cosy in here," he said now. "I envy you the prints. I know a bit about them, and those are highly desirable."

"I'm aware of that, young man," said Alf. "So don't bother offering to buy them. They were my dad's, but after the accident he put them up in the loft. I got them down again after he passed on."

"A hunting accident?" prompted Gus.

"Yeah. The son of a visiting nobleman was thrown in the field. Broke his back, poor devil. Dad got blamed, because he had shoed the horse, and it somehow got lamed. We thought it jumped badly over a hedge, but it was never proved. My dad got the sack, and never really got over it."

"Sacked by Roussel, was he?"

"Yeah. Theo's Dad. Theo's your landlord, I suppose?"

Gus nodded. "Don't see much of him, though. I think he keeps away in case I ask him to spend money on the cottage!"

Alf laughed. "So what have you come for? Do you want some questions answered? I hear there's been an unpleasant event in poor old Roy Goodman's family? And what about him and his intended having their banns challenged? My God, that was a turnup! Stupid old fool should know better, I reckon. There's bound to be skeletons in the cupboard when you get to his great age."

"Not Roy, surely? He seems such an honourable person. Though last time we talked you mentioned a breach of promise involving him and some woman? What was all that about?"

"That was years and years ago, and I only heard about it secondhand. Apparently he was walking out with Ethel Goodman—his cousin from over Settlefield way—and she claimed he suggested they got engaged. Anyway, it was all over the farming community, because they was cousins, and that ain't reckoned to be healthy, is it? A few months went by, and the word went round that he had broken it off. She was heartbroken, and her dad, who was a bit of a man, said he'd get his lawyers to sue for breach of promise."

"And did he?"

"Dunno. It all went quiet, and people forgot about it. But the poor girl never married. Still alive, in a nursing home in Settlefield. Lost her marbles completely, so they say."

"I suppose she wasn't in the family way, or anything like that?"

"Why?" Alf asked suspiciously.

"Well, because it is possible. And if there is a son, say, somewhere, it could well have been him challenging Roy and Ivy's banns. I doubt if it would be a legal challenge, even so, but it could put the cat among the pigeons in a big way. See my point?"

"Oh yes, I see it," Alf said. He got up and put a shovelful of coal on the fire, then turned to the window and stood looking out. "It's goin' to snow again, Gus. You'd best be on your way," he said.

Twenty-six

THE SNOW HAD been falling all night, and Ivy was awoken early by the bright, clear light filling her bedroom. The sun was up, and when she got out of bed and went to the window, it was—to put it in Katya's words when she brought in Ivy's early-morning tea—"a beautiful fairyland! It reminds me so much of home, Miss Beasley."

"It's all very well now," replied Ivy, turning to take her tea. "But by the time the farm traffic and delivery vans to the shop have ploughed backwards and forwards, it'll all be dirty slush."

"Then you and Mr. Goodman must put on boots and walk around the garden. There are snowdrops under the hedge, and celandines in the spinney. Mr. Goodman could take photographs. He likes to do that, yes?"

"Quite right, my dear. We shall ask you to come with us, in case, like babes in the wood, we get lost. Everywhere looks different under snow. Now, I must be up and about. Lots to do today. Thank you for my tea."

* * *

IN DEEPER WOODS down Hangman's Lane, Gus and
Deirdre were laughing like children as they walked hand in
hand through the heavy fall of snow, and watched Whippy
leaping in a series of arcs in an attempt to see where she was
going.

"How long have you had her, Gus?" Deirdre asked.

"Can't remember. She must be six or seven now. I'd be lost
without her."

"I know."

The two trudged along in companionable silence, until Gus
said, "I think I've got some important new information, and I
don't know what to do with it, Dee-Dee."

"What's it about? Alf's Susan, or Steven's murder, or Ivy's
banns? We've got a lot on at the moment."

"That's the problem. It could relate to the murder and the
banns, but it was Alf who gave me the information yesterday.
I went up to see him, and he was communicative for once.
Asked me in, and you'd be amazed how clean and bright it is
inside that cottage."

"Is that the important information?"

"No, of course not. It's to do with Roy, and, incidentally,
Ivy, too. We all know about his contention, though he admitted
it was secondhand, that Roy was engaged to be married in his
youth, and then broke it off for someone richer. This was a *very*
long time ago, of course, and Roy denied it hotly."

"I could never see that it matters much, though," said Deirdre. "After all, it would be extremely unlikely that such a nice
and probably good-looking young farmer would not be an
attractive proposition for the local girls."

"You're right, absolutely right. And I think it would have
been much better if he had laughed it off, saying he had quite
forgotten it, instead of denying it so furiously. But he did, and
I think that was what upset Ivy most. And, of course, there is
the obvious link with the interrupter of the banns. Though
again, that in itself can only be a small hiccup. If Roy had
decided against marriage altogether when young, there would
not now be even a sniff of something untoward."

"There's something else, isn't there," said Deirdre, looking up at the sky. "Something we haven't thought of. Perhaps we should turn back. The sky looks full of snow, or maybe rain. Come on, turn around. We can follow our own footsteps."

"But I think I *have* thought of it," Gus continued, whistling for Whippy to follow them. "Supposing the Ethel girl was pregnant?"

Deirdre stopped suddenly in her tracks, and Gus barged into her. "Gus!" she said. "Do you think she could have been? And does Roy know? And if he does, he must be going through hell! Oh Lord, Augustus, this is a much more dangerous situation than we—or, at least, me—have thought."

Deirdre always spoke the careful English of the nouveau riche, and her lapse in grammar indicated to Gus how shocked she was. And he loved her for it.

"So, my lovely, what on earth are we going to do?" he asked.

"Think," said Deirdre, as they emerged out onto the lane. "You are going to make some coffee, and we will sit and think. And if Miriam Blake interrupts us, I shall tell her we are about to be overcome by lust, and will she please leave us alone."

"You wouldn't!"

"Try me," answered Deirdre. "I'm formidable when roused."

THE REST OF the day was necessarily curtailed for Ivy and Roy by further falls of snow. There was no question of going out with the trundle. Even Roy could see that he would most likely be bogged down and have to be rescued.

After lunch, Ivy suggested they set up a pontoon school, but Roy said who would play with them? They couldn't ask Deirdre and Gus to venture out in the snow, and Roy whispered that there wasn't one single other resident who could count up to ten, let alone twenty-one.

This was, of course, not true, but Ivy was silent for a while. Then she spoke, like the oracle. "Pinkers and Katya. I think they will agree to play, if *you* ask them, Roy. You know you can charm the birds off the trees."

"Are you sure, dearest? I don't think La Spurling would approve."

"She's not here to approve or disapprove. Off you go, now. I saw Pinkers in the office."

It was some time since the small interview room had been used for the previous pontoon school, and to Roy's amazement, Miss Pinkney hurried off with great enthusiasm to find extra electric fires to warm it up ready for the players.

"You will have to teach me how to play, Mr. Goodman," she had said shyly. "Shall I go and find Katya? I think she is in the kitchen with Anya. Perhaps Anya would make up the fourth?"

"We need *you*, Pinkers, to give us the stamp of approval," Roy said firmly.

"NOW, IVY, HOW are we doing? Is it time for a tea break?" Roy was enjoying himself with the three women, and, what was more, he was winning. Katya and Miss Pinkney, new to the game, had nevertheless picked up the rules and strategy very speedily and the time had passed quickly.

"Anya is bringing us tea at any minute," said Katya. "This is fun, isn't it, Miss Pinkney?"

The assistant manager looked nervously at the door. "I keep thinking Mrs. Spurling is going to walk in any moment," she said.

"Blame it all on Roy, dear," said Ivy. "She's already had a rocket from him, and won't be in the mood for another one. Anyway, she's gone off to Ipswich to see her aged mother, so she said. Poor soul. A bit of a busman's holiday for her. We must be nice to her, Roy, to make up."

As if on cue, there was a knock at the door. Miss Pinkney jumped up, red in the face, and opened it.

"Oh, thank goodness it's you, Rev. Dorothy!" she said.

"Well, thank you, Miss Pinkney!" the vicar replied. "I don't always get such a warm reception. But I see you are busy—pontoon, is it? Great game. Perhaps I could join you sometime?"

"You'd be very welcome," said Roy politely, thinking Mrs. Spurling couldn't possibly forbid it if the vicar was involved.

"It was really Miss Beasley and Mr. Goodman I came to see. Just to report on the banns fiasco."

Katya immediately jumped to her feet and left, and Miss

Pinkney said she must make a call from her office. Ivy and Roy were left, and Rev. Dorothy smiled at them.

"Not a lot to report, I'm afraid," she said. "But that in itself may be good news. If that man does not reappear, then his objection will be null and void, and we can go ahead with the second time of asking on Sunday next."

"So is there no trace of him?" said Ivy. "Surely someone must have recognised him. I tried to make a list of all the people in church, but as I sit at the front, that wasn't much good. Deirdre Bloxham and Augustus Halfhide might have better luck, but with this snow still around we have not been able to get together. Our regular meeting is tomorrow, and we'll make it by hook or by crook."

"There is one small clue," said the vicar. "After everyone had gone from the church, the cleaner came in and found a man's white handkerchief. It was in the pew where our interrupter was sitting, and there was an initial in one corner. The letter 'F,' it was. I have handed it to the police, of course, but I thought you would want to know."

There was a short pause, and then Ivy said quietly, almost to herself, " 'F' for who, I wonder?"

There was a gentle knock, and the door opened. Anya came in with tea and cookies, saying that it was a bit dreary in the interview room, and perhaps they would like to move to the lounge?

"Katya sent a message to say you were not to worry," she added. "She will clear up the cards and put the room straight before Mrs. Spurling gets back."

"No need, unless there is an interview in the near future," said Roy. "Our next session will include the Reverend Dorothy, so I am sure not even Mrs. Spurling will object. Tell Katya she might as well leave it as it is."

Twenty-seven

IVY COULD NOT believe what she saw out of her window next morning. Everywhere was dripping. Torrents poured into the drains, and a small stream of melted snow ran swiftly down the slope in the road from the shop towards Springfields.

"Thawing!" she said loudly, and, opening her door, half ran down the corridor, still in her sensible red nightie, to knock up Roy. "Are you awake?" she shouted joyfully. "Its been raining and everywhere is dripping and there's not a sign of snow anywhere!"

"Come in, my dear!" he called. "I am quite decent."

"I'm not," said Ivy, looking down at herself and sobering up. But it was too late to turn back, so she opened Roy's door and sidled in.

"It must be my birthday," said Roy, grinning at her from his bathroom. He was still in his pyjamas, but with a rather dashing silk dressing gown over the top. "My beloved fiancée has entered my room in her filmy, revealing nightdress! Come to my arms, Ivy, while we have the chance!"

Ivy instinctively folded her arms across her chest, and,

blushing fiercely, crossed the room and planted a warm kiss on his cheek.

"I'll have you know," she said, "that my nightdress is good warm winceyette, which reveals nothing at all! I only came to tell you the snow's gone, and we can get out and about again. Foolish of me, I know."

Roy took her hand and led her to a chair. Then he sat on the edge of his bed and said that in that case, he would have to wait until they were properly wed.

"But let's make the most of this lovely moment," he added, "and plan what we are going to do today."

"It's the Enquire Within meeting this afternoon," said Ivy, drawing her nightdress well down over her knees. "I hope we can persuade Deirdre to remember who was in church last Sunday. She's lived in Barrington for longest, except for you. And you were sitting at the front with me, so you couldn't have seen much."

"Then this morning we shall arrange for Elvis and his taxi to take us to a certain furniture store in Thornwell. After all, we are to be newlyweds, and must choose a comfortable bed. We can't rely on La Spurling! If we can get a salesman talking, so much the better."

"Good idea," Ivy said. "And now I really think I should get back to my own room. We don't want—"

A loud knock interrupted her.

"Come in," called Roy. His smile was broad, and he realised he was looking forward to a confrontation with Mrs. Spurling.

"Ah, there you are, Miss Beasley." It was Katya, looking worried. She hurriedly shut the door behind her, and said that if Miss Beasley was ready to return to her room, she would make sure the coast was clear.

"Excellent," said Ivy. "I'll see you at breakfast, Roy dear," she said.

"Do come again, beloved," he said. "You will be very welcome, day or night."

Katya swallowed hard. "Yes, indeed, Mr. Goodman," she said. "Now, come along, Miss Beasley. Time to get dressed. The snow has gone, and the sun is breaking through. What a surprise to see the rain this morning!"

They stopped outside Ivy's door, and Mrs. Spurling's raised voice came up the stairs very clearly. "Who has been playing cards in the interview room?" she shouted.

"Oops!" said Katya. "In you go, Miss Beasley. I must face the tigress in her den!"

"Don't forget to mention that the vicar is joining our pontoon four. That should fix her," said Ivy, vanishing into her own room.

Mrs. Spurling was not so easily put off. She approached Roy and Ivy at the breakfast table, and asked them acidly if they would mind asking permission to use the interview room for gambling in future. "I might have had an interview arranged," she said.

"But you didn't," said Ivy. "And if you say playing an innocent card game for matches is gambling, then you've led a very sheltered life, as I believe I have said before. We enjoyed our game very much, and I suggest you organise something like it, perhaps whist, for other residents? A good way of passing a wet afternoon, and better than staring at rubbish on television for hours on end."

Defeated as usual, Mrs. Spurling marched off to her study, head bent and muttering to herself.

ELVIS, WITH HIS specially adapted taxi clean and sparkling, appeared promptly at ten o'clock, ready to take Ivy and Roy to Maleham's furniture emporium.

"And how are all the plans going?" he said. "Soon be the happy day."

They realised that Elvis knew nothing about the fiasco with the banns, and so they gave him a brief account. "What did this bloke look like? The one who interrupted in church?" he asked.

"Burly sort of chap," said Roy. "Red-faced, balding. Oh, and I just remembered. Perhaps you noticed it, too, Ivy. He had an earring in one ear. I'm sure of that now, because I dislike the current fashion intensely. Earrings are for ladies, as far as I am concerned."

"Tall or short?"

"Medium, wearing a black leather jacket."

"Could be anybody," said Elvis. "I pick up dozens like that every month. Can you remember anything else about him?"

They were silent, until Ivy suddenly said, "Yes! I can! He may have dropped a handkerchief with an 'F' in the corner, as he went out of the church."

Elvis drew into Maleham's car park and switched off the engine. He turned round and looked at them. "Sunday before last, did you say?"

Ivy nodded. "Why?"

"I picked up a bloke who looked like what you just said on the road outside Barrington. I'd dropped off a passenger, and this man hailed me. I don't always stop, but he only wanted to go to the railway station in Thornwell, so I took him. I tried to make conversation—makes the job more interesting—but he wasn't saying a dicky-bird."

"Not even when he got out at the station?" Roy had begun to collect himself, ready to drive out of the taxi in his trundle, but Ivy had sat up straight, all alert to Elvis's revelation.

"Let me think. Yeah, there was something. I think I asked him where he was going. On the train, like. He paid me his taxi fare and said it was a short journey. Going as far as Colchester, he said. He was sniffing, and helped himself to a tissue out of my box I keep for passengers. I got the impression he was making it up as he went along."

"And did you definitely notice the earring?" Roy asked. "I do remember that, so it is important."

"Oh yes, I noticed it." Elvis explained that he had considered getting one himself, but his wife had said she would divorce him if he did, and so he'd dropped the idea.

After that, he saw Ivy and Roy safely inside the furniture store, and said he would be in the car park waiting for them. "Take as long as you like," he added. "I've got this book to finish. Due back at the library. So, see you soon. Happy shopping!"

Mr. Maleham was in conversation with a customer on the ground floor, and when he saw Roy with a stick and walking with difficulty, he immediately rushed across to them. "Good morning! Can I help you at all?"

"Good morning," said Roy. "If you could direct us to your bed department?"

"Ah, now, that is upstairs, but we have a lift. Allow me to take you up. Won't you take my arm, madam?"

"No, thanks," said Ivy. Smarmy type, she thought, and bristled. "I can manage quite well."

"We do have a wheelchair handy for disabled customers' use, if you wish, sir?" Maleham offered.

"The lift will be fine," said Roy. "Thank you kindly."

When they emerged into the department, Mr. Maleham called over the salesman who had taken over from Steven Wright, and instructed him to take care of Mr. and Mrs. . . . er? He looked enquiringly at Ivy.

"Miss Beasley and Mr. Goodman," she replied tartly.

Mr. Maleham sighed. One of those, he thought to himself, and walked off, leaving his assistant in charge.

"We are to be married, you see, young man," said Roy. "And we shall need a nice comfortable bed, easy to get into and with a reasonably hard mattress."

"Well, I'm blowed," said the assistant. "What a lovely thing! You two been married before?"

"Mind your own business," said Ivy quickly. "Now, what's your name?"

"Sam, Samuel Frost, but you can call me Sam, Grandma."

"And you can call me Miss Beasley! I'm nobody's grandma, nor ever will be."

"How about that bed over there," said Roy hastily. "Do you see the one I mean, Sam? It looks so lovely, with a stripey blue and white duvet. I suppose you make them up to look more attractive? After all, there's nothing very beautiful about a mattress!"

"Too right, though I says it as shouldn't. Now, come this way. Follow me, and then you won't trip over the rugs and lamps and stuff."

"You've had an accident in here recently, I believe?" said Roy innocently. "Wasn't a tramp found dead, tucked up inside a bed of yours?"

"Oh yeah." Sam looked around furtively. "We're not supposed to talk about it. But between you and me, it wasn't a tramp. It was our department manager, and it looks like he was murdered. No signs of natural causes an' that. They haven't told us anything more about it, but it does make me nervous, I don't mind telling you. I'm temporary manager, and sometimes when there's no customers in, it can get a bit creepy."

"Well, nothing will happen to you with Roy here," said Ivy fondly. "He's very handy with that stick!"

They finally settled on a very comfortable-looking double bed, not too high off the ground, and with a medium-hard mattress. Roy was delighted with the refinement of a mechanism that sat the prone sleeper up in bed, ready for morning tea, though Ivy protested that it would not be necessary.

"I'll see if I can get you a discount," Sam said. He had really taken to the old gentleman, and felt sorry for him about to be shackled to sharp old Miss Beasley.

"No need, young man. We shall require it to be delivered before the fifth of May to Springfields residential home in Barrington. Now, shall we go to your office and do the necessary paperwork? Ivy, my dear, why don't you go and look at those lovely dressing tables with heart-shaped mirrors? I'd love to buy one for you!"

"It'd take more than a heart-shaped mirror to improve my appearance!" she said, blushing a fiery red. "But thanks, anyway. I'll just have a wander round."

THE DRESSING TABLES were round a corner, out of sight of the office, and Ivy sat on a stool and looked into the heart-shaped mirror. What an old bat, she told herself. What a turnip! Confirmed spinster, unpopular with most people and not caring tuppence. And here she was, loved and respected by the dearest man in Barrington. Tears came to her eyes and she dabbed at them with her handkerchief.

"Everything all right, dear?" said a voice behind her. She turned round and saw a squat, dumpy figure in black.

"Perfectly all right!" said Ivy crossly. "Are you a customer or a member of staff?"

"Customer. I'm looking for a bedside table for my hubby. He's bedridden, thank God."

Shocked, Ivy asked her what she meant.

"He was under my feet for forty years. Followed me about like Mary's little lamb. But he weren't no little lamb! Miserable old devil. Anyway, it's a great relief now. He can't move out of his bed. The nurses come every day and attend to him. I just take his food on a tray, an' get out of the room as quick as poss."

For once, Ivy was speechless. Then she asked who was looking after him at this moment.

"My son, Frank. Frankenstein, we should have called him! Looks like the back end of a bus. Still, he's not a bad lad. Takes care of his dad while I'm out. I often come in here for a bit o' peace. It's very nice, and they don't get many customers, except at weekends. Then I go to the supermarket next door. Frank looks after his dad, unless he's got a special Saturday job to do. Works on the railways. I don't know why I'm telling you all this, dear. Just thought you looked a bit upset. But you're all right now, aren't you? I'll leave you to it. Them mirrors make you look awful, I always think!"

"Just a moment," said Ivy, getting to her feet. "I was thinking of wearing earrings for my wedding, and I suppose I'll have to have the lobes pierced, won't I?"

"No problem. Go to Hillses the Jewellers in Church Street. My Frank went there for just one lobe to be done. He's had no trouble with it. One small ring, he wears. Can't say I approve, but he's a grown man. Knows his own mind. Anyway, dear, maybe we'll meet again sometime in here? Really nice to talk to you. Getting married, did you say? All the best, then."

"Thank you," Ivy said. "You've been so nice. What did you say your name was?"

"Beryl. Beryl Maleham. And yes, before you ask, I am related! The high and mighty store owner is a distant cousin. That's why he lets me come in and wander round without being bothered. Cheerio, dear. See you soon, I hope!"

Twenty-eight

"WOULD YOU LIKE me to order your taxi again this afternoon to take you to Tawny Wings for your meeting?" Mrs. Spurling was trying hard to be helpful. She would not admit it, but Mr. Goodman becoming so sprightly—there was no other word for it—had come as a shock to her. For years he had been quiet, undemanding and polite. But since Miss Beasley had arrived and their romance had blossomed, he had become a different person. She suspected he was now much more like he was in his prime.

There was a lesson to be learned here, she thought. Perhaps she underestimated other residents who could be capable of much more than at present? The thought of half a dozen Miss Beasleys and Mr. Goodmans filled her with terror! Still, the idea of whist, or even some easier card game, held regularly, was not such a bad idea. Ever since her husband had run away with the cook, she had coasted along. Time to change, she told herself. And if Miss Beasley could find herself a husband, she was sure she could do the same.

As she looked at herself in the small mirror over her desk,

she caught sight of Mr. Halfhide coming up the path. He might do for a start! Quite attractive in his way. But she would be in competition with the merry widow, Mrs. Bloxham, who was not only merry, but very rich. Well, he would do to practise on.

"Good afternoon, Augustus!" she said, as he came into reception. "I do hope you don't mind Christian names? After all, we have known you here for a long time. Have you come to see me?" She simpered, and Gus backed away hastily.

"Not today, thanks," he said. "I've come to pick up Roy and Ivy for the meeting. No need for his trundle. There are only a few steps to walk to my car, and he likes to think he can still manage, I think."

"Very true, Augustus," she replied. "We must all keep our youthful skills in trim, don't you agree?"

Good God, the woman's cracking up! Gus wondered what had caused this sudden change of character. La Spurling had suddenly become all soft at the edges. He sidled past her and made for the lounge, where he expected to find his two colleagues waiting for him.

"Ivy? What have you two been up to?" he said in a stage whisper. "Mrs. Spurling has had a startling makeover."

"Roy's fault," said Ivy blandly. "He came over all masterful, and she fell under his spell. If anyone asks me, I'd say it won't last. She'll be back to her unlovely self by teatime; you'll see. Meantime, Gus, have you come to collect us?"

"Your chariot awaits, madam," he said, bowing elaborately.

"Don't even try," answered Ivy. "Leave it to my Roy. He's one of nature's gentlemen."

DEIRDRE WAS WAITING for them with a big smile. "Come on in. I've got a surprise for you." She took Roy's arm and led him gently into the entrance hall.

"I can manage the stairs, dear," he said.

"No need! Enquire Within has a new office. Follow me, everyone."

She led them through a door on the far side of the hall, into a room full of watery sunlight. "This was Bert's workroom at home," she said. "I faced up to the fact that he wasn't ever coming back to use it, and turned it all out, repainted it, and set it up as the permanent Barrington office of our enquiry agency. What do you think, Ivy?"

Ivy looked around at the polished desk with a vase of fresh flowers, the obviously new and cheerful curtains, and the businesslike filing cabinet in the corner. "Deirdre Bloxham," she said. "What can I say?"

The others waited with bated breath to hear what Ivy would say.

"I think I can speak for us all," she said finally, "when I say that you are generous, good-hearted and a very valuable member of our team. And what's more, you're not bad-looking into the bargain."

"Hear, hear!" said Gus.

"Thanks," said Deirdre. "Now, Ivy, are you going to take the senior member's chair?"

Ivy shook her head. "If you insist," she said, and went swiftly to sit down. "Now we can start the business of the meeting. We have a lot to tell, haven't we."

They started with the morning trip to Maleham's. "We got Elvis to take us into Thornwell," Ivy said. "He didn't know about our banns, and when we told him what the interrupter looked like, he got all solemn and said he had picked up a man answering to that description on Sunday morning, getting on towards lunchtime. The man wanted to go to the station, and said he was catching a train to Colchester."

"Did he have an earring?" asked Deirdre. "I reckon that was the most distinguishing feature, as they say."

Roy nodded. "Yes, Elvis remembered particularly because his wife had forbidden him to get one himself."

"Very interesting, you two," said Gus. "Sounds like the man had been hired by someone to come to church and challenge the banns. Colchester, did you say? Might be worth following up that lead straight away."

"We haven't finished with our morning's work yet," said Ivy, looking at Roy.

"You take over, Ivy dear."

"Well, we got into the store successfully and met the creepy owner, Mr. Maleham. He took us up to the bed department in a lift and left us to it. A nice young assistant took over, named Sam, if I remember rightly. Roy?"

He nodded. "Sam it was," he said.

"So then we had a good look around, and decided on the bed we wanted. Roy went off to do the paperwork, and I wandered out of sight. Found myself amongst dozens of dressing tables, some with heart-shaped mirrors. Seeing myself from all angles was a horrid sight! Anyway, this woman came up and started talking. Turns out she is a cousin of Mr. Maleham, and he allows her to have a change of scene every so often, wandering around the store with no intention of buying. Light relief from looking after a bedridden husband, apparently. She was a real chatterbox, so I let her run on. People tell you their life stories sometimes!"

"So what came out of it, Ivy?" said Deirdre.

"As well as a husband, she has a son, Frank. She wasn't very complimentary about his appearance, but said he was a good lad with his dad, taking over from her to give her a break. She described him. Frank, that is. To use her words, he looks like the back end of a bus. Big and burly, and, it transpired, with an earring."

An admiring silence followed up this report, and Ivy subsided, looking smug.

"Now we're getting somewhere," Gus said. "We started with rich Uncle Roy and his heir, Steven Wright. Then we have Steven found dead in Maleham's store. Meanwhile, Ivy and Roy have their banns challenged, and Ivy has found a woman in Maleham's store, with a son who answers the description of the challenger.

"Cut to Alf Lowe, and from him a contention that Roy was years ago engaged to a cousin, ditched her, and was threatened with breach of promise in his youth."

Deirdre nodded, and said, "And now I can take over, with my discovery of a couple named Jossland, farming near Settlefield. Young Mrs. Jossland was a Goodman before her marriage, and she has an old aunt, Ethel Goodman, who is from a branch of the family of dear Roy."

"One link missing, at least. Probably more than one," said Ivy. "Don't forget Steven Wright was married, not particularly happily. Wendy, isn't it? But who is or was Wendy, apart from being Steven's wife? The missing link, and maybe unimportant, but worth finding out."

"And to return to the heart of the matter," said Roy, "who is now most anxious to get hands on my so-called fortune? Apart from the donkeys, whoever it is, we need to know how far he or she is prepared to go? I must impress on Ivy as my intended wife, and the rest of Enquire Within who are fast uncovering family secrets, that we are all vulnerable, and must be on our guard."

"And that includes you, Roy," said Ivy. "It doesn't bear thinking about, but with you out of the way, the whole thing comes up for grabs. Unless you have sewn everything up very carefully?"

They all looked expectantly at Roy. He hesitated and seemed about to answer the question. But then he looked at his watch, and said wasn't it time for Deirdre to put on the kettle and make tea? And he, for one, was feeling peckish. Had she by any chance some of Miriam's chocolate shortbread in the cupboard?

Twenty-nine

GUS DELIVERED IVY and Roy safely back to Springfields, and as Ivy had predicted, Mrs. Spurling was her old sharp self.

"Next time you go out in this weather, Mr. Goodman," she said, "I suggest you allow me to order your specially adapted taxi, so that you have as little time as possible to get wet. Tea is served in the lounge, and there's a good fire, so do go and warm yourself. And you, too, Miss Beasley."

Gus frowned. "I can assure you, Mrs. Spurling," he said, "that I have two large golf umbrellas, and can park my car in Tawny Wings' driveway so that my passengers have all of two steps to be inside Mrs. Bloxham's porch, safe and dry."

"Very well, then. But please remember, Mr. Halfhide, that residents of Springfields are under my sole care, and I am responsible for them twenty-four hours of every day."

"Calm down, dear," said Roy in his best soothing voice. "We have had tea with Mrs. Bloxham, but I am sure we can manage another cup. Shall we say tea for three in Miss Beasley's room in ten minutes? Thank you so much."

Mrs. Spurling turned on her heel, but then remembered a message for Miss Beasley.

"In an envelope, hand delivered. I have put it in your room."

"Delivered by whom?" said Roy anxiously.

"A strange-looking man, bald, with a leather jacket and one earring. Such a ridiculous adornment for a grown man! He wouldn't give me his name. Just said the message was important."

"Lucky you remembered it, then," muttered Gus, alarm mounting.

"Right," said Ivy. "Up we go, and see who's sending me billy doos."

THE WHITE ENVELOPE was on Ivy's bedside table, and Gus picked it up. "Would you like me to open it?" he said.

"Why? Do you think it might contain a bomb?"

"Don't jest, dearest," said Roy. "Why don't you let Gus open it, just in case."

Ivy burst into one of her rare raucous laughs. "Certainly not! It might contain something very private," she said. "Give it here, Augustus."

He handed it over, and she slit it open with a paper knife. She then gingerly withdrew a single sheet of white paper, with bold capitals in red ink. She put on her spectacles and began to read.

IVY BEESLEY! WHY DON'T YOU SAVE YOURSELF A LOT OF TRUBBLE AND BRAKE IT ALL OFF? OR ELSE YOU ARE NEXT. A WELL WISHER.

There was a stunned silence, and then Ivy screwed up the paper and threw it in the bin. "What rubbish!" she said. "And what's more, my well-wisher can't spell!"

Gus crossed the room and hastily fished out the crumpled paper and envelope. "We must take this seriously, Ivy," he said sternly. "From Mrs. Spurling's description, we know this was delivered by the same man who was in church, challenging the banns. What do you think, Deirdre and Roy?"

Deirdre was pale, and her hand trembled as she clutched Gus's sleeve. "Over to you, Gus," she said.

Roy had grabbed Ivy's hand, and now said very firmly that

since his nephew and heir, Steven, had been found dead in bed, and that not his own, they should take this anonymous letter very seriously. "Time to ring Frobisher. I shall do it at once, if you will give me the missive, Gus."

"It is addressed to me," said Ivy, and put out her hand.

"Very well," said Gus. "But please keep it somewhere safe. I am in absolute agreement with Roy. We must ring Frobisher at once."

"He'll be off duty," said Deirdre, looking at her watch.

"How do you know?" said Gus.

"Because he was a great friend of mine at one time, and I am familiar with his work timetable. Isn't that good enough?"

"Well, I suppose nothing's going to happen tonight, is it? I'm quite safe in Springfields. It would take Raffles to get into this place. Tomorrow, let's meet here at ten o'clock, and that will be time enough to ring the police." Ivy sat back in her chair and smiled at Roy. "And don't worry, my love," she said. "I have every intention of sticking to you like glue until we're well and truly wed."

Thirty

"WHOEVER HEARD OF an enquiry agency headed by an eighty-year-old spinster?"

"Agatha Christie?" suggested Inspector Frobisher. The inspector was explaining to his driver why they had to be at Barrington at ten o'clock sharp. "But the heroine of Enquire Within is no mild-mannered posh lady, I assure you. Miss Ivy Beasley and her team have had some remarkable successes in their time, and not all achieved as a result of villains being nice to old ladies."

"We're heading for a house called Tawny Wings? You're having me on, sir."

"'Fraid not, lad. There it is, over there. Park in the drive."

The inspector walked across to Deirdre, who was waiting by the open front door.

"Good morning, Barry," she said with a grin. "Or should I call you Inspector Frobisher?"

"Lovely Deirdre, you can call me what you like, and at any time of day or night," the inspector murmured in Deirdre's ear, as they made their way into Enquire Within's office. Ivy, Roy and Gus were waiting to unload what they knew and, most important, present the inspector with Ivy's anonymous letter.

Ivy's face was thunderous, as Roy handed over the crumpled paper. "Load of rubbish!" she said. "Much the best thing if we had left it where I put it—in the bin."

Frobisher read it silently, and then placed it in his document case. "With your permission, Miss Beasley," he said politely, "I will take this and have some tests done. Clues might emerge, as I am sure you are aware."

"If it's clues you're after," said Ivy, "we have a description of the man who delivered it."

"Fire away, Miss Beasley," he replied. The old girl was in good form.

"Bald, heavy and ugly."

"And nasty-looking," added Deirdre.

"And with one gold earring in his cauliflower ear," said Roy, managing to look perfectly serious.

"In other words," said Gus, now smiling, "the perfect image of a common criminal."

"So you might as well give that rubbish back to me, and this time I'll make sure it is destroyed, as it should be." Ivy held out her hand.

"Not really," said Frobisher firmly. "This large, bald and ugly criminal with one gold earring is clearly up to no good. Have you, any of you, thought of a reason why such a man might want to do harm to a nice old lady in a residential home?"

Where to start? After Ivy had hotly challenged his description of her as a "a nice old lady," the next half hour was taken up by the team's account of two possibly linked dramas. First they mentioned what Frobisher would already know. They referred to the shocking challenge at the reading of the banns in Barrington church, and then the oddly comfortable deathbed of Steven Wright, nephew of Roy Goodman, who was engaged to Ivy Beasley. And now this anonymous letter addressed to Ivy.

"Round and round the mulberry bush," said Ivy. "But where does it start? That's the trouble with circles. They don't have ends or beginnings. Do you take what I mean, Inspector?"

"Exactly," said Frobisher. "Very well put."

"Time for coffee, I think," said Deirdre. "I do hope you'll stay and have a coffee with us, Ba . . . Inspector?"

* * *

WHEN INSPECTOR FROBISHER left Tawny Wings with strict instructions to all of the team to be on their guard, none of them seemed to want to leave. Deirdre looked at her watch.

"Shall I make us a snack and more coffee, and then we can carry on with our meeting?" she suggested.

"Good idea," said Gus. "We need to plan what we're going to do next. I assume bringing in the police does not mean we ditch our investigations?"

"Good gracious me, no," said Ivy. "I shall have to phone Springfields and say we'll be back later."

"I think I'd better do that, Ivy," Roy said. "You know how unpleasant La Spurling can be."

Deirdre disappeared into the kitchen, and Gus followed her, saying he could make a very good roast beef sandwich, and Roy and Ivy were left in the office.

"Useful session, don't you think, my dear?" Roy said.

"I suppose so. But there was one thing I didn't mention. I thought it best to keep quiet about my meeting with Beryl Maleham in the store. You remember? You sent me off to look at heart-shaped mirrors, and I met this woman who couldn't stop chattering."

"Had a son called Frank, who they should have named Frankenstein?"

"That's the one. She told me where to get my ears pierced. Her son had had one ear done and was very satisfied. Oh Lord, Roy, are we onto something?"

"Could be, but lots of men get their ears pierced these days, I'm sorry to say. I think this means another trip to Maleham's to see if we can get in contact with your Beryl. Even if she's not there again, we could ask for a phone number, or an address. You could pretend you really liked her and wanted to meet for a cup of tea?"

"I didn't dislike her," said Ivy thoughtfully. "If you think it would be helpful, I'm perfectly willing to try."

MEANWHILE THE CONVERSATION in the kitchen had at first gone along much the same lines, except that Gus was keen to have another chat with Alf Lowe as well as following up clues to the author of Ivy's threatening messages.

"More to find out. So I go and talk to Alf, and you pay another social worker's call on the young couple and their adorable baby," Gus said, and planted a quick kiss on the back of her neck as she set off with a loaded tray

"Oh, and by the way," he added, "what's Frobisher's Christian name?"

"Dunno. I've forgotten," said Deirdre.

Thirty-one

SATURDAY WAS MARKET day in Thornwell, and Elvis came early to pick up Ivy and Roy. They were both dressed warmly, and Miss Pinkney had extracted a promise from each that they would have a hot drink in a nice warm coffeehouse halfway through the morning.

"I really don't know that I should agree to your going. The sky looks like snow again."

"Don't worry about us, dear," said Ivy. "We have had eighty odd years to learn how to look after ourselves. We shall be safely back by lunchtime."

Elvis was in talkative mood, and they chatted easily about the weather and the political situation until they reached the outskirts of town. "Shall we go into the shopping centre first, Ivy?" Roy said. "Then we could call in at Maleham's on our way home."

"Still looking for a bed?" said Elvis. "There's other places we could go to, if you want. There's a big furniture store in Oakbridge. Maybe next Saturday?"

"No, we do have good reason to visit Maleham's again," Roy said.

"Something to do with that man I picked up? Him with the earring?"

"Yes, that's right," said Ivy. "I met his mother in the store, and she says he helps out sometimes, moving heavy furniture about and so on. It's weekends, mostly, when he's not working on the railways."

"Right, folks. Here we are, then. I'll drop you by the market and pick you up same place at half past eleven?"

"Make it eleven," said Ivy. "We'll have coffee first, and then be ready. Thank you, Elvis."

Roy drove his trundle out of the specially adapted taxi with panache, and they set off to browse around the market square. It was a large trading area, with the stalls protected by blue-and-white-striped awnings. Unlike some markets, where the majority of goods for sale are cheap clothing, mostly for women, Thornwell had managed to maintain a real mixture of interesting bargains. There were the usual secondhand books, fruits and vegetables, bread and cakes, but also a collectors' stall, where Roy had picked up several interesting items over the years.

"Let's start with Ikey Preston," he said now. "He might have some little gem you like. A wedding present from me to you."

"I don't need any presents," Ivy said severely. "And anyway, have we had permission from Rev. Dorothy to go ahead with the second reading of the banns tomorrow?"

"Of course we shall go ahead," Roy said, stopping beside the collectors' stall. "We have heard no more, and I shall confirm with a call to Rev. Dorothy when we get back to Springfields. Now, good morning, Ikey, what treasures have you got for us?"

Roy was not to be dissuaded, and Ivy finally selected a small brooch with seed pearls and garnets woven into a gold heart. "You are an old softie, Roy," she said, as he reached up to pin it onto her coat.

"I'm sure a thank-you kiss would not come amiss," said Ikey, grinning broadly. "Good luck, you two. See you next week, Mr. Goodman?"

"There'll be no more presents until Christmas!" said Ivy, and Roy smiled.

"Time for coffee," he said.

* * *

THE COFFEEHOUSE WAS in the market square, close to where they would meet Elvis, and they chose a window seat with views of the busy shoppers.

"What would we do without Elvis?" said Roy, tackling a sugary jam doughnut.

"We'd be stuck at Springfields, and if you ask me, we'd soon be—" Ivy suddenly stopped speaking and stared fixedly out of the window.

"What is it, Ivy? Someone you know?"

"Not sure," she said. "Over there, Roy. Look at the fruit stall. That man with his back to us. Isn't that Frankenstein?"

Ivy was pale, and Roy peered anxiously out of the steamed-up window. "Wait until he turns around. We'll be able to see then. Oh look! Here he comes. No, Ivy, it's not him. This one's got a beard! You can relax, beloved."

They were subdued when Elvis returned to help Roy into his trundle and then drive them both on their way to Maleham's. "Too cold for you today, Miss Beasley?" he said. "You're looking a bit peaky. I've got the heating on full blast."

"No, no. We had a little shock. All a mistake, though. I'm perfectly all right, thank you. Now Elvis, here we are. We shan't be long. Roy, you don't need the trundle. Hang on to my arm and we can manage. We just have to ask a few questions. See you in a few minutes, Elvis."

They entered Maleham's, and were immediately approached by a pleasant girl offering help. "We've already given you an order for a bed, but we wish to look for a suitable matching wardrobe," said Roy. They had agreed they would go straight up to the department where Beryl had told Ivy she loved to browse.

"We can manage the lift ourselves, thank you," said Roy. "Very simple. I'll hold on to Ivy and we'll march off together!"

The sales assistant smiled indulgently. What a nice old couple! It was quite cheering to see how excited they were about their future, especially since they couldn't have much of a future left!

The lift was in the far corner of the ground floor, and with no difficulty at all, they pressed the right button and were conveyed safely to the bedroom furniture department. Apart from a young couple musing over a four-poster, there were no customers around. Ivy told Roy to sit down on a lavishly upholstered stool, and went round the corner of the office to look for Beryl. She thought she caught sight of her, but the woman disappeared through a door marked STAFF ONLY. Not Beryl, then.

"No sign of her," she said to Roy, returning to where he was still obediently waiting. "At least, I don't think so. We'd better go back downstairs and ask if we can have her details."

"They may regard them as confidential," warned Roy.

"We can only ask. I'll think of some good reason why we want to get in touch."

The lift was back on the ground floor, and Ivy and Roy waited until it returned and opened its doors to let them in.

"Press ground floor, then," said Ivy. "Ugh! Somebody's been smoking in here. I'm sure that's not allowed."

The lift came to a trembling halt, and the light went out. Ivy felt her way to the necessary panel of buttons.

"Bottom button, Ivy," said Roy. Ivy obeyed, but the doors remained shut. He frowned. "Try the next one up. That should do it."

But still the doors remained shut, and after that Ivy pressed all the buttons angrily, one by one, and still nothing happened.

Ivy peered through the dark window of the lift. "It's a brick wall," she said nervously. "I think we're stuck between floors, Roy. And that cigarette smell is making me feel sick."

"Try the emergency button again. It's bound to get us going again. Don't worry, my love. Someone is bound to realise the lift's stuck, and then we'll be out and on our way home."

Thirty-two

ELVIS HAD FINISHED his library book, listened to the news on the car radio, and now looked at his watch. It was half an hour since Ivy and Roy went off into the store. Ivy had said a few minutes, hadn't she? Ah, well, they had probably been held up by an overzealous salesman. He would give them another five minutes, then go and check that they were all right. He had been taxiing them around for a long time now, and was fond of the old couple. He wouldn't want them to come to any harm.

"EXCUSE ME," SAID the young man who had been trying out the four-poster. Sam, the cheerful sales assistant, looked hopeful. But the young man wanted only to point out that the lift wasn't working. "My wife's expecting, and feels a bit dizzy. We need to get out into the air as quickly as possible."

"So sorry. Best to use the stairs, if you need to hurry. That lift is very unreliable. I do apologise. When is the baby due?"

"Any minute now, if we don't get out of here. We'll be off down the stairs. Come on, love, hold on to me."

Sam sighed. Another lost sale. Still, a new couple had just arrived in the department, and were asking about bedside tables. He put on his best smile, and forgot all about the lift.

THE ATMOSPHERE IN the dark box was decidedly stuffy. Roy was finding it difficult to breathe properly, and Ivy insisted that he should sit on a small stool in the corner. "But what about you, my love?" he said, feeling his way over and sitting down gratefully. "You must be getting tired. Why don't you sit on my lap?"

"I'm fine," said Ivy, doing her best to keep her spirits up. "I'll leave your naughty suggestion until I'm desperate!"

"We're sure to be rescued soon," said Roy.

"Do you think we should try shouting for help?"

"Why not? Ready? One, two, three, shout!"

They both chorused a hoarse "Help!" and waited hopefully. But there was no reply, and Roy said he thought the lift was a gimcrack modern one, and probably soundproof. He was worried that Ivy, in spite of her efforts to seem cheerful, sounded shaky.

"Try your mobile, Ivy. You can dial an emergency number."

Ivy took out her phone, and clumsily felt her way round it, but could get no signal. "Not surprising, shut up in a brick box," she said, and took a deep breath. "Oh Roy, I think I'm going to be sick!" she said.

"No, you're not," he said firmly. "Come here and sit on my lap. I promise not to take advantage of you!" He held out his hand, and Ivy smiled bravely, and perched herself on his knobbly knees. He put his arm around her and kissed her cheek. "Whatever happens, my dearest," he said, "I want to tell you that since I met you, I have been happier than at any other time in my life. I love you dearly, and always will."

Ivy put her arms around him, holding on tight, and they sat like this, waiting to see what Fate held in store for them.

THE LIFT SUDDENLY juddered, and the light came on. "Sit tight, dear," said Roy, "just in case it stops again."

But it continued on its slow journey to the ground floor,

where it stopped, and the doors opened. The first face they saw was that of Elvis, looking extremely anxious.

"I'll sue the buggers!" he said loudly. "Fancy leaving an old couple stuck in a lift for over half an hour! Here, you," he said to a worried assistant, "fetch the manager at once."

"I'm here already," said Mr. Maleham, pushing his way through the crowd that had gathered outside the lift. He looked inside and saw a pale-faced old lady perched on the knees of an equally sickly-looking old man. He made a quick decision to defuse the tense situation, and laughed.

"You've not wasted any time, sir," he said, offering his hand to Ivy, and helping her out of the lift. "Is this your taxi man? Ah, then perhaps all three of you would come along to my office and I'll do my best to make amends for this unpleasant experience."

A very grumpy Elvis followed the others to the office, and reluctantly accepted a small glass of brandy.

"I keep it for emergencies," Mr. Maleham said, handing glasses to Ivy and Roy. "I do hope you will sit down and relax for a few minutes. I shall investigate what went wrong with the lift, of course, but meanwhile I do apologise most sincerely. You were both very brave. Nothing worse than being shut up in a small, dark space."

"Oh yes, there is," Ivy said, her colour returning. "If anyone asked me, I'd say being found dead in a bed in Maleham's Furniture Store was worse."

Mr. Maleham swallowed hard. This old bat was quite likely to cause more trouble, he decided, and said that the police were very close to finding the culprit. Steven Wright had been a valued employee, and was much missed, he added.

"He was also my nephew," said Roy flatly. "And I miss him, too. I am quite ready to leave now. And you, Ivy? Come on, then, Elvis. Let's be on our way. Thank you for the brandy, Mr. Maleham. We shall take no further steps, but I advise you to get the lift fixed at once. Other trapped customers may not be so tolerant. Good morning."

Mr. Maleham stood up, anxious to get rid of them. But Ivy stayed in her seat. "One more thing, Mr. Maleham," she said. "A small request. Can you give us a telephone number or address for your relation, Beryl Maleham? I met her in your store, and we had a really good chat. I'd like to get in touch, and invite her over to Springfields for a cup of tea. She seemed quite low, I thought."

"Certainly, certainly," said Mr. Maleham. "Here's my address book. Now, Beryl, Beryl, married my cousin. Yes, here it is. I'll get my secretary to jot it down for you. So kind of you. I'm sure she'll be really pleased. Now, if you'll excuse me?"

SAFELY BACK IN Elvis's taxi, Ivy and Roy were silent, still a little shaken up, and thinking back over their experience.

"Straight back to Springfields now?" said Elvis.

"Yes, please," said Ivy. "But could you pick us up on Monday? Say about ten o'clock? I must make a call to Beryl when we get back, and hope to visit her with a an invitation to tea."

"Not 'I,' dearest," said Roy. "*We* will visit her together, or not at all. And that is an order."

Elvis waited for a dusty answer from Ivy, but all she said was, "Of course, my dear. You know best."

Thirty-three

ELVIS SAW HIS passengers safely back in Springfields, and was about to drive off when he noticed a piece of folded paper tucked under his rear windscreen wiper. He got out again, slid it from underneath the wiper and unfolded it. The message was in red ink capitals, and he read it with a sinking heart.

TO IVY BEASLEY. DO WHAT YOUR TOLD, OR NEXT TIME THERE WONT BE NO RESCUE. NO MORE BANS, OR ELSE!

Elvis took the piece of paper between thumb and forefinger and walked back into Springfields reception. He held the paper out of sight, and asked Miss Pinkney, who was on duty, if she had the address for Mr. Halfhide, friend of Ivy and Roy. Always anxious to be helpful, she quickly found the number and Elvis left. He did not want either Ivy or Roy to see him returning into reception, and was quickly in his taxi and making his way round the Green into Hangman's Lane.

Miriam Blake was in her front garden, and saw the taxi arriving outside Gus's cottage. Why would he want a taxi? He had his own car now, and that was parked up the end of the row, under the trees. She was sure he was at home, and knelt down to attack nonexistent weeds, so that she was in earshot of a conversation.

Gus looked out of his window and saw Elvis. He had met him once or twice up at Springfields, and went quickly to the door, hoping nothing was wrong.

"Can I come in a minute, sir?" Elvis said. "It's to do with your friend, Miss Beasley."

"Ivy? Nothing wrong, I hope."

"Dunno, yet."

"Well, come in, come in." Gus ushered him into his small living room, and out of the corner of his eye noticed Miriam standing close to the low garden wall. "Now, what is this all about?"

Elvis silently handed the paper to Gus, and watched him read it and heard him groan.

"Oh no. Not another one. Where did you find it?"

Elvis then gave him a detailed account of what had happened at Maleham's, and said he had noticed the message only when he was leaving Springfields.

"But what a horrible thing for Ivy and Roy to go through! Trapped between floors in a lift!"

"With no light nor nothing," said Elvis.

"So how are they? And have they seen this horrible thing?" He threw the paper onto a small table by the fire and motioned to Elvis to sit down.

Elvis perched on the edge of a rickety dining chair, and said that he thought they'd had enough shocks for one day, and that was why he had decided to bring the message down to Gus. "You said something about another one, Mr. Halfhide," he said. "This is not the first, then?"

Gus shook his head. "There's something very nasty happening, I'm afraid. All because Ivy and Roy are intending to marry."

"That'll be about money, then," said Elvis wisely. "It's always money. Root of all evil, an' that."

"Anyway," said Gus, "I'll keep it for the moment and have a serious think about what to do."

"Don't forget them banns are due to be given a second

reading tomorrow, Mr. Halfhide. I should bring in the police, if I was you."

"We already have, Elvis. They're on the case. But if you think of anything useful, you can always tell us. Enquire Within is working flat out to find out what's going on."

"Just don't let the vicar call them banns; that's all I'm saying. Now I'll be off. Thanks, Mr. Halfhide. They mean quite a lot to me, those old things, actually."

"We'll be on our guard," said Gus, opening his front door. "And don't forget, you can call me day or night."

Elvis was about to get into his taxi, when he turned back. "There was one thing," he said. "Did Miss Beasley or Mr. Goodman tell you about that bloke I picked up in the taxi? Resembled the man who challenged the banns. Well, when I got out of the taxi to go and find them in Maleham's, I could swear I saw him again, coming out of the back of the store. O' course, there's lots of men wear earrings an' that, but he sort of swaggered, if you know what I mean. Might be worth following up."

"DEIRDRE? GUS HERE. Can I come up and see you for a bit? Something important has come up."

"Oh Gus, I'm sorry. I'm due up at the Hall for a drink with Theo."

"Cancel it. This really is important, Deirdre. And time is of the essence."

Silence. Then Deirdre said that in that case he should come up to Tawny Wings straight away, and she would put off her drink with the squire. "He's lonely; that's all. And I can go up later. Come up and we'll have a scratch lunch."

Gus fixed Whippy's lead, and set off. Miriam was still in her garden, and she greeted him warmly. "Supper tonight, Gus?" she called. "Rabbit pie with roast potatoes, and spotted dick for pudding!"

Gus smothered an impulse to give her a ribald answer, and explained that he might not be back in time.

"Well, if you are, just come in," she shouted.

"She's unsquashable, Whippy," he muttered, and the little dog put her ears back in reply.

* * *

"NOW, AUGUSTUS, WHAT'S so important? Something new to do with Alf, or Ivy and Roy?" Deirdre ushered him into her warm sitting room.

In answer, Gus handed her the message. "Stuck under a windscreen wiper on Elvis's taxi."

"Oh my God, now what? Has Ivy seen this, or Roy?"

"No, Elvis brought it straight to me. Those two have had a nasty experience today, stuck in a lift, and he thought this might be the last straw."

"And it's Sunday tomorrow. Well, I can give you my opinion straight away. We get hold of Ba—Frobisher, and hand it over to him. Meanwhile . . . Well, meanwhile what?"

"One of us must talk to Rev. Dorothy, and tell her all about it. Then I'm sure she will agree to postpone the banns. She'll think of something."

"Maybe invent one or two church rules about banns that have been challenged?"

"So, will you come with me?"

"What, now?"

"No time like the present," said Gus. "Come on, Whippy. If nothing else, we shall find out whether the Reverend Dorothy is a dog-lover."

"She can stay here, if you like. We'll probably be coming back here?"

Gus, thinking that this would be one in the eye for Roussel, agreed.

Thirty-four

"SHE'S MUCH TOO attractive to be a reverend," whispered Deirdre, as Dorothy hailed them from the bottom of her garden. Tall and willowy, and with the stiff white collar of her office, which she miraculously made attractive, the lady under discussion smiled broadly and said how pleased she was to see them, and what could she do to help?

"It's about Miss Beasley and Mr. Goodman," explained Gus, with his most winning smile. "I believe their banns will be called for the second time tomorrow?"

Dorothy nodded. "We've been unable to trace that man who ran off from the vestry," she said. "I can only think it was a practical joke, though it was very far from funny! So, yes, I intend to go ahead. Is there a problem?"

Gus explained, and brought out the message. "This is the second message we've received," he said. "I am sure you're right, and it's just some idiot's idea of a joke, but I am not prepared to risk it." He had no idea what he would say if she asked what exactly he would do to prevent it, but hoped that he sounded authoritative enough.

Dorothy stared down at the paper in her hand. "I must say

I agree with you, Mr. Halfhide," she said slowly, "and I presume you will hand this to the police straight away? Do I understand that Miss Beasley and Mr. Goodman know nothing about this second message? And if so, are you going to tell them?"

Deirdre spoke up. "I see no point in worrying them with it. We can surely think up some reason why the banns can't be called tomorrow, without giving them another horrible shock?"

Dorothy replied that in her opinion Miss Beasley was more or less shockproof. "And surely if Enquire Within is still working on the case, you'll have to tell the other two?"

"She's right," Gus said to Deirdre. "Shall we ask them up to Tawny Wings for supper tonight, and break it to them after a glass or two of wine?"

"Ivy's teetotal, she always says, though she frequently breaks the rules," Deirdre said. "And anyway, what shall I do about the squire?"

"Mr. Roussel?" said Dorothy, looking puzzled. "Does he come into this somewhere?"

"Not at all," said Gus firmly. "He is of no importance whatsoever."

AFTER SOME HESITATION on the part of Miss Pinkney, who, though quite happy for Gus to pick up Ivy and Roy and take them to Tawny Wings for supper, was worried in case Mrs. Spurling should look in last thing to check that everyone was safe and sound. Then Ivy settled the matter by saying that she was not a prisoner in Springfields, and would be ready to deal with Mrs. Spurling if the question should arise.

"COME ON IN," said Deirdre, as they arrived. "I've rustled up something rather special for supper, but let's have a drink first and relax."

Ivy's eyebrows were raised. "I am perfectly relaxed, Deirdre," she said. "As far as I am aware, we have no reason to be otherwise. But I know Roy likes a small whisky around now, and I am partial to a sweet sherry. Thank you very much for inviting us. A nice surprise, wasn't it, Roy?"

"I think so," he replied slowly. "Though I can't help wondering if Gus and Deirdre have something to tell us? Maybe something unpleasant?"

Gus and Deirdre exchanged looks. No fooling the old man, then. "We might as well tell them and get it over with. Then we can enjoy supper," said Deirdre.

Gus reluctantly took out the now-crumpled piece of paper from his pocket and handed it to Ivy.

"Oh dear me, not another missive from my well-wisher," she said calmly, and read it out to Roy in a perfectly steady voice.

Roy, on the other hand, looked quite nervous, and as Ivy was moving towards the fire, obviously about to consign the message to the flames, he put out a hand to stop her.

"Give it to me, dearest," he said. "I think we should hand it over to Inspector Frobisher. He would not be pleased to hear we had destroyed it."

"Quite right," said Gus, and rescued it from Roy to return it to his pocket. "I shall be going into Thornwell on Monday and will drop it at the police station."

"So the banns will be called again tomorrow? I really see no reason to pander to this lunatic." Ivy's face was red with annoyance, and her voice sharp.

"Well, actually," said Deirdre, clearing her throat, "apparently there are still one or two formalities regarding the challenge to sort out. We met Rev. Dorothy, and she explained. Should be fine by next week."

"That's right," said Gus. "Nothing to worry about, though. Now, how about those drinks, Deirdre? Would you like me to do the honours?"

AFTER IVY AND Roy had been taken back to Springfields, Gus collected Whippy from Deirdre and made his way home. He parked his car, and walked back to his cottage. To his dismay, he saw a figure, unmistakeably Miriam, waiting for him by the front door.

"Augustus Halfhide!" she said, when he was close. "This is the end! All those times you have eaten my food, and asked me to mind Whippy, and dozens of other favours, and you haven't even the decency to let know you wouldn't be back for supper! I repeat, this is end of our relationship. Find yourself another slave! Good night!"

"But Miriam, my dear, I remember you offering supper, but I didn't say yes or no, and you said 'just come in.' Isn't that right?"

She stood in front of his door, arms akimbo. "Trust you to twist the truth!" she said fiercely, not budging.

"It is the truth," Gus replied mildly. "And I am rather tired, if you wouldn't mind allowing me to go into my house. I am sure we can sort all this out in the morning. You know I value your friendship highly, and would never have knowingly hurt your feelings." He sighed, and wondered if he had gone an encouraging step too far.

Miriam stood silently for a moment, then, like a deflating balloon, put a swift forgiving kiss on his cheek, and moved to one side. "Oh, all right, then," she said. "Let's forget all about it. Rabbit pie's still edible, and what's more you can eat it!" She laughed, pleased with the old joke.

He nodded, patted her on the shoulder and moved to unlock his door.

"Oh, and by the way, you had a visitor. Big bloke, with a bald head. I didn't go outside, though he looked vaguely familiar. Starting to grow a beard, or fashionable stubble. One or the other. He knocked and knocked, but of course you were not there, and he finally went away, looking furious. I would have gone out to help, but it was nearly dark by then and, as I said, he was a big bloke."

"Did you notice if he had an earring?" said Gus urgently.

"No, of course not. I said it was nearly dark. Anyway, why shouldn't he have an earring? Lots of men do. Can't say I approve, but I'm old-fashioned, I suppose."

"What time was this?"

"Not sure. Sometime after the six o'clock news. Why, anyway? Was he important? Should I have gone out?"

"No to all those questions. Now, off to bed, Miriam. I look forward to rabbit pie lunch tomorrow. Night-night, love."

Miriam went off very happily to bed, and dreamt that a big man wearing diamond drop earrings was holding her hostage, and Gus came along to rescue her, declaring she was the only one for him.

Thirty-five

THERE HAD BEEN a hoarfrost in the night, and when Deirdre drew back her bedroom curtains she saw a glistening white world in front of her. The sky was a heavenly blue, and sunlight filled the garden. She would not have been at all surprised if a fairy had landed on her windowsill and offered to fly her to fairyland.

But Deirdre was made of stern stuff, and such whimsy was immediately banished from her thoughts. She had work to do today, even if it was the Sabbath. She had lain awake for an hour or so last night after the others had gone, and thought about Theo Roussel, who had sounded so sad and disappointed when she had called him to cancel their drinks get-together. He complained that he had not seen her for ages, and was she by any chance avoiding him?

She didn't know the answer to that one herself, and skirted the question, saying that she would be at home anytime he liked to call in. She suspected the truth was that middle age was catching up on her, and she couldn't be bothered to carry on a relationship that was clearly going nowhere.

Now she put all thoughts of love and marriage out of her

head and considered what she should do today to carry on
enquiring. The little Jossland family came into her head. That
lovely baby! Perhaps she should have insisted with Bert and had
one or two of her own. Anyway, Bella had said they would be
pleased to see her again at any time, and she decided to drive
over to Settlefield. Perhaps this morning? She doubted they were
churchgoers, but you could never tell these days. But it wasn't
that far, and she could always come home if they were out.

AT THE FARM, William Jossland had got up early as usual.
He had a small milking herd, and was out in the yard before
six. Bella had fed Faith, and the tiny girl was now sleeping
sweetly, snuffling in her milky dreams. The morning sunshine
streamed into the bedroom, and Bella slid quietly out of bed
and into the bathroom. She would give William a surprise, and
have breakfast all ready with something special, as it was Sunday. Bantams' eggs? The little flock of black-and-white bantams
was hers to care for. She had taken a fancy to them in the
Oakbridge cattle market, and William had indulged her, saying
bantams were useless layers, but if she wanted a hobby it was
better than yoga or some such nonsense.

She put the chalk-white eggs on to boil for a couple of minutes, and set the table. She could see William out in the yard,
and knew that he would be in very shortly, ravenous and
cheerful.

Such a pity they had to waste a lovely day visiting Aunt
Ethel Goodman. As they were the only relatives in their generation, they felt obliged to visit the old lady once a month, regard-
less of the fact that she had no idea who they were, and usually
snored her way through their visit.

"Breakfast's ready," she said, as William came stamping
into the kitchen. Lumps of mud fell off his boots, and he stood
them outside the door, coming in with his thick socks squelch-
ing on the stone floor. "Walked over the pond, and the ice
broke!" he said, kissing her fondly. "How's our young lady?"

"Fast asleep," said Bella. "Let's see if we can have breakfast
before she wakes. I suppose we'll have to take her to visit Aunt
Ethel? I hate the smell of that place. It seems all wrong, taking
a new baby there."

"Rubbish," said William. "We needn't stay long, anyway. The old thing has no idea who we are or where she is."

"Poor old lady," said Bella. "Can she go on much longer? It's not much of a life, is it?"

"Who knows. She might be having lovely, lurid dreams of the past. And the staff say she's still strong as an ox. No, she'll go when she's ready. The last of the Goodmans, more or less."

"Well, that branch, anyway. Oh, listen! Wasn't that Faith? Why don't you go and get her and she can have a cuddle while we're having breakfast."

DEIRDRE DROVE INTO the farmyard around ten thirty, and parked in a spot she hoped would not be in William's way. Now she was here, she was struck by how unsuitable it was for her to be calling on a Sunday. But farm life was different, surely? Cows had to be milked, livestock fed and watered, eggs collected, every single day of the week. Perhaps she should just turn around and go home. But they had probably spotted her by now. Anyway, they would not be likely to see her off the premises with a shotgun!

She decided to ask how they were, and if they had any problems, apologise for it being Sunday, and leave. Unless, that is, they insisted on her going inside, and then she would play it by ear.

Before she reached the flight of steps leading to the back door, it was opened and Bella stood there holding Faith in her arms and smiling broadly.

"How nice to see you, Mrs. Bloxham! Come on in and have a coffee. William's gone up to check on the water supply in the barns. He went through the ice on the pond this morning and was not best pleased!" She laughed cheerfully, and Deirdre followed her into the warm kitchen.

"And how is little Miss Jossland today?" she said.

Bella handed her over and Deirdre sat marvelling at the tiny person in her arms. "Just to think she will grow into a beautiful young girl," she said.

"It does make you think," Bella said. "We have to go and see my old aunt, Ethel, this morning, and since Faith arrived I've tried to remember that this horrible old woman was once a lovely baby, too. Visiting is from ten to twelve, and we usually stay about half an hour, so I'm afraid we can't talk for long this morning."

"Is she in a good home?" Deirdre said, her brain working fast. "I have another client I visit, and she's fed up with where she is."

"Auntie's been in the Firs for years. Alzheimer's got hold of her when she was only about sixty-five. Poor old thing. She had an unhappy romance in her youth, apparently. We don't talk about it! So anyway, the Firs seems to be quite a nice place. It's a nursing home, really, so they don't have many bright ones in there."

"I must have a look at it sometime," said Deirdre, and was delighted when Bella rose to the bait.

"Why don't you come along with us?" Bella said. "We don't stay long. Not much point, really. You could have a look around, I'm sure. And who knows? Maybe Aunt Ethel Goodman will be stimulated by a visit from a stranger. Though I doubt it!"

"Well, if you're sure," Deirdre replied, and looked round as William came in, cursing the weather and saying couldn't Bella go on her own to visit Aunt Ethel? Then he saw Deirdre, and managed a smile.

"Nice to see you, Mrs. Bloxham. Sorry we can't sit and chat this morning."

"I've suggested Mrs. Bloxham comes with me to do the Aunt Ethel visit," Bella said. "Why don't you give it a miss this morning? We can be all girls together!"

"Really? Would you mind, Mrs. Bloxham? It would be really helpful just now. The path across to the pigs is like a skating rink, and I have to see to it before one of us gets a broken ankle."

"Of course I don't mind," Deirdre said. "I'm here to do what I can to help. And anyway, it will be useful for me to see the Firs."

"Afraid Aunt Ethel Goodman won't have much to say. In fact, nothing. But Bella will be glad of some company. Right, splendid. I'll be off up to the pigs, then. See you later, love and little love. And Mrs. Bloxham. Bye."

THE FIRS WAS a large, redbrick house, dating back to the thirties, and had belonged to a builder who had spared no expense in making a quality home for himself. Modern wings had been added, however, with narrow corridors barely wide enough for the several wheelchairs, and these contained the private rooms of the residents, each with a door that opened out onto a scrubby garden. The roomy ground floor of the old house had been converted into lounges and a main dining room for the inhabitants. There were one or two vases of wilting flowers, and the smell of disinfectant was powerful.

Deirdre followed, struck immediately by the difference between Springfields, which was more like a four-star hotel, and this place. But now they arrived in Aunt Ethel's room, and drew up chairs by the side of her bed. She was asleep, and snoring. Deirdre looked closely at her, trying to see some similarity between her and dear old Roy, and noticed that one eye was half-open. Was she feigning sleep?

"Shall we wake her?" she said to Bella.

"We've tried, but she never does. They say she does sometimes, but never talks. Just moans. That's why I dread coming here, and am really grateful to you!"

"Yes, we can just chat, and then go away again. Do you think she knows we're here?"

"You can't tell, can you?"

"Well, we'll just ignore her, and talk about something else. Would you like to hear about my other work? It's an enquiry agency, and we take on cases of all sorts, usually one at a time. But at the moment we've got three things we're investigating."

"How exciting!" said Bella. "What is your agency called, just in case we have a mystery to solve on the farm?"

Deirdre described Enquire Within, and when she named the other members of the team, Bella looked surprised. "Goodman? Mr. Roy Goodman? He must be one of the other family branch over at Barrington. What a coincidence! And who are you investigating? Or is it all confidential?"

"Not really. It's all been in the papers. You must have seen the report on Steven Wright, found dead in bed in a furniture store? That's one thing. And then there's a funny old chap living in Barrington who wants us to get rid of his wife. Legally, I mean! He's called Lowe. Lowe by name and low by nature, I reckon. Still, I mustn't go on about confidential—"

The sleeping figure stirred and her eyes opened. Then she

said, suddenly and perfectly clearly, "Alf Lowe, he's a rotten sod!"

Bella and Deirdre froze.

"Never was any good," said Ethel. "Rotten sod. Burn in hell, I 'ope."

And then her eyes closed and she began to snore once more.

"Good heavens," said Bella. "What was all that about?"

"Something in her past, I expect. How strange," added Deirdre. "It must have been something I mentioned. Alf Lowe, she said, didn't she? How extraordinary."

Now it was Faith's turn to stir and stretch. She gave a tiny yawn, and began to squeak.

"Feeding time coming up," Bella said. "We'd better be off now. Auntie's not going to say anything else, is she?"

"Probably not," Deirdre said. "Perhaps we could have a quick look around before we go? It has been a most interesting morning."

"Well, you certainly managed to get more out of Aunt Ethel than anyone else has. Must have been the sound of a new voice, do you think?"

"Could've been. I know my cousin, Miss Ivy Beasley, has lots of conversations going with usually silent old persons in Springfields, just by provoking them, and being her usual sharp self."

"Don't tell me she's another distant relation!"

Deirdre laughed. "No, but she is engaged to Roy Goodman, so not far off."

Thirty-six

TEA AT SPRINGFIELDS was always special on a Sunday. Anya in the kitchen had baked several different cakes, so that residents had a good choice, and Miss Pinkney took a great deal of trouble organising relatively easy quizzes that the old persons could answer or not, as they felt able or willing.

Ivy usually shone on these occasions, having spent a lifetime listening to BBC Radio Four, where she gleaned all kinds of general knowledge information, ranging from the current vice president of the United States to the word for a young female cow. But today she was still simmering with fury at the absence of the banns being read.

"It seems to me," she said now to Roy, who was hoping Ivy had given up protesting, "that we are just giving way to black-mail. It's just the same as if a ransom was demanded and we paid up."

"Well, dearest, we must be thankful that you haven't gone missing, and so that problem does not arise. Why don't we just forget about banns for the moment? By next Sunday I am sure everything will be cleared up, and we can go ahead and look forward to our wedding day." Roy had accepted the story about the friend turned up unexpectedly in town this morning, and no more had been said.

"Next question," said Miss Pinkney, in a loud voice. "Who wrote *The Wind in the Willows*?"

"William Shakespeare," answered Ivy crossly. "Some people say it was Kenneth Grahame, but he got the idea from the Bard of Stratford. If you ask me, it would have been better left alone. All that stupid stuff about rats and badgers and toads and rabbits. Vermin, I call them. Every single one of them."

This was too much for Roy, who burst out into loud laughter. "Oh, Ivy Beasley," he said. "What would we do without you?"

The residents having tea joined him, some not knowing quite why they were laughing, and Miss Pinkney said she would give Ivy a point for originality.

It was at this moment that Deirdre walked into the lounge.

"Good afternoon, Mrs. Bloxham," said Miss Pinkney, now glad of the interruption. "Will you have a cup of tea with us?"

"Thank you," said Deirdre, and she walked across to join Roy and Ivy. "Hi, you two. Have I got news for you!"

"Good afternoon, Deirdre," said Ivy, still cross. "And where on earth did you get that ridiculous greeting from?"

"Never mind that," answered Deirdre. "Just settle down and listen for a bit. I had a most interesting morning, and I'm bursting to tell you about it. I'll have a cuppa with you, and then I'm off to tell Gus. I expect you'll want to call a special meeting tomorrow, Ivy."

When Deirdre had finished a detailed account of her morning with the Josslands and the visit to Aunt Ethel Goodman, neither Ivy nor Roy said anything at first. Then Roy said, "A really good morning's work, Deirdre. As a matter of fact, I do remember Ethel, a second cousin twice removed, or some such, but after the split in our family, I heard no more about her. Now it seems she had a connection with Alf Lowe, here in Barrington?"

"And what connection?" said Ivy. "This is really something to get our teeth into, Deirdre. Well-done, gel."

"What we really need to do is find out more about Alf's early life. I don't have much hope that Aunt Ethel will come up with anything more, though she is probably sitting on the answer to our investigations! Still, there will be other ways."

"We need Gus. You said you were off to winkle him out, Deirdre? Why don't we meet tomorrow morning at Tawny Wings and have a brainstorming session?"

"A what?" said Ivy.

"Oh, just a phrase I picked up from a newspaper. I rather liked it," added Roy lamely. "But, dearest, if you object, it shall never pass my lips again."

"Good," said Ivy. "Now, Deirdre, off you go and find Gus, and confirm tomorrow. Meanwhile, no doubt you can tell us who is the current vice president of the United States?"

"Abraham Lincoln," said Deirdre. "Somebody like that, anyway. So, cheerio, you two. See you tomorrow."

I REALLY MUST walk through the village more often, thought Deirdre, as she crossed the Green and watched a group of children having a snowball fight in the fading light. How charming! It reminded her of her childhood in Thornwell, when groups of children in the back streets had only dirty, slushy snow to play with. Now it looked so crisp and white. Good enough to eat. However, when one tough-looking character sent a large snowball in her direction, perfectly aimed at her fur hat, so that snow cascaded down the back of her neck, she faced the chilly reality.

But then she cheered up again, as she turned into Hangman's Lane, where the Budd family in the first cottage in the Row were building a snowman under the outside light in their garden. Two small boys, mother and father, were hard at it, collecting up fistfuls of snow and producing a quite remarkable likeness to Gus Halfhide, who lived at the end of the Row.

"Afternoon, all," she said, as she passed.

"Hi, Mrs. Bloxham," called Rose Budd. "Who do you think this is?"

"Mr. Augustus Halfhide," said Deirdre, laughing. "I'll tell him to come and have a look. He might lend you one of his hats."

She reached the end of the row, and knocked at Gus's front door. No answer. Then Miriam's light came on, and there was the sound of her door opening, and out Gus came, followed by a curious Miriam Blake.

"Hello, Deirdre! I wasn't expecting to see you today."

"So I see," said Deirdre icily, her warm feeling of goodwill to all men evaporating fast. "Can you spare a couple of minutes? I have something rather important to tell you."

"Of course." He turned to Miriam and thanked her politely for a pleasant afternoon, and then came out to open up his cottage. "Come on in, Dee-Dee. Can I offer you something to drink?"

"No, thank you. And if you dare to offer me a glass of Miriam's disgusting primrose wine, I shall throw it at you."

"Now, now. You know there's nothing between Miriam and me. Just neighbourliness, that's all. Come and sit down and tell me what's to do."

Deirdre, making a revenge decision to renew her warm relationship with Theo Roussel, sat down on an upright chair and cleared her throat. "Well, I have had a busy day, gathering information for Enquire Within," she began sternly. Then she gave him the same detailed account as had impressed Ivy and Roy, and said they must meet tomorrow to decide how to proceed further in researching the early life and times of Alfred Lowe. "Not only will this be useful in finding out about his relationship with Aunt Ethel Goodman, but could well uncover more about his wife, and why she is wanting a divorce now," she added.

"So we meet tomorrow morning to discuss it? Sounds most interesting. Tell me more about Aunt Ethel and her young relations. A farming family of Josslands, did you say? And the wife, Bella, formerly a Goodman?"

"Yes, well, we can talk about it tomorrow. I just need to confirm to Roy and Ivy, and then I'll be off home. I'm having my postponed drinks engagement with Theo later this evening, so don't try to get hold of me. Anything else can wait until tomorrow."

"Just hold on a minute," said Gus. "There was one thing. Apparently a thuggish-looking man, bald and heavy, and with a stubbly face, came looking for me when I was out. Could be just one of those Jehovah's Witnesses. I did have a copy of *The Watchtower* shoved through my letterbox. On the other hand, it might have been Ivy's mysterious well-wisher."

"Jehovah's Witnesses are usually very presentable," Deirdre

said. "Grey suits and good haircuts. Always polite. Sounds more like the man Elvis saw coming out of Maleham's store unloading bay. Ask someone else round here who might have seen him. Oh, and make sure you go and look at Budd's snowman. A remarkable likeness."

"Of whom?"

"You'll see. Good-bye, Gus. Be there at Tawny Wings at ten thirty tomorrow."

Thirty-seven

IVY WAS UP with the lark, and by the time Roy came down to breakfast, she was buttering her second piece of toast and looking obviously at her watch.

"Morning, dearest," said Roy, hooking his stick on the back of his chair. "Did you sleep well?"

"Not really," said Ivy. "My conscience was troubling me."

"Ivy? How on earth could you have a bad conscience? The most honest and straightforward person I know is Miss Ivy Beasley."

"Ah, well. I owe you an apology. I was a real crabby old spinster yesterday, when you said we would have a brainstorming session, and I mocked you for using that expression. Everything you say sounds wonderful to me, and I'm sorry, and I promise not to be such a miserable old stick again." She sniffed and dabbed at her eyes with her handkerchief.

"My dear Ivy," Roy began, "you were perfectly right, and to me you are neither crabby nor miserable. But thank you, my love. Let's start the morning again. Good morning, Ivy! You're looking young and beautiful as ever. And we have an interesting meeting to go to at Tawny Wings, so I won't take too long over breakfast. What's on the menu? Oh good, scrambled eggs with bacon. Now, have another piece of toast to keep me company, and then we'll make tracks up the hill to Deirdre's."

THE PAVEMENTS IN the village were still treacherous, so when Gus called to offer them a lift, they accepted reluctantly. "Not that we don't love to ride in your car, Gus," Roy said. "It's just that once a farmer, always a farmer, and I still miss the early-morning routine, when the air is fresh and you feel you could move mountains. Though it was usually a dung heap that needed moving!"

And so, in good spirits, the three arrived on time at Deirdre's front door, to find it locked and with no signs of life anywhere about.

Gus, looking grim, said that he understood she had been visiting the Honourable Theo Roussel last evening, and had maybe been encouraged to stay until it was light for her journey back home.

"Don't be so ridiculous, Gus!" said Ivy. "We all know what happens when those two get together. We shall just have to sit in the car until she appears. And don't forget we're here on Enquire Within business, so no quarrelling between the two of you."

At that moment, the big cream-coloured car purred into the drive, and a blushing Deirdre got out.

"So sorry, chaps," she said. "Just had to go out on a little errand. It won't take me two ticks to get the fire going in our office. Gus, can you come and help?"

"You've got a nerve," he said under his breath, as they laid a fire with sticks and coal, and put a match to the screwed-up newspaper.

"No worse than you, with that Miriam," muttered Deirdre. "We'd better have an electric fire as well. Don't want the oldies getting a chill. There's one in the kitchen."

"Yes, ma'am," said Gus acidly. He went off, deliberately stamping his snowy boots on the highly polished parquet floor.

Once they were all settled with cups of hot coffee, Roy was first to speak.

"We have all been told now about Deirdre's interesting discovery over at Settlefield, and have come to the same conclusion,

I believe, that we must find out more about any early relationship between Alf Lowe and Ethel Goodman. I have a particular interest in this, as you can imagine. Some of these people are relations of mine, and since Alf Lowe has cast aspersions on my behaviour as a young man, we may be able to shed some light on that, too."

"Well said, Roy," said Gus. "So, Deirdre, tell us again, would you, exactly what they said about Ethel before you went to see her."

Deirdre was still feeling embarrassed about not being at home when they arrived, but last night had been something of a reunion with Theo Roussel, and she still felt a residual glow. She reminded herself that her colleagues had come out on a snowy morning and were not in the first flush of youth.

"Of course," she said, smiling sweetly, "I'm happy to do that. Well, I went on a sudden impulse, really. Then I thought maybe Sunday was not a good day, but they welcomed me very nicely. They said they had to go on a monthly visit to see Aunt Ethel, so couldn't chat for long, and then Bella suggested I go with them. The old lady is a Goodman, and Bella's great-aunt. She never married, they said, and was now totally confused. They apologised that she was nearly always asleep, didn't know who they were and showed no sign of wishing to talk."

"She must be about the same age as me," Roy said. "So that would make her either a cousin of my father or—"

"His sister," said Deirdre. "Funny you never heard of her, though, Roy?"

"Mm," said Ivy. "I hesitate to suggest this, Roy, but she could have been disgraced in some way. You know, not acknowledged by the family, that kind of thing."

"You're right," said Deirdre. "The usual thing was getting yourself in the club, up the spout, in the family way. Call it what you like."

"Ah," said Gus. "Now we're onto something. And it all points to Alf Lowe, doesn't it? I must call on him again, and see if I can get him to talk."

"And maybe if I go again with Bella Jossland to visit Ethel, she might come out with something more. I could drop a few names that might mean something to her, and see if it sparks a memory." Deirdre put another log on the leaping flames, and asked whether they were ready for another coffee.

"I wouldn't say no." Ivy's feet were still cold, and she felt a little shivery now. Roy looked at her closely.

"Are you all right, Ivy dear?" he said.

"Just a bit cold," she said, and Gus immediately moved her chair nearer the fire. "Can't have you out of action, Ivy," he said. "Let me feel your hands."

They were stone cold, and he rubbed them between his own.

"Thanks; that's fine now," said Ivy. But she was still pale, and Roy began to worry.

"Perhaps a shot of whisky in Ivy's coffee would be a good thing," he said, and Deirdre nodded.

"Good thinking," she said. "And maybe we should cut the meeting short. We've actually decided on what we do next."

"I never touch strong liquor," said Ivy, "but perhaps in this case . . ."

"There'll be jobs for you and Roy," said Gus, aware that they would be primarily interested in clearing up the problem with the banns and anonymous letters to Ivy. "In fact," he added, "might I suggest you have another go at finding that Maleham woman, to see if she can shed any light on either Steven's death or this thug who comes and goes with threats in red ink."

"But first we have hot coffee and whisky, and make sure Ivy is warm and comfortable," said Roy.

BY THE TIME Gus had helped Ivy out of his car and into the lounge at Springfields, she was quite her old self, protesting that she was perfectly all right and not to make a fuss.

Mrs. Spurling was on duty, and was full of "I told you so" strictures. "You will have to remember your age, Miss Beasley," she said. "We don't want any more hiccups to get in the way of your wedding. Which reminds me," she continued, "Rev. Dorothy is making her weekly visit here this afternoon, and asked particularly if she could have a word with you and Mr. Goodman. I assured her that you would be here, so I hope you have no plans for going out again in this wintry weather?"

"I wonder if she has some news for us?" Roy said. "I shall not be content until Ivy is my lawful wedded wife. By the way, Ivy, are you happy with 'love, honour and *obey*'?"

"Good gracious me, no," said Ivy briskly. "Nobody has that nowadays. But you know I shall always give due consideration to anything you suggest."

"Mm," said Roy.

WHEN REV. DOROTHY arrived at Springfields, Ivy and Roy were sitting in Ivy's room, snoozing companionably together.

"Sorry to disturb you!" she said, coming in after knocking softly on the door.

"Not at all," said Roy politely. "It's very nice to see you again, isn't it, Ivy?"

"Yes, indeed. Have you news for us?" said Ivy, coming straight to the point.

"Well, yes and no. I have cleared the way for calling the banns this coming Sunday, and so that will be the second time of asking. But I am still worried about those threats you received, Miss Beasley. What have the police advised?"

"Caution," said Ivy stubbornly. "They advised caution. So I don't see why we can't have the banns read, and then be extra cautious after that. What do you say, Roy?"

"I suppose you're right, dearest," he said slowly. "Though I must say I still feel uneasy. But I know Ivy thinks we should not pander to threatening letters, so perhaps we should go ahead?"

"Very well," said Rev. Dorothy. "Just so long as you appreciate that extra caution must be taken. I know that you two are often out and about on your own, but perhaps that could be changed. Maybe one of your friends, Deirdre Bloxham or Gus Halfhide, would always be with you when you're away from Springfields?"

"That might be difficult," said Ivy. "But we can certainly try it."

Thirty-eight

NEXT MORNING, THE thaw had once more set in, and everywhere was dripping. Small rivulets coursed down the gutters and overflowed the village drains, most of which had been installed in the nineteenth century, and were ripe for replacement.

Elvis drew up his taxi outside Springfields, and stepped straight into a deep puddle. "Damn and blast!" he said loudly. "What on earth do Ivy and Roy want with going into Thornwell this morning? They should stay warm inside, and watch telly, like all the others." But he knew that when that happened, his good friends would have lost the freedom that kept them so active and bright in their old age. And they were soon to be married! He was really looking forward to playing his part in the ceremony, ferrying Roy up to the church, and then going back for Ivy and Gus, who was giving her away. He had not yet been told who would replace Steven Wright as Roy's best man, but he harboured a secret hope that maybe he would be asked.

"Good morning, Elvis!" said Ivy cheerfully, now completely recovered from her chilly moment. "Is it a little warmer today?"

"It's a right mess everywhere," he said. "And I've got a wet foot from treading in this puddle."

"No problem," said Ivy, and immediately went back into Springfields, soon to reappear with Roy and his trundle, and bearing a pair of dry socks. "Put these on," she said. "My father always used to say if you had dry feet, the rest of you would come to no harm."

"Hear, hear," said Roy, and so Elvis dutifully changed his socks, and they set off for Thornwell.

"Where to today?" he said, once they were on the main road.

"Here's the address," said Ivy, and handed him the piece of paper given to her by Mr. Maleham's secretary.

"What do you want in that part of town?" he said.

"What's wrong with it?" Roy could see Elvis's face in the driving mirror, and he was frowning.

"It's the rough quarter," Elvis replied. "Used to be so bad they advised non-residents to stay away. Especially at night! It's not quite so bad now, but I still wouldn't go there after dark. Do you know who lives there?"

"Yes, a Mrs. Maleham. Cousin of the furniture store. Surely she must be all right?"

"Yes, well, I suppose so. Do you want me to wait?"

Ivy began to say no, they would be perfectly all right if he came back after about half an hour. But Roy remembered they were supposed to be cautious at all times, especially as they had only Elvis with them. He said that he would be happier if Elvis waited outside, and Ivy did not disagree, for once.

"HERE, FRANK, THERE'S one of them special taxis drawing up outside. What's going on?" Beryl Maleham peeped round the side of the curtain, and saw Elvis opening the door.

"Hey, it's that nice Beasley woman I met in the store!" she continued. "You know, her that's getting married late in life. And her bloke's with her, as well. How nice of her to come and visit."

"I expect you'll be talking weddings, with big hints to me," said Frank. "I'm off upstairs if they're coming in here. You can do the honours, Mum."

* * *

ELVIS LOOKED AT his watch. It seemed like ages since Ivy and Roy had entered the house, but only fifteen minutes had gone by. The woman who came to the door was smiling and looked friendly as they went inside. How would he know if they were all right? He supposed he would just have to wait until the half hour was up, and then find an excuse to knock and investigate.

He began to think about this Mrs. Maleham. What was one of that family doing living in this disreputable quarter of town? The store was an old established one, and now they were in the new shopping place, they would be even more successful, surely? But Mr. Maleham, the boss, had seemed to him a bit of a slippery sort. He couldn't get rid of Ivy and Roy quickly enough after they'd been shut in the lift. Or was Elvis imagining things? After all, there were quite a few customers in that day, and it was natural that Maleham wouldn't want a fuss made publicly about a broken-down lift.

He opened his new library book—another of his favourite Inspector Montalbano stories—and began to read.

"HOW CLEVER OF you to find me!" said Beryl. "Did you ask in the store?"

"Yes, we did. It was the day we got stuck in the lift. We'd gone hoping we might see you again, but you weren't there that day. So we asked, and Mr. Maleham gave us your address. He said he thought you would be pleased to see us," Roy added hopefully. He wasn't happy. The house was untidy, and an unpleasant smell of stale frying oil wafted in from the kitchen.

"Oh yes, I am pleased. Can I make you a cuppa? Miss Beasley, isn't it? And your name?"

"Goodman," said Roy. "And yours is Beryl, Ivy tells me."

"And are you friends? I am sure I remember Miss Beasley telling me she was going to be married soon. Asked me about earrings, didn't you, dear?"

"That's right," replied Ivy. "Roy is my fiancé." There was something not right here, she was thinking. She felt uneasy, and did not like being called "dear" by anybody but Roy. Perhaps they would exchange a few pleasantries and then leave. It was a good thing that Roy had asked Elvis to wait. "How is your husband, Mrs. Maleham?" she said.

"My husband? Oh yeah, same as usual! He's upstairs, bed-bound, as they say."

"A nice little house you have here," lied Roy. "Have you lived here long? And do you have good neighbours to help with your husband? These streets of old houses benefit from close proximity to next-door friends, I believe."

What the hell is he talking about? Frank, lurking upstairs, wished they could get on to the subject of marriage and calling the banns. He was under instructions to make sure they were postponed indefinitely, and more urgently, he needed to make sure of next Sunday, at least. But it wouldn't do to let them see him. They'd have a pretty accurate idea of what he looked like by now.

"My son lives with me," said Beryl. "I told Ivy about him. He's good with his dad."

"He's at work, I suppose?" Ivy asked. "Maybe we can meet him someday. Always useful to know of a good, strong young man to help you in times of trouble. We've got our Elvis— drives that taxi out there. Not that he's much use with our present problem."

"What's that, dear? Perhaps I can help?" said Mrs. Maleham eagerly.

Roy tried hard to signal to Ivy not to mention banns, but too late.

"I told you we are getting married, but we're held up in calling the banns," she continued. "You know that bit where they say if anyone who knows just cause or impediment etcetera, etcetera? Well, this man jumped up and said he knew a reason why we shouldn't be wed. Never been known to happen within living memory in our church."

"Oh my gawd," said Beryl. "What a turnup! You must've been devastated."

"Yes," said Roy, "we were. But it's all sorted out now. We really must be going, Ivy. Look, there's Elvis getting out of his cab. Nice to have met you, Beryl. Perhaps we might meet again. Ivy was hoping you'd be able to come over for tea at Spring-fields."

He gave Ivy a small push towards the door, and they left, promising to keep in touch.

Elvis got them safely back into the taxi, and they started off on the return journey. "Anywhere else you want to go? Was that Maleham woman pleased to see you?"

"Yes," said Ivy, "but—"

"No, that'll be enough for one morning," Roy interrupted. "Back to Springfields, please. Mrs. Maleham's house was not a nice place. We shan't be asking you to take us there again, shall we, Ivy?"

Ivy made no reply.

Thirty-nine

ROY AND IVY arrived back at Springfields with long faces. "Ah, there you are," said Mrs. Spurling. "Not a morning to be out and about. Wet feet and wet heads, I expect. Perhaps you'd like to go to your rooms before lunch and dry out?"

"I am perfectly dry, thank you," said Ivy. "Roy must answer for himself."

Oh dear, thought Mrs. Spurling. The course of true love not running smooth this morning? "The forecast is good," she said, "so perhaps the sun will tempt you out tomorrow, when an outing will be more favourable."

"Perhaps," said Ivy, and walked straight up the stairs to her room. She spent five minutes changing her stockings, which were in fact soaked, and then heard a small, tentative tap on her door.

"Come in, Roy," she said.

He opened the door and hovered insecurely. "May I have a little talk with you, Ivy dear?" he said.

"Of course. Come in properly and shut the door behind you. You never know when Big Ears is about."

He came in and sat on the edge of a chair. "I know you're cross with me, Ivy," he said, "but I had a very strong feeling in

that house that something was really wrong. Perhaps dangerously wrong. I can't explain it, but that's why I insisted on us
leaving straight away."

"You were right," said Ivy placidly. "There *was* something
wrong, though whether dangerously so, I'm not sure."

"Ivy! What did you see?"

"It was more what I heard," she said. "There was somebody
at the top of Mrs. Maleham's stairs, fidgeting and breathing
heavily. In other words, there was an eavesdropper, and I think
I know who it was."

"Well, so do I, I think. Her husband? The bedbound one? I
don't see that he could do us much harm? But did we do the
right thing to get out of there as soon as possible?"

"Probably," said Ivy. "If Beryl's husband was bedbound, he
wouldn't be sitting at the top of the stairs, would he? But for
now, why don't we go down to lunch, and I'll tell you who I
reckon was the eavesdropper. Can't be sure, of course, but
we'll see."

THE CONTINUING THAW had frustrated Deirdre, who
had spent the morning checking for burst pipes and leaks all
over the house. Then, when she went to get her car, it would not
start. Too damp! She was due to be at her hairdresser's at four,
and had planned to call once more at the young Josslands' on
the way. She meant to follow up Ethel Goodman's outburst with
another visit, and wished to clear it first with the young ones.
She knew she would probably need their permission or approval,
in order to get past the nursing home's visiting rules.

She had called the service department of her motor business
in town, and they had said they would be out immediately. "It's
probably the plugs," she had said, and they had answered respect-
fully that they would soon have her on the road.

Now they had been and gone, and the engine was purring
along once more. She took the road to Settlefield, and soon
approached the farm. William was crossing the yard carrying a
couple of buckets, and stopped to meet her with a smile. "I'm
afraid Bella and Faith are out," he said. "Mums and Babies Club
in the village hall. Can I help?"

Deirdre explained that she would really like to visit Aunt

Ethel Goodman again, to see whether she could stimulate her with some local talk. But she would not do so, of course, without their permission.

"You could certainly have had that," said William. "But I'm afraid the old girl finally pegged out last night. They phoned us this morning. She was eighty-something, you know, so she'd had a good innings! Mind you, they said it was a bit of a surprise, as she really had nothing physically wrong with her. I'll tell Bella you called. Come back when you like. Always welcome!" He set off again with his buckets, and there was not much Deirdre could do except turn the car around and head for the hairdresser's.

"Not your usual cheery self, Mrs. Bloxham?" said her stylist. "Nothing seriously wrong, I hope?"

"No, not really. Just something very annoying, but I'll get over it. And don't cut me too short. Doesn't suit me."

"My, my, we are in a bad mood! How about a nice cup of coffee?"

"Oh, go to hell," said Deirdre, and subsided behind the pages of a fashion magazine.

THE AFTERNOON SUN hastened the thaw, and by the time Ivy and Roy had rested after lunch, most of the snow had gone, and the roads and pavements were quite clear. "Shall we take a stroll up to Tawny Wings and call on Deirdre?" Roy suggested. "If she's not in, we can come straight back. We can tell her about our visit to Mrs. Maleham, and your suspicions about the man lurking at the top of her stairs."

"We could do," said Ivy. "But perhaps a walk up to the cemetery would be better. It's not so far, for one thing, and it gets dark so early."

"The cemetery?" said Roy. "Why there? It's a gloomy old place. Do you have an ulterior motive, beloved?"

Ivy shook her head. "Not really. Just thought it would be interesting to look at a few graves. Maybe some of your forebears?"

"And maybe encounter Alf Lowe at the door of his cottage?"

"Ah. Well, maybe that, too. But perhaps we should wait until tomorrow and set off earlier?"

They were no sooner settled in the lounge with a whist

foursome than Deirdre arrived, looking immaculate but very cross.

"Sit down, gel," said Ivy. "You look as if bears had eaten your porridge. We'll finish this hand, and then somebody else can take our place." Ivy scooped up her winnings, and they moved to a quieter corner of the lounge.

"Now, then, what's happened to put you out of sorts?"

"It's Ethel Goodman. She's gone and snuffed it! Just when I was sure I would get more useful information out of her. I called at the farm, just to get the okay from them, and William Jossland told me. It was unexpected, apparently. Nothing wrong with her, except old age and senility."

"Then her death could not have been all that surprising?" said Roy. "None of us can last forever."

"Oh, cheer up, do!" said Ivy. "If that old girl hadn't retired to her bed and made no effort whatsoever, she'd probably be still alive and doing a bit of baby-sitting. No, Deirdre, it's no use getting upset. Just listen to what happened to us."

Ivy recounted the visit to Mrs. Maleham, and said that she and Roy had come to an important conclusion.

"Which is?" said Deirdre, surreptitiously taking a biscuit off a passing tea plate.

"The eavesdropper upstairs was probably her son, Frank. He keeps turning up like a bad penny, and although we didn't see him, we reckon he's our bovver-boy with the earring. The same one who delivered Ivy's first threatening message, and the same one who Elvis saw coming out of the back of Maleham's store on the day we were shut in the lift."

"And the same one who called on Gus while he was out, and . . . ?" said Deirdre, becoming animated and much more cheerful.

"And who stood up and challenged our banns," said Ivy. "And who left in the church a handkerchief with an 'F' embroidered in the corner. Beryl told me herself that time in the store, when I first met her, that her son was big and ugly. Frankenstein, she said. Don't you remember, Roy?"

"Of course," he replied. "And I think you may be right, though we do need more proof before passing all this on to Inspector Frobisher."

"I agree with you, Ivy; it looks very suspicious," said

Deirdre. "And if it is her son, Frank, do we think he's acting on his own, or being hired by somebody to prevent you marrying Roy? And I hate to bring it up again, but do you think there's any possibility that Ethel Goodman was hastened on her way by person or persons unknown, to stop her coming out with anything too revealing?"

"Such as what?" said Ivy.

"Such as why someone is so anxious to stop you marrying Roy, of course!"

"I think we know why, Deirdre," said Roy, with a sigh. "It is to prevent Ivy from inheriting my estate."

"Yes, but put yourself in the mysterious stranger's shoes. If you were a stranger trying to stop Ivy inheriting, wouldn't the simplest way be to make sure that Ivy was out of the way? And then you, Roy, would be next on the hit list, so that a person so far unknown would be next in line to inherit."

"I cannot bear to think of my Ivy being in danger," he said, once more avoiding the need to reveal exactly what he had done in his last will and testament.

"Then why don't you change your will right now?" said Deirdre baldly. "And let it be known that you've done so. I'm sorry, Roy, but I can't see the need for all this pussy-footing around."

"And I can't see why you can't mind your own business, Deirdre Bloxham!" said Ivy fiercely. "Roy's private financial situation is his own affair, and I for one am quite happy that it shall remain so. Now please change the subject."

"Don't be cross, dearest," Roy said. "I quite understand Deirdre's point of view, but things are more complicated than that. I assure you that when you are my wife, Ivy, you will want for nothing. More than that I cannot say, just at the moment."

"Right. Change of subject," said Deirdre. "Find out if Gus has been to see Alf Lowe, and, if so, whether he has gleaned anything useful from him. I've a good mind to call on him myself, and break the news about Ethel Goodman's demise. His reaction might be worth watching."

"Well, I think perhaps we should leave that to Gus," said Roy tactfully. "I do understand you are feeling frustrated on all sides, Deirdre love. But let's leave Alf to Gus, and then maybe on Thursday at our meeting he will have something to tell us."

Forty

THE CURTAINS IN Alf Lowe's small bedroom were heavily lined and when he drew them tightly across the window, he sometimes slept on in total darkness until midmorning. Today he had stayed in bed all day, falling in and out of sleep. This evening, however, he had been woken by loud knocking on his door. It had turned out to be a man wishing to read the electric meter. "Don't think I'm letting you in at this time of night!" he had said finally, and shut the door in the man's face.

He had returned to his bed, thinking he might as well wait until tomorrow to get going again. Last night had been disastrous. Everything had gone to plan at first. Then the sight of the onetime love of his life, now a shrivelled, balding old woman in a narrow bed, with her mouth open and snoring, had unsettled him much more than he had expected.

He had set off for Settlefield in his battered old Ford, giving himself plenty of time to go slowly in the dark. Then, safely arrived, getting into the nursing home had been easy. He had managed to dodge the security light, find his way in by a garden door, and then luck had been on his side. The first room he had tried was Ethel's, and there seemed to be no staff in sight. He had crept up to her bed and whispered loudly in her ear, "Eth! Wake up! It's your Alf!"

Her reaction had been immediate. Her eyes had opened and she sat up in bed and almost strangled him with her arms around his neck. "You've come, you old sod!" she had said in a strong voice, and a vivid memory assailed him, of himself as a young man, climbing into Ethel's window on the farm, and the warm welcome he had received. My God, she had been hot stuff! And so she had remembered him. He knew it was now or never. She was clearly quite capable of telling all about her adopted baby.

For years Alf had kept quiet about the child he was fairly sure was his. At the time it was a disaster, and he knew his father would kill him. Deeply religious, the old man had strong Catholic views on sin and disobedience. Then he heard it had been adopted. He had quickly spread a rumour that the father had been Roy Goodman, who had definitely had an affair with Ethel around that time. Ethel had spread her favours, and Alf and Roy had taken turns. The rumour had spread, but Roy had denied it hotly and brushed him off like a bothersome fly. Ethel's parents had had plenty of money to arrange for the adoption, and the whole thing had died down. Only recently had Alf begun to think about old Roy's current engagement, known all round the village, and the possible financial ramifications once he was married to Miss Ivy Beasley.

Alf had always thought that when the time came, if he outlived Roy Goodman, he would revive the story of Roy's own son, and his rightful inheritance. The fact that Ethel was a Goodman would count for something, but not necessarily enough. Now, with Ivy Beasley on the scene, it had been necessary to make a plan to sabotage the wedding.

In the way of villages, it had some years ago become known that old Ethel's baby had been adopted by a couple named Maleham, in Thornwell. Alf had tracked down the family, and discovered that the baby was now a middle-aged man named Frank, and he had listened to Alf's plan. Delighted with the idea of a large inheritance, he had agreed to help, and also to keep it under his hat.

Alf turned over restlessly in his bed, and resumed his worries about the previous night. As Ethel had started to struggle in the bed, muttering that she must get dressed for her wedding, Alf had freed himself from her arms and pushed her onto her pillows, where she relaxed and was quiet. "All a long time ago," he had whispered in her ear. "Remember Roy? Roy Goodman? You had a good time with him, didn't you? Don't forget he was your baby's father, Ethel. Looked just like him, didn't it! If anybody comes asking, don't you forget that, there's a good gel. Bye, bye, then, Eth dear." That should do it, he said to himself, and straightened up.

He left as he came in, shutting doors and avoiding the security alarm. By the time he had got back home, he had been shaking from head to foot with sheer exhaustion. And now, after getting rid of the meter man, he crawled back into bed. Perhaps he should have a sandwich? Hunger could stop you sleeping, couldn't it? But the last thing he wanted was food.

Forty-one

"MORNING, GUS!"

It was Miriam, chirpy even at the ungodly hour of six thirty, when Gus had got up to let Whippy out into the garden for a pee.

"Morning, Miriam," he said. "Very cold again. Must dash. I can hear the phone."

"I can't hear anything," she replied. "You've just got ringing in your ears. I get it sometimes. I go to the surgery to have them syringed."

"No, no. Really, it is my phone. See you later."

He dashed back into the house, leaving the door open for Whippy to return. The sky was leaden, though the forecast had promised sunshine in East Anglia. He looked at the clock, and decided it was not worth going back to bed. He had a tricky task to do today, and then this evening he planned to invite himself to supper with Deirdre. Provided Miriam didn't get in first! He was weak, he told himself. Too weak to say no. But then, Miriam was a brilliant cook, and if he played his cards right, he need only fend for himself two or three times a week. He had no experience of cooking and had no intention of trying to improve.

So, this morning, the tricky task. He would leave Whippy in the kitchen, and walk up to Alf Lowe's cottage to see if he could talk his way inside for a chat. It was no good taking Whippy. Alf was anti-dog, so he'd not stand a chance.

He wondered if Alf was an early riser. Probably not. Well, after breakfast he would set off to the shop for a few things, have a gossip with James, and then walk up Cemetery Lane to Alf's cottage.

"SO WHAT HAPPENED to the sunny day?" said Ivy, as Mrs. Spurling passed their breakfast table.

"Give it time," she said shortly. She was in no mood for Miss Beasley this morning. Tiddles, Ivy's black cat, had found its way into the kitchen and eaten a large chunk from a whole salmon cooling on the slab. "Perhaps you would allow me to have a word with you after breakfast," she added.

"What about?" said Ivy. She knew perfectly well what had happened. When Tiddles had come into her room earlier, Ivy had identified a strong smell of fish coming from the cat's smiling jaws.

Roy saved Mrs. Spurling from replying. He came into the dining room, wished her a polite good morning and settled down opposite Ivy. "And how is my lovely lady this morning? Fresh from her beauty sleep?"

"Dear God, give me strength!" muttered Mrs. Spurling, as she walked swiftly away to her office. Roy Goodman was such a nice old boy. Could he not see that Ivy Beasley was a stringy old spinster, with thin grey hair and evil black eyes that bored into her latest victim? She sighed. Of course he couldn't. Love is blind, isn't it? And anyway, she added to herself, trying to be honest, old Ivy can look quite smart when she's dressed up. And when she smiles at Roy, it transforms her face.

The phone was ringing when she got to her office, and when she answered it she did not recognise the voice. "Hello, who is this?" she said.

"Never mind who I am. I want to speak to Miss Beasley." The man speaking was clearly trying to disguise his voice, and Mrs. Spurling said, "If you want to talk to Miss Beasley, I must have your name."

"Tell her an old friend wants to give her a message."

"Certainly not," said Mrs. Spurling. "I can give her a message, but I need to have your name; otherwise I cannot help you." There was silence then, and she put the phone down with a bang.

"Who was that?" said Ivy, coming into the office, as requested.

"A wrong number. Now, Miss Beasley, it is a small matter of a fresh salmon half-eaten by your cat."

"His name is Tiddles. And yes, I know he ate some of it and I'm very sorry. Just add the cost of replacing it to my account. And if Anya hasn't thrown the rest away, could you make sure it is saved for Tiddles's supper? Is that all? I must go upstairs and get ready to go out. We plan to get some exercise this morning, and walk up to see some Goodman graves. I love graveyards; don't you, Mrs. Spurling?"

Mrs. Spurling was speechless.

"It's the gravestones," said Ivy happily. "Very interesting, some of them. I had a book once, full of odd sayings on gravestones. One I remember very well. You should have read it, Mrs. Spurling. 'Here lies the body of Elizabeth, wife of Major General Hamilton, who was married forty-seven years and never did *one* thing to disoblige her husband.'"

"It was my husband who did the disobliging, Miss Beasley. Now, if we could get back to Tiddles?"

"Certainly. I'll have a word with him." So saying, Ivy walked off to join Roy and plan their walk up Cemetery Lane.

GUS SET OFF soon after breakfast and took Whippy for a quick walk up to the woods and back. He met no one, and was able to rehearse what he would say to Alf in order to gain entry to his cottage. There was no real reason to suppose that even if he got in and they had a chat, Alf would be more forthcoming. Having made the rash accusation that Roy had got a girl in the family way and then dumped her, he seemed unwilling to say anything more about it. Perhaps it wasn't relevant to their current investigation, but perhaps it was. Gus had a feeling about it, and in the field of investigation his feelings were usually worth pursuing.

First the shop. He was happy to find it empty, except for James, who was stacking shelves.

"Morning, Gus! How are you and Whippy? Where is she, by the way?"

"Back at home. I'm hoping to call on Alf Lowe, and I know he's not a dog lover."

"Alf? Is he poorly? He hasn't been in for his paper this morning."

Perfect, thought Gus. The perfect excuse to knock on his door. "I'll take it up to him if you like. Maybe he's overslept."

"Thanks. Then perhaps you could let me know if he's all right. I'm an unofficial message taker here. If there's an old person needing help, I usually hear about it before anyone else. Now, what can I get you? Dog biscuits?"

Gus collected up a bagful of such essentials, and continued on his way. At Alf's front door, he knocked softly at first; then, getting no answer, he knocked again, loudly this time.

"Wait a minute, y'bugger!" came a voice from inside. Then the door opened a crack and Alf, looking almost unrecognisable with a stubbly face and hair all anyhow, peered out. "What do you want?" he grunted.

"I've brought your newspaper, Mr. Lowe. James at the shop was a bit worried because you hadn't been in at your usual time to collect it." Gus handed it over, and Alf grabbed it and began to shut the door. From long practice, Gus put his foot in the opening.

"Are you all right? Can I get anything for you?"

"Clear off. That's what you can do," said Alf. But he stopped pushing the door against Gus's foot. "I'm not up to much at the moment," he said. "Nothing wrong. Just old age, I reckon."

"Can I come in and we could have a chat?" Gus said, without much hope.

To his surprise, Alf pulled the door open and stood to one side. "Come on, then. A bit of a talk might buck me up. But I'm not answering any of your stupid questions."

"I'd be pleased to help, Mr. Lowe. You can choose the subject, and I'll listen."

"Huh! That's a new one! But I'm up to your tricks. What's yer name, anyway? I've seen you round the village, but don't know who the hell you are."

"Augustus Halfhide, but my friends call me Gus. You can call me Gus."

"So we're friends, are we? You'd better sit down, then. I might need a friend or two." Alf was looking considerably more cheerful, and Gus sat in the most comfortable chair, trying hard to look relaxed. He smiled at Alf, and waited.

"How's that old Beasley bird at Springfields? Is she still planning to marry old Roy Goodman for his millions? Got an eye for the main chance, that one."

Gus held his breath. An odd subject for Alf to raise, surely?

"Ivy Beasley? Oh, she's fine. A good friend of mine, actually, though I expect you know that. Keep your ear to the ground, don't you, Alf? I bet not a lot goes on in this village without your knowing. Am I right?"

Alf nodded. "That's village life for you. You're a townie, if I'm not much mistaken. No, in villages nothing goes on in secret for long. There's always someone who finds out, and then it spreads like wildfire."

"But this isn't really your village, is it? I understood you grew up near Settlefield. Farming family, was it?"

Alf's eyes narrowed. "You didn't come here to talk about farming, did you," he said.

"Farming's as good a subject as any other."

"Oh, all right. Yes, Lowes were farmers for generations. It goes like that round here. And we all married each other. Result, a few loonies. But mostly we all got on and helped each other out. I ended up in Barrington after my wife left me. And, by the way, you can stop worrying about that. Case closed, as they say. She's emigrated to Australia with another bloke. Never coming back, she said. Good riddance, I said, and those will likely be my last words to 'er."

"Is that why you've been a little upset?"

"Upset? I been celebrating—that's why I'm a bit middlin', if you want to know. Now, before you get on to the subject of Roy Goodman and his floosies, I reckon it's time for you to go. I s'pose that unlikely wedding is going ahead? Someone should tell Miss Beasley what she's in for. Though he's prob'ly past it by now. Cheerio, boy. And thanks for the paper."

Forty-two

"HEY, LOOK, ROY, isn't that Gus? Coming out of Alf Lowe's cottage?"

Roy manoeuvered his trundle onto the pavement, and agreed that it certainly looked like Gus being waved off by Alf Lowe. He sped up, with Ivy doing her best to follow at a quick pace, but by the time they reached Gus, the door had been closed and there was no sign of Alf.

"Hello, you two!" said Gus. "Where are you off to?"

"The cemetery," said Ivy. "We thought we'd cheer ourselves up. Winter seems to be going on forever."

"Can I join you?" said Gus.

"We're not coming apart," said Roy, and chuckled.

"The old ones are the best," said Ivy. "And of course we'd love you to come with us. Anything useful to tell?"

"Not sure," said Gus. "But maybe."

They set off again, Roy leading the way in his trundle, and Ivy and Gus following closely. Barrington graveyard was not the most entertaining place Gus would have chosen, but he knew Ivy loved graveyards, and there was a seat, probably very wet, where they could rest before returning to Springfields. He did the gentlemanly thing, took off his rainproof jacket and spread it over the bench.

"Your seat, madam!" he said.

"You're in a good mood, Augustus," said Ivy. "Sit by me, and tell us all about Alf."

"Well, for a start," began Gus, "our case concerning his wife is closed. She's gone off to Australia and is not coming back."

"Can't say I'm sorry," said Ivy. "Never come between man and wife, my mother always used to say."

"He was obviously feeling rotten when I arrived, but claimed he'd done too much celebrating his victory over his wife, and he did seem to improve as I sat chatting."

"Chatting? What did you chat about?" said Ivy sharply.

"Farming," said Gus. "Farming families in and around Settlefield in the old days. His family had a farm, but he didn't stay in it. Perhaps I should have asked why, but he was clearly getting fed up with me. But the interesting thing was, he brought up the subject of you, Roy, and your floosies. I quote. He seemed interested in you, too, Ivy, and asked me if you were still intending to be married, the two of you. Now, why should that concern him? He did actually ask me twice."

Ivy got to her feet. "I can feel the wet coming through the buttonholes on your jacket, Gus. I think we should be getting back, and then we can check with Deirdre that tomorrow's meeting is okay. We can discuss Alf Lowe then. I think you've stumbled onto something, but we need more information about Roy's floosies. And don't say you've told us all you know, Roy, because there may be something you haven't known or have forgotten."

"I suppose it's no good my denying it, Ivy?" Roy said pathetically. "Come along, then, let's go back to Springfields." He turned his trundle and headed for the cemetery gate. "Why don't you come in with us, Gus? I am sure La Spurling will find you some lunch. You can work your magic with her, I know."

"Good idea," said Gus. That will take care of lunch, he reflected, and then I can look forward to supper with lovely Deirdre, if she will have me.

UNFORTUNATELY FOR GUS, Deirdre had a prior engagement. When Gus popped into her kitchen on his way home, she was delighted to see him, but when he mentioned supper, her face fell. "Sorry, Gussy, no can do. Himself up at the Hall has promised to take me out to that new and expensive restaurant in Oakbridge."

"Cancel him," said Gus confidently. "I promise to bring fresh fish and chips from the shop in Thornwell. Piping hot, and wrapped in several layers of newspaper."

Deirdre laughed. "Not much of a choice, is it? No, Gus, I haven't seen much of dear old Theo lately, so I really must go with him this evening. Shall I see you tomorrow at our usual meeting?"

Disappointed, Gus said that yes, he would be at the meeting. "As it happens," he added, "I had an interesting talk with Alf Lowe this morning, and if you had chosen fish and chips, I was planning to fill you in with the details. However, I must be brave, and the whole story will be on the table tomorrow."

He left Tawny Wings, and wandered slowly back home, thinking about Alf. He had looked really grim when he first opened the door. Was it just his usual morning face? Or had there been something bad worrying him? Perhaps, after all, he had realised he still felt some affection for his wife, and the thought of never seeing her again had troubled him unexpectedly.

But why had he been so interested in Ivy and Roy? What was it to him whether they were married or not? He continued down Hangman's Row, and turned into his front garden. Poor Whippy must have been lonely without him. Perhaps Alf should get a dog to stop him brooding. As he put a hand out to open his front door, he saw a piece of white paper stuck halfway through the letter box. He walked in and withdrew the paper. There was no envelope, and when he unfolded it, he saw familiar red ink. And one very big exclamation mark.

It was dark in the hallway, so he took it through to his kitchen, where light streamed in, even in dull weather.

SOMETHING BAD WILL HAPPEN TO THE BEASLEY WOMAN IF THEM BANNS ARE RED ON SUNDAY. STOP THEM, OR ELSE!

Gus's heart sank. But why deliver it to me? Ivy's not *my* woman. This must have been brought by him with the earring.

I suppose he thinks I have more authority than two old codgers in an old folks' home. He sighed, and at that point a figure crossed by his kitchen window, knocking lightly as she passed.

"Hello, Miriam," he said dully. "Is Whippy in the garden?"

"No, she's right in front of you. What's that you're reading? You look quite pale."

Gus did not answer, and she continued, "What you need is a nice fish pie with peas and chips. Homemade, of course. Come round about seven? What do you fancy for pudding?"

"Poison pie," he answered. "And can I bring a friend?"

THE RESTAURANT NEAR Oakbridge was exclusive, and when Deirdre and Theo Roussel arrived in Deirdre's swish car, it was in good company. A couple of Bentleys and a Porsche four-by-four were already parked.

"Gentlemen farmers, I suppose," said Deirdre. "My Bert would have approved. He loved a good car, you know. His heart was in cars. Always had been."

"I hope he saved a bit of his heart for his wife," said Theo. He was not particularly interested in Deirdre's Bert. Once a motorcar salesman, always a motorcar salesman, in Theo's opinion. However much money he had made, and he had made plenty, he was not likely to have been a guest at Barrington Hall.

"Oh yes. Childhood sweethearts, we were," Deirdre said nostalgically.

"I seem to remember a certain teenage Deirdre when she was playing the field, and mostly with me." He leaned across the table and stroked her cheek. "You are just as beautiful now as you were then. What do you fancy to eat, my love?"

"Fish and chips," she said. She didn't hold with soppy talk, and reacted badly. "Straight out of the newspaper."

Theo laughed uncertainly. "Well, we could ask, I suppose," he said.

"No, of course not. I was just joking. I think paté for starters, and then I'd love roast pheasant with all the trimmings. This is a really nice place, Theo, and it's lovely to be out with you again."

Theo relaxed. It was going to be all right. He knew his chief rival for Deirdre's favours was his tenant in Hangman's Row, and he occasionally thought of turning him out. But that wouldn't solve anything. And anyway, Gus wasn't a bad chap, on the whole.

"Have you had success with any mysteries lately, you and the others? Miss Beasley and Mr. Goodman still an item?"

"Oh yes, they certainly are. And in answer to the other question, we are deep into anonymous messages and deathbed crime. Possibly."

"My, that should keep you busy! But now let me look at the wine list. I need to choose carefully, so that my lovely guest will be sufficiently mellow to take coffee with me back at the Hall. In due course."

"If you're talking about wine," said Deirdre bluntly, "it'll have to be good. My Bert used to say I'd got a head like a camel. At least, I think it was a camel."

Forty-three

OUTSIDE IVY'S BEDROOM window a group of crows were quarrelling in the treetops and the hoarse sound penetrated Ivy's sleep. She opened her eyes, and could see through the curtains that the sun was up already. A knock at the door brought Katya in with her morning cup of tea, and she sat up in bed.

"Please draw the curtains, Katya," Ivy said. "Am I late waking? It looks like a fine day out there. And listen to those noisy old crows! Do you think spring is here at last?"

Katya laughed. "So many questions so early, Miss Beasley! Yes, it is a lovely day, and Mr. Goodman is already in the breakfast room. Can I help you to get dressed?"

"No, thank you, my dear. I am still quite capable of that, unlike some of the lazy residents in this place. I actually heard one of them, who shall be nameless, say that she did not pay all that money and be expected to make her own bed. No, I shall be fine. Please tell Roy I'll be down in no time."

So now it is Thursday, she thought, and the week was going fast. She splashed cold water over her face, and pulled on a sensible tweed skirt and lambswool jumper. Lace-up shoes and warm stockings anchored by suspenders completed her outfit for the day, and she made her bed quickly, not forgetting hospital corners, and went downstairs to find Roy.

"Good morning, beloved!" said Roy. "A lovely morning at last, and perhaps spring is on its way. Now, do you fancy scrambled eggs and bacon? I can recommend it. And brown toast and marmalade? And coffee?"

Ivy kissed the top of his head, and blushed a little. "No, I shall have my usual boiled egg, white toast and Marmite, and a good strong pot of tea."

Roy laughed. "No good going to France for our honeymoon, then," he said.

"France? What's wrong with Blackpool? We never had holidays except once when I was a child, and then it was Blackpool. My mother was very critical of everything, but I remember thinking it was the best place ever."

"Blackpool it shall be, then. And, by the way, Gus phoned earlier and said he was coming fifteen minutes early to pick us up for the meeting. Wants to tell us something, so he said."

"Perhaps he's going to say that Deirdre has accepted him and we can have a double wedding?"

"I doubt it, but that does remind me that our banns should be called this Sunday. No problems now, surely."

"Rev. Dorothy seemed confident," Ivy replied. "Things seem to have sorted themselves out. Now Alf doesn't want our services, that only leaves your nephew's strange death for us to carry on investigating."

Roy nodded. "I wasn't particularly fond of him, but I wouldn't have wished him dead. Perhaps I should give Frobisher a ring and see if the police are any nearer finding the reason he died. That at least. And, Ivy dear, don't forget the anonymous threats to your safety."

"Never mind about me. I hope we're not going to forget Steven's wife? Wendy, isn't it. I don't think we or the police have given enough thought to Wendy."

At this moment, Gus came into the dining room, wished them a cheery good morning, and ordered himself some coffee. When it came, Katya produced more toast and real butter, and said it was all with the compliments of Miss Pinkney, who was on duty today.

"And don't tell La Spurling!" added Roy.

When he had settled down, Gus became more serious and said he had something unpleasant to show them.

"Another letter," said Ivy flatly.

He handed the crumpled sheet of paper to her, and said he was sure that they were all empty threats and no harm was going to come to either Roy or her. "But we must continue to be cautious, Ivy. I know you wish to ignore them, but I'm sure Frobisher would want you both to be very careful."

"Of course," agreed Roy. "I think I shall go this minute and call Inspector Frobisher before he goes out. You will guard Ivy, won't you, Gus?"

He took his stick and limped off as quickly as he could before Ivy could say a word.

When he returned, his face was grim. "Well, I'm glad I phoned. He had some bad news for us on two fronts. First, they found traces of some kind of food poisoning in Steven's stomach at the autopsy, and second, the matron of the nursing home where Ethel Goodman died is asking for the police to do an investigation. She is not satisfied that the old lady died from natural causes, and has the home's reputation to think of. Even more important for us to be wary, Ivy."

"Oh my goodness," said Ivy, knocked off her perch for a few minutes. "Well, that means we still have plenty of work to do," she continued, rallying. "I must say I am not surprised by the news about Steven. I noticed that he was a greedy man. Always ate several pieces of cake when he came here, at the same time comparing Springfields' cooking with his wife, Wendy's. As for Ethel, it seemed so likely that she could have died at any time at her great age, so that does come as curious news."

"Apparently her young Jossland relations at the farm, the ones Deirdre has been to see, are not satisfied, either. At first they just took it as inevitable, but then, talking to the matron, they learned that Ethel was not in any way physically ill or weak. She was just old and obstinate. Could speak, but wouldn't."

"She spoke to Deirdre, if you remember," said Ivy. "And, oddly enough, the name she mentioned was Alf Lowe, and not favourably."

"Time to go up to Tawny Wings," said Gus. "We can fill Deirdre in, and then have a planning session."

* * *

"BUT WHY DID the man with the earring deliver that note to you, Gus? The others have been more or less planted where Ivy would find them." Deirdre had been dismayed at the sight of the third anonymous threat, and supported Roy in his concern to keep Ivy safe.

"If I'd been there, I could've asked him," said Gus. "I've given it some thought, and I can only think that he knows about Enquire Within and thinks I will persuade you two to give up the idea of marriage. After all, you cohabit at Springfields already."

"There should be more to marriage than just living in the same house," said Deirdre sternly. "You of all people, Gus, should know that." Gus nodded humbly. His own marriage had come to grief some time ago, and his ex-wife had involved him in a very unpleasant murder case quite recently.

"If anyone is interested in knowing what I think," said Ivy, "I say that I intend to ignore the threats, take sensible precautions, and, with my dear Roy and our good friend Elvis, pay another visit to Mrs. Maleham, mother of Frank, who not only sports an earring, but also works weekends in the furniture store warehouse. It is entirely possible that he knew Steven and probably didn't like him."

"Ivy!" said Deirdre. "Isn't that terribly rash? After all, you might be putting the pair of you straight into the lion's den!"

"I doubt it. Not with Elvis in his taxi waiting outside only yards away from us."

"Why don't you invite her to tea at Springfields, dearest, as you planned?" said Roy. "That would be a safer option, surely?"

"Because there would be no heavy-breathing listener at the top of the stairs. I mean to sort that out. No, I shall ring Elvis this afternoon, and arrange for him to pick us up tomorrow morning."

"Then I shall come with you," said Deirdre.

"And so shall I," Gus added.

"Don't be ridiculous," said Ivy. "You will have to trust that Roy and I can make it a perfectly natural and innocent visit. I shall say we were shopping in town, and thought it a good opportunity to pop in and see her. I might suggest she arranges for her husband to be brought to Springfields to live, though I doubt whether they could afford its exorbitant fees."

"So what shall I do, if you won't let us come with you?" said Deirdre.

"Why don't you visit your Jossland couple, and see if you can get anything further about Ethel Goodman. Why did she blurt out 'Alf Lowe' in that way, and who might know about her early life on the farm. That would be really useful," suggested Ivy.

"Which leaves me," said Gus. "I think I shall have another chat with Alf. He certainly warmed up last time. And I reckon he knows a lot more than he's telling."

"I think maybe we should all meet again on Saturday to report. I have this funny feeling that things are coming together."

"Inspector Frobisher is not going to rely on funny feelings," said Ivy sharply. But on seeing Deirdre's face fall, she softened and said she knew what Deirdre meant. "Just go easy, gel," she said. "We don't want the Malehams getting suspicious. Though at the moment I can't see a direct connection between Alf and Ethel to Beryl Maleham and son Frank."

"Saturday, then?" said Deirdre. "Ten thirty here. I'm having my hair done at twelve o'clock and then lunch with Theo."

"The sooner you choose which one you're taking to the altar, the better," said Ivy. "I don't hold with all this shilly-shallying."

"Hear, hear," said Gus.

Forty-four

THE SUN HAD continued to shine all morning, and when Ivy and Roy took a turn around the garden, with Ivy waving her stick at the crows' nests, they decided spring was definitely just around the corner and they should have a little jaunt after lunch.

But after lunch, Roy said he needed his nap before they set out to nobble Deirdre and persuade her to take them for a ride around the villages. "You won't need your trundle," Ivy said. "We'll just have a sightseeing ride without getting out of the car."

"Are you coming up now for a nap, then?" Roy asked.

"Not for a few minutes. I'll follow you shortly. I just have to see to Tiddles first."

Roy went off, promising to be down again in half an hour's time. "I'll just shut my eyes for a short while," he said.

Ivy had forgotten to give Tiddles a worm pill with his main meal at breakfast time, but now she intended to wrap it in a piece of meat for a little snack. She started off to look for him, but failed to find him in any of the usual places. She knew he was not in her room. She had shut the door on him as she came downstairs. Perhaps he had been tempted into the garden by the sunshine and the noisy crows? There was no one in reception, and she reckoned she could be out and back again quite safely without bothering to go upstairs for a coat.

She began to look around the garden, calling for him as she went. He usually came straight away, expecting a treat. There was a dense shrubbery down one side of the house, and she suspected he might he in there, stalking nesting birds and deaf to her calls. "Tiddles? Tiddles! Come to Ivy, come along," she shouted.

Peering through a spiky holly bush, she caught her foot in a trailing weed and almost fell. Struggling upright again, she decided Tiddles must have gone hunting. There was a farm around the corner where he loved to go, occasionally coming back with a half-dead rat in his mouth and dumping it on the doormat in reception.

She was back inside before anyone noticed her absence, and in no time was snoozing in an armchair in the lounge whilst waiting for Roy to appear. She was awakened by the pleasant feeling of someone kissing her cheek. She sat up sharply and saw Roy grinning at her.

"Wakey, wakey, Ivy Beasley," he said. "Did you dream of me?"

"Certainly not," she said. "And now look what you've done!"

At least four of the old lady residents were laughing, and Roy's friend Fred called out from the other side of the room, "Go to it, boy!"

Roy was unabashed and said that he was all set for a ride with Deirdre. He had telephoned her, and she was looking forward to seeing them. Apparently she had nothing to do and was thinking of visiting the Josslands, but said that could wait until tomorrow. Best not to go too soon, perhaps, as they might be mourning their old aunt.

"There's Deirdre, my dear. Let me help you up, and then you can fetch your coat," Roy said, offering Ivy his arm.

Deirdre walked into the lounge, and wondered why everyone seemed to be laughing. Then she saw Ivy, grim-faced, arm in arm with Roy, and guessed that the old boy had been teasing her. "Cheer up, Ivy," she said. "Are we ready?"

"Ready in two ticks," Roy said. "We'll just find our coats. Though it's always warm in your car."

"If you feel like it, we might stop somewhere for a cup of tea?" said Deirdre.

"We'd better warn La Spurling," said Roy. "She'll shove us in the cooler if we're late back."

"Really, Roy! Sometimes I wonder about your upbringing," said Ivy, and disappeared upstairs for her coat.

WHEN THEY WERE safely settled in Deirdre's car, Ivy warmed up and said this was really nice.

"Lovely to have a trip out without having to talk business!" Deirdre agreed.

"Don't know about that," said Ivy. "We always have to be alert. Ears and eyes open."

"We can try to forget it for one morning," answered Deirdre, determined to make this an enjoyable outing, if only for dear old Roy.

Ivy was quiet for ten minutes or so, and then said, "Aren't we somewhere near Settlefield? I'm sure I saw it on a signpost we just passed."

"Not far," Deirdre replied.

Ivy relapsed into silence for a minute or two, then said, "Shall we go and call on your friends, Deirdre? Just to say hello? We might see that baby you're so fond of."

"We can't just turn up, three of us, Ivy dear," said Roy. "Not without calling them to see if it is convenient. After all, he's a busy farmer and she's a young mum."

"All the more reason to go without notice," Ivy said. "They won't rush around tidying up. What do you say, Deirdre? You know them pretty well."

"Mm, well, I suppose it would be okay. They're a very nice couple. He'll be out on the farm, anyway, probably. Oh look, here's another turn to Settlefield. Sit tight."

She executed a neat turn to the right, and soon they approached the lane leading to the farm.

AS DEIRDRE HAD supposed, William Jossland was out with the tractor, and Bella greeted them warmly. She insisted that they help Roy up the steps into the warm kitchen, where she put on the kettle for tea.

"What a lovely surprise!" she said. "We are always hoping Mrs. Bloxham will drop in to see us, but it is wonderful to meet Roy. A real, live Goodman relation! Such a pity we never met before. That ridiculous feud, so long ago. Anyway, now we've found you, we shall keep in touch."

"Is Faith asleep?" Deirdre asked. "Ivy and Roy have heard so much about her. I'm sure they'd love to have a peek."

On cue, a wail from above sent Bella off to bring her downstairs, and the next ten minutes were spent passing her around for a cuddle. When it was Ivy's turn, the cuddle lasted exactly sixty seconds, before she handed the warm bundle on to Deirdre.

Finally Roy thought it appropriate to mention Ethel. "We were so sorry to hear about your aunt," he said. "Still, she was a good age. I don't remember her very well, I'm afraid."

Bella was immediately serious. "Yes, we were sad. But the old lady had been almost unaware of any kind of life for quite a while. I remembered having birthday cards from her when I was little, but otherwise she didn't figure much in family gettogethers. There was always a kind of mystery surrounding her! Everyone called her 'poor Ethel.' I do remember that."

"Do you recall anyone named Lowe in her life? Alf Lowe?" asked Ivy, and Deirdre frowned at her. No business talk, hadn't they agreed?

Bella shook her head. "Why?" she asked.

"Just wondered," Ivy said, and smiled defiantly at Deirdre.

"Though wait a minute," Bella said. "I know she had lots of boyfriends when she was young, and I seem to have heard that name. Could've been one of them. I'll ask William when he comes in. Josslands and Goodmans certainly knew each other, so he might remember hearing the name."

After tea and a good plain sponge cake from the local Women's Insitute, the three waved a cheerful farewell to Bella and Faith, and, promising to come back soon, they went on their way.

WHEN DEIRDRE DREW up outside Springfields, she was surprised to see Mrs. Spurling waiting at the roadside.

"We did say we might be out for tea," she said, getting out of the car.

"Oh yes, Mrs. Bloxham, you did. But I wanted to catch you before the others come out of the car."

Then she palmed a folded sheet of paper across and tucked it into Deirdre's coat pocket. "Another one," she whispered. "Found it halfway through the letter box. I've notified the police."

"Oh blast!" said Deirdre. "And we had such a nice afternoon. But thank you, Mrs. Spurling. I'll get in touch with Mr. Halfhide, and we'll decide whether to tell Ivy."

"I'm afraid the inspector said he'd be here in half an hour, so she'll have to know. I do hope I've done the right thing."

"Of course you have," said Deirdre, patting Mrs. Spurling's arm. "I'm so sorry that Springfields has had to be involved. We do appreciate your help."

Somewhat reassured, Mrs. Spurling helped Roy out and back into the lounge, with Ivy following, glaring at other grinning residents who dared to remember the kiss.

Then Gus arrived, and they broke the news to Ivy. This time, she did not dismiss it out of hand, but paled and said that if she could get her hands on the author of these letters, she would personally wring his neck.

"May I see it?" Roy said. As he read it aloud, he saw why Ivy was now really worried.

" 'No banns on Sunday!' " he began, " 'Or your preshus cat will meet a sticky end. We got him now. No banns, or else he's had it!' "

A shocked silence greeted this, and then Gus said, "I'll get this evil devil, if it's the last thing I do!"

"Don't worry," said Ivy, visibly pulling herself together. "This is outright war now. And here's Inspector Frobisher to lead us into battle."

Forty-five

INSPECTOR FROBISHER ARRIVED punctually, smiled affectionately at Deirdre and settled down with the four enquirers in the conference room, which had been warmed and dusted with great efficiency by Mrs. Spurling.

There had been time before the inspector arrived to tell Gus about their afternoon's call on the Josslands, and he had said his visit to Alf had been a washout, as he wasn't there, or wasn't answering the door.

"Now, Miss Beasley," said the inspector, "as you are the target for these threats, perhaps you would like to tell us your best guess as to who might be sending them. I know you well enough to know that you will have been giving it some analytical thought, and I'd appreciate it if you could share the result with me."

Clever man, our inspector, thought Gus. Flattery will get you everywhere.

"Well," said Ivy, "I do have an idea, but I'm afraid it won't get us very far."

"Never mind; just tell us, Ivy dear," said Roy.

"Right, well, for a start, I don't think the deliverer is the originator of the messages. I think some shifty character is being paid to deliver them. Probably paid well, as there is considerable risk of being caught and duly punished."

She paused for dramatic effect, then continued with a question.

"Have you thought, Inspector," she said, fixing him with a steady look, "of talking more seriously to Wendy?"

"Wendy?"

"Yes, Wendy Wright, wife of Steven Wright, who was a nephew of Roy. I have been wondering about Wendy. She was, you know, very badly treated by Steven. Added to that, she might, mistakenly, perhaps, have thought that with Steven out of the way, she might have been next in line for Roy's money?"

"Well, of course we spoke to her at the time," said Frobisher, collecting his wits," but she had a cast-iron alibi. After we were satisfied with her answers to our questions, she went off to Australia to stay with relations. Poor soul was very upset, naturally, and we were quite happy for her to go, provided we are kept informed if she changes her address out there."

He frowned. Was the old girl deliberately being awkward, keeping him at bay? Using Wendy Wright as a red herring? He wondered if she realised how vulnerable she was, and just how serious those threats could be. If the cat had been abducted, she could be next.

"But, Ivy," Roy said now, "leaving Wendy aside with a cast iron alibi, don't you think we should tell the inspector about the listener at the top of the Malehams' stairs?"

"What's this?" said Frobisher, beginning to lose patience. "Look, you four, we are not playing a jolly cops and robbers game. I know you have had success in the past, but this involves one of your own group. Someone means to stop the wedding; we all know that. And the reason, as Miss Beasley has so rightly said before, is Mr. Goodman's considerable wealth."

"Anyone would think I'm a millionaire," protested Roy. "Just comfortable, as they say."

The inspector nodded, and continued, "Steven Wright was the heir, but now he is gone, things have changed. When Miss Beasley becomes Mrs. Goodman, she will more than likely inherit. Begging your pardon, Mr. Goodman! Not very polite to talk about you as if you were dead, but we guess that you will want to provide substantially for your wife. So no other candidates as beneficiaries. At least, no serious ones. We have found a young couple in Settlefield who are distantly related to Mr. Goodman, but she has confirmed that there has been a lifetime's feud with that branch of the family, and until very recently the Josslands were strangers."

"We know about them," said Deirdre, smiling sweetly. "I have become quite a friend of the family. Bella was a Goodman, and they have a lovely baby named Faith. Don't you think that's a splendid name?"

"Yes, well, of course," said Frobisher, not sure how relevant this was.

"And you haven't mentioned Ethel," she said, and talking of babies, she added to herself.

"Ethel?"

"Yes, Miss Ethel Goodman, very recently deceased. Lived in the Firs nursing home in Settlefield. Aged eighty-something."

Frobisher sighed. "Ah yes, Ethel. A somewhat severed branch of the Goodman family. We have had a request for an investigation. Tell me more, Deirdre."

"Nothing much more to tell, except that she has lived there for years, vegetating among the oldies. There are rumours about her being cut off from the rest of the family. But only rumours." As for the rest, Deirdre said to herself, there's more work to be done there, and I'm going to do it.

"I doubt if there is much danger from that quarter, then, though we shall see," said the inspector. "Looks like the Goodmans are dying out, if you'll excuse my saying so."

"Yes, Bella's side of the family are all gone. Sad, really, don't you think? Would you like a coffee, Ba . . . Um, inspector?" asked Deirdre.

"A cup of tea would be very welcome, thank you. Now, what else have you to tell me, you four?" He could see from their exchanged glances that there was something more, but nobody replied.

"Right, well, then, shall we start with the listener at the top of the stairs?"

Ivy looked at Roy, and gave the slightest shake of her head. "I really think we should be looking again at Steven's wife and

her relationship with him," she said. "We have been told there
is some suggestion of poison? It would have been possible for
her to have given him something that wouldn't act until he got
to work, and then he might have stretched out on the bed thinking his nausea would pass. But it didn't. Don't you think that's
possible, Inspector? Or," she continued, "she might have com-
missioned someone to do it for her, leaving her with, in your
words, Inspector, a cast-iron alibi?"

Frobisher gave it some thought. "Difficult, Miss Beasley.
Steven did not go home the night before he was found. According to Wendy Wright. If she had given him poison herself, it
would have been some very delayed kind, since she hadn't seen
him since waving him off to work the morning before."

"So she said," Ivy persisted. "You were obviously taken in
by her crocodile tears, Inspector Frobisher. I must say I am a
little surprised."

"I think you must accept that we gave her a very thorough
questioning before agreeing that she could leave the country,"
he replied, becoming irritated. "But of course I will have
another look at her evidence."

There was a knock at the door, and Mrs. Spurling came in
with a tray of tea and cake. "I do hope you will be finished soon,
Inspector," she said. "I have to take care that my residents are
not overtired by all this t'do."

"Don't worry, Mrs. Spurling," said Roy kindly. "We are
perfectly all right, and Inspector Frobisher is well aware that
at our age, our memories are not all they should be."

"Very well. Will you be mother, Mrs. Bloxham, and pour
the tea?"

AFTER THE INSPECTOR had gone, the four continued to
sit in the conference room, discussing what had been said.

"What was all that about Wendy Wright, Ivy?" said Gus.
"Were you serious, or was it a diversionary tactic?"

"No, no," said Ivy. "I was quite serious. I think it is highly
likely that she wanted to get rid of him, and so would I if I'd
been in her shoes. He was cruel, Gus. Two people stuck in a
marriage like that can make life hell for each other. Though in
this case, the cruelty seems to have been all one way."

Now was the time to tell about her talk with Wendy's neighbour, and with an apology for misleading him, she gave a brief report.

Roy frowned. "Thanks for telling me, Ivy," he said. "I knew you were up to something! You are a rotten fibber, you know, dearest. Anyway, as far as Steven's married life went, I knew very little. I saw him so seldom that I can't recall Wendy coming with him. Oh, now, wait a minute. She did turn up here once. She had dropped him off, and then driven into town to do some shopping while he checked up on me. I do remember that he was unpleasantly annoyed with her when she returned a little later than planned."

"That's not enough to trigger a poisoning, is it?" Deirdre said.

Ivy bridled. "Possibly not, but try to imagine what it must have been like, if he was a real bully all the time. Maybe she couldn't take any more, and just flipped."

"Now, girls," said Roy with a smile. "Little birds in their nests agree!"

Deirdre fluffed out her feathers and said could they please change the subject and talk about Ivy's really dangerous situation, and her reluctance to tell the inspector about the Malehams, Beryl and Frank, the man with the earring?

"After all," she said, "you and Roy were very worried about your last visit to them. And surely that listener at the top of the stairs was highly suspicious?"

"Yes," Ivy replied, "but we have no proof that it wasn't her bedridden husband. He could've been going to the toilet, breathing heavily with the effort. And Beryl has always been very friendly. I don't want to bring more trouble to her if there is no good reason. No, Roy and I will go again soon, and ask some awkward questions."

"I shouldn't worry about Beryl Maleham," said Deirdre. "She's probably a real mother hen, and perfectly able to protect herself and her chick."

Gus began to laugh. "Not much of a chick, from the description we've got," he said. "And we don't know how much information La Spurling is feeding to the inspector. Ivy doesn't call her Big Ears for nothing."

"What's funny, lad?" said Roy. Just at this moment, laughing seemed inappropriate.

"I just had this bizarre thought that maybe Mrs. Spurling is the brains behind the whole thing. Or somebody else we haven't thought of. Sorry, Ivy; I know we're up against something really serious. Sorry, Roy."

Ivy took this personally, and was furious. "You might just as well say that I am the one who's pulling the strings," she said. "Why not? I am the most likely to benefit in the end. Suppose I am anxious to throw the scent off me and onto some other likely character, and then, when we're married, and I am the only possible beneficiary left, I arrange to remove Roy to heaven, bless him. . . . Really, Augustus, I am surprised at you!"

And then, for the first time ever in the experience of Deirdre, Roy or Gus, Ivy burst into tears.

Forty-six

GUS HAD BEEN mortified yesterday, and had spent half the night thinking of a way to restore Ivy's faith in him. His own wife had been so tough, and he had never seen her cry. And his mother had died when he was small, before he had had time to notice whether she was crying, or be alarmed by it.

And Ivy, of all people! No wonder he felt so shattered. He should have realised that the wicked threats made to her, and then the disappearance of Tiddles, had weakened her defensive shell, until finally he had been the one to pierce it. Oh Lord, what on earth could he do to mend it?

It was a cold grey morning, and he sat huddled in the warm dressing gown Ivy had given him for Christmas, drinking coffee and chewing a piece of cold toast.

In the midst of her tears, she had rushed upstairs to her room, obviously not wishing anyone else to see her, and he had heard no more, except for two calls. The first from Roy had assured him that she was fine this morning, perky as ever, and determined to find Tiddles. She had already made several forays to hunt for him, and planned to put notices all round the village alerting people to keep a lookout for him. Her resolve to catch the author of the threats was now doubled.

The second had been from Deirdre, full of accusations of heartlessness, and advising a sincere apology.

Now he saw a shadow cross the kitchen wall and knew it was Miriam, on her way to see him. She gave a brief knock at the door and came in. "Gus? Not up and dressed yet? Aren't you feeling well? There's a nasty flu bug going around. Apparently Alf Lowe has been taken to hospital in Thornwell, suffering with a high fever. O' course, he's got no one to look after him. I could've done it, if they'd asked me. Still, I don't particularly want to catch it. Though I'll look after you, if you've got it," she added hastily.

"Well, you're safe, because I haven't got flu," said Gus. "Just a nasty attack of guilty conscience."

"What've you done, then," said Miriam, laughing at him.

"Offended someone so badly that they dissolved into tears," he said.

Miriam stopped laughing. "Not that Deirdre Bloxham? She's hard as nails. Mind you, I bet she could put on a good performance when required."

"No, not Deirdre," replied Gus. "Anyway, I have to get going now, so shall I come in for coffee about eleven? You can send Whippy back here now. I'll give her a late breakfast."

"Whippy? I haven't seen her this morning."

"Oh no, not Whippy, as well!"

"I haven't touched her!" said Miriam.

"No, of course not," Gus said. "But Miss Beasley's cat, Tiddles, has gone missing."

There was a scratching at the door, and Miriam opened it. A shivering Whippy came in, and Gus gave her a big hug.

"She's like a child to you, isn't she," said Miriam. "See you at coffee time."

UP AT SPRINGFIELDS, Elvis shut the taxi door and went through the gate to collect Ivy and Roy. He had had an early call from Ivy, asking him to pick them up around ten o'clock, to be taken into Thornwell. They planned to visit a friend in hospital, Ivy had said. Mrs. Spurling had warned them about the bug going round the village, bad enough to send Alf Lowe into hospital, and against Roy's advice, Ivy planned to visit him.

"We could easily pick up the infection, Ivy dear," he had said. "It's a virulent strain, so they say."

Mrs. Spurling, too, had been very unwilling to sanction the visit. But knowing that Miss Beasley was quite likely to disregard her advice, she said nothing except to caution them to be home in time for lunch, which was grilled salmon, untouched by cats, and very expensive.

Now Elvis was alarmed. His passengers were really old, and he was fond of both of them. "Do you really want to go in there, among all them germs?" he said, as he drew up outside the hospital.

"Oh yes. If it was dangerous for us, they'd not let us in. He might be quarantined," replied Ivy confidently. "Give us about three-quarters of an hour. That should be enough," she added.

"I'll wait," said Elvis. "Just in case they turn you out straight away."

They walked into reception, and were told that Mr. Lowe was much better and probably had had only a bad cold. Yes, they could pop up and see him. He should be home tomorrow.

"But beware," said the receptionist. "Apparently he's in a very bad mood, and swearing at all and sundry!"

"He knows us," Roy said. "And don't worry. We can give as good as we get, especially Ivy here!"

A passing nurse offered to take them along to Mr. Lowe's ward. "It's on the ground floor, but I could still find a wheelchair, if you like," she said, watching Roy struggling with his stick. He had said no to bringing his trundle in, knowing that the corridors of the hospital were always busy with people running about on emergency errands.

"All right so far," he said. "Give me your arm, Ivy dear."

They moved off slowly, and the nurse insisted on taking Roy's other arm. "I shall find a wheelchair and bring it for you when you leave," she said.

ALF WAS SITTING up in bed, reading a newspaper. He lowered it, and his face darkened. "What the so-and-so are you two doing here?" he said. "I'm going home tomorrow. Not ill at all. All a ruse to imprison me."

"It's called goodwill," said Ivy, taking off her gloves, and sitting down by the bed.

"Don't come too close," said Alf. "You might catch what I haven't got."

Roy smiled. "You seem in fine fettle to me," he said. "Still, now we're here, we might as well entertain you for a few minutes. There must be some village news to give you."

"Nothing about that village interests me," Alf said grumpily. "Now, if it was Settlefield, I might be curious. Anything from me old stamping ground?"

"Settlefield? There was something, wasn't there, Roy?"

"Ah, yes. I don't suppose you remember her, but old Miss Goodman has passed away. Ethel Goodman, one of the Settlefield branch of the family. I didn't know her, of course, and she was very old. Eighty-two, I believe."

"Eighty-one," said Alf, and then closed his eyes, as if in pain.

"You all right, old chap?" said Roy.

"Bit of a spasm," said Alf. "Better have some kip now. Nice of you to come. Cheerio." And he leaned back on the pillow and gave every sign of drifting into sleep.

Ivy and Roy went as silently as possible out of the ward, and made their way back to reception.

"Soon back?" said the receptionist. "I do hope he wasn't too offensive."

"Not at all," said Ivy firmly. "He just needed a rest. Said he was glad we'd come, so we'll look forward to seeing him back in the village. Good morning."

Elvis was waiting for them, and they were soon on the road to Springfields. After a couple of miles, Ivy turned to look at Roy. "One thing, dearest," she said. "How was Alf so very sure of Ethel Goodman's age? That bears thinking about."

"Yes, funny, that. I noticed it, too, and I think he realised too late that it was an unwise remark. And when he closed his eyes, I'm sure a tear ran down his cheek."

"Here we are, then," said Elvis. "And if I'm not mistaken, that's the vicar's car outside Springfields."

* * *

REV. DOROTHY WAS waiting for them in the lounge, looking anxious. "Good morning, Miss Beasley, Mr. Goodman,"
she said. "Could I have a word?"

"Of course," said Ivy. "Why don't we go up to my room?
Sorry we weren't here when you arrived. We've been visiting
the sick."

"Oh dear! Anyone I should know about?"

"He's coming home tomorrow. Alf Lowe, it was. They
thought he had the nasty flu that's going about, but it was just
a bad cold. He's always had a weak chest, apparently."

"Where does he live?"

"Cemetery Lane. Lives on his own, but keeps the house
decent. Married, but separated. Grumpy, most of the time."

"Right. I'll call. I'm pretty thick-skinned. You have to be in
this job!"

Settled in Ivy's room, with coffee brought in by Katya, who,
on seeing the vicar, crossed herself surreptitiously as she left
them, Ivy opened the conversation.

"Let me guess why you've come," she said. "It's about my
missing cat, Tiddles? Have you spotted him?"

Rev. Dorothy shook her head. "Sorry, no sign, I'm afraid.
No, the reason I'm here is once more the banns question. I
found this on my doormat this morning." She handed Ivy a
piece of paper, folded carelessly.

"My goodness," said Ivy cheerfully, "this is definitely better
grammar than the ones I usually get," she said. "Not much of
a threat, though, is it?"

"What does it say, dearest?" said Roy, who was not smiling.

"It says that if Rev. Dorothy reads our banns tomorrow in
church, she will never read anything again. Ever."

She handed him the paper, and he looked at it closely. "This
sounds like desperation," Roy said. "It is too ridiculous for
words."

"I can see your point," said Rev. Dorothy. "It doesn't specify
how I am to be silenced, does it? Mind you, that doesn't mean
our blackmailer hasn't thought of some way."

"What are you going to do with it?" Roy asked.

"Give it to the police, of course. I'm not in favour of giving way to such threats, but I live alone, as you know, and I shan't feel safe until this whole business is cleared up."

"And the banns?" said Ivy sadly.

Rev. Dorothy frowned. "I'm afraid I am not prepared to take the risk. I am so sorry, but I have already contacted my superior and he has ordered me not to proceed for the moment."

A long silence followed this, and then Roy reached out and took Ivy's hand. "The registry office, beloved? Or shall we run away to Gretna Green?"

Ivy took his hand in both of hers, and said that if anyone asked her, she would say it was her right to be wed in church to the best man in the world, and nobody was going to stop her. A couple more weeks were not long to wait for the rest of her life's happiness.

Rev. Dorothy sniffed hard, and fumbled for her handkerchief. "Bravely said, Ivy. You know I shall do all I can to help, for my own sake as well as yours!"

Forty-seven

INSTEAD OF THEIR usual postprandial snooze, Ivy and Roy retired after lunch to Ivy's room to have a serious discussion about latest developments.

"Should we ask Gus and Deirdre to come down here?" Roy was very anxious about Ivy's apparent refusal to be depressed. But perhaps that one collapse into tears was all she needed to rearm.

"Not yet," she said. "I think you and me need to discuss our next move very carefully. That letter to the vicar was a big mistake on the blackmailer's part. Smacks of desperation, as you said."

Roy nodded reluctantly. "I think so, Ivy, but I really think we should urge Inspector Frobisher to get on with it. They've had long enough, in my opinion. I wake up every morning in trepidation for the next missive."

"Yes, well, me, too. A little bit. But I refuse to be scared off by an idiot who can't write proper."

Roy looked at her curiously.

"Yes, and that's a joke," said Ivy. "I had a very good education at our village school, and can write a letter with the best of them. So we are dealing with a dropout, perhaps slow learner, who has no small opinion of himself, and thinks he is onto a quick profit. But he is not the one pulling the strings. I could swear to that."

"What about Wendy Wright? Do you think she might really be the one?"

"Maybe not. The police don't think so, as we saw. But it won't hurt Frobisher to do a bit more digging there."

"So you haven't ruled her out. Who else, Ivy? If you're not sure she's the one, who is? I hope you're not concealing anything from me!"

"No, I've been thinking some more about the Malchams. I was not sure enough to tell the police about Frank and Beryl, but now we've got this message in a different style. It begins to make some sense. Frank, with earring, working part-time at Maleham's, still living with his mother. She, resentful and perhaps with a grudge against Steven Wright. The pair of them could be in cahoots."

"But why should Beryl be interested in Frank inheriting my money? She would not know there was any possibility of that happening. There's still that missing connection between the Malchams and the Goodman family. Honestly, Ivy, I have a very good mind to do what I threatened and give most of it to the donkeys. We'll keep enough to pay our fees here, and offload the rest. Then we'll sell our story to the local newspaper, so everyone knows, and then we'll be married in church and live happily ever after."

"No need, my dear one," Ivy said softly. "I think we are not far off finding the missing piece in our jigsaw. Let's give Gus and Deirdre a ring now, and ask them to come to tea tomorrow. You are looking much too worried, and a nice snooze now will do you good."

Roy sighed deeply. " 'What dreams may come when we have shuffled off into a nice snooze?' " he misquoted.

"Off you go, now," said Ivy, "and I'll give Deirdre a ring. Then I shall stretch out and count ducks."

"Not sheep?" said Roy, picking up his stick.

"Stupid animals," Ivy said. "Some of them go round twice."

* * *

"HAS IVY CALLED you, Gus?" Deirdre was sitting on a
kitchen stool with a glass of red wine to hand. She had phoned
him as soon as Ivy had finished speaking, but had had no reply.
Next she tried his mobile, and he answered.

"Where are you, anyway?" she continued.

"Out to lunch," said Gus. "And yes, if, as you say, Ivy
sounded even more stern than usual, then something's up. Did
she suggest any more than asking us to tea tomorrow?"

"No. Just said it could be important, but not immediately
urgent."

"Right. So tomorrow it is. Are we going to church in the
morning to hear the second time of reading the banns?"

"Oh no, that was something else she said. There's been
another hitch, apparently, so we are not to break the habit of a
lifetime and go to church for no special reason. Her words,
Gus. There's life in the old thing yet."

"Right. So, any news about Tiddles? Perhaps she has had a
lead on that particular mystery?"

"Tiddles wasn't mentioned," she said, laughing. "I personally think the cat's shut in somewhere nearby, and the blackmailer knows it's missing and is making capital out of it. Ivy
has planned to alert the whole village, and has already phoned
James at the shop. He called Theo at the Hall, and asked him
to look in the stables, where his lost cat was found a while ago.
And he phoned me."

"Right-o. So what are you doing this evening? May I call
around suppertime?"

"Why not?" said Deirdre, and signed off.

Gus turned to look at Miriam, who was just coming in from
the kitchen bearing a steaming jam sponge pudding. She
banged it down on the table, and said that she had a good mind
to tip it over his head. "What a cheek, Gus Halfhide!" she said.
"Eating my delicious lunch, which I slaved over for hours, and
at the same time making a secret date to have supper with that
woman up at Tony Wings, whoever he is. And that on top of
coming in at least two hours late!"

"*Tawny* Wings is the name of the house, Miriam. And I
know I shall be lucky to get fried egg and beans, so there is no

need for you to worry. We have Enquire Within business to discuss. And I'm sorry about being late. Blame Whippy. She got lost in the woods, and I'm worried about her being abducted, like Tiddles."

"Oh well," said Miriam. "I suppose I have to believe you. Do you want some of this pudding, or are you leaving room for egg and beans?"

SUSPECTING THAT GUS had been lunching with Miriam Blake, Deirdre decided to take a ready meal from the freezer. They were expensive, but delicious, and she was tempted to claim she had made it herself. An innocent enough lie. One of her own small list of culinary achievements was bread and butter pudding, and she set about making a substantial version, with cream and lots of sugar and sultanas. She would insist on Gus having two helpings, and that would teach him to exploit two women friends at once.

When he finally arrived and knocked at her manorial front door, she was so struck by his humble expression that she relented and asked him to come in and be cheered up with a whisky and ginger ale to keep out the cold. Not that it was cold in her large drawing room, where she had a leaping log fire as well as efficient central heating. She sat him down in a comfortable chair, and after pouring the whisky, she opened the subject of Ivy's tears. For a moment, she thought he was going to weep, too.

But spies don't weep, and he merely said he felt absolutely terrible. His father had been very strict about making little girls cry, right from when he was at nursery school. "No gentleman, however small, would even consider it," the old boy had said.

"Well, if it is any comfort to you, she sounded fine. Quite her old self, and very firm about our tea party tomorrow afternoon."

"Do you think she has anything new to tell us?"

"Oh yes. That's the way she works. Very painstaking about getting it right before involving us. They went to see Alf Lowe in hospital, you know. I think it's something to do with him. You never got to see him, did you?"

"No, he'd gone by the time I got up there. I shall go again on Monday, if he's home."

"Coming home tomorrow, apparently. It was only a cold, and they're sending an ancillary nurse to make sure he's comfortably settled. He shouldn't be living on his own in this weather, really. But he refuses all help, silly old fool."

When they had finished supper, they sat by the fire chatting amiably.

"This case has been very puzzling," said Gus, "and I get the feeling Ivy and Roy are handling it mostly by themselves. I suppose that's natural, since it is their proposed nuptials that are at the root of it."

"And one victim dead already. If those threats are really serious, then the killer may strike again. Or am I being over-dramatic?"

"No, not at all. They're serious, all right. But Ivy's safety depends on how long they are prepared to wait for the wedding to be called off permanently. Or, for her to snuff it from natural or other causes, like fear and worry. I doubt if she's cried real tears since she was a child."

"What about Tiddles?" Deirdre threw another log on the fire, and wriggled back into her deep armchair.

"Tiddles is at greater risk. But we shall find out more tomorrow."

Deirdre yawned. "Gosh, I'm tired," she said. "Early bed tonight, I think."

"Like some company?" Gus asked quietly.

"Why not?" answered Deirdre.

Forty-eight

ROY AND IVY went to the early-morning communion service in church, to avoid a barrage of sympathy from well-meaning churchgoers. As a result, they were back at Springfields and first in for breakfast.

"I've been thinking," said Ivy. "What difference is it going to make, our being married? Apart from sharing a bed, that is. I mean, we're a bit old for passion, aren't we?" She whispered the last words, and in truth it had taken a lot of courage for her to even mention such things.

Roy grinned. "Never too old for a bit of rumpy-pumpy under the duvet," he said. "Trust me, Ivy. I'm a good teacher."

"Is it true, then, Roy, that you were a bit of a lad in your youth?"

Roy frowned. "Where is this leading, beloved? Not over to Settlefield and the late lamented Ethel Goodman, I hope?"

"Possibly," said Ivy. "After all, it is difficult to forget entirely that Alf Lowe accused you of getting a girl in the family way, and then deserting her."

"Huh! He could talk! Known for it, he was. But are you

thinking Ethel might have been that girl? There was never any talk of her being up the duff, as far as I remember."

"If by that you mean being pregnant, yes, I am thinking of that. And you might not have heard anything because of that silly feud between the two families."

"True," said Roy. "But nothing much is secret in villages, and I do, or rather did, have one or two friends in Settlefield who would have mentioned it, I'm sure. No, I think you're barking up the wrong tree there. I think Alf Lowe was just being malicious. He can't help it."

"Well, he should be home today, so I think it would be a Christian act to call and make sure he's all right."

"Whatever you say, dearest. Your wish is my command."

"Nonsense! And when we're married, I am going to do whatever *you* wish."

"Not to mention a spot of the other," said Roy.

THOUSANDS OF MILES away, Wendy Wright was sunning herself in her friend's garden. The telephone rang, and after a minute there was a shout to say the call was for her.

"It's for you, Wendy. Some man called Frobisher. I think he said he was a policeman. What have you been up to?"

Wendy went indoors and was away for five minutes or so. When she returned, her friend could see she was upset.

"It was the police from Thornwell," she said. "They want to ask me some more questions, and although they didn't actually ask me to return to answer them, I could guess that's what they really want. So, as they said there was no immediate hurry, I agreed to return in a few days. I've been meaning to go back, anyway. You've been so kind, and I'm feeling a lot stronger."

"Is it about Steven's death? Have they got any new clues?"

"He didn't say. I think they're still a bit mystified as to how the poison got into him. But just lately I've remembered him being sick after we'd been out to dinner. It was very violent. He was sure something in the dinner poisoned him. Maybe there was some lingering after that. Or it could've been something else that actually killed him."

"Or somebody," said the friend.

"Yeah, but isn't it more likely that Steven stayed late, working after everyone had gone, like he often did, and got into that bed because he was feeling rotten—maybe faint and sick—not knowing that he was going to die as a result?"

"Goodness knows," said her friend. "You should not try to work it out. Leave it to the police; else you'll undo all the good we've done while you've been here."

AFTER ROY'S CONVERSATION with Ivy at breakfast time, he had been thinking hard, trying to remember his early days, when his Settlefield friends had often come over to Barrington for young farmers' meetings, or just a drink in the pub. His sister had been engaged for a while, to one of them, but had then married one of the Wright family, and produced Steven. He'd been an only child, and had no doubt been spoilt with too much cosseting. Not strong as a small boy, he had never joined in much with the farming community, preferring to play at home with his fond mother.

Roy's sister was, of course, a Goodman of the Barrington branch and had married "out" by choosing a stranger for her husband. She'd disapproved of Roy and his early laddish ways, but towards the end of her life, they had been close, often having nostalgic conversations on the telephone. When she died, he had felt sad, as if some part of him had been amputated. He had nursed hopes of Steven, and had been a generous uncle. But Steven was not an easy person to like, and had not, in Roy's view, improved with maturity.

Now, stretched out on his bed after a good lunch and not feeling in the least sleepy, Roy wished he could talk to her and see what she remembered of Alf Lowe. The Lowes were smallholders near Settlefield, and did not mix with the richer farming set, who looked down their noses at anyone with the odd few acres. But she might have been able to see some possible connection between him and the Malehams, though for the life of him, he could not think what it might be.

He looked at his watch. Time to go down for the tea party. It was a lovely day, and when he went to find Ivy, the sun streamed in through the lounge windows. She was sitting in their usual corner, and Gus had already arrived.

"Deirdre might be a few minutes late," said Ivy. "She called and said she had an unexpected visitor."

"Let's hope he or she was not clutching a piece of white paper with red capitals," said Ivy sharply. "We've had quite enough of that nonsense."

On cue, Deirdre appeared at the lounge door and waved at them.

"Looks cheerful enough," muttered Ivy to Roy, who nodded and with difficulty got to his feet.

"Sit down, Roy dear," said Deirdre. "Though it is really nice to see gentlemanly manners occasionally." She looked pointedly at Gus, who shot to his feet.

"Please take my seat, Mrs. Bloxham," he said with exaggerated politeness.

"Okay, okay. Sorry I'm late, Ivy, but I had a stranger at my door, trying to get in to talk to me. Foot in the door. The usual thing. But my Bert taught me a way of dealing with that. We keep a heavy hammer handy, and one blow from that on the intruding foot works wonders."

"But he left you a piece of paper?" guessed Ivy.

Deirdre nodded, and handed a crumpled message, now familiar to the others, across the table to Ivy.

"Oh, really, this is ridiculous," she said, and put the paper down in the centre of the table so all could read it.

TO IVY BEASLEY, YOU HAVE BEEN SENSSIBLE SO FAR. NOW BRAKE IT OFF, OR YORE TOMCAT MEATS HIS WATERRY END.

"Spelling gets worse, but that sounds nasty," said Gus. "I presume the oaf who brought it cleared off quickly?"

"Hobbled away, more likely," said Deirdre cheerfully. "And he didn't have an earring. Not today, anyway. It was quite difficult to see his face, as he was obviously growing a beard. Not much more than black stubble, but looked very odd with the bald head. And definitely no earring. I looked specially."

"Well-done, Dee-Dee." Gus looked at her admiringly. "You are a brave lass. So what do we think about this one, Ivy?"

"I say again what I've thought about all of them. We ignore them, and carry on as usual. O' course, the minute the police got involved, things changed. I'm not saying they shouldn't be, but now there isn't a soul in a twenty-mile radius who doesn't know Mr. Goodman and Miss Beasley are having trouble getting wed."

"Then if you don't mind, Ivy, may I take charge of this latest message? I'll take it to the police station tomorrow." Gus picked up the paper and folded it carefully before tucking it into his jacket pocket.

"I'm so sorry about Tiddles," Deirdre said, anxious to avoid another tearful exit from Ivy. But she needn't have worried. Ivy said that if anyone asked her, she would say that Tiddles was capable of taking care of himself, and would reappear. She felt it in her bones.

Katya appeared, bearing a tray of scones, with jam and cream, and a luscious-looking fruitcake. "Now, Miss Beasley, will you pour the tea, or would you like me to do it?"

"I'd really like Mrs. Bloxham to be mother," said Ivy sweetly. "She's been a good girl today, so we'll give her pride of place."

Deirdre thought to herself that if pouring tea was the reward, then there was little incentive in being brave. But then she felt her eyes smarting with a salty tear as Ivy smiled at her. "Thanks, Ivy," she said. "Tea with milk, everybody?"

"THAT'S A NASTY bruise, Frank," said Beryl. "How on earth did you get that?"

"Caught my foot in a pothole on the pavement outside Tesco's. You got any of that bruise cream, Mother?"

"Upstairs in the medicine cabinet," she said. "It's a bit old. We haven't needed it since Dad stopped throwing himself about and tripping up on everything. Should be all right, though. And while you're up there, for goodness' sake have a shave. You look like them dropouts in the church porch in the market square."

Forty-nine

GUS AROSE EARLY, and set out with Whippy for her morning walk. It was another sunny day, though there was a sharp little wind. He had put on the Fair Isle knitted dog coat that Ivy had made for her, and they kept up a good pace along Hangman's Lane until they came to the entrance to the woods.

"Just as well dogs don't need wellies, Whippy," Gus said, as they pushed through dripping undergrowth. "Must have rained in the night."

"Talking to yourself, Gus?"

He looked round swiftly, hoping not to see a beefy character with an earring. But it was his landlord, the Honourable Theodore Roussel, holding a large black Labrador on a lead, and smiling benevolently at his tenant.

Gus laughed with relief. "Last person you talk to before the men in white coats arrive, I'm told," he said.

"Not as bad as that, I hope? Shall we let them off their leads? Less chance of a fight that way."

They duly unhooked the dogs, and walked on, chatting amiably. Each knew the other enjoyed Deirdre's favours, but jealousy had evolved into a wary tolerance, most of the time. Finally, Theo said he would be turning back, and Gus turned, too.

"How's the enquiry agency going? Caught any murderers lately?" Theo laughed as though he'd never heard anything so ridiculous.

"On the way to catching one, I think," said Gus. "There is one thing puzzling us at the moment, and you might be able to help."

"Fire away. Only too pleased."

"Well, you probably know Maleham's Furniture Store in Thornwell?"

"Not really," answered Theo, frowning. "All gimcrack rubbish, I believe."

"Possibly," said Gus. "But it is an old family firm, and I wondered if you had come across any of them in the past? Frank Maleham, particularly?"

"Sorry; no help, I'm afraid. Any other way I can assist?"

"Lowe, then. Alf Lowe? I believe his father was a game-keeper for you at one time?"

"Oh, heavens, yes. Dreadful fellow. Had to get rid of him in the end. Not Alf, of course. His father. But I do remember hearing that Alf was a great one for the girls when young! He was a good-looking lad, I believe, and played the field. One of his girlfriends was a relative of your colleague, Roy Goodman. Quite a scandal at the time, so I was told. Of course, things were different in those days. Pregnant girls without husbands were treated cruelly, and sent away, just as if they had committed a serious crime instead of a moment of unbridled passion, what?"

They had arrived back outside Gus's cottage, and Theo strode off chuckling.

Gus fed Whippy and topped up her water bowl. "Here I come, Alf," he said aloud, "Time to tell all. Now, back soon, little dog," he added, and stroked her velvety head.

AS HE APPROACHED Alf's cottage, he was pleased to see a light in his window, and smoke curling up from the chimney. He knocked, and shouted through the keyhole, "Alf? It's Gus Halfhide. Don't get up. I'll let myself in."

No reply. But then he heard a key scraping, and a voice shouted, "Yer silly bugger, it's locked!"

Gus waited, and then the door opened a crack. "Whatcha want?"

"To see how you are and if you need anything. Or just a chat, if you feel like it."

"Best come in, then." The door opened another six inches.

Gus squeezed in and shut the door behind him. "Now, you sit down by the fire, Alf," he said. "I hope you didn't have to light it yourself?" He could see a full log basket and a scuttle of coal by Alf's chair.

"No," said Alf, and then he cackled. "A pretty young lady came in and helped me get dressed, and then she did the fire and made me some breakfast. How's that for aftercare service?"

"Very good," said Gus. "Let's hope they keep it up. So, did they treat you well in hospital? Plenty of visitors?"

"Nobody except them two from Springfields. The never-to-be-wed Ivy Beasley and Roy Goodman. I suppose it was quite nice of them to bother. But I got the feeling they just wanted to pump me for information. Anyway, they didn't stay long."

Because you made sure they didn't, thought Gus. He wondered how Alf knew about the banns problem, but on second thought realised that the whole village knew. No doubt about that.

"So what've you been up to with the widow Bloxham?" Alf said, with a knowing wink.

"She is a colleague and friend," Gus replied. "We meet regularly on business."

"And funny business, too, eh?" Alf laughed at his own wit, and said that if Gus had nothing to do, would he like to make them both a cup of coffee? "The things are in the kitchen, which is cleaner than it's ever been."

"The pretty young carer?"

"Got it in one, Gus. Anyway, I'm glad you come. I was beginning to get a bit fed up with my own company."

Gus made the coffee, and sat down opposite Alf. "What shall we talk about?" he said, pleased that Alf seemed to be warm and relaxed.

"How's about you telling me about poor old Ivy and Roy? It's only what's to be expected, really. Ridiculous, getting married at their age. And him rich as Croesus! You'd think he'd want to hang on to his money, instead of hitching himself up to a grasping spinster." He looked at Gus as if weighing up some serious problem.

"Well, you may be right. But Roy has nobody else to leave his money to. And in any case, you can be sure he is in regular touch with his lawyer. He'll have his will sewn up nice and tight."

"Don't you believe it!" said Alf. "Them Goodmans wouldn't spend a penny on solicitors, not if they was forced at gunpoint!"

Gus pounced. "They say Ethel Goodman, the old unmarried lady who's just died, was sitting on a fortune."

"Not likely!" said Alf. "She was cut out of her parents' will when she was a girl. Poor old thing. Just enough to pay the old folks' home, and even then she was subsidised by the state."

"Cut out of their will? Why on earth did they do that?"

"Oh, I forget now," Alf said, yawning loudly. "Good gawd, Gus, I ain't done nothing today, and I'm tired out. You'd better go now, and I'll have a bit of a nap. Come again when you want. And lock the door behind you, then shove the key back through the letter box."

As Gus walked back down Cemetery Lane to Springfields, he considered Alf's reaction to his question about Ethel Goodman. It was as clear as if he had kicked him physically out of the cottage. Alf was not prepared to talk about Ethel's disgrace, and now Gus knew why.

ROY AND IVY, blissfully unaware that they were being insulted by Alf Lowe, sat companionably in Ivy's room, playing cribbage. Roy claimed that it helped him to think clearly, in spite of the fact that Ivy won nine times out of ten.

Katya tapped at their door, and said that Mr. Halfhide was below, and should she send him up?

"Gus? Yes, of course, ask him to come up, and bring us some coffee and cookies, if you have time, dear," said Ivy.

"We didn't expect you this morning, Augustus," said Ivy, as he came in looking pleased with himself.

"Just passing, Ivy," he said. "I've been to see Alf Lowe, and I thought you'd like to know how I fared with the old devil."

"Sent you packing, did he?" said Roy, smiling.

"No, quite the contrary. He asked me in, and we had coffee together. He looked pale, but he's being well looked after by his carer. I think you might see him resident here before long," he added.

"That's neither here nor there," said Ivy briskly. "What progress did you make?"

"Right. One, Alf says that you, Roy, are as rich as Croesus. Two, he disapproves of old people getting married. Three, he shut up like a clam when I asked him about Ethel Goodman's disgrace. But before that he had said she hadn't a penny to her name and her parents had cut her out of their will."

All three sat silently digesting this. Then Gus said, "There's more. I met the squire, and we had a chat. Got onto the subject of Alf Lowe and his colourful past. Theo remembered one of the lads getting a Goodman girl into trouble, and her being sent away in disgrace. We agreed that morals were much stricter in those days."

Then Ivy frowned, cleared her throat, and asked Roy if he knew whether there had been an illegitimate baby in all this. "Not getting at you, beloved. Just wondered if there had been talk of such a thing. Sounds likely that it was Ethel, poor Ethel, remember, who was sent off for a good while under a cloud. And maybe returned, tolerated but not forgiven?"

Roy shook his head. "That's women's talk, I'm afraid, Ivy. And sadly there are no women of that generation to ask. I suppose the young Josslands might have heard the old folks gossiping. Just don't know, Ivy. Oh, and by the way, Gus, I'd like to know where the totally false rumour that I am a millionaire came from. It is beginning to irritate me."

Ivy put out a hand to take Roy's. "Don't fret, dearest," she said. "I would love you, and marry you, if you hadn't two ha'pennies to rub together."

Fifty

"SODDING CAT ESCAPED," said Frank. "Got out when I was feeding it."

"Your fault," said Beryl. "An old rabbit hutch is no place for a cat. I don't know why you brought it home, anyway. Nasty old stray tomcat. It scratched my hand when I tried to make a fuss of it. If you really want a cat, I'll get you a nice tabby."

"You'd think it'd be grateful, being rescued, wouldn't you?" said Frank. "Anyway, don't bother, thanks. I've had enough of cats already. Are you going up the store this afternoon? I got the day off, and thought I'd go and have a ride round the villages."

"Not in my car, you aren't! That dent on the wing is a real mess. Go on your bike, if it's still roadworthy. And yes, I am going to the store, so I'll need the car myself. Why don't you go into Oakbridge on the train?"

"That'd make a nice change, wouldn't it?" said Frank, with heavy irony. "No, I'll come in with you. There's always something to do. Uncle Malcham might give me a cup of tea, and I don't think he'd mind."

"Old skinflint! He wouldn't give you the time of day. Still, you can help your mates in the warehouse."

"And don't say it, Mother! I know what you're thinking. 'Get yourself a nice girl and have a family of your own; then you wouldn't have so much time on your hands being idle.' Well, chance would be a fine thing. All the girls I could get interested in are fixed up already. You'll just have to put up with me for a bit longer."

ELVIS THE TAXI driver had a difficult assignment this afternoon. Ivy Beasley had phoned him earlier, and said in a whisper he could hardly hear that she would like him to collect her and take her into Thornwell. She wanted to buy a secret birthday present for Roy's birthday in two weeks' time. What with the anonymous threats and trouble with the banns, she had completely forgotten.

She had told Roy that she had an appointment with the dentist. As he had arranged to join a whist game in the lounge, he was finally persuaded to let her go on her own, but with Elvis keeping an eye on her and bringing her safely back to Springfields.

When Elvis arrived to pick her up, to his surprise she asked him to go straight to Maleham's Furniture Store.

"But what about the birthday present, Miss Beasley?" he said.

"I haven't forgotten," said Ivy, "and we can do that as well. Sorry, Elvis, but it is necessary, believe me. I need to have a look at something in the bedding department. I might even buy the present there, and then I can make an appointment with a dentist, so my lie is only a small one. Do you know of a reliable dentist in Thornwell?"

"Never use them myself," said Elvis proudly. "My mum was a devil about sweets and sticky drinks when we were little. Result: good teeth! My sister's the same, though she has them whitened every so often. But I know there's one spoken highly of in the middle of town. Would that do?"

Ivy nodded, and said she would appreciate it if Elvis could keep her secret.

"I'm not too happy about it, Miss Beasley," he said. "I don't like deceiving Mr. Goodman. He's always been so kind to me. Are you sure this is a good idea?"

"Perfectly sure, young man," Ivy said sharply. "Sometimes white lies are a good thing. Now, off we go. First stop, the furniture store."

BERYL MALEHAM DECIDED to vary her usual programme of wandering around the store on the ground floor, and then ending up in the beds department upstairs. Today she dropped Frank off at the warehouse double doors and parked her car at the back of the building as usual. Then she made her way round to the front of the store and ascended to the beds, planning to work her way down and have a cup of tea in the little café newly installed by the front entrance.

As she pottered round, admiring new designs, she wondered if she had been too harsh on the boss, her Maleham cousin. He never complained about her frequent visits. But then, looking at it another way, wasn't her respectable presence a much better thing than a department with not a single customer in sight?

When she reached the upper floor, she drifted round happily, and finally settled herself in a jazzily upholstered armchair. The price of it astonished her, and she decided it would be last thing she would want in her bedroom. But it was so comfortable that in spite of her best efforts to stay awake, her eyelids began to close.

"Well, if it isn't Beryl!" said a familiar voice. Beryl looked round guiltily, and saw Miss Beasley beaming at her.

"Hello, Ivy!" she said. "Fancy seeing you again." She laughed and said it was a nice coincidence, and was she now Mrs. Goodman?

"We're nearly there," said Ivy. "One or two minor hitches, but you know what it is like, getting married in church. So many rules and regulations. Were you married in Thornwell?"

"Yep, but it was a registry office for us. A bit of a shotgun wedding, you might say."

"Ah, so that's when Frank came along. You'd not be without him, now, would you?"

"Well, there's a lot more to it than that. But let's not talk about the past. Are you still planning on a May wedding?"

"Oh yes," said Ivy. "But there'll be no patter of tiny feet for

me! I don't regret it, Beryl. When I look at children today, so
badly behaved and out of control, I don't regret it one bit. No
wonder they grow up into hooligans!"

Beryl stood up from her comfortable seat, and said why
didn't they get the lift down, and have a cup of tea together in
the new café? "It does a good tea, and we can treat ourselves
to a slice of window cake. What d'you say, Ivy?"

"A cup of tea would very nice," Ivy said, though she was
not sure about this development. She had promised to wait for
Elvis by the beds, while he went to the toilet on the ground
floor. It was quite possible that he would be going up the stairs,
while she was going down in the lift to the café. On the other
hand, if she mentioned waiting for Elvis, Beryl might change
her mind and leave.

"Right, Ivy, let's go and treat ourselves," Beryl said, taking
charge. But Ivy hesitated, and as a result she was finally inside
the lift and the doors closed before Beryl could join her.

As she turned to press the button to open the doors again,
she saw that she had company.

"Afternoon, Miss Beasley," said Frank Maleham. "What a
pleasant surprise."

Fifty-one

ELVIS CAME OUT of the men's toilet and headed for the lift. He had been bursting; otherwise he would never have agreed to leave Miss Beasley. She had promised to stay in the beds department until he joined her, and he hastily pressed the lift button to go up one floor. To his irritation, he saw it was stuck on the basement level, and he pressed again, several times. Quicker by the stairs, he decided, and ran up two at a time.

Miss Beasley was nowhere to be seen, and he panicked.

"Have you seen an elderly woman wandering round up here?" he asked a nearby customer. She shook her head. "Sorry, mister. No elderly women, unless you count me, and I don't think you're looking for me, are you?"

Elvis ignored her laughter, and quickly returned to the ground floor. He pushed his way through shoppers, but could see no signs of Miss Beasley. Perhaps she was stuck in the lift again? But why would she be in it at all? She had given her word that she would stay in the beds department.

He crossed to the lift, which now opened in front of him. A man and woman, with an awkward pushchair, emerged, but no Miss Beasley.

"Have you come up from the basement?" he asked them. They looked mystified and said that as far as they knew, it was only a storeroom down there. "Sorry, mate," the man said, and they walked away.

Only one thing to do, Elvis decided. He rushed into the lift as the doors were closing, and pressed the button for the basement. But someone on the ground floor had summoned the lift before he got in.

Finally, by blocking the entrance to the lift on the ground floor, in spite of customer protestations, he pressed the basement button and emerged into what was, as the man had said, a large storeroom in total darkness. He fumbled around for a light switch, calling all the time for Miss Beasley. At last he found the switch, and the room was flooded with light. But there was no answering call from Ivy. There was nobody to be seen or heard, and he took the lift back up to the ground floor.

Perhaps she had gone outside to look for him in the car park? He ran around at top speed, anxiety mounting. Back to the store, then. He waited for a car to pass in front of him, and as it went slowly out into the road, he saw Ivy, sitting in the passenger seat and waving frantically.

THE POLICE WERE kind and helpful, and asked Elvis whether he had taken note of the number plate, the colour of the car, or the make. He had not registered the number or letters; nor could he be sure of the colour or make. He thought it was black, or possibly blue, and it could have been a Ford or a Toyota. Hatchback? He wasn't sure, but thought not. All he could really remember was that it was Miss Beasley in the passenger seat, and she was being driven away from him. And yes, he thought the old lady had a mobile phone.

Having thought carefully and given a more detailed description, and been assured that they would do all they could to intercept the car, he then had the terrible task of telling Roy what had happened. First, he must inform Mrs. Spurling, and then perhaps she would agree to tell Roy. He had a sudden urge to get into his taxi and drive away, miles and miles away, and never return. But of course he could not do that. Ivy and Roy were his friends, and he must not desert them.

Mrs. Spurling was surprisingly calm. "Probably had a senior moment and asked the stranger to bring her back to Springfields. Since you had not kept your word never to let her out of your sight, she must have decided she had to make her own way home. Need I say, Elvis whatever-your-name-is, that I shall recommend never using your taxi again!"

"Can I speak to Roy Goodman, please?" said Elvis, his voice unsteady.

"Certainly not," Mrs. Spurling said. "I shall wait half an hour to see if she turns up, and then break the news myself. Good-bye."

"THIS IS NOT the way to Barrington," said Ivy, frowning at Frank, who sat at the wheel of his mother's car, keeping his speed down to thirty miles an hour. He needed time to soften up this old biddy, and tell her exactly what would happen to her if she didn't do what she was told.

"We're going the pretty way," he said. "I got things to tell you. What you're going to do, an' that."

"I know perfectly well what I'm going to do," said Ivy sharply, fishing in her capacious handbag. "I am going to phone Springfields and tell them to alert the police. And if you lay your hands on me, it'll be the worse for you."

Frank gave a yelp of laughter. "Got yer black belt, Miss Beasley? Wow, I'm really scared. An' give me that!" he added, snatching her mobile and putting it in his pocket. "They'll know soon enough that you're missing. But not for long, you silly old bat. I don't want a stupid woman on my hands. Just agree to what I say, an' I'll drop you off in Cemetery Lane in Barrington. If you don't, o' course, you might end up in the cemetery underground!"

"You don't frighten me, Frank Maleham. What is your mother going to say, when she finds her car's been stolen? She'll report it to the police straight away, and it won't take them long to put two and two together and start looking. Not one of the brightest, are you?"

"How d'you know I'm Frank Maleham and this car is my mother's? I could be anybody, on the lookout for a car to borrow." He blustered, but Ivy knew that she had shaken him off his perch, if only temporarily.

"Better listen for the siren, Frank," she said. "And the flashing blue light. You know what the police are like. Any excuse to play cops and robbers, and they'll be racing through town on our trail."

Frank quickened up, until the car was doing seventy miles an hour on the narrow lane leading eventually to Barrington. He planned to find a suitably remote place to stop and have a go at frightening Miss Beasley into submission. Then, after that, he would find the way back to Barrington and drop her off before getting back to Thornwell. With any luck, his mother would still be in the store. She usually stayed until closing time, and he could park her car without her knowing it had been for a run.

As they sped along, with Ivy holding on tightly to her seat, he worked out what he would say if they were caught. Ivy was old; that was obvious. He would say he had found her wandering in the car park, lost and frightened. The only thing he could get out of her was her address: Springfields, Barrington village. So he had borrowed his mother's car to take her back. A charitable act, that's all, Officer, he would say, and he congratulated himself on the perfect get-out.

They stopped in a field entrance, where the grass was long, indicating that farm traffic was unlikely.

"Now, Miss Beasley, you just listen to me."

Ivy said nothing. She would not look at him, but stared fixedly out of the window.

"That wedding you're planning to old Roy Goodman. It won't do. I got very good reasons why it won't do, but you don't need to know them. But I got orders to stop it. My orders come from a very ruthless source, an' if you don't agree to stop it, he'll make sure the happy couple are down to one unhappy old fool. Or, it could be one unhappy old spinster. Need I say more?"

To his extreme irritation, Ivy turned to look at him, began to smile and then laughed loudly, holding on to her hat in case it should slip. "Frank Maleham," she began, still spluttering, "you have been watching much too much television. You've made several mistakes in this heist—is that the word?—starting with taking a car by now known to the police. And there are other foolish things you've done. We might as well agree to cook up a story explaining what happened, and go straight back to Springfields. If you accept that, I shall say nothing about your attempt at abduction."

"What other mistakes?" said Frank. Things were not going according to plan, not at all.

"Well, you've forgotten Elvis, my taxi driver. He will have the police searching high and low for me. He knows all about your threatening letters, and they'll give their search the highest priority."

Frank said nothing, but his face was pale and sweaty. Ivy chose her moment, and said, "So shall we do a deal? You give up your blackmail and leave Roy and me to a few years' happiness, or I tell the police—is that a siren?—what really happened this afternoon. What do you say? Do we settle for saying you were taking a confused old lady back home, and no questions asked?"

MRS. SPURLING LOOKED at her watch. Twenty-five minutes had gone by since Elvis's call. So, in five minutes, she had to find Roy and tell him that his fiancée was missing. How could she possibly do this without the poor old fellow keeling over with a heart attack? She sat in her office in front of her computer, her head in her hands, thinking desperately of a solution to a problem that, in all her years of caring for old people, she had never had to face.

"Yoo-hoo! Are you all right, Mrs. Spurling?"

She looked up and saw Deirdre Bloxham peering in at her door. "Oh yes, quite all right, thank you. Just resting my eyes for a couple of minutes. Have you come to see Mr. Goodman? He's playing in a whist four at the moment."

"I'll wait," Deirdre said cheerfully. "Shall I go up and see if Ivy's in her room?"

Mrs. Spurling blinked rapidly and said, "She went into town in Elvis's taxi, but should be back shortly. Shall we give her half an hour or so? I'll take you into the lounge. Mr. Goodman might have finished his game by now. Come along, Mrs. Bloxham. I am sure he'll be pleased to see you."

Fifty-two

AS FRANK AND Ivy drew up outside Springfields, a siren was heard screaming through the village. A police car drew up behind them, and two policemen emerged, running. Then they conferred, and approached the Maleham car.

Mrs. Spurling was by now out of Springfields and on her way to the car. She reached it just as Ivy descended carefully onto the pavement. "Thank you very much, Mr. Maleham," she heard her say. "Very kind of you to rescue me. Will you come in for a cup of tea?"

The burly man, who had got out at the police request, turned his head, and Mrs. Spurling caught the sunlight flash on the single gold earring.

"Miss Beasley!" she shouted. "Thank God you're safe! Come along in, my dear."

One of the policemen stepped forward. "We'll need to ask a few questions, sir," he said, taking Frank's arm. Perhaps you could find us a private room, madam." They trooped in, and Mrs. Spurling ushered them into the chilly conference room.

Frank followed meekly, and sat down next to Ivy.

"Now, just for the record, Miss Beasley, will you give us a detailed account of what happened, from the time you left Maleham's Furniture Store?"

According to Ivy, Frank Maleham was the hero of the hour. He had taken pity on her, lost and confused in the car park, and when she asked him to take her back to Springfields, he had readily agreed. His mother's car was in the car park, and he had the key in his pocket. Rather than leave Ivy to get lost again, he had decided to take her immediately back home.

"My mum usually stays all afternoon in the store," he interposed.

"How did you come to have her car key in your pocket?" asked one of the policemen.

Frank looked at the clock on the wall. With luck, this could be wrapped up in ten minutes, and then he'd be home for the football on telly.

"Mum always gives it to me to hold on to," he explained. "She's forever losing it, else."

Mrs. Spurling had turned on the electric fire, but even before it had warmed the room, the police were satisfied that there had been no evil intent in Maleham's offer to give a lift to Miss Beasley, and they departed, not forgetting to congratulate Frank on his good citizen act.

"Well, dearest," said Roy, when they were settled in Ivy's room for a peaceful hour or so. "You certainly had an adventure! But what were you doing at Maleham's? I thought you were at the dentist's? I shall speak sternly to Elvis when we next see him."

"Not really his fault," she said. "I assumed he had forgotten where he had to meet me, and we somehow missed each other. No need to upset him, beloved. After all, he is our friend, and we'd be lost without him." She avoided answering his dentist question.

As they both drifted into a doze, Roy dreamt of roast pheasant for supper, and Ivy went once more over the point at which Frank Maleham had grabbed her from the lift in the basement and manhandled her out of a side door into the car park and his mother's car. Before sleep took her into a well-deserved rest, she trusted that Beryl had not wanted to leave the store before Frank returned.

* * *

WHEN FRANK GOT back to Thornwell, he parked the car exactly where it had been before, and made his way into the warehouse. Here there was some curiosity about his temporary absence, but he settled down with his mates with an uncomfortable feeling of a job only half-done. He had been taking a large box to the bedroom department when he had spotted his mother with Miss Beasley. He had made sure they hadn't seen him, and, thinking quickly, he had come up with a plan that needed only patience to carry out. His ruse was to stand by the basement lift doors with his finger on the down button, and after several false attempts, his quarry had arrived on her own, looking confused. If his mother had been with her, then he had an alternative plan ready, but it was not needed.

He had put out the lights to scare her into submission, and this had worked. But only for a short while. Then the old bird had rallied, and outwitted him with ease. He had nothing to show for their excursion, except a negative result. Ivy Beasley now had the upper hand, and unless he could think of a way of reversing the situation, next Sunday the banns would be called and the two lovers would have only one more hurdle to jump. As he remembered that banns have to have a third time of asking, he cheered up a little. There was still enough time to find a way.

Closing time came, and he wandered out into the car park to see whether his mother had left already. If she had, it was bus queues and a long walk uphill to their house. There was no sign of her car, and so he trudged off to find the bus stop. Finally, after going over the afternoon's events yet again, he half smiled, realising he had never for one minute worried about the possibility that Miss Beasley would break her word to keep silent.

BERYL, ARRIVING HOME, glanced at the petrol gauge on the dashboard. It registered empty, with a little light warning her that she was almost out of fuel. She frowned. She had owned this car for so long that she knew exactly when she had to fill up, and she could have sworn there should be a little more petrol than was showing. She shrugged. Tomorrow she had to go to Oakbridge to see a friend. She was not sure she would make it to the filling station on the corner. Indoors, with a cup of tea, she made a note to remember.

"Hello, Frank," she said, as he came wearily through the door. "Did you stay late? Sorry I couldn't wait for you. It gets dark so early now, and I hate driving under streetlights. Oh, and by the way," she added, remembering the petrol, "you didn't take my car out while I was in the store, did you?"

"O' course not, Mother. What should I do that for? Don't you start getting all suspicious and checking up on me; else I shall have to find other accommodation!"

"That could be no bad thing," muttered Beryl, as she poured him a cup of stewed tea.

"I heard that," he said. "And this tea is disgusting. Put the kettle on and make me a fresh cup."

"Don't you issue orders to me, Frank Maleham!" Beryl shouted at him from the kitchen. If he was spelling for a fight, she was capable of giving as good as she got.

BACK AT SPRINGFIELDS, Ivy was tucking into a coffee sponge, and several cups of tea to wash it down. She had surprised herself this afternoon, and was feeling dangerously inviolable. Roy had accepted her explanation, as had Mrs. Spurling and Miss Pinkney, and she announced that she would be ringing the vicar after tea to discuss again the advisability of reading the banns this coming Sunday. Frank Maleham had confirmed himself as the culprit and she had frightened him off. There would be no need to delay things further.

Then she remembered something he had said. He was under orders from an unnamed source. Well, they had more or less decided that already. Maybe Frank was dealt with, but he was only the messenger. She hoped he would not get shot, but he might be replaced. No, it was not over. They had to find the source.

"Roy, dearest. Have you thought any more about Wendy Wright?" They were sitting in their corner of the lounge, and she leaned towards him and took his hand. As he was eating a piece of cake at the time, this made things difficult, but he smiled at her and said the only woman he thought about was a lovely lady named Ivy.

"Idiot!" she said. But her face softened, and she said perhaps they should ask Inspector Frobisher whether he had heard anything more.

ROY MAY NOT have been thinking about Wendy, but the inspector certainly was. The more he thought about the story she had just told him on the office telephone, the more a new and clearer explanation for the death of Steven Wright had emerged.

She had described the fateful dinner party and his subsequent violent sickness, and said she would be arriving at Heathrow tomorrow evening. He had offered to meet her and bring her back to Thornwell. "We can talk in the car on the way back," he had said. He was far from thinking she had had any deliberate hand in the poisoning of Wright, but he needed details of the dinner party, names, addresses and telephone numbers of anyone he had been in contact with during his last twenty-four hours, and so on.

He looked at his watch and stood up from his desk. Time to be packing up and leaving unfinished business until tomorrow. As he opened his door to walk out of the police station, his telephone rang. He hesitated, sighed, and turned back to answer it.

"Thornwell police. Can I help you? Oh, it's you, Miss Beasley. My chaps tell me you had an interesting afternoon. All safe and comfortable now?" He knew she was a sharp old tab, but he could not help having a soft spot for her.

"Fine, thank you, Inspector. I just have a question to ask you."

"I am about to leave the office, but carry on."

"Sorry about that, but it may be urgent. Have you had any further communication with Mrs. Wright, Steven's wife? I have been remembering one or two occasions when it was clear they didn't get on, and I wonder if further investigation might come up with something?"

The inspector smiled. She was no slouch, this old dear. "As a matter of fact, I am meeting her off a plane tomorrow, and shall be having talks with her on the question of the poison found in Steven's body. Does that suit?"

"Well-done, Inspector," Ivy said. "Let me know what transpires, please."

He was about to give her a short lecture on police confidentiality, but remembered in time that she was still under threat from anonymous messages, and merely said he would certainly be in touch.

"Good-bye, Inspector," Ivy said, and turned to Roy, who was sitting obediently in her room, blinking at the last rays of winter sunlight.

"So what did he say, Ivy?"

"She's flying home tomorrow, and will be questioned by him immediately."

"Do you really think she had anything to do with the death of her husband?"

"Possibly," said Ivy. "If he'd been my husband, I'd have been tempted, I don't mind telling you!"

Fifty-three

"GOOD MORNING, MISS Beasley! How are we this morning?" Rev. Dorothy tried hard to sound bright and breezy, but the sound of Ivy's voice reminded her of an ongoing problem. Banns or no banns? That was the question, and she was sure Ivy was about to attempt a change of mind.

"Are you free this morning? I wondered if you could spare me a few minutes."

Ivy's voice was firm.

"Of course. Why don't you and Roy come up to the vicarage for a coffee? It is a lovely morning. But it's cold, so you must both wrap up well. I've got a lovely patch of snowdrops I'd like you to see."

"Right," said Ivy. "We shall see you at about half past ten? And don't bother about snowdrops. Plenty of those in Springfields' garden. Still, being as God is in charge of yours, they might be bigger and better, I suppose."

Rev. Dorothy put down the phone and roared with laughter. No wonder Roy Goodman was so keen to make old Ivy his wife! She'll keep him going till he's a hundred, if not more.

She heard the old grandfather clock strike nine o'clock, and decided she just had time to go to the shop and buy chocolate biscuits. She would sweeten up her visitors and prepare them for another refusal.

AFTER HER CONVERSATION with the vicar, Ivy turned to Roy and said she had something important to tell him. They were sitting as usual in her room, and she drew her chair up close to his.

"Good heavens, dearest, I do hope you are not going to suggest we call the whole thing off?"

"No, of course not. I haven't given you the whole picture of yesterday's adventure, and as I don't mean to keep anything from you, ever, I think now would be a good time to tell you. You see, I wasn't quite honest with the police, but in a good cause."

She then told an increasingly alarmed Roy the full story of her abduction by Frank, and everything that followed.

"But, Ivy, you must tell Inspector Frobisher! After all, he will want to arrest Frank Maleham straight away. Who knows what the stupid fool will do next?"

"Well, that's just it, really, Roy. Frank is a stupid fool, but not much else. He said he was obeying orders, and I believed him. If I turn him over to the police, our chances of discovering his puppet master will be just about nil."

"Puppet master?" said Roy, opening his eyes wide. "An unusual phrase for you, beloved."

"Television, last evening," she said, "and I thought it was a good description of foolish Frank. Somebody's pulling his strings, and we must find him. Or her."

"You never cease to surprise me, Ivy dear. But you are quite right. I just insist that you do not, on any account, go out alone again, until this whole business is cleared up. And now it's time we were preparing to go to the vicarage. No doubt you will tell me in due course what you intend to say to Rev. Dorothy."

"WHAT BEAUTIFUL SNOWDROPS, my dear," said Roy to the vicar, as she greeted them from her front door. "We have them at Springfields, but they are nothing compared with yours. Such harbingers of spring, don't you think?"

Ivy stared at him, but his expression was totally innocent of all guile.

"Thank you, Mr. Goodman! I do love them. They cheer me up every year. A kind of solace for all the bad weather of winter."

What on earth are these two going on about? thought Ivy. "Shall we go in, then?" she said tartly. "I'm cold, and Roy looks blue. It's a really sharp east wind this morning."

Inside the vicarage sitting room, they found a roaring fire and comfortable chairs, and Ivy relaxed. "No coffee for me, please. A tea bag will do me. Never touch coffee. I always say it's bad for you, but Roy doesn't agree with me. Still, when we're married, we shall come to a compromise. I shall continue to drink tea, and Roy will join me."

Rev. Dorothy laughed. "Now, speaking of your marriage, I expect you have come to discuss whether we can go ahead with the banns on Sunday?"

"Exactly," said Ivy. "I have now had further information which leads me to believe there will be no more threatening letters. In fact, I think the whole business will subside, and we can settle down. So you go ahead, Rev. Dorothy, and call our banns twice more."

"Ah, yes, well . . . I am not so sure that it is all so straightforward. Does Inspector Frobisher know about your decision?"

"No," said Roy quickly. "And I must say that I think it is a unilateral decision. Dear Ivy is very sure that all will be well, but I must confess I am not so convinced. Ivy has bravely dealt with the messenger, but we have not yet found the originator of the messages. Until we do, and discover the reason behind their demands, I think we should wait. It cannot be long now."

"So you would like me to arbitrate about Sunday?" said Rev. Dorothy.

Neither replied, and finally Dorothy said she would go into the kitchen and make more tea and coffee, to give them a chance to come to a decision.

"I do hope, Ivy dear, that our marriage is not going to be a constant struggle for supremacy?" Roy took her hand and kissed it. "In fact, just to show you how much I love you, I am going to ask you to think for a few seconds, and then give me your opinion. Whatever it is, I shall abide by it. How's that?"

"I was going to say exactly the same thing!" said Ivy. "So we're back to square one."

They said nothing more until Rev. Dorothy returned, and then Roy said, "I think we have agreed; haven't we, Ivy?"

"Yes, we'll go ahead."

"But I thought we agreed—?" Roy looked at her and shook his head gently. "Can I say I am overruled?" he said, and laughed.

"Well, I still think we should wait."

"Then I must give the casting vote," said Rev. Dorothy, "and I'm afraid I agree with Roy, for my own safety as well as for the two of you. Don't forget I also received a threatening letter. I think all will be well once we have got this ridiculous business settled. I won't ask you how you fixed the messenger, but I'm sure you will want to tell Inspector Frobisher. Now, let's change the subject," she added.

"Fine," said Ivy, "as long as it's not snowdrops."

FROBISHER'S GREETING TO Wendy Wright at the airport was warm. She looked such a pleasant woman, and although his long experience had taught him that appearances were unreliable, he found it difficult to imagine her as a malicious poisoner.

"I do like flying," she said, handing over her suitcase for him to carry. "It always seems as if you are leaving all your problems behind and starting afresh."

"But one usually has to come back to them! I am so sorry to have to call you back to Thornwell. And the weather is not exactly welcoming. Anyway, let's return to the police station, and then after we've gone through everything, you will be able to open up your house again and relax."

"Mm, not so sure about the house. I was thinking of selling it. Too many memories, and I am fancy-free now. I can live anywhere that appeals to me."

Something about the triumphant way she said "fancy-free" jarred with the inspector. But he concentrated on his driving, and they exchanged only pleasantries now and then, until they reached Thornwell.

"Now, if you will come into my office, I will ask a few questions and make the necessary notes. In here, please."

Wendy noticed the change of tone in his voice. She was now a witness to Steven's sickness attack, and possibly a suspect in the cause of his death. She took a deep breath and followed him.

After the necessary preliminary cautions, Frobisher said, "Firstly, we now know that your husband died from a dose of salmonella poisoning. Perhaps you would tell me step by step about your supper date with friends? First, what food had Steven eaten that day before you went out?"

"Breakfast was cereal and coffee—he had black coffee. Then we had a sandwich later on. Wholemeal bread and cheddar cheese from the supermarket. Well within its sell-by date. At our friends', we had a choice. There were eight married couples, and the wives had supplied one dish each. Steven is very picky about his food, so I took his favourite cold fish with mayonnaise, and we both had good helpings of that. I don't think that was the cause, because I had no ill effects. He might have had some pudding. He loved sweet things, and I noticed there was a curdled creamy thing. Looked a bit dodgy to me and I warned him about it. But he could have had some when I was chatting to other people."

"Ah," said Frobisher. "So what time did you leave their house? And had Steven complained of stomach pains before you left?"

Wendy shook her head. "Don't think so," she said. "We had to stop on the way home for him to have a pee, and then in the night he began to throw up."

"Were you worried about him?"

Wendy looked uncomfortable. "Well, to tell the truth, Inspector," she said, "we had had a row, and I was cross with him for drinking too much. That's what I thought had made him sick. And until you said about the salmonella poisoning, that's what I still thought."

"And next morning?"

"He had the trots—diarrhoea, I mean—but after a while that stopped. He looked pale and wouldn't eat or drink anything. He stayed at home, and I coaxed a little food into him. Only cereal and toast. Same thing next day, with a bit of this and that, but then he went into work after lunch on the Saturday and didn't come home that night. Or ever again. I thought he was off with his floosie—he had one, you know—and the next thing I heard was that he had died in a Maleham bed."

"Had you parted on good terms when he went off to work the day before?"

"Not really. We quarrelled most of the time. I'm being honest with you, Inspector, though it's probably not in my best interests."

"Oh yes, it is, Mrs. Wright. Being perfectly honest with a detective inspector is in your very best interests. Now, were you surprised to hear that he had crawled into one of Maleham's comfortable beds and died there?"

"Of course I was! I immediately felt guilty!" She began to cry, but went on speaking through wrenching sobs. "I should have insisted he stayed at home. After all, he'd been off work. I should have made him drink lots of water. He must have been really dehydrated. And now you say it was salmonella poisoning. How long before it takes hold? Will you find out if anyone else from that night was affected?"

Frobisher nodded. "Of course, Mrs. Wright. Perhaps you will give me names, and addresses if you have them, of all the people who were there. It is a fact that salmonella does not always kill people, and it can take up to seventy-two hours to produce symptoms. Children are at greatest risk, and elderly people. And sometimes others who have a poor natural immunity to infection."

"Poor immunity, did you say? Yes, Steven did have that! We had to avoid places where he might catch flu or even colds. Oh, do you think it was that, then?"

"It is possible. But I have a great deal more work to do now. And thank you for being so frank with me. Please let me know if you are leaving Thornwell for any reason. Can you find your own way home? Good morning."

Fifty-four

"WE HAVEN'T HEARD from Deirdre, have we, dearest?" For once, Roy and Ivy had decided to stay in the lounge and watch television. But after about half an hour, when all the other residents, full of lunch, had gone to sleep and were snuffling and snoring, Roy thought that it was time for a change of scene. "I wonder if she's seen the Jossland couple again?"

"She's going there this afternoon," Ivy replied. "She rang this morning and said she was going, and did we want to go, too? I thought you looked a little tired after our exciting visit to the vicarage, so I said no."

"It *was* exciting," said Roy, smiling, "if only because you and I established a happy way of working as one."

Ivy looked at her watch. "If you'd like to go with Deirdre, it's not too late to give her a ring?"

"Fine. Let's go, then. I'll just get our coats and we'll be off. The sun has come out, and the fresh air will do us good."

Roy established that Deirdre was about to leave, but would pick them up in about half an hour. He accepted gratefully. Ivy said she was not to bother; they would find their way up to

Tawny Wings and be there ready to go to Settlefield in thirty minutes precisely.

So much for acting as one, thought Roy, and helped Ivy on with her coat. Then he took his stick and went to fetch a manual wheelchair, knowing that the trundle would not go into Deirdre's car.

Once on the road, spirits rose with all three, and Deirdre volunteered the information that Gus was intending to pay another visit to Alf Lowe. "He seems to get on well with him lately. The old boy has a skin like a rhinoceros, but Gus takes no notice. He says he's sure Alf is sitting on secrets that will help us get to the bottom of the threats. It's your money that's at the root of it, Roy. We are all sure of that, but exactly why, we haven't found out yet."

"Donkeys," said Roy enigmatically. "Donkeys is the answer. Ivy and I are quite determined on that—aren't we, beloved?"

"No comment," said Ivy. "Oh look, there's the turn to the farm. It *is* nice to have an outing, Deirdre. Very kind of you to think of it."

"Not at all. They know we're coming this time, and seemed pleased when I suggested it."

As they drove into the farmyard, William and Bella were waiting for them.

"Out you get, lad," William said to Roy. "No need for the wheelchair. Take my arm, and we'll be up the steps into the kitchen in two shakes of a lamb's tail!"

"And how's my little Faith?" said Deirdre. "Is she walking yet?"

Bella laughed. "I know she's a fantastic baby, but no, not yet. William says I am already a pushy mother, and reminds me that you have to crawl before you can walk!"

When they were all settled with cups of tea and cake, with Faith crooning at them from a play mat on the floor, Ivy asked whether they'd managed to sort out Ethel's estate. "Sometimes it takes *years*," she said.

William looked at Bella, and grimaced. "Not with Aunt Ethel," he said. "She had virtually nothing to leave. We know that in the dim, distant past she was disgraced and cut out of her father's will. But she worked hard for years, and we thought she would have saved a bit. Not that we wanted it, but it was sad to find out she had more or less nothing left."

"The nursing home fees took most of it, we reckon," said Bella. "Up you come, Faith," she added, picking up the baby and handing her to Deirdre. "Go to Auntie Dee-Dee. "

"We'll get no more sense out of my cousin," Ivy whispered to Roy. "Ask them a question about Ethel's disgrace."

William was on his feet on his way to the cows, and Bella had gone upstairs to fetch a clean nappy. When she returned, Roy said pleasantly, "Did you ever find out what Ethel did to be so unkindly treated?"

William laughed as he went out, saying that it was a case of the wrong side of the blanket. "Bella will tell you the whole story," he said. "Nice to see you all. Come again soon. Sorry I have to leave you, but the cows won't wait."

"So it was an illegitimate baby, was it?" Ivy said baldly. She'd had enough of all this flaffing about.

"Ivy likes to call a spade a spade," Roy said apologetically.

"She's right," said Bella. "I don't know much about it, but there was a baby, and we think it must have been adopted. It is certain that it never came back to Settlefield. Once or twice, when Ethel was still living in her little cottage here, she had begun to be a bit confused, and once or twice she mentioned a lost baby. We always assumed that she had had a miscarriage or an abortion, but apparently not. In her will, which was pathetically short, she referred to a child. All she said was, 'the remainder of my possessions are to go to my child.' No name, or indication where such a child might be found. Sad, isn't it, Miss Beasley?"

Ivy nodded. "It is very sad, Bella, but those were very different times from today. Now you're lucky if you can find a child that has two parents married to each other." She leaned forward and prodded Faith's stomach awkwardly. "Who's a lucky little girl, then?" she said.

"She's not a parrot, Ivy," said Deirdre, suppressing a laugh. But at least Ivy had tried.

"SO NOW WE know Ethel Goodman had an illegitimate baby, which was taken for adoption immediately after birth. Is that right, Roy?"

Ivy was sitting bolt upright in Deirdre's car, full of certainty that they were on the right path at last. Roy looked at her and frowned. "You know what this means, Ivy?" he said.

"Oh yes. It means you may have a living heir to your fortune, after all. Unless you get your bequest to the donkeys into your will as soon as possible."

Deirdre looked in her driving mirror and could see that Roy had a half smile on his lined old face. Why wouldn't he come out with it now? None of them knew what he had in his will, except that Ivy would be well provided for. Was he being deliberately secretive? Was he actually enjoying all this attention? Only one thing to do, and that was to ask him outright.

"Roy, I do hope you'll forgive my asking, but have you made a will? I know sometimes people think they have, and either it has slipped their minds, or it is hopelessly out of date, leaving everything to somebody who has died before them."

"You can rest assured that everything is in order, Deirdre. I have very good lawyers."

"But when did you last see them, dearest? Not that I care, but Deirdre has a point," said Ivy.

"And thank you for your concern, Deirdre," Roy answered blandly. "I do appreciate it."

"Right, well, perhaps we'd better talk about something else," Deirdre said, aware that she had not had a straight answer to her question. "I do have a nice piece of news to give you."

"Out with it, my dear!" said Roy. "We could do with good news just at the moment."

"Well, William and Bella have asked me to be a godmother to baby Faith! Isn't that wonderful?"

Ivy was about to make a caustic remark about godmothers, who have all the glory and none of the hard work bringing up a baby, but she bit it back. Poor Deirdre had obviously wanted a baby years ago when Bert was alive. And although this was second best, it had given her a lovely surprise.

"Congratulations, Deirdre!" said Roy. "I'm sure you will make a very good godmother. Little Faith is a charmer already. When is the christening?"

"In a few weeks' time. They want to have it quite early, before spring planting and lambing starts. Though apparently some lambs are born in January these days, or even earlier."

She had lived a long time in a village, but Deirdre was an urban person at heart, and was not too sure of the country calendar.

"If you ask me, it's interfering with nature," said Ivy. "Lambs out of season, chickens in wire cages, calves being killed before they have time to grow up. It's not right, and we shall all suffer for it in the end."

"Maybe, maybe not," said Roy placatingly. "At least you and I have reached an age where we don't have to bother with these things. I must say that as a retired farmer, I can speak from experience, and am only too relieved that things are a lot easier on the farm these days. Nothing stays still, Ivy, and even now, things that in my day we thought were the bee's knees in modern farming methods, are now looked on as old-fashioned."

"Hear, hear, Roy! Well said!" Deirdre drove into Barrington and parked outside Springfields. "Now, are you going to offer me another cup of tea?"

"Certainly not," said Ivy. "Me and Roy have a little glass of sherry about this time, and we would be very happy if you would join us?"

"You're on," said Deirdre. "Great stuff, cousin Ivy. In we go!"

Fifty-five

ALF SAT HAPPILY in his armchair by the fire, watching his carer dust round his precious ornaments.

"You're being careful, 'ent you?" he said. "Them china figures are worth a bomb, so I've been told. Maybe I shouldn't tell you that. How do I know you're not sussing out houses worth turnin' over?"

His carer turned indignantly, hands on hips. "Mr. Lowe! You are joking, I hope? Now, would you like another cup of tea before I go?"

Alf chuckled. "Only teasing, girlie," he said. "I'm very grateful for all what you're doing for me. I shall be sorry when I'm well enough to get back to doin' me own housework for meself!"

"Yes, well. I'll put the kettle on. I've got a spare minute or two, so I'll have a cup with you if you promise to behave." She had been told that the old man was still very frail, so she must avoid upsetting him.

So it was that when Gus knocked at Alf's door, and shouted that it was only Gus, and he would let himself in, he stepped into the cottage to find a pretty young woman sipping tea in a chair opposite the old ruffian.

"Morning, Gus! This is my young lady, Jean Brown. Aren't I lucky? The old dog's not done yet!"

The carer stood up, smiled at Gus, and said she would wash up and then be off. "I'm afraid Mr. Lowe is feeling much better," she said. "Here, sit down, and while the kettle's hot I'll make you a cup of tea. Or would you rather have coffee?"

After she had gone, with another burst of raillery from Alf about looking forward to their naughty weekend, Gus looked at him closely. The old boy's cheeks were still pale, but there was a light in his eyes that hadn't been there for months.

"You're certainly looking better, Alf," Gus said. "Had some good news, have you?"

"You could say that," Alf replied. "My wife has given up wanting a divorce. At last! No more pestering from Susan. Not that all the pestering in the world was going to give her what she wanted. Anyway, she's ditched the man who wanted to marry her, and another idiot where she's living has taken a fancy to her, and is quite happy for them to be living in sin. At her age! Good luck to him, I say!"

"So no more worrying about a vow made when she was very young?"

"She *were* young, yes. I managed to play the field until I turned thirty. Anyway, that's enough about me, as they say. Tell me about your love life?"

Gus paused, and then in a genuinely curious voice, said, "How old are you, Alf? The truth, now."

"No reason to lie. I'm eighty-two next birthday. And I mean to live to be a hundred."

"Good man," said Gus, laughing. "I reckon you'll make it."

Then he gave him an edited version of his own foray into marriage to a society girl, and the saga that led to their separation and divorce.

"Is she still around?" asked Alf.

"Somewhere," answered Gus, and changed the subject. "I must be off soon, but I have been meaning to ask you about a family my colleague Deirdre has been getting chummy with. Jossland, their name is. William and Bella. They live over at Settlefield, where you came from?"

Alf's expression changed. He looked wary and suspicious. "What about them?" he said.

"Nothing, really. I just thought you might remember the family. Bella's side were farmers, like your own. In fact, I believe the girl was a Goodman, and a relation of our Roy. Funny how things go round and round. It occurred to me you might be interested to hear about them. They've got a baby, apparently, and Deirdre's gone completely daft over it."

"Babies! The less I know about babies, the better I like it. My wife, her overseas, was always going on about them. I refused to have anything to do with it."

"Never wanted a son or daughter yourself, then?" said Gus.

Alf yawned deeply. "Time I had a sleep, Gus, old chap. Nice of you to come again. I look forward to it. Not many people I welcome in here, but I've took a fancy to you. Mind how you go, and post the key through the letter box."

His eyes closed and his head rested back among his cushions. Gus knew better than to accuse him of pretending, and let himself out of the door, posting the key as instructed.

INSPECTOR FROBISHER LOOKED at his afternoon's appointments, and saw that Miss Ivy Beasley was due to come in at three thirty. This reminded him that he was still not quite satisfied with Wendy Wright's explanation of her husband Steven's death. Certainly the poison identified had the right characteristics. Delayed action, capable of causing death. But wasn't her claim that he had a malfunctioning immune system rather sudden and unconvincing? It had never been mentioned before, to his knowledge. Perhaps the old boy, Roy Goodman, would remember something about it.

He looked at his watch. Nearly half past three. Perhaps he would have a few minutes with his eyes shut, emptying his mind before the old biddy arrived. He wondered what she wanted. That episode when she had gone missing from a furniture store in Thornwell was surely closed? A good-hearted bloke had given her a lift to Springfields, and all was well. From what he knew of that residential home, it was upmarket, with high fees. If the story got into the local paper, it wouldn't do any good to Springfields's reputation! Perhaps Miss Beasley was about to sue them for neglect. Confused and lost, the man had said. Well, that wasn't the Ivy Beasley he knew and loved. And here she was, arriving punctually as usual.

"Good afternoon, Miss Beasley. And Mr. Goodman, too. Nice to see you again. How can I help?"

"Good afternoon, Inspector," Ivy said. "We don't really need your help. In fact, we have some information which might help you. I am going to hand over to Roy, as I have made a bargain which I intend to keep."

What is she talking about? Confused, maybe? Frobisher turned to Roy, and said perhaps he would like to elucidate.

"Not sure about that," said Ivy, with the ghost of a smile. "But he will tell you all about it."

Frobisher sighed. Perhaps he should send for a cup of tea for them all, but then he thought that might prolong the agony. No, he would see them politely off the premises as soon as possible. Unless they had some new and really useful information, of course.

Roy began with Ivy's dentist appointment. "Not true, Inspector, I'm afraid. It was just an excuse for my Ivy to go enquiring on her own in Maleham's Furniture Store, from where she was abducted."

"What? That's not what was said originally. Are you sure about this, Miss Beasley?"

Ivy clamped her lips together, and gestured towards Roy.

"She is sure, Inspector," said Roy. "She was taken by force from the store basement, driven off into the countryside and, ultimately, after making a bargain with her abductor, unloaded at Springfields Retirement Home."

"But she was apparently unhurt?" said Frobisher. He was beginning to think they were having him on. But why?

"No, no, nothing like that. The culprit was not at all violent, except for a little pushing and shoving to get her into the car. No, Ivy is quite capable of standing up for herself."

"I've noticed," said the inspector drily. "So what was the reason for this abduction?"

"Money," said Ivy.

"Donkeys," said Roy.

"Now, you two, I've had enough of this! Either you stop

having fun at my expense, or I'm afraid I shall have to close this interview."

"Oh, sorry, Inspector," said Ivy, apparently full of remorse. "I would just ask you to remember that my life has been threatened. The fact is that I was told I must drop my intended marriage to Roy Goodman, or else. And the 'or else' was distinctly threatening."

"Right." Frobisher took his pen, a clean sheet of paper, and fixed them with a stern expression. "Name? Address? Where does he live? Was he the man we congratulated for being a good citizen? Have you met him before, and how do you know he was the man delivering threatening messages?"

Roy sighed. "Carry on, Ivy," he said.

"If you will give me that paper, Inspector, I will write it all down for you. It will save time, and as you are about to say, you are a very busy man."

"REALLY, IVY, I am surprised at you," said Roy crossly, when they were in Elvis's taxi returning to Springfields.

"Why, dearest?" she said.

"It was most embarrassing. That poor man clearly thought we were wasting his time with senile imaginings. If you're not careful, this sort of thing will prejudice our chances of further assignments in Enquire Within."

"I did no more than I said I was going to. No more and no less. I wrote down details that I could remember. His underlings would have taken Frank's particulars at the time he brought me back to Springfields, as a matter of course, but he probably falsified them. I doubt if he will do anything more about it. Frobisher, I mean. If he did take it further, Frank will convince them that I was in fact short of a marble or two. And I have not broken my word. Well, maybe chipped it a little, but that's all."

"Mm, well, we'll see. Tomorrow's our meeting at Tawny Wings, and I for one am hoping we'll be able to clear up the whole thing. Thank you, Elvis," he said, as they turned into Springfields' drive. "Now, you go ahead, Ivy. I want a word with our friend here. Off you go."

Fifty-six

ROY AND IVY had spent what was left of the afternoon snoozing in Ivy's room. Instead of separating into their separate ways, Roy had said he would be quite happy in Ivy's armchair, and she could stretch out on her bed as usual.

At five o'clock, Roy woke with a start. For a moment he could not remember why he was in an armchair and not his own room. Then he saw Ivy still asleep on her bed. He stood up quietly and went over to look at her. She had taken off her glasses and her hair had slipped out of its tightly restricting net. She had a half smile on her face and he suddenly saw her as a young girl, warmhearted and innocent, as yet to suffer from a bullying mother and an angry, henpecked father.

He took her hand and stroked it gently. "Ivy, my dearest," he whispered.

Ivy stirred, frowned and opened her eyes. Her face was suddenly brightened by a broad smile. "Roy Goodman," she said. "Are we married?"

Then she woke up properly, straightened her hair, put on her glasses and lowered her legs to the floor. "Good gracious," she said. "What time is it? Are we late for tea? Really, Roy, you should have woken me earlier."

"Ah, my Ivy's back," he replied. "No, we are not late, and I wouldn't dream of disturbing your beauty sleep. And you are beautiful when asleep, Ivy, though I'm sure you won't believe me."

"You are quite right. No woman of my age is beautiful. Neat, clean and tidy. That's the best we can hope for. Now, what is our plan for the rest of the day?"

"I think we should review all we know in our enquiry so far, and then be prepared for tomorrow's meeting. What do you think?"

"Sounds fine to me. There are still missing pieces in the jigsaw."

"Perhaps Gus and Deirdre will be able to fill in the gaps. Gus may have picked up more from Alf, and Deirdre could have gleaned helpful straws from what seems to be her daily telephone conversation with the Josslands. Being a godmother has quite gone to her head, silly girl."

"Perfectly natural, Ivy dear. She has always wanted to be a mother, apparently, and I think it was a lovely idea of the Josslands'."

"Well, that's as may be. Now, let's go down and have tea, and then we can retreat back up here and go through our findings methodically."

"Yes, ma'am," said Roy with a smile. "Anything you say."

"Oh, and by the way, what were you talking so privately to Elvis about? Not cooking up any nasty surprises, I hope?"

Roy smiled. "As if I would. No, I was asking him if he would do me the honour of being best man at my wedding. And he was so pleased, dear Elvis, that he drove off with the hand brake still on. Clouds of blue smoke coming from his taxi!"

TEA HAD BEEN what even Ivy had to admit was delicious. Griddle cakes with honey, chocolate cake and lashings of clotted cream. Feeling replete and happy, she and Roy went back up to her room, and settled down.

"You start, Ivy. Let's hear the result of your methodical

thinking. If you see my eyelids drooping, please prod me with my stick."

"Don't be ridiculous, Roy! Nighttime is for sleeping. Now, shall we start with our most important client? I think that's you, Roy, so off you go. What did you know about Steven and his family before he died in Maleham's bedroom department?"

"Right. First, he was the son of my sister, who was obviously a Goodman, and she married a rather unpleasant man named Wright. Steven was their only child, and grew into a similarly unpleasant man. He was also my only close living relative, my sister and her husband having died some years ago. He married a nice girl called Wendy, originally from Birmingham. He visited me very rarely, and each time stayed for perhaps thirty minutes. He agreed to be my best man, though it was not, he let slip, in his interest financially that the wedding should go ahead."

"So that's where I came in," said Ivy. "We announced our engagement, set a date for the wedding, proceeded to have the banns called. With no warning whatsoever of illness or incapacity, Steven was found dead in Maleham's bed. Subsequent police investigations showed that he died of salmonella poisoning."

"And had during a recent evening been violently sick after a friend's dinner party, so there was some warning," added Roy.

"Wendy leaves the country, after being exonerated from any blame, having a cast-iron alibi."

"So that rules her out," Roy said. "I'm glad of that. I always liked her, and felt sorry for her, him being so unpleasant. I do remember thinking at one point he would be very lucky if she stuck with him."

"She's back in this country, I believe, so perhaps it would be nice for you to give her a call? Perhaps you could ask her about his previously unmentioned faulty immune system? Remember? The inspector asked you about that. He was obviously doubtful, but it may be quite true."

Roy frowned, but agreed. "Kind thought, Ivy. I'll do that tomorrow."

Ivy's phone rang, and she picked up the receiver. "Hello, Deirdre? No hitch in our meeting plans tomorrow, I hope? No?

Right. What time, then? Nine thirty? I'll consult Roy." She put her hand over the mouthpiece and said Deirdre had a lunch appointment, and could the meeting start earlier tomorrow? Roy nodded, and Ivy said into the phone, "That's all right. Who are you lunching with? No, let me guess. Bella and Faith? Thought so. Right, see you tomorrow at nine thirty. Good-bye."

"Now, who's next?" Ivy said.

"I think *you* are the most important person in all this, even though you are sure you have put an end to the threatening messages. Frank Maleham said he was only the messenger, and that he took orders from somebody, whose name he wouldn't reveal. Surely our priority now is to find that somebody?"

"Quite right, my love," said Ivy, "Though I'm beginning to get a glimmering of an answer to that one. Tomorrow, when we put all our heads together, we should get all the details straight."

"I suppose you're not going to tell me who the glimmering might be?"

"No, not just yet, else I might confuse everybody. If you put the wrong piece in a jigsaw, it messes up the rest."

"Right, so, who else? There's Beryl Maleham?"

"Innocent," said Ivy.

"And Frank, we know about. More to discover about Ethel Goodman?"

"I think we know most of it, but it will need sorting out."

"Alf Lowe? I think Gus is bound to have more to tell us about him."

Ivy did not reply for a minute or two. Then she looked at her watch. "There's that good programme on the telly starting now. Shall we put it on?"

Roy raised his eyebrows. "Methodical session over?" he said.

"Enough, I think, until tomorrow." She reached across and switched on the television.

Fifty-seven

"MY GOODNESS, YOU two have finished breakfast in record time!" said Miss Pinkney, smiling broadly. "Off out already? Anything I can do for you before you go? And will you be back for lunch? It's lovely to see you both so active these days. And are we on again for May five?"

Ivy stopped. "Yes, no, yes, yes. In that order. And thank you very much for asking, Miss Pinkney. If only a certain other person shared your enthusiasm! We saw La Spurling earlier, and were given a warning about wrapping up warm, watching out for slippery pavements, keeping an eye on the clock to make sure we were back in good time for lunch, etcetera, etcetera."

"Never mind," Miss Pinkney replied. "She is responsible for you, after all."

"Well, we'll be off now and see you later, dear. Roy is just climbing aboard his trundle and then we're on our way to Tawny Wings."

"Enquire Within business meeting?"

"That's right. The most important so far, probably."

Roy's trundle hooter was heard calling for Ivy, and she hurried out, only to turn back and retrieve her umbrella from the stand by the office. "I promised Her Who Must Be Obeyed!" she said to Miss Pinkney, who waved them off cheerfully.

Deirdre ushered them into the meeting room, where Ivy was pleased to see a bright fire giving off a good heat. "Morning, Deirdre; morning, Gus," she said. "All well, I hope." She then made for the chairman's chair, and settled herself in a way that meant business.

"Now," she said, "I formally declare this meeting open. We have a great deal to get through this morning, and as Deirdre is going a-godmothering at lunchtime, we'll make a start straight away. Perhaps you'd like to sum up where you have got to so far with your enquiries, Deirdre?"

"Nothing much further forward, really, Ivy. As we now know, Ethel Goodman had an illegitimate baby quite late, in her thirties. She was still living with her parents on the farm, and was absent, ostensibly doing a household management course. Came back very unhappy and nobody spoke to her. That's something Bella remembered overhearing. Apparently Bella used to sit under the table at her grandmother's house, hiding under the chenille tablecloth with bobbles round the edge, listening to grown-up conversation. Anyway, Ethel was treated as a pariah, and cut out of her parents' will. Eighty-one when she died, leaving virtually nothing, except a sad little reference to 'my child' in her will. There is apparently some unsolved puzzle about her death, but I've heard nothing more."

"Thanks, Deirdre. Now, Roy, would you like to sum up what we discussed last evening?" Ivy blew him an awkward kiss, and he smiled fondly.

"Of course, dearest. Well, folks, Ivy has been busy, and has now decided there will be no more messages. Our priority is still to find out who was giving the orders to Frank Maleham. Person or persons unknown, so far. We also decided that poor Steven's death was a poisoning accident involving salmonella, which can be a killer if the victim has a weak immune system. Between his being ill after a dinner party, and, two or three days later, having a violent attack in Maleham's, crawling into a bed, and dying, there was an interval which almost fits in with the description of an attack of salmonella poisoning."

"Why almost?" said Deirdre.

"Almost," replied Roy, "because the delay was rather longer

than would be expected. And one small thing needs to be veri-
fied," he said professionally. "We need to establish whether he
did indeed have a weak immunity to infection."

"Thank you, Roy. So that leaves you, Gus, to tell us all you
know about Alf Lowe."

At this point, much to Ivy's irritation, there was a sharp
knock at the front door, and Deirdre went to investigate. After
an altercation of female voices, she reappeared, looking red
and cross, and behind her came Miriam Blake, striding into
the room purposefully.

"Miss Blake!" said Ivy. "We are having a private meeting!
If you wish to discuss anything with us, please get in touch this
afternoon."

Miriam stood her ground. "What I've got to say concerns
what I think you might be talking about this morning," she
said. "And when I've said it, I'll go, but not before. I got this
feeling when I got up that Gus and you lot might be on the
wrong track."

A surprised silence greeted this, and then Ivy cleared her
throat and said, "In that case, you'd better have a seat and say
what you have to say. But make it quick. We've a lot to get
through."

Miriam sat bolt upright in a hard chair, and began. "From
what I've heard, or overheard, you would probably say, I reckon
you need to know something about Frank Maleham. I saw him
outside Gus's cottage, actually delivering one of them messages
for Miss Beasley. Now, you may not know this, but Frank Maleham was a mate of mine at one time, and up to now I've not been
willing to shop him. We used to go to folk dancing in Thornwell
Town Hall once a week, and he was kind and thoughtful. He
was always my partner. But then we drifted apart."

"Miss Blake," said Ivy sternly. "First of all, we are not gun-
ning for anyone at present. And secondly, we haven't time to
listen to details of your past love life."

"Just *listen*, Miss Beasley!" Miriam said. "It's very important. One fact you won't know, because he never liked it talked
about, is that Frank Maleham was adopted. His so-called mum
and dad couldn't have kids, so they adopted him when he was
a new baby."

More silence, while Miriam blew her nose hard.

"Did he know who his real parents were?" Deirdre asked.

Miriam shook her head. "He reckoned his mum must have been somebody local, but he didn't really want to find out. Mind you, he probably knows now. Him and Beryl Maleham was always very close. Still are, and she wanted everybody to think he was her proper son. Sad, isn't it?"

"Never mind whether it is sad or not. Have you anything else to tell us? We are very grateful to you for coming and helping us along. What you have told us about Frank is valuable information. Now, we must get on." Ivy stood up and walked to the door. "Good morning, Miss Blake, and thank you for coming."

Miriam dawdled, reluctant to leave the spotlight. But in a minute or two she was gone and Ivy came back into the room.

"Well, that was a turnup, wasn't it?" said Gus.

"Yes and no," said Ivy. "I had a suspicion from my conversations with Beryl in the store that he was not her own son. Not many mothers would refer to their only sons as Frankenstein. But useful to have it confirmed. And, of course, he must be about fifty and that would fit in with what we know about Ethel Goodman's mysterious baby."

"So who was Frank's father?" said Deirdre, glancing anxiously at her watch.

"Plenty of time yet, Deirdre," Ivy said. "As to the real father of Frank Maleham, I think Gus can make a good guess. Tell me if I'm wrong, Gus."

Gus sighed. "I don't like the place this is leading us," he said, "but yes, I think I may have the answer. Frank Maleham's birth mother was possibly Ethel Goodman, and his father, well, I'm not absolutely sure. . . ."

He paused, and Ivy said, "Get on with it, man, do!"

"It could be, and I repeat, I am not truly sure, but from a number of things he's said in our conversations, Frank Maleham's father could be the old reprobate Alf Lowe."

Fifty-eight

"SO," SAID DEIRDRE, going over to Gus and giving him a quick kiss on the top of his head, "if you'll excuse me, I'll just go and cancel my lunch date. There'll be other times when I can see my goddaughter, and now we have some very serious thinking to do. Okay, Ivy?"

Ivy nodded. "Good girl," she said. "We'll wait 'til you've made the call; then we'll start again."

Deirdre disappeared, and the others talked about the weather, the news and what was on the box that evening. They waited until she returned, and then Ivy began.

"Right. If—and it is quite a big if—Alf Lowe is Frank Maleham's father, then it is very likely that he is also the one who gives Frank his orders. In other words, Alf Lowe has an urgent reason for preventing Roy and me from getting married. And if so, what is it? And if you say 'donkeys,' Roy, I shall divorce you even before we're married."

"Pretty obvious, I would have thought," said Deirdre. "Frank, if he *was* Ethel's son, is half Goodman, and therefore stands in direct line to inherit Roy's money, so long as Ivy doesn't get there first."

"And always supposing Roy hasn't sewn it up tight, and he has told us that he has. But Alf doesn't know about that, and still means to have a share of it if he can prevent the wedding," said Gus. "I wouldn't put it past him to be behind the whole thing, Steven's death and all. But then again, I've got quite fond of the old devil, and can't quite see him in the role of murderer. Wicked schemes such as clumsy blackmail, yes, but not actually killing someone."

"Well, I am still not sure that Steven's death was accidental poisoning," said Ivy, "but with luck we should have that sorted out soon. Then there have been threats to my life, and Roy's, but they were empty threats, I am sure. So who else is there left to rouse suspicions of a really serious crime?"

"Ethel," chorused Roy and Deirdre. "Did she fall or was she pushed, in a manner of speaking," Deirdre continued. "Although she was old and confused, doctors have agreed that her heart was good, and she showed no signs of having had a stroke. Nothing much to go wrong. So why did she die that night? She'd apparently had a good supper, and had quarrelled vigorously with the night nurse who came in to settle her down for sleep. This was apparently par for the course, according to Bella."

"Did your Jossland friends tell you if the police are still investigating?"

"Oh yes, Ivy. They've not found anything useful, and with someone of that age, even though no cause was immediately apparent, a natural death could quite well be the case. But they're still looking."

The phone rang in the hall. "Oh, not another interruption!" Ivy said. "Go and answer it, Deirdre, and don't be long."

After about five minutes, Deirdre returned, looking solemn. "It was Inspector Frobisher," she said. "About Aunt Ethel, coincidentally. While the cleaners were giving her room a good turnout, they found a small framed photograph in a drawer, tucked behind some woollies. O' course, she was bedridden, so nobody had looked in there for a long while. He wants to come and see us, and show us the photograph to identify it, if we can."

"When?" said Gus, sitting forward, suddenly alert.

"Now. I said he could come straight away, while we are all together. It was nice of him to ask, really. He could have just turned up."

"Perhaps he's nervous of being left alone with you, Deirdre dear," said Ivy acidly. "Oh well, I suppose we'd better wait. This might well get us several steps forward."

TO THE OTHERS' great surprise, Gus had said he must shoot out and feed Whippy, but he'd be back before the inspector arrived. Ivy had objected, but he had gone before she could argue. Deirdre had made sandwiches and coffee, and the three sat round trying to relax, and failing dismally.

Gus, however, had dashed up Cemetery Lane until he reached Alf Lowe's cottage. He knocked loudly, and heard the old man shouting in return that there was no need to knock the door off its hinges. "It's not locked, and I'm coming," he yelled.

"Ah, Alf. Should you be on your feet?" said Gus.

"Much better, lad. Come on in and sit down. You look out of breath."

"No, I can't stay. I just need to ask you a couple of questions. Did you get Ethel Goodman in the family way? And is Frank Maleham your real son? And did you ever give Ethel a photograph of yourself?"

Alf paled before his eyes, and sat down heavily in a chair. "You've bin busy, Gus. Yeah, Ethel had Frank adopted, though I said she should keep him, poor little sod. She wasn't much cop, that Ethel. Selfish woman. Tried to get me to marry her, and said I was the boy's father. She was getting on, and desperate. She'd been around all the local blokes, though, and I blamed it on Roy Goodman. He just ignored it, and his family was rich. In the end, she got sent away, and the baby was adopted. I'd've got nowhere in a court case. But, to be honest, I always thought the baby *was* most likely mine."

Gus looked at his watch. "I have to get back, Alf," he said.

"There's more," said Alf stubbornly. "When I heard about the marriage, I thought of Frank, an' how the Beasley woman, as Roy Goodman's wife, would inherit the entire estate if old Roy snuffed it before her. So I found out where Frank was, and told him that Roy could well have been his father, just as likely as me. He didn't seem surprised, and joked that when he looked in the mirror he saw me! Anyway, he got the point and did the rest, with my help. Wrote the letters himself and delivered them. Waste of time, really, as it happens. We had no real proof. And Ethel was too far gone in that home to do any good with remembering, though she recognised me!"

"Have you seen her lately?"

"She's dead, 'ent she?"

Gus could see he was trembling, and decided he'd done enough. One more thing he had to say. "Alf, the police are enquiring about Ethel's death. If there's anything to tell, for God's sake, tell the truth, this time. Must go, but I'll come and see you later."

GUS WAS BACK inside Tawny Wings just in time.

"There's Frobisher's car just turning in," said Deirdre. She had had no time to ask Gus what he was up to. She did not believe for one minute that he had to feed Whippy.

"Good day, everybody," Frobisher said, nodding to each. "No, thanks, Deirdre, I won't have a sandwich. This shouldn't take long." He brought out the photograph and handled it gingerly so as not to smudge any lurking prints.

"May I see it?" said Gus. Frobisher held it out in front of him, and watched his face closely.

"Anyone you know, Mr. Halfhide?"

"Not too sure. Try the others. Deirdre, particularly, as she has lived in Barrington longer than me."

Deirdre looked. And caught Gus's eye. She hesitated, and then said it was so faded it really could be anybody.

"Mm, and how about you, Miss Beasley?"

"Deirdre's right," she said. "And my eyes are not what they used to be. Show Roy, Inspector. He's been around Barrington longer than any of us. Born and bred, as they say."

Frobisher frowned. "So how are your eyes, Mr. Goodman?"

Roy looked quickly round the others, and said he agreed that it was very faded. "Could be any of us lads around here years ago," he said. "Looks quite young. Or it could be somebody's relation from abroad? Very difficult to tell, Inspector. Sorry we can't be more helpful."

Frobisher sighed. "Very well," he said. "Then I must approach the person who is most likely to have given Ethel Goodman a photograph of himself at that time."

"Can you tell us who that would be?" Gus said.

"Oh, no, Mr. Halfhide. Since you know already, it would be wasting my time. Good day to you."

In complete silence, the inspector left the Enquire Within office and drove off into the village. Gus dashed out into the road to see what direction he took; then he walked slowly back.

"He went up Cemetery Lane," he said bleakly. "Well, we did our best to help, didn't we? As Alf said, there was no proof."

FROBISHER STOPPED HIS car outside Alf's cottage, and got out. A tall, funereal yew tree cast a shade over the road and the cottage, and the road was once more icy. He slipped and grabbed the car door, cursing. He knew that this was going to be a difficult interview and wished he had brought his assistant with him. But there would be no need for extra help. Alf Lowe was a frail old man, still physically able and mentally sharp, but not up to doing a runner.

He knocked on the door, and there was no reply. Tentatively turning the handle, he pushed the door open. He saw a bright fire in the grate, a rocking chair still moving slowly to and fro, but as far as he could tell, nobody at home. He walked through to the bedroom, and found what he now dreaded finding. On the bed, a battered old suitcase, half-full of clothes, and on the floor, Alf Lowe, spread-eagled out at his feet and no longer breathing.

"Bad luck, Alf. You nearly made it," he muttered, and took out his mobile to summon assistance.

Fifty-nine

AFTER AN AMPLE breakfast to stand them in good stead for what the day would bring, Ivy and Roy made their way up to an urgent meeting at Tawny Wings, and although spring was in the air, and the early-morning frost had vanished in bright sunshine, their moods were sombre. Frobisher had returned yesterday to tell them that Alf had died from an apparent stroke. The open suitcase, half-full of summer shirts, was a clear indication that he had hoped to be off to sunny climes before the police got to him.

"He had tickets ready in his wallet," Frobisher explained. "It seems he was expecting a visit from us, and was making hasty preparations."

"So my swift visit to him was too late?" said Gus. "I do apologise, Inspector, and I hope you won't consider it impeding the course of justice, but I did have a quick word with the old fellow. Nothing more than a hint, of course."

Deirdre, sitting behind Gus in the rather crowded office, saw his crossed fingers behind his back. What an old softie he was! No wonder he was no good as a spy.

Frobisher nodded. "You were seen, Mr. Halfhide. My chaps

were already there, waiting in a plain car until I arrived. They peeped in after you had left, and saw the old boy frantically packing. So I do not intend to take you in on suspicion of murder."

Deirdre interrupted sharply. "For heaven's sake! Gus was his only friend. Poor old sod had been really ill, and could have popped off at any time."

"Relax, De—er, Mrs. Bloxham," said Frobisher. "There is no question of murder in this case. But now we come to Ethel Goodman, and I am afraid that here there was a strong suspicion of intention to kill."

"What? Alf intended to kill her? When?"

"We have found traces of Alfred Lowe's footprints outside Miss Goodman's nursing home. He entered through a garden door, and had her curious family not raised the question of her previously robust health at the time she died, Alf would probably have got away with it."

"You mean Bella and William raised the alarm?" said Deirdre.

Frobisher sighed. "That is so. The young couple did not particularly like the cantankerous old woman, but expected her to go on for several more years. Once they had raised the matter, we were obliged to investigate."

"But you don't think he killed her?" Gus asked. He could not imagine old Alf, bad-tempered and rude as he was, actually committing murder. But he was cunning enough to have broken into the home to see her, and perhaps attempt to persuade her to keep her mouth shut.

"Difficult to say. There was no evidence of violence, but fear could have finished her off. And now, if you have no more questions, I must be getting back to the station. I am sorry, Mr. Halfhide, that your friend died. But I must warn you that I shall be unable to feel compassion in any similar cases in the future. And by the way, that photograph I showed you was a particularly good likeness of the young Alfred Lowe. Good morning, all. Are you going to see me out, Deirdre?"

When she returned, she was blushing. "What did he say to you out there?" said Ivy, who missed nothing.

"He said to thank you all for the usual helpful spadework

we put in. Said he would be able to wrap up the case more quickly as a result."

Ivy pursed her lips. "Huh! Well, we have a few loose ends to sort out. So why don't you make coffee, Deirdre, and we'll have a discussion. And cheer up, Gus! At least old Alf had found a friend for the last few weeks of his life. And you took a risk, you know, running up there to warn him the police were onto him."

"Yes, well, less said about that, the better," Deirdre said. "I like to think I was able to encourage Barry Frobisher to be lenient."

Ivy's attention had been caught by an expression of sadness on Roy's face.

"What's up, Roy dearest?" she asked.

"It has occurred to me over the last day or so that *I* am the sole reason for Ethel getting killed, or dying from fright, and, indirectly, Alf Lowe hastening his own death. And also for Ivy being viciously threatened, as well as myself, the Reverend Dorothy and possibly Gus."

"Rubbish!" said Ivy briskly. "How on earth do you make all that out?"

"I have never boasted about having money, nor have I lived extravagantly or betted on horses or dogs, nor done anything to indicate that I was in possession of what to some people would seem a fortune." Roy passed a hand wearily over his eyes.

"But even so," he continued, "the word clearly got around to some that it would be worth trying to get hold of it. My fault, entirely, and I'm sad it should end in this way, souring the lovely feelings Ivy and I have developed for each other in Springfields."

"Roy! That was a long speech," said Gus. Ivy was sniffing into her handkerchief, and Deirdre openly dabbed her eyes with a tissue.

"And absolute rubbish!" repeated Ivy. "But there is just one thing, Roy, and I have pondered long and hard as to whether I should mention it. But here goes. Don't you think that if you had said loud and often that your will had completely tied up all moneys to named beneficiaries, that information might have saved some trouble?"

"Possibly, my love. But I reckoned that if the blackmailer was not absolutely sure that my money would all come to you, Ivy dear, he would be less likely to arrange for your removal from the wedding plans. He, or she, would have to look further."

"Not a bad plan," said Gus, consolingly.

"Thanks, but now I see it was a forlorn hope." Roy hunched back into his chair, looking beaten.

"As my mother used to say," said Ivy, taking Roy's hand, "it's easy to be wise after the event. We'll give Alf a good send-off in the cemetery, and then get on with planning for our wedding."

The phone rang, and Deirdre picked it up. "Who did you say? Oh, Wendy Wright. Can I help you? Miss Beasley called you, you say. Hang on a minute. She's right here."

Ivy took the phone. "Hello, Wendy," she said. "I hope you don't mind my using your Christian name? We shall soon be distantly related! Good. Well, it's just one question about your husband, Steven. Did he suffer as a child from catching every bug that was going? He did? Right. Was there any treatment for it? You're not sure. Now, how are you getting on? We must meet. Perhaps you would like to come to tea tomorrow? Good. We'll see you then. Good-bye, Wendy."

"Ivy, what have you been up to?" said Roy.

"Not sure yet," said Ivy. "I hope you don't mind my inviting her here to Springfields tomorrow?"

"Of course not. It was a very nice thought, beloved."

Or was it? Gus looked at Ivy and wondered.

Sixty

IVY AND ROY sat in the lounge at Springfields, awaiting the arrival of Wendy Wright. There were few fellow residents, as all had been invited to a matinee performance of the Cinderella pantomime in Thornwell. Ivy had said wild horses would not drag her to a pantomime of any kind, and Roy said he must stay with his fiancée, as they were expecting a teatime visit from his niece-in-law, Wendy.

Ivy saw her first, "My goodness," she said. "She's overdoing the mourning wifey bit. Look at her! Dressed in black from head to foot!"

"Ivy! The poor girl has every right to be in black, if it helps her through this difficult period."

"I bet she didn't wear black beside the pool abroad," said Ivy, and then, as Wendy approached, her tone changed, and she welcomed her warmly.

"How are you, my dear?" said Roy. "Are you managing everything now you're back? You must have a house full of reminders of poor Steven. But time heals, so I'm told. We are very glad you were able to come today."

Wendy thanked him with tears in her eyes. "You are quite

right, Uncle Roy," she said. "But I mean to get a job as soon as possible. No good moping around the house, I've told myself. And how are you and Ivy getting on with wedding plans? I haven't been back long enough to ask before. Now that Steven has gone, I do hope we won't lose touch."

"So you mean to stay in Thornwell now?" Ivy sat back in her chair, hands folded in her lap. "Oh, here's Katya with our tea. Thank you, my dear. This is Mrs. Wright, widow of Roy's unlucky nephew."

Roy frowned. Surely an inappropriate adjective for Ivy to use?

Wendy coloured. "Oh, not so much unlucky as unwise, Miss Beasley," she said. "He had a lifelong problem with inadequate natural immunity to infection, and I am afraid he refused to take treatment that was offered."

"I expect he thought he could handle it himself. Avoid people with colds and flu, and watch his diet? That kind of thing?"

Wendy looked at her sharply. "Yes, of course. Exactly that kind of thing. I am not sure if you knew, but we had dinner with friends, and he was very sick afterwards. Said he had tasted something bad. It turned out to be salmonella poisoning."

"Yes, we did hear about that," Roy said. "But why don't we change the subject, if you don't mind, Ivy? I'm sure Wendy doesn't want to have to relive that upsetting time."

Ivy continued as if she had not heard. "What did you have to eat at your friends' that night, Wendy? It must have been something pretty virulent? Here," she added, offering a plate of chocolate biscuits, "have another one."

Wendy drew a deep breath. "No, thanks," she said. "I've not had much appetite for quite a while, not since Steven died, in fact."

"Naturally," said Ivy. "You must now be very wary before you eat anything not prepared by yourself. That is surely to be expected; wouldn't you say, Roy?"

Roy was worried. What on earth was Ivy up to? The poor woman, deep in mourning black, was looking very upset. Frightened, even.

"Oh yes," Wendy replied. "I was always very careful with Steven's diet."

"I had a friend with the same condition as Steven," Ivy said. "Same problem. Insisted on his wife preparing all his food, even when they dined out. You probably did the same, Wendy?"

"Yes, of course. It was a way of life with us. I always ate the same as Steven to save time."

"So what on earth could he have eaten that night? I imagine you and the rest of the guests were fine?"

Wendy's hands were twisting together agitatedly, and Roy sent urgent signals to Ivy to change the subject. But Ivy kept her eyes on Wendy, and said, "Could it have been something else he ate? Like some leftovers for breakfast? Your neighbour told me that her dog had been sick after you gave her the remains of an omelette that day?"

To Roy's surprise and horror, Wendy burst into terrible sobs and rushed towards the door, where she was met and held by Inspector Frobisher.

"Now, now, Mrs. Wright, what is the trouble?" he said. "Why don't you come and sit down and tell us all about it."

He took her by the arm and escorted her to where Ivy sat, perfectly composed, and Roy struggled to stand up, consumed with anxiety.

"I've asked young Katya to send in more tea," said the Inspector. "We must give this lady time to recover. We can have a little talk before I have to ask you, Mrs. Wright, to accompany me to the station."

Wendy Wright pulled herself away from the inspector's supporting arm. "Let go of me!" she said angrily. "I don't want any of the old witch's tea! Let's get out of here and down to the station. None of you knew what Steven was really like! He enjoyed making me suffer, and several times I thought of going away for good, and yes, I do mean suicide!" She began to cry, but quickly recovered herself.

"Steven was very clever, Uncle Roy," she continued, "and I knew it'd be hell's own job to leave him. He wouldn't permit it, and would always be after me. I was desperate after that party, and I got the idea from him being so sick and that reminded me how the wrong food could do for him. He ate something bad there, though it wasn't my salmon. There was a curdled cream pudding. Looked very dicey to me, and I tried to stop him having any, knowing that it would make him even more determined to eat it! So next morning, after he'd recovered, more or less, I remembered some rotten old chicken I'd saved for the neighbour's dog, and I disguised it in an omelette I made for him at breakfast. He didn't eat much, though obviously enough to make him ill again." She bit her lip, and no one spoke.

Then she began again. "So you see, there was nothing to tell whether it was the cream pudding or next morning's chicken omelette."

She began to cry again, and muttered something that no one could hear.

"What was that, Mrs. Wright?" asked the inspector gently.

She scrubbed at her eyes with a small handkerchief, and looked at Ivy. "I said, Miss Beasley, that I am glad he's gone, and I meant it."

"I'm sorry, gel. I'm really sorry," Ivy said.

Eventually calming down, Wendy submitted meekly to being led by Frobisher out of the room, leaving a shocked silence behind her.

After a few minutes, Ivy spoke again. "Well, so now we know. I am sorry, Roy, and mostly sorry for you. I wish it had never had to happen."

"Poor creature," he answered, "poor, poor lady. How could Steven have treated her so badly? What would my poor sister have thought? There must have been bad blood in that Wright family. My sister would not have killed a fly. Well, this has been a terrible day. I hope never to see another like it."

Sixty-one

IVY AWOKE TO a gentle knock at her door, and saw that someone was drawing back the curtains, admitting bright morning sunshine and the sound of a blackbird singing on his usual branch outside her window.

The person was, of course, Roy, and he smiled at her. "Good morning, my love," he said. "I do hope you will forgive my coming in, but I found Katya outside your door bearing a tray of tea and biscuits, so I thought we might share? And," he added, "I brought you these."

He handed her a small bunch of pale yellow primroses, still with drops of dew on the leaves, which he had carefully arranged in an egg cup from the kitchen.

Ivy reached for her glasses, checked her hairnet was in place, and blinked briskly to clear her vision. "Goodness, how lovely, Roy. Have you been out in the garden in your slippers? They look quite wet!"

She slipped out of bed and fetched a towel from her bathroom. "Here, sit down, and I'll dry your feet," she instructed.

But Katya was having none of it, and insisted on both of

them sitting at the little table by the window while she gave Roy's feet a good rub and then poured the tea.

"Now, Roy," said Ivy. "It's not my birthday, so why the beautiful flowers?"

"Have you forgotten? Our banns will be called once more this morning, and we shall be there to hear them. I have spoken to Reverend Dorothy, and she says the police have assured her that Frank Maleham is safely in custody, so there will be no hitch this time."

"Don't tempt fate! Many a slip 'twixt cup and lip, as my old mother used to say."

"Dearest Ivy," answered Roy, "I shall be holding your hand, and no harm will come. You'll see."

WORD HAD GOT around the village, and half the congregation were rooting for Miss Beasley and Mr. Goodman, while the other half, though perhaps not acknowledging it, were hoping for another dramatic interruption.

Gus and Deirdre, obeying Ivy's orders, were sitting with the betrothed couple in the front pew. Roy, as promised, held Ivy's gloved hand tightly, and she sat close to him, as if to gain warmth and courage from his presence.

It was a communion service, and the long queue waiting for the bread and wine smiled encouragingly as they passed the front pew. At last it was time to call the banns, and Reverend Dorothy smiled broadly as she began.

"I publish the banns of marriage between Ivy Beasley, spinster of this parish, and Roy Vivian Goodman, bachelor of this parish. If any of you know cause or just impediment why these two persons should not be joined in holy matrimony, ye are to declare it."

The silence was thick with tension, and Ivy counted up to five, holding Roy's hand in a vicelike grip.

"Then this is the second unchallenged time of asking," Rev. Dorothy pronounced, and to Ivy's surprise and joy, the entire congregation burst into spontaneous heartfelt applause, and the organist played from memory, and not very accurately, Handel's triumphant hymn tune, "See the Conquering Hero Comes."

Everyone joined in, and Gus changed the words to "conquering heroine" as Ivy sang loudest of all.

After the "Amen," all sat, except Ivy, who remained standing and turned round to face the congregation.

"Friends," she began, with an unaccustomed wobble in her voice, "I would just like to say that if anyone asked me, I would say Barrington is the best village in England. Thank you all for your support for me and Roy, and you are all invited to the wedding on May the fifth."

"Are you sure about that, dearest?" said Roy, as she sat down.

"Of course not," she answered, and knelt down to pray. As silence fell on the assembled company, a very small miaow was heard from the back of the church. A cat marched up the aisle and leapt onto Ivy's pew. "Ah, there you are, Tiddles," she said, and got to her feet. "Time to go, Roy," she added, and with the cat tucked under her arm, she set off for home.

ANN PURSER

The Measby Murder Enquiry

🐾

The author of *The Hangman's Row Enquiry* presents a brand-new mystery, as cantankerous spinster Ivy Beasley finds that spending her golden years in the quaint village of Barrington won't be as quiet as she thought.

Ivy hasn't been in assisted living at Springfields for long, and she's already found new friends, formed a detective agency called Enquire Within and solved a murder. Now, as autumn falls, Ivy and her team—Roy, Deirdre and Gus—have more mysteries to solve in between card games.

Enquire Within has been asked to look into a murder in the village of Measby—a crime that, to Ivy's surprise, hasn't even shown up in the papers. Similarly intriguing is the new Springfields resident, Mrs. Alwen Wilson Jones, who claims she was conned out of a large sum of money. But as clever old Ivy discovers, Mrs. Wilson Jones, like everyone else in Barrington, has secrets—like a possible connection to the murder in Measby . . .

"Purser always comes up like roses." —*Shine*